# Coleman Hill

June Thomas Cook

**PublishAmerica**
Baltimore

© 2008 by June Thomas Cook.
All rights reserved. No part of this book may be reproduced, stored in a retrieval system or transmitted in any form or by any means without the prior written permission of the publishers, except by a reviewer who may quote brief passages in a review to be printed in a newspaper, magazine or journal.

First printing

This is a work of fiction. Names, characters, places, and incidents either are the product of the author's imagination or are used fictitiously. Any resemblance to actual persons, living or dead, events, or locales is entirely coincidental.

PublishAmerica has allowed this work to remain exactly as the author intended, verbatim, without editorial input.

ISBN: 1-60474-959-8
PUBLISHED BY PUBLISHAMERICA, LLLP
www.publishamerica.com
Baltimore

Printed in the United States of America

# *Dedication*

This book is dedicated to my husband Neal, who without his unselfish love, support and encouragement, the Coleman story would have never come to life.

To my grandson Vince, daughter Kelly and son-in-law Josh, I love you with all my heart and want only that you remember me with pride.

To my parents Midge and Jerry, who passed down to me the gifts of imagination and creativity which enabled me to write my novels. I only wish that they could be here to share the joy of my first publication.

Last but certainly not least, my deep appreciation to the late Mr. Ed Rowland of Jones County, Georgia, for sharing with me his vast knowledge of farming and providing information that proved invaluable in my research to make this story credible. His gracious help and years of experience were a great asset.

# *Acknowledgments*

I would like to acknowledge my late father and mother-in-law Herbert and Doris Cook, for providing the many actual events depicted in this story that occurred during their lifetime while growing up in rural Georgia, and who instilled in me the value of family loyalty and devotion that was the salvation of the Coleman family and all families.

I would also like to offer my deep appreciation to my two dearest and longtime friends Sonya and Annette, as well as my beloved family members Sharon and Kay and sister-in-law Cheryl, for their direction, support and encouragement in my writing endeavors.

Also, my appreciation goes to fellow author Phillip O. Harris Sr., whom without his help and suggestions, this book may have never been published.

I must acknowledge Jasper County, Georgia, for the inspiring and scenic pasture land which provided the backdrop for the fictional, North Georgia town of Myrick.

And finally, to PublishAmerica for making COLEMAN HILL a reality three decades after its inception.

# *Prologue*

The Kenworth slowly pulled the long grade coming out of Rome, headed for Chattanooga. The truck and its driver, high up in the cab, had made this trip three times a week for the past five years, three months and one week. The driver was able to pinpoint the exact day and hour it all began. It had not been his intention to follow in his father's footsteps after graduating from high school. His father had advised him to seek another profession—any profession other than truck driving.

"Driving a truck for a living gets old fast—faster than most jobs," he told his son. "It's a job that gets in your blood and as the years go by, you can't get away from it. No one wants to hire you for anything else because they think you're not qualified to do anything but drive a truck and you get locked in."

But here he was, driving down the same road, on the same route he had driven eight-hundred and nineteen times before. It was monotonous, for certain, except for the occasional accident he encountered and hopefully wasn't involved in. Fortunately his route, which required driving overnight, unloading in the mornings and returning the following afternoon, didn't cross much traffic in the late night hours. The two-lane, narrow highways and roads were usually deserted except for the occasional opossum, deer, fox and polecat that he often struck. A slight bump or dull thud was all he felt on impact. The sheer size and enormous weight of the tractor and fully loaded reefer it pulled saw to that.

It was 9:00 p.m. and he was precisely on schedule. At any given time, he was aware of his exact location by the face on his Timex wristwatch.

Over the years, to ease the monotony and help pass the time, it became a game for him. He knew that if he were on schedule, at exactly 9:55 p.m., he would be a little less than two miles outside the city limits of the small, north Georgia town of Myrick. It annoyed him if something threw him off schedule and interrupted his *time-keeping* game, for then he would be forced to drive faster to make up the time lost.

Listening to the drone of the engine as he settled back in his seat after shifting into tenth gear, he began mulling over his life in general. Why in the hell did *he* have to drive a truck in order to eke out a living? Why hadn't he listened to his father? Yet at the same time, he knew certain "classes" of people seldom broke free from their own social ranks. The rank assigned them at birth. Occasionally, there were the fortunate ones who "lucked-up" and became wealthy, but they were few and far between. He knew *he* would never become one of those lucky few. It just never seemed right to him that the rich people's kids had the same opportunity to go to college as their parents and poor kids like himself, were forced to accept minimum wage jobs straight out of high school like *their* parents. Now, at twenty-four years-old, he was already married with one child and another on the way. They lived from payday to payday with nothing left over at the end of the month. His destination in life had already been mapped out for him. It was written in stone. His fate was sealed. He was "locked in".

His prophetic thoughts began running through his mind as the reflections from the white lines on the highway flickered in a strobe-like image against the ceiling of the truck's cab. Why did the rich always seem to get richer as they went their merry way through a life of privilege, while the poor man struggled for every dime he earned and always seemed to get farther and farther behind? Why was it that the more manual labor he performed, the less he was paid? It was *his* class, the working class that was the backbone of our society and kept our country running smoothly. Not the rich assholes in their mansions and Mercedes. On the other hand, he knew everyone couldn't be rich and fortunate because someone had to flip the burgers and take off the trash.

"Ah, hell! Son-of-a-bitch," he cursed out loud, applying the brakes and shifting into a lower gear as he began slowing the big rig to a complete stop. Immediately he began mentally assessing the damage before even stepping out of his truck. *I've still got one headlight, no steam is coming from the radiator and I don't hear a fender scrapping against a tire.* He felt like he was in pretty good shape, but had better stop and get out to check just to be sure.

Since there was no emergency lane and the highway was flanked on both sides by narrow, soft shoulders, he stopped dead still in the middle of his lane for fear of getting stuck or turning the huge trailer over if he pulled off the road. He knew of drivers being crushed by the enormous weight of the trailer as they walked around to check for damage after making the mistake of pulling off onto a soft shoulder. Due to the fact that it was nighttime with little or no traffic on the two-lane highway, he felt it would be relatively safe—or the lesser of two evils.

After grabbing the flashlight from under his seat, he swung open the door and climbed down from the big rig. He walked to the front of his cab and confirmed his initial prognosis. There was a large bend in the bumper with some of the grill broken and missing and his right headlight was knocked out, but the old Kenworth was still drivable. Only minor damage. He turned and began walking about a hundred and fifty yards behind his trailer, shinning the flashlight beam across the road from side to side as he searched for the cause of the damage.

Suddenly he saw a thick cloud of steam rising from the ditch to his right. "Yep, just as I figured," he mumbled to himself. "Damn! Just my luck."

Lying in the ditch was a solid black, Angus beef cow weighing in, he guessed, around eleven-hundred pounds. Fortunately, for him, it hadn't been a large bull and that he had just managed to clip the animal with his bumper, or he wouldn't be able to continue driving his rig. Legally, it was the farmer or livestock owner who was responsible for any damages caused when his animal broke through a fence and wandered into the highway. He knew, however, from other truckers that it was nearly impossible to find a farmer who would admit that it was his cow that had caused the accident. The livestock owner would rather accept the monetary loss of his cow than have to pay for the other person's damages. His boss, however, depending on his mood, might decide to deduct the repair costs from the driver's paycheck. Either way, somebody wound up on the losing end.

He walked back to his truck and opened the cab door. Reaching behind the seat, he pulled out the heavy wooden baseball bat he carried with him at all times. Walking along the length of the trailer, he gave each tire a firm slap with the bat, checking for low tire pressure or flat tires. Satisfied all the tires were still good, he stood for a few seconds behind the trailer, allowing the cold night air to caress his face. He wished he could shut off the refrigeration unit along with the diesel engine so that he could enjoy, if just for a brief moment, the quiet, peaceful sounds of the country night. It seemed as if he was never able to escape the constant and monotonous sounds of the diesel engine and reefer unit, combined with car horns, sirens and other road noises.

He reached inside his coat pocket and pulled out a crumpled pack of Pall-Malls and lit one. Taking a long, slow drag from his cigarette, he began walking back to his truck cab. He happened to glance up and saw a huge, magnificent, Southern mansion about a mile away on top of a large hill overlooking the town. It was well lit with a dozen or so cars parked along the winding, circular driveway. Looking at his watch with the aid of the taillights on the truck cab, he saw that it was 10:15 p.m. and knew he was just outside Myrick. *One of those rich assholes throwing one of his fancy parties,* he thought to himself. *Enjoying the finer things in life while I'm out here on a cold night, driving up and down the road in this rig busting my ass for a living. People like that ain't got no worries in the world and neither do their kids.* To him, life didn't seem fair.

Already behind on his schedule, both the one in his head and the one on his Timex, he climbed back into his truck and continued heading toward his destination. The big diesel engine revved up, gears ground into first and slowly the driver and his load were once again on their way, climbing up the ten ranges of gears as they ascended into the foothills of the Appalachian Mountains.

As the taillights faded into the darkness, the peaceful sounds of the country night returned. A little farther up the road, past the city limits, the faint sounds of laughter and music could be heard coming from the big, white columned house atop the hill overlooking the town.

# Book I

# *Chapter One*

    The town of Myrick, Georgia, with its' nearly 3,000 residents, was centered in the northwest corner of the state, only a stone's throw from the Georgia-Alabama state line. The Creek Indians had inhabited the area long ago. During the Civil War many of its' majestic plantation mansions were either riddled or completely destroyed by confederate cannon balls and ransacked by blue coat soldiers on their way to the future of Atlanta.
    One of the largest and most impressive of those few remaining, exquisite dwellings was the Coleman mansion, situated high atop an immaculately manicured green hill overlooking the small, old cotton mill town. Twenty-four round Corinthian columns supported the roof of the magnificent, fourteen-room, white stucco mansion, built on the Greek revival style and accented by tall black shutters flanking the twelve-foot windows. Inside, elegant crystal chandeliers, Carrara marble mantled fireplaces and massive imported European mirrors were in nearly every room, with elaborate plaster cornices and ceiling medallions adorning the fourteen-foot high ceilings. Fan-shaped transoms and sidelights accented both entrances of the central hallway that ran through the center of the one-time plantation mansion.
    Surrounding the home were magnificent Magnolias and century old, massive Oak trees. A six-foot, red brick wall, capped with white stone and pillars encased the one-acre estate. The house was constructed in the 1830's using slave labor by a wealthy cotton plantation and land baron named Jonas Barrow, for whom the county was named. The property had

been handed down through the Barrow family from generation to generation. Now, the town of Myrick stood where Barrow's three thousand acre cotton plantation once rested.

In the early 1900's, the forty-three long, forty-mile wide Barrow County was home to one of the wealthiest politicians in the state. Former criminal court Judge and State Representative Benjamin Aldridge Coleman, Sr. established the town's cotton mill, employing approximately half of the 3,000 residents. The remaining inhabitants eked out a meager existence by farming or sharecropping acres of rolling cotton, peanut and soybean fields, while others scrapped by with dairy and cattle farming.

Myrick represented the typical, small Southern cotton mill town where a person knew everybody and their business. A town where no one bothered to use their turn signals because the person behind already knew where they were turning. In the lower part of the town, the South side, down by the mill, were dozens of small, saltbox style, wood frame houses, built and maintained by the mill owner to house the mill workers and their families. The tiny, less-than-modest dwellings stood in stark contrast to the historic old mansions on their upper or Northern side of town. The reason being, in Myrick, as in most Southern communities, there were two predominate social classes—the very rich and the very poor, better known as the haves and the have-nots.

Now, Ben Coleman, Jr., eldest son and namesake of the Judge and politician Benjamin Coleman, Sr., owned the impressive Barrow estate. Coleman, Jr., the wealthiest, most powerful man in Myrick, and one of the most influential men in the state, considered himself the last of the true Southern aristocracy. He acquired the sprawling estate in early 1950 after purchasing the property for a mere one hundred thousand dollars from its financially ailing owner and great grandson of the original owner. The Barrow family had been forced over the past century to sell off most of its three thousand acre rich farm land track by track in order to preserve and maintain the enormous old mansion itself, until all that remained was the single acre it dominated. Ben Coleman renamed the property, certainly for its' aloof location, Coleman Hill. There, he settled with his pregnant wife and two year old daughter and together they would raise three children. The stately mansion and its owners were the town's most familiar and envied vestiges. Yet while most townspeople envied the Coleman family for their wealth and privilege, others resented it and looked on them as arrogant snobs. They were, with the exception of one.

The lights, dancing off the prisms of huge chandeliers, could be seen shining through the windows of the ground floor of the magnificent mansion high atop Coleman Hill. Catherine Coleman was once again entertaining the town's few, yet most prestigious dignitaries as she did frequently. Guests included Mayor Burton, Judge Willis and Dr. Carter, along with several wealthy business owners. Since Myrick wasn't what one might refer to as a particularly exciting town with regular social activities and events available, Mrs. Coleman relished any excuse to throw one of her lavish, formal dinner parties to break the small town monotony. This also provided her with the opportunity to display her show-place home and play gracious hostess to the town's most influential residents.

Black servants scurried about from guest to guest carrying antique, silver-serving trays laden with imported caviar and cold duck. On the ornate hand carved, rosewood sideboard lay the finest Irish linen table napkins beside heirloom porcelain china and Waterford crystal. Only the exquisitely jeweled lady guests, with their formal attire and finest diamond jewelry, out-shown the fine culinary decor. Brilliant reflections of light sparkled from their gems beneath the dim glow of crystal chandeliers as they mingled atop the eighteenth century, hand-woven Persian rugs.

Catherine Coleman floated about the vast rooms like a blue puff of smoke, as she saw that her guests were being properly served, while gathering bits of tantalizing town gossip. Across the room, her husband Ben, standing in command of a small group of men all dressed in imported silk suits, was absorbed in boring business and professional prattle. Mrs. Coleman, wife of the town's cotton mill owner and considered the most refined and aristocratic woman in Myrick, was, at forty-five, a strikingly attractive petite woman. With her dark auburn, shoulder-length hair perfectly coiffed, her long slender fingers freshly manicured and her youthful, unlined face painted to perfection, her delicate features and porcelain complexion revealed no visible signs of aging or sagging. Thanks to good genes and one of Atlanta's finest plastic surgeons. She could have easily passed for a woman fifteen years younger than her fifty-two year old husband. Born in Nashville, Tennessee, Catherine Warren was viewed as the town's coldest and most aloof snob, who found absolutely nothing in common with those not on her social or economic level. Her father had resided as Dean of a prestigious women's college in Tennessee where she was born. Her father retired and the family moved to Rome, Georgia when she was a junior in school. Catherine's social, blue blood mother was from a wealthy plantation owning family in Virginia.

Being an only child, Catherine was indulged and spoiled incessantly, and because her own interests came before anything or anyone else, was disliked by nearly all acquainted with her. Her many young gentlemen suitors were quickly turned off by her shallow, self-centered disposition and, were it not for a wealthy young opportunist by the name of Benjamin Coleman whom she met at a Christmas party given at her parents' home, the beautiful socialite would have most likely remained single for many years to come. Ben Coleman's dark eyes lit up with dollar signs when he was first introduced to the refined socialite fresh out of finishing school. Although Coleman certainly didn't need her money or influence, for there was an abundance of that in his family, he felt there was always room for more. He also saw Catherine equal to him socially as well as financially. This was most important to a man from his walk of life for intelligent, affluent young men, from such wealth and privilege, would dare not marry beneath them.

Ben Coleman's reputation as a snob equaled his wife's. His notoriety as a powerful, ruthless and cunning businessman, driven by greed and who seldom played by the rules was widely known. There was a well-known story around Myrick that Ben Coleman had stood patiently by his own father's deathbed for three days and nights with pen and sanction in hand, waiting for the old man to regain consciousness long enough to sign over the family business solely to him. By doing so, he prevented his two younger brothers from receiving their fair share of the cotton mill. When the elder Coleman finally regained consciousness, just before he died, Ben, Jr. shoved the papers his lawyer had drawn up in his father's hands. Coleman assured his father they were his own burial wishes, sparing their mother the unpleasant task of making the final arrangements. Only hours after the old man had trustfully signed the documents, Coleman stood at his bedside and watched his father draw his last breath. Satisfied that his father was finally out of the way, he turned and left the room, coldly telling the family butler on his way out, "See that he's cremated. No need to spend a lot on a fancy casket and funeral. Money should be spent on the living, not the dead."

Most everyone in town believed the well-circulated tale, especially those who worked for him at the cotton mill. His employees often referred to him in whispers as "The cheap old bastard" or "The old asshole". Around Christmas he was known as "Scrooge", because the mill-hands never received so much as a holiday greeting and only got Christmas Day off during the entire holiday season. Workers put in twelve-hour shifts, five days a week, fifty-two weeks a year with alternating shifts on Saturdays. There was little sick leave and no paid vacations with minimal healthcare provisions. The only holidays observed were Thanksgiving and Christmas, which were the only two days out of the year the mill ever closed. Even the lowest paying jobs were scarce in the north Georgia town, giving Coleman an additional advantage.

Coleman was not only known for his greediness, but also for his underhanded and shady dealings with town officials such as Sheriff Bowman and Mayor Burton. It was suspected also that the town Judge was in Coleman's back pocket. Although these assumptions were only based on suspicion and not fact, those who worked in and around the courthouse, had good reason to believe the town's wealthiest businessman was paying off city officials for special privileges and favors.

Equally well known about town for their pretension, arrogance and power were the Coleman's three extraordinarily beautiful daughters. At twenty, Angela, the eldest and most out-going of the three girls, was inappropriately nicknamed Angel by her mother—inappropriate, because the curvaceous, raven-haired beauty was anything but an angel.

With long, thick black hair and big brown eyes, her sensuous, full lips were her most noticeable attribute. The college sophomore was every male co-ed's dream and every mother's nightmare, for her sexual misconduct had earned her quite a reputation on campus.

Since the evening had begun, Angel had been holding court in a quiet corner with several handsome young men, most of which were popular boys enrolled in the same college in nearby Athens. From the young age of fourteen, the most uninhibited of the three sisters had established certain notoriety among the local boys and high school football team. Apparently the locker room talk never reached the sharp ears of her proper and refined parents, for they thought of her as they did their other two prized off-spring, as the sweetest, purest wisps of Southern charm ever sired in their blue-blood aristocracy.

Angel knew she didn't have to worry about her reputation getting back to her sexually straight-laced parents, for there were few who would dare confront her powerful father with some tawdry facts about his daughter's character. The middle daughter, Amy, with her tall, slender frame and perfectly sculpted face, was another striking beauty. Her sparkling brown eyes, creamy complexion and soft, curly brown hair accentuated her classic high cheekbones and square jaw, making the high school senior very photogenic and perfect model material. Her beauty alone could have easily made the eighteen year-old one of the most popular girls in school. But, like her mother, her aloofness and egotism thwarted away potential suitors and even girlfriends in droves. Yet, of all his daughters, Ben Coleman held the greatest affection and expectations for Amy, for she was the brightest and most studious of the three girls. Despite the fact she had inherited her mother's looks, vanity and air of superiority, Amy was extremely intelligent and articulate.

Joining the guests, a half-hour after they had arrived, Amy descended the winding staircase like a regal princess wearing a formal, sky blue, knee-length sheath dress. Her curly brown tresses, cascading loosely above her shoulders, framed her finely chiseled face. She offered a faint nod and aloof smile to the guests as she strolled across the room, turning heads as she walked over and sat down in a quiet corner beside her younger sister, Anna.

Painfully shy and self-conscious, sixteen year-old, Anna Marie was the Coleman's youngest and least doted on daughter. Throughout the evening, as always when her mother threw one of her extravaganzas, Anna sat nervously alone in the most secluded corner she could find. She dreaded and despised these useless displays of wealth and superiority and begged her mother to let her remain peacefully upstairs in the refuge of her room. Her mother refused, as usual, insisting that all three of her lovely daughters' presence was required. Catherine Coleman loved nothing more than having her most prized possessions on display. Her daughters were easily the most beautiful girls in town—the entire county—perhaps the state for that matter, and Catherine reveled in the compliments they collected.

Anna, with her long, natural ash blonde hair and deep ocean blue eyes, stood out from her darker haired siblings. For her sisters had inherited their parents' dark hair and eyes, and it seemed unlikely for them to have sired a daughter in such stark contrast. Her older sister Angel often joked that Anna was the "lone white sheep in a dark sheep family." But, Anna was, without a doubt, the most beautiful of the three Coleman girls, yet oddly and surprisingly, the one who was painfully shy and withdrawn. Anna lacked any of the confidence and self-esteem, which her older sisters possessed in abundance. It simply wasn't her blonde looks that set Anna apart from her siblings. It was her personality. While Angel and Amy were conceited and self-absorbed in their own egos, Anna had little if any self-esteem. It wasn't an absence of beauty or brains that contributed to her lack of confidence, instead it was her lack of self-worth and feelings of inadequacy. It seemed to stem from the emotional neglect and lack of interest she received from her parents. While they spoiled and doted on their two oldest daughters, their youngest seemed to go unnoticed and overlooked. Angel's analysis of her younger sister's position in the family, as the "lone sheep", had more than a ring of truth. She wasn't just physically the only white sheep but she was treated like one as well. It wasn't that Anna was a bad child who misbehaved or caused her parents concern. To the contrary, she was a perfect role model for any daughter. Yet for some reason, unbeknown even to her own sisters, she was simply ignored—by her father more than her mother.

This indifference fed her underlying insecurities and caused her to withdraw from everyone. Unlike her sisters, who remained aloof and self-absorbed, Anna was repressed and introverted. The beautiful, curvy teen retreated to a self-imposed inner shell. A loner by choice, she spent hours in her room either reading or day dreaming, searching for an escape from her own anxieties and lack of self-worth.

"It's hard to figure who revels in these little parleys more—Angel or Mom," Amy said as she watched their older sister lead the three young men gathered around her in the corner in some hearty laughter.

"She's always the life of the party, that's for sure," Anna replied. "I'm glad somebody is enjoying themselves. I wouldn't even be here if it weren't for Mother dragging me downstairs."

"I don't think any of us would, to tell you the truth. Just look at it this way," Amy said, leaning over her sister's shoulder. "It's a good way to develop those all important 'social skills' that Mother keeps harping on." Amy disliked these functions almost as much as Anna, but for different reasons. Amy simply saw them as unnecessary and boring, while Anna looked on them with dread and anguish. Amy managed to execute the role expected of her, that of a well-honed socialite, while Anna retreated to the nearest corner, attempting to become invisible. Not possessing her sisters' popularity and confidence, Anna had little to help her through these torturous gatherings. She was, however, thankful for Amy's company. Amy, being the more sensitive of the two older girls, sensed Anna's anxieties and usually offered her presence, providing Anna with someone to converse with in order to keep her from standing out too much as the awkward one. Aloof and distant, with most everyone, Amy was much different toward her little sister. With Anna, she appeared caring, loyal and supportive even though those feelings stemmed mainly out of sympathy she felt toward her younger sibling.

Considered the most vain and shallow of the three, Amy spent hours in front of the mirror primping and preparing for these events. Once she was satisfied with her reflection, she turned her attention to Anna in an attempt to boost her sister's sagging ego, making sure Anna looked her very best. She fussed over her long blonde tresses as much as she did her own.

"Have you been to the buffet table yet?" Amy asked.

Anna shook her head. Despite the fact that she was starved, she could not bring herself to get up and make the painful journey across the room to the buffet table to sample some of Estelle's fabulous hors d'oeuvres and canapes.

"Come on, let's get something to eat," Amy said, taking her sister's hand. "I'm starved. I haven't eaten since breakfast. I've been waiting all day for a slice of Estelle's red velvet cake."

Estelle Pittman was the Coleman's cook and housekeeper. She had been with the Coleman family for nearly two decades. She carried well over two hundred pounds on her large frame and was a dark chocolate brown with salt and pepper hair, which she kept short and tightly curled. At sixty-one, she was from the old school South where Negroes stayed in the background and only spoke to the whites when spoken to.

The two sisters made their way to the long buffet table and began filling their plates with samples from every silver tray and chafing dish. Before they got to the end of the table, two handsome young men approached them and began flirting with Amy, ignoring Anna completely. This was something Anna was used to. Slowly she turned and inconspicuously made her way back to the secluded corner, alone. As she sat quietly munching on the goodies that filled her plate, she would occasionally look up and sneak a glance at the guests mingling about, catching disjointed bits and pieces of conversations and exchanges. She glanced over to the corner where Angel stood laughing and talking freely with her gentlemen friends, then to the buffet table where Amy entertained her admirers, all the while making herself even more aware of her own inadequacy and isolation. Stray bits of conversations between two elegantly dressed middle-aged women standing behind her, suddenly took her attention.

"She's such a lovely girl, but nothing like her sisters," she overheard one of them whisper softly over a glass of champagne.

"I know," agreed the other woman. "Anna seems so shy and withdrawn. I've often wondered if there isn't something wrong with her."

*Something wrong with her?* The words hit her hard, cutting through her like a knife. She felt like a circus freak. Anna was beautiful like her sisters, an honor student, yet she was different and it was obvious—to everyone. Perhaps that's why her on parents paid so little attention to her. She felt like that one puppy in the whole litter that got pushed to the side and trampled on. She glanced up and saw another guest staring in her direction. Suddenly, she found it impossible to swallow the bite she had in her mouth. She felt as if she were about to choke. Anna sat her plate down and got up from her seat. Quickly she made her way out of the room and toward the staircase where she made her escape.

"Where are you goin' child?"

Anna paused at the bottom of the stairs, recognizing the familiar, friendly voice.

"I know you haven't eaten anything."

Anna turned and faced Estelle. In many ways, the old maid was more like a mother to Anna than her own mother. She loved the old black woman who had nursed she and her sisters through all their childhood illnesses and crisis. Estelle understood Anna's feelings better than anyone and was always there to offer comfort and encouragement.

"I'm not feeling so good, Estelle. I'm going upstairs to my room. Don't tell Mom where I've gone unless she asks. Okay?"

The old woman gave a wink and nodded. "I'll be up shortly with a plate. Don't you worry, I won't tell her."

"Thanks Estelle. I'd really like some of your cake." With that, Anna turned and ran up the stairs to the safe refuge of her room where she remained the rest of the evening. She would deal with her mother's scorn later.

The brutal Georgia sun was finally sinking behind the horizon, retreating only to return early the next day to sear everything beneath it. It was mid-July, the hottest, most miserable time of the year in Georgia. It was at this time of year that temperatures often rose to the triple digits and the air became so thick and humid it made it difficult to breath. This was when those who were fortunate or wealthy enough, sought refuge in the nearby North Georgia mountains which offered shelter from the agonizing heat. July and August were the months most Georgians reserved for their vacation time, where they escaped to higher ground, to be sheltered by thick trees and woods, which lowered the ground temperature a good ten degrees.

Gene Longhorn, however, was not one of those fortunate, nor wealthy enough to escape. Instead, he was one of the poor unfortunate souls who were destined to toil his life away in an attempt to eke out a meager living with his own blood, sweat and tears. From a dirt poor, uneducated family, and only a high school education himself, twenty-one year-old Eugene Anthony Longhorn hadn't the opportunities or the advantages to better his life. This produced much anger and bitterness as well as some underlying depression. One of three children, born to a half-Creek Indian father and an Italian mother, Gene was the youngest child and the only one in his family who actually worked hard for what little he made. His father, Joseph Longhorn, owned a two-acre automobile junkyard beside their six-room wood-frame house that he managed, along with his oldest son Joe, Jr. Gene's mother and younger sister were killed in an automobile accident when Gene was thirteen. While Gene worked hard labor in all kinds of weather, ten to twelve hours a day as a farm foreman, his father and brother sat around drinking beer and eating, waiting for someone in need of a used car part to drop by. Joe, Jr., who was seven years Gene's senior, also drove a wrecker for the wrecker service they also provided. Their workdays were easy compared to Gene's, who earned his pay with muscle and sweat.

From the age of thirteen he had worked on a farm for an elderly landowner by the name of Harry Porter. Porter owned a thousand acres of prime pasture land where he raised Black Angus beef cattle and Holstein dairy cows. Porter stood about five-feet, four-inches and weighed just under a hundred thirty pounds. His thinning hair was still mostly brown and only peppered with grey. Porter had never married or sired any offspring and, at seventy-four, had outlived virtually everyone in his family. All he had left to show for his life was a one-hundred and twenty-four year-old deteriorating plantation house built by slaves before the Civil War, a thousand acres of rolling pasture and an eight year-old Chevrolet pick-up with less than six thousand miles on the odometer due to its owner's deteriorating eye sight. The only time the truck left Porter's yard was when the old man sent Gene into town to do his weekly shopping and to pick up his medications at the corner drug store.

Sweat glistened off his well-tanned, muscular back and chest as Gene Longhorn glanced down at his watch and began rolling up the water hose inside the milking barn. His final chore each day was to make sure the concrete floor was hosed down and free of cow manure. It was a little past six p.m. He washed his calloused hands at the outside faucet before getting into his nineteen sixty-four royal blue Chevelle Malibu Super Sport which had landed in his father's junkyard two years ago. After sinking every dime he could manage to scrape up into the junked super charged automobile, the mighty 327 V8 engine roared with power and shinned like the day it rolled off the showroom floor. It was the only thing Gene Longhorn owned that he could be proud of.

He left the Porter farm and turned onto Highway 11 where he drove the six miles to his house. Along the way, he passed an old, heavyset black woman walking down the road with a bundle of fresh collard greens tucked under one arm and carrying a Piggly Wiggly grocery sack in the other. He knew what she would be serving her family for dinner that evening. He was getting pretty hungry himself after working in the fields all day. It was almost six-thirty. His brother closed the junkyard office at six sharp so he was already home. Their father, who stayed home most of the day, had dinner prepared as usual and waiting on the dinner table. Both Joe Longhorn and Joe, Jr. were about the laziest, most gluttonous humans on the face of the earth. Both tipped the scales at well over three hundred pounds and neither man stood over five-feet, six-inches tall. While their mother had been a slender, petite woman, Joe, Jr. had obviously inherited his father's fat gene cells. In stark contrast, Gene was the exact opposite of his brother and father. Standing at nearly six-feet tall and weighing more than a hundred pounds less than either of them, Gene was a handsome young man, inheriting his mother's dark Italian looks with his thick black hair, dark brown eyes and olive complexion. His broad shoulders and lean, yet muscular body was tanned a golden brown from hours of hard farm labor. There was no doubt he would have had many girl suitors if only he'd had the money to squire them. Every dime he earned went to his unemployed father to help provide them with the gargantuan amounts of food he and Gene's brother managed to consume. What little that was left went toward the restoration of his super-charged automobile.

Gene parked in front of the old wood-frame house that was in desperate need of repair and a fresh coat of paint. He went inside where his father and brother were already seated at the dinner table.

"Just in time," said Joseph Longhorn, as his youngest son walked through the door. "Better sit down and grab a plate before it gets gone."

"I'm gonna go wash up first," Gene replied, heading toward the only bathroom in the tiny house. When he finished, he returned and took a seat at the small kitchen table beside his father.

"You know, me and Dad have been talking about gettin' you to start lookin' after the junkyard on Saturdays so we can have the whole weekend off," Joe, Jr. said, biting into a plump fried chicken breast.

"I can't do that," Gene snapped. "I'm already working seven days a week for Porter. I can't take off Saturdays. I've got my own work cut out for me. At least you two have Sunday off which is more than I get."

"Well everybody else gets to take two days out of the week off. Why shouldn't we?" replied his brother.

"Why shouldn't I?" Gene snapped. "I've always had to work seven days a week. You two don't do half a day's honest work the whole six days you call yourselves working. All you do is sit around on your fat asses, drinkin' beer and stuffin' down sandwiches all day, waitin' for somebody to drop by and buy a part off one of them junk cars. I'm the one out there bustin' my balls working ten hours a day, seven days a week." He paused, sat down his glass of iced tea and looked his brother square in the eye. "I tell you what. I'll make a deal with you. You go do my job on Saturdays and I'll be glad to fill in for you at the junkyard. How does that sound?"

"That don't sound like such a fair trade to me," chuckled their father, his huge belly jiggling like Jell-o as he laughed. "If I was you I'd keep my Saturday job and just appreciate Sunday," he advised his oldest boy with a wide grin.

"Why don't you get him to work the yard on Saturday?" Gene asked his brother. "He ain't doin' nothin' anyway. Let *him* give you the day off."

"I'm retired," his father replied quickly. "I put in my twenty-three years at the cotton mill. Besides, I'm on disability. I *can't* work."

"You can't work because you can't fit behind a steering wheel, but you could sit behind a desk and take people's money when they come in the office. How hard could that be?" Gene asked his father.

"All I'm sayin' is everybody needs some time off now and then," Joe, Jr. sighed.

"Tell me about it," snapped at his brother. "When was the last time you saw me with a day off? I've been workin' my ass off everyday of the week since I was thirteen. And I still ain't got nothin' to show for it."

"You got a nice car," his father reminded his son. "The envy of every kid in the county."

"That's *all* I've got," Gene replied.

"You know what your problem is?" Joey asked, looking at his brother as he inhaled a fried chicken leg.

Gene remained silent and just stared back at his brother.

"Your problem is, you've got a bad case of assyitis."

Gene continued to stare at his brother across the table in silence.

"You know," Joey went on to explain. "When your optical nerve gets crossed with your rectal nerve and it gives you a shitty outlook on life."

Their father howled with laughter. Gene however, remained silent and gave his brother an icy cold stare, finding no humor in his observation.

"Well, the truth is, there ain't nothin' around these parts," his father said. "You'll never make nothin' if you stay here. The only ones that come close to makin' anything are the ones that work in the mill and they just make enough to get by. Nobody will ever get rich working for old man Coleman. He'll see to that."

"Dad is right," Joe, Jr. agreed. "But what are you gonna do? If you ain't got no college education, nobody is gonna offer you a decent job. And who's got the money for college in the first place?"

"It don't matter if you got a fancy degree or not," their father said. "They don't pay nothin' around these parts no way. Besides nobody ever got rich workin' for somebody else. You're either born with money or left with it or you'll struggle all your life just to make ends meet. The only people around here with money are people like the Colemans who's had it handed down to them generation after generation. Old money is what made them rich."

"Yeah? Well, nobody has ever left me anything. I've had to work my ass off all my life for every dime I ever made," Gene snarled.

"That's life, boy," his father replied. "You're either born with it or you'll never have nothin'. Least if you stay around here you won't. You might be able to find a better job down around Warner Robins or Macon. You might find work at the air base down there. Or maybe at the Ford plant down in Atlanta. I hear they pay pretty good at places like that, but unless you work the cotton mill, the best you'll ever do is make minimum wage. At least at the mill you get some healthcare benefits."

"Yeah, that's more than what I'm getting' workin' for old man Porter. This town and everything in it is nothin' but a dead end." Gene finished his meal in silence. He felt trapped and defeated. Talking about his dilemma only made him realize how unlucky he was. Unless his luck broke or some drastic changes came his way, he was destined to be a loser just like his father and brother the rest of his life with no more to show for his hard labor than what they obtained. The only difference was, he worked ten times harder than both of them put together for what little he had. Life was unfair, that was for sure. It seemed the harder he worked, the less he gained. All his hard work and efforts would only make him old and worn out before his time. He glanced across the table at his father and brother who sat there fat and seemingly satisfied to have next to nothing. Food was all they lived for. As long as they had enough to fill their bulging bellies each day, they were happy as a couple of pigs rutting in a mud puddle—which is what they reminded him of at that moment. But for him, there had to be something better. There had to be more to life. He just had to find a way to escape from the existence to which he was born. But how? He had to find a way. And the sooner, the better.

# *Chapter Two*

Sunday dinner at the Coleman home was always served promptly at one o'clock in the afternoon and immediately following church. This Sunday the entire family gathered around the long mahogany dinning table. Angel was home from Athens for the weekend. Her mother insisted she try to come home at least every other weekend since the college wasn't that far away. Even though college was out for the summer, Angel continued to live in Athens where she shared an apartment with a girlfriend.

Since Estelle had every Sunday off, she prepared a large dinner on Saturday and placed it in the refrigerator for Mrs. Coleman to warm in the oven following church. Today, Estelle had prepared a rib roast with green beans and new potatoes.

As soon as Catherine led the table blessing, she began passing around the large china serving bowls.

"Amy, we need to begin discussing your fall college quarter now that summer is coming to an end. You have your entry exams behind you now so we need to register you by the end of the month. That's something we should have already done and have behind us."

Amy had been dreading this moment for months, but the time had finally arrived when she had to tell her parents she had no intentions of following in her older sister's path and attending the University of Athens.

"Mom," she began nervously. "I've been meaning to discuss something with you and Daddy, I'm not going to Athens in the fall."

Her parents looked at their daughter in stunned disbelief. "What do you mean you're not going to Athens? Arrangements have already been made. You've already been accepted," her mother exclaimed.

Her father stared at Amy with his cold, steely eyes. "Of course she's going. Already a couple of months out of school and she's become lazy. That's why it's important to begin college as soon after graduation as possible. The longer you wait, the lazier you become and before you know it, you've put it off indefinitely. No," her father added firmly, "you're starting fall quarter this September. End of discussion."

Amy had always been and would remain Ben Coleman's favorite daughter. Just as it was unexplainable that Anna was the least favored, for some reason known only to him, Amy was his most preferred. He was more affectionate with her than his other two daughters and doted on her constantly. For several years, up until her early teens, Angel had been Daddy's little darling. Then oddly, that changed overnight and the oldest girl suddenly turned somewhat hostile toward her father and had less to do with him. No one understood why. Their mother thought the reason for the sudden change had something to do with Angel transforming into young womanhood and resenting her father making her his little princess. It was around this same time Angel began to enter her *tomboy* stage. A stage she had yet to emerge from.

"If you don't want to enter fall quarter, then what do you plan to do?" Angel asked her sister, placing a heaping slice of Estelle's cornbread on her plate. "You must have something in mind."

There was a long, nervous pause, then finally Amy replied, "I want to go to modeling school in Atlanta," she replied, fearing her father's reaction.

"I absolutely forbid it!" her father shouted with a hard icy glare. "You are not going to Atlanta to do any thing of the kind. You can just get that foolish idea out of your head right now."

"It's my life, Daddy. My future. People have told me I'd make a successful model. The money is good and I'd get to travel. I'm eighteen now and an adult. It's not like I would need a chaperone or someone to travel with me. Besides, I'm old enough to make my own decisions now."

"Oh really," Ben Coleman replied. "Well then, you'd better start making your own money as well because I'm not paying for any modeling school. You're going to college where your sister can look after you the first year and help you get settled in. So you can just forget any foolish ideas about modeling. Besides, that's not a profession I want for my daughter. That's for girls who don't have the money or brains to further their education. You're fortunate enough to have choices in life. My daughters are going to make something out of themselves and become successful women instead of having to become waitresses and store clerks."

"Or a mill worker," Angel smiled with sarcasm. "God forbid any of us become *common folk*."

"Listen," Coleman said, pointing his finger at his oldest daughter. "I've worked hard all my life so that my children wouldn't have to settle for common labor jobs."

"Your father is right," Catherine added, supporting her husband. "Your father and I have always insisted on nothing but the best for all of you girls. We can't stand by and allow you to throw your futures away foolishly. College isn't an option in this family, it's a requirement. So let's drop this discussion and move on."

Ben Coleman continued to stare at his daughter in silence. Finally he added, "I don't want to hear anymore about Atlanta or modeling. Do you understand me?"

Amy kept her head bowed, picking at the food on her plate. "Yes sir," she replied, her voice barely above a whisper. She remained quiet throughout dinner.

As they were finishing their meal, Angel announced that she wanted to drive down to the Dairy Queen for an ice cream sundae for dessert before packing to return to Athens. She invited her sisters to join her. They all agreed and the three girls excused themselves from the table. They got into Angel's red, Ford Mustang convertible and headed for the local Dairy Queen. Anna took her position as the youngest sister in the back seat of the sports car, reserving the front for her two older siblings.

"You do know, don't you, that it's not so much his concern over our future as how it will make him look to his friends?" Angel told Amy, as she lit up a cigarette once she was safely away from the watchful eyes of her parents. "Just think how it would look if he has a daughter who refuses to go on to college and earn a degree."

"I know that," Amy agreed, as they cruised down Main Street, past the town square, which held the ten-foot statue of confederate General Robert E. Lee. "It's not our welfare he's concerned with. It's his precious public image and how our decisions reflect on him and Mom."

"It's all about him," Angel added. And the easiest way to control us is to threaten to take away his money. Money is power to him. And since all our money comes from him, we don't have the freedom to do what we want or make our own decisions."

"Money makes you a whore," Amy declared in disgust. "It forces you to do things you don't want to do and it's always men who dangle it in front of their women to make them do whatever they want. Dad wants me to go to college so he threatens to take it away if I go to Atlanta. He knows I don't have any way to support myself while I go to modeling school. I couldn't afford an apartment plus pay for my tuition on my own."

"Why don't you just get married and move out?" Anna suggested.

"Marriage is nothing more than legalized prostitution," Angel replied. "You're still doing what some man wants you to do so he'll take care of you."

"That's right," Amy agreed. "The only way you'll ever have independence and freedom to do what you want is to have your own money."

"That's why I'm working for my degree," Angel said. "Be financially independent," she advised her youngest sister. "Don't rely on a man to support you. It might have been good enough for Mother and her generation, but I sure as hell don't want to have to live my life like her."

"Neither do I," agreed Amy. "But I hate the thought of having to give in to the old man and make him happy in order to achieve some independence."

"Like I said," Angel reiterated. "Money makes you a whore. One way or another."

"Well, you could come to Athens and move in with me while you pursue modeling," Angel suggested. "But it would mean driving from

Athens to Atlanta everyday. Mom and Dad wouldn't even have to know you're staying with me. You could get a job after school and make enough money to pay for your car insurance, clothes and some food. I would provide you with a place to stay and maybe I could slip you a few bucks now and then. Maybe you could even get some modeling jobs to help out. All you need is a nice portfolio and some contacts."

"Yeah and do you know how much a portfolio would cost me? Around two or three-hundred dollars. And besides, if Daddy ever found out that you were helping me go against him, he would stop paying for your apartment and force you to go live in the dorm."

"So who's going to tell him?" Angel asked. "I'm not. You're certainly not. Just let him think you moved to Atlanta and are working after school to support yourself."

"He'd never believe that. He knows I couldn't make enough working a part-time job to pay for modeling school and an apartment, plus all my other expenses. He's not stupid."

"Well, do what you want," Angel concluded. "It's just a thought."

The shinny red convertible signaled and turned into the Dairy Queen just outside of town. Angel stepped on the gas and turned in front of the blue Chevy that had the right of way. Since there was a long line at the drive-thru window, they decided to park and go inside. The Chevy turned in behind them and parked a couple of spaces away. The driver got out and walked toward the entrance of the small restaurant and took his place in line. Sunday afternoons were the busiest time for the only ice cream stand in town. The three girls took their time climbing out of their car and strolled inside the cool, air-conditioned restaurant where not only tasty frozen treats were sold, but some of the best brazier burgers and chili dogs in town.

While her sisters continued to be engulfed in their conversation, Anna stepped forward at the counter beside the young man her sister had turned in front of earlier. The waitress behind the counter grabbed her pencil and asked who was next.

"He was here first," Anna replied, gesturing to the young man who stood beside her.

"We'll have three medium hot fudge sundaes with walnuts to go,"

Angel interjected over Anna's shoulder, ignoring her sister's offer to allow the young man in front of them to be served next.

"But he was ahead of us," Anna reminded her.

"So? Haven't you ever heard, 'ladies first'?" Angel replied.

The confused waitress glanced up at the three girls and the young man standing in front of her. She simply wished someone would just confirm his or her order so she could move the line along.

"Go ahead," the young man told her, nodding toward the three girls beside him. Although he didn't know them, one glance told him they were little rich girls with more money than manners, tooling about town in a brand new automobile bought and paid for by their wealthy parents. To him, they weren't worth a confrontation. While people like him had to work and struggle for everything they had, these little princesses were handed everything on a silver platter. Not only did they have all the money they could ever want or need, but they were attractive as well. God just seemed to smile down on some more than others. The unfairness of it all infuriated him but there was nothing he could do to change things. Such was life.

Once the waitress had jotted down their order, Angel turned away, without so much as a nod of appreciation to the man who had allowed them to move ahead of him, and resumed talking to her sister.

Anna shyly glanced at him and with a polite smile said, "Thank you."

The young man looked at Anna and saw a girl who, although was every bit as lovely as her two companions, was completely different. This girl was rich and beautiful, yet polite.

After processing the girls' order, the waitress turned to him. " I'll have a double brazier cheese, large order of fries and a chocolate shake for here," he said. He then glanced back to steal another look at the young lady who had caught his eye. She was staring at him. She flushed and quickly turned her head when he caught her looking at him.

"Guess you think I must eat a lot," he smiled.

Anna turned back to face him. "Why?" she smiled back.

"Well, that's a lot of food for one person."

"You're a big guy," she replied, still smiling.

"And a hungry one," he added. "I've been working all day and I've worked up an appetite."

"Where do you work?"

"I work for Harry Porter. He has a farm outside of town."

Anna thought for a moment. "Is he the one who owns that big old plantation house that sits way back off Highway 11?"

"Yeah. That's him."

"I've always admired that old house. It's huge. And it looks so old," Anna said.

"And it's also pretty run down," he added. "Old man Porter don't even live there no more. It's fallin' in. He moved a trailer in over there beside it and moved out of the house."

"Really? Why doesn't he fix it up?"

"Costs too much money. Harry says he could build two houses for what it would cost him to make that old house livable again."

"How old is it?"

"It's been in his family for over a hundred years. It was built before the Civil War."

"Wow," Anna gasped, her blue eyes wide in amazement. "I'd love to go in there sometime. I love old houses."

Angel was so absorbed in her own conversation with Amy that she didn't noticed their younger sister talking to the man next to them. She stopped when she noticed Amy's attention had diverted to Anna. When she turned around and saw the two involved in their own conversation, she was surprised that her sister was chatting with a perfect stranger. Just then, the waitress arrived with their order and Angel handed her the money across the counter.

"Come on Anna, let's go," Angel said, taking her sister by the arm and leading her away as if she were leading a small child out of harm's way.

"Bye," Anna smiled at the young man. "Nice talking to you."

"Same here," he nodded in return. "Take care."

Gene Longhorn watched as the three girls walked to their car and drove away. Suddenly it dawned on him where he'd seen two of the girls. They were the Coleman sisters. He had gone to school with Angela and her sister Amy. He had graduated a year or two ahead of them. But he'd never seen the other girl before. The one they called Anna.

Anna came downstairs and walked into the kitchen where she joined Amy and her mother who sat at the table discussing their trip to Atlanta that morning. At least twice a month Catherine would gather her daughters and the four of them would drive to Cumberland Mall where they shopped for expensive clothing and accessories along with household items that couldn't be found in a small rural town like Myrick. This weekend however, Angel wouldn't be joining them because she was staying in Athens and would be home the following weekend.

"Why don't we just wait until next weekend when Angel can go?" Anna suggested to her mother, not really caring to make the trip herself.

"Because Amy wants to look for some new fall clothes to start college with this September," her mother replied. "I'm sure you could use some new fall things yourself to start back to school."

"Yeah, I suppose so. But I just don't like that long drive down there and back. If it just weren't so far away," Anna said.

"Oh, it's not that far," replied Catherine. "We'll have lunch at that restaurant in the Mall that you like so well. It'll be fun. We'll be home by late afternoon. Besides, your father and I are supposed to have dinner with the Carters tonight so I need to be home early. You girls have been invited if you'd like to join us."

"I have a date tonight," Amy reminded her mother.

"With whom?" Anna asked, surprised because her sister seldom went out on dates. Amy had the opinion throughout high school that no one in the small town was *worthy* of her and that Myrick had nothing to offer where men were concerned. And for the most part, she was right. The majority of the boys her age were from poor, mill working families with very little money and even less to offer. The ones who did equal her socially and monetarily, were unattractive and uninteresting.

"Chuck Willis," Amy replied.

"Is that Judge Willis's son?"

Amy nodded. Charles E. Willis, Jr., known throughout high school as Chuck, had graduated with Angel two years ago and was attending college in Athens. He was home from school for the summer and he and Amy had become quite chummy recently.

"Where are you going?" Anna asked.

"Out to eat and to a movie. That's pretty much all there is to do around here on a Saturday night. This place is so dead. I hate Myrick."

"Well that's all you'd be doing if you lived in a big town," Catherine told her daughter. "There's nothing wrong with dinner and a movie. That's all your father and I did while we were dating."

"There's more restaurants with better food in the city and stage plays, ballet and the opera, not just movies at the local theater," Amy insisted.

"I guess you're right," Catherine agreed. "Your generation needs more stimulation than mine. We were willing to settle for less."

Estelle, who had been washing the breakfast dishes and listening quietly to their conversation, finally spoke up. "The youngins' today are a lot different than when we was growing up, Miss Catherine. A hamburger and a drive-in satisfied us. But this generation wants more excitement."

"That's right," Amy agreed. "And you're not going to find it around here because that's all Myrick has to offer."

The back door to the kitchen opened suddenly and Cassandra, Estelle' sixteen year-old daughter walked in. "Hello," the attractive black girl greeted.

"Hi Cassie," Anna replied. "Why aren't you sleeping in? It's Saturday morning."

"How come you aren't?" Cassie asked with her familiar toothy grin.

"Mom and Amy want me to go to Atlanta shopping with them this morning."

"Oh, going to the big city, are you? While I have to settle for what I can find at K-Mart."

"Well why don't you go with us to Atlanta? Since Angel isn't here, there's plenty of room."

Catherine nervously shifted her weight in the chair. She wished her daughter wouldn't invite Cassie to come along. Besides the fact she was black, she was their maid's daughter. But to Anna, she was a good friend, perhaps her *only* friend other than her own sisters. Unlike her parents and sisters, Anna didn't view people of color on a lower social level. To her Cassie was her equal. The color of her skin made no difference. Cassie was good and kind. She was a sweet girl and Anna enjoyed her company.

"Cassie, I guess you best hang around here today," Estelle told her daughter, aware of Catherine Coleman's social attitude and racial prejudice. "The bathrooms need a good goin' over at home and there's laundry from yesterday that needs ironin' and puttin' away."

"Well I can do all that this afternoon after I get back from shopping," Cassie told her mother.

"Hey, I've got an idea," Anna said. "Why don't I stay here and go shopping with Cassie instead?"

"Sure. That's a great idea," Cassie agreed.

"Anna—"

"Oh please, Mom," she begged. "I wasn't looking forward to that long drive to Atlanta anyway. You and Amy go ahead. I'll stay here and go shopping with Cassie."

"Go ahead, Mom. Let her stay here. We'll go," Amy said, letting her sister off the hook.

Catherine thought for a moment. She didn't want Anna seen fraternizing with their Negro maid's daughter. However, Anna was different from her sisters—from the entire family for that matter. *Color blind*, Ben Coleman would say.

"Well, alright then," Catherine finally agreed with reluctance. "I guess you would have more fun with Cassie anyway. Bring my purse and I'll give you some shopping money."

The two girls got into Cassie's old blue Toyota and drove about a mile out of town to their local K-Mart store. They spent a couple of hours looking at clothes, shoes, accessories and cosmetics. Other than the small, locally owned department store in downtown Myrick, K-Mart offered the only real shopping opportunities without having to drive to nearby Rome or all the way to Atlanta. There was even a small snack bar in the back of the department store that served hot sandwiches and cold plates.

"Are you gettin' hungry?" Cassie asked as they headed toward the check out line.

'What time is it?"

"Twelve-thirty," Cassie said, giving her watch a quick glance. "Do you want to grab a bite here or down at the Dairy Queen? They have really good cold plates at the drug store."

"A cold plate sounds good," Anna agreed.

They left K-Mart and drove back into town. Cassie parked in front of the corner drug store across the street from the town square. The girls got out and went inside. They sat down at a booth and grabbed a couple of menus. Although it was 1969 and segregation was being erased throughout the South, there was still plenty of racial prejudice in small towns like Myrick. Thus, a black and a white girl sharing a table in a public restaurant was neither a common nor welcomed sight. Some time passed before a waitress finally walked over to their table with an order pad. The plump woman in her mid-forties gave the two girls a discriminating glare.

"What can I get for you?" she asked.

"We'll have two cold plates," Cassie replied.

"And what to drink?"

"Coke for me," Cassie answered.

"Sweet tea, for me," Anna replied.

After jotting down their orders, the waitress quickly turned without saying another word and went back behind the lunch counter. As they sat there chatting, Anna's attention fell on the young man climbing out of a Chevy pick-up that had just pulled up to the curb. It was the same guy she'd had the brief conversation with at the Dairy Queen last Sunday.

"Hey," Anna whispered to Cassie across the table. "Do you think that guy coming in here is cute?"

Cassie turned and glanced over her shoulder at the young man walking through the door. "Yeah, for a white guy, he's pretty cute, I guess. Do you know him?"

"Not really. I just ran into him at the Dairy Queen last weekend. I don't know his name. He seemed really nice though."

The two girls seated at the soda fountain booth were the first things that caught Gene's eye as he entered the corner pharmacy. He immediately recognized Anna and a spontaneous smile appeared on both their faces. He nodded and began walking toward them.

"Hi," he greeted with a friendly smile.

"Hi," Anna replied. "I thought I recognized you from the Dairy Queen."

"Yeah. You're Anna, right?"

"Yes. How did you know my name?"

"The girl you were with that day. I heard her call your name."

"Oh, that was my sister, Angel. They are my sisters. I'm Anna Coleman."

"Yeah, I think I went to school with them, but I graduated a year or two ahead. I don't remember you, though."

"You were probably already out of school by the time I got there. I'm the youngest. I was a Freshman when Angel was a Senior and Amy a Sophomore. I'm a Junior now. I'll graduate next year."

Gene hadn't expected Anna to be that young. He was five years older.

"Hi," Cassie smiled. "I'm her distant cousin. Real distant." They all laughed.

"I'm sorry," Anna apologized, forgetting her manners. "This is my friend, Cassie Pittman. We both go to Myrick High."

"Nice to met you," Gene nodded. "I'm Gene Longhorn."

"Are you working today?" Anna asked.

"Yeah, I'm afraid so. I had to run into town to pick up some medicine for Mr. Porter. He usually has me runnin' errands for him on Saturdays since he can't drive anymore himself."

"I got those prescriptions ready now," Doc Wheeler shouted to Gene from behind the drug counter at the back of the store. "They're ready when you are."

"Okay. I'll be right there," Gene shouted back. "I guess I better get on back there and pick up those prescriptions. Y'all eatin' lunch here?"

"Yeah, if they ever decide to bring it to us," Cassie said. "All we ordered was a couple of cold plates. How long does it take to throw some tuna and macaroni salad on a plate and run it out here?"

"Well, I'm gonna run on back to the pharmacy and I'll be back in a minute," he said.

"Okay," Anna smiled.

Anna waited until he had walked away. "He is so cute," she cooed to Cassie, leaning across the table.

"Yeah, but isn't he a little too old for you? He's older than Angel," Cassie said.

"Well, he doesn't look that old."

"I bet your father would have a fit if he came callin' on you. Your mother would too, for that matter."

Anna thought for a moment. Cassie was probably right. Although it wouldn't be simply his age that would be the only determining factor. Who his father was would also have a bearing on the matter.

"If I was you, when he asked me out, I'd sneak off with him," Cassie suggested. "I wouldn't try to bring home and introduce him to my parents."

"Oh, I doubt I'd ever be able to get away with that," Anna replied.

"Tell them that you're goin' off with me," Cassie told her.

The way her parents felt about Cassie's race, she'd be just as well off telling them about Gene, Anna thought to herself. Just then they caught a glimpse of the waitress behind the soda fountain counter.

"Excuse me," Cassie said. "Are those cold plates about ready?"

The woman gave Cassie a cold stare. "I'll see," she replied, disappearing once again.

"Then again, you may be countin' your chickens before they're hatched," Cassie said. "He ain't asked you out yet. After finding out how young you are, he may have second thoughts."

"You're right," Anna sighed with a disappointed frown.

"Still waitin' for those cold plates?" Gene asked, returning from the drug counter.

"We're about to give up and go down to the Dairy Queen," Anna replied.

"That's where I'm headed," he said. "I thought I'd grab a burger before driving back to the farm."

"They seemed to have lost your orders," the waitress said, reappearing once more. "It'll be awhile longer."

"Look, just forget it," Cassie snapped. "You didn't loose our orders. You just don't want to serve no coloreds in here. Well forget it. I'd be afraid to eat anything you served me now anyway. Come on Anna, let's get out of here."

The girls slid out of the booth and started to leave.

"Y'all are welcome to join me for a brazier burger if you'd like," Gene offered. "I'm headed there now."

"We'd love to," Cassie replied.

"Sure," Anna agreed with a shy smile. "Sounds good."

The waitress gave them a hard stare as they left the store and went outside. Just as they stepped outside, Cassie ran into a young black boy she knew from school and who attended her church. They stopped to chat for a moment while Anna and Gene continued walking to their cars parked by the curb.

"Hey Anna," Cassie called to her friend. "Would you mind if me and Clarence rode around a little while and you guys go on without me."

Anna was a little unsure about being left alone with Gene. After all, she had just met him.

"That's fine," Gene shouted back to Cassie. "I'll give her a lift home after lunch."

Anna glanced up at him, not knowing what to say.

"That's okay with you, isn't it?" he asked.

"Yeah. Okay," she replied. "If you're sure you don't mind."

"Of course not."

Anna glanced back at Cassie and smiled. "I'll see you later, Cassie," she said.

"Okay. Bye now," Cassie yelled back at her friend as she climbed into her car with the male companion.

Gene walked over to the passenger's side of the pick-up and opened the door for Anna. He helped her step up and slide onto the seat. She thanked him. Then he walked around and got in on the driver's side. They talked about Myrick and whom they went to school with as they drove the short distance to the Dairy Queen. Again, Gene got out and opened the truck door for Anna and helped her out. He was such a gentleman, she thought. He held the door open for her as they entered the small burger stand.

"What do you want," he asked her.

"Whatever you're having," she replied.

Gene ordered two double brazier cheeseburgers, fries and two large Cokes and paid the waitress behind the counter.

"Oh, you don't have to pay for mine," Anna said, opening her handbag. "I'll pay for my food."

"Don't bother," Gene smiled. "It's my pleasure."

Anna returned his smile. "Thank you," she said. She wondered if this would be considered a *real* date. It was the first time a guy had ever paid for her meal. In fact, it was the first time she had ever been alone with a guy. She was nervous yet very excited. When the waitress handed them a tray filled with their order, Gene took it and led them to a corner booth near the back. She took her seat across the table from him and watched as he removed her food first from the tray and placed it in front of her. She thanked him and waited for him to begin eating before she touched her own food.

"You eat here a lot?" she asked him.

"Yeah, and I eat a lot when I'm here," he cracked with a smile.

"They do have good burgers," Anna agreed.

The two continued their conversation, getting better acquainted as they learned more about each other, falling instantly *in like*. Neither had much if any dating experience for different and various reasons and both were extremely pleased, if not relieved, to have found one another with so little effort. After they had finished their meal, they continued to chat for almost an hour learning as much as they could about the other. Finally, Gene glanced at his watch.

"Damn! It's after two-thirty," he exclaimed. " I need to be getting' back to the farm. Old man Porter will be wondering where I got off to."

"I'm sorry," Anna apologized. "It's my fault. I talk too much."

"Don't be silly. I've enjoyed every minute of it. Listen," he said, and then paused, carefully considering his next move. "Would you like to go out tonight? I mean since it's Saturday night and all."

Anna tried to control her enthusiasm. "Oh, sure. I'd love to," she replied. "But wait, I'll have to ask my parents first."

"Okay. Why don't I call you around seven-thirty and make sure we're on for tonight and then I'll come by and pick you up around eight."

"Alright," Anna agreed. "Here, I'll give you my number." She jotted down her home phone number on a piece of paper and handed it across the table to him. Then they got into his truck and Gene began driving her home. When she began giving him directions to her house, he stopped her.

"I know where you live," he grinned. "Everybody around here knows where Coleman Hill is."

After he had dropped her off, Gene sped back to the farm. All the way back he kept thinking about Anna and hoping that he would call her house five hours from then and have her tell him she was ready and waiting. But he had a gut feeling that wasn't going to happen. It was just too good to be true. He simply didn't have the kind of luck it would take to get a girl like Anna. She was beautiful and sweet and from one of the wealthiest families in the county. Not to mention, she was five years his junior. She was still just a kid. The few girls he had briefly dated in high school couldn't begin to compare with Anna. They weren't even in her league. But neither was he.

When Anna arrived home that afternoon, she was in a state of panic. Her mind was a battleground. Should she take a chance and be up front with her parents and ask their permission to go out with Gene or should she just take Cassie's advice and slip off with him. Once they told her she couldn't see him and then got caught sneaking out, she would be in double trouble. But if she took the risk and lied to her family about whom she was with, perhaps she would be lucky enough to get away with it. She was glad her mother and Amy hadn't arrived home from Atlanta yet. That gave her time to phone Cassie and discuss the matter with her.

"I say don't ask your mom and dad," Cassie advised. "I can tell you, they're gonna say no when they find out he's not from a wealthy family and isn't in college. Think about it Anna. Do you really believe your dad will allow you to date a guy five years older than you? He's a grown man! You're still in school. You're still a kid compared to him. Besides, he comes from nothing. He's a farmhand. If you really want to see him again take my advice and just slip off with him. I do it all the time and I haven't gotten caught yet. My mom doesn't know half the guys I go out with. Just tell your parents you and I are going to the movies tonight. I'll back you up. Besides, my mom knows I've got plans to go out tonight anyway. I'll just tell her you're going with me to the show. Instead of letting Gene pick you up at your house, I'll pick you up instead and drop you off somewhere

where he can meet you. Then when you're ready to come home, have him drop you off at the Dairy Queen and I'll pick you up and take you home myself. Or, tell your parents the truth and see what they say. But we both know what their answer will be. And then if you want to see him, you'll still wind up having to slip off and it will be harder then because your dad might start checking up on you to make sure you don't see him. It's better this way. Less chance of raising suspicion."

Anna thought about everything Cassie said. Finally, she decided she was right. It was her best chance to see Gene again. Perhaps her *only* chance.

"Okay," she said. "Be at my house at a quarter till eight."


Anna was anxiously sitting beside the phone in the den waiting for Gene's call at seven-thirty. Her parents had just left for dinner at Dr. Carter's house and wouldn't be home until eleven or so. After much begging and pleading, Anna had finally gotten permission from her parents to go to the movies with Cassie.

"It's not good for you to be seen hanging around blacks," Coleman warned his daughter. "You can go this time, but I don't want it to become a habit. People will start to talk. I won't have it," he insisted.

"Anna, I'm sure you can find other friends," her mother added. "I know you and Cassie have grown up together and attend the same school, and I love Estelle, but you don't want to become too chummy with them. It doesn't look good."

Anna had no idea how she was going to slip off with Gene again. Cassie was her only excuse for going out. She had no other friends. She couldn't get her sisters to cover for her. Angel would probably be just as against her seeing Gene as her parents and she didn't know if she could trust Amy to lie for her. However, of the two, she might be able to confide in Amy better than Angel. She and Amy had always been closer mainly because they were nearer in age and Amy was more devoted to her. But for now, she would use Cassie as her cover and worry about the next time when it came around. That is, if there *were* a next time. The thought suddenly occurred to her that she might not even *want* to see him again.

Once the nearly impossible decision was made of *how* she would manage to keep her date, she was then faced with the next most difficult decision of what to wear. For nearly an hour she stood in front of the tall cheval mirror beside her closet trying on nearly every summer outfit she owned. It was one of the most memorable occasions a girl would ever experience—her first date. She had to look extra special. She began with her Sunday dresses, which were too formal, and then her sundresses, which were too bare, then on to her slacks, which weren't appropriate for a first date. Finally, she settled on a pale aqua blue sleeveless dress with a square neckline and full skirt. She examined her choice once more in the full-length mirror and was pleased with her reflection in the glass. She sat down at her antique vanity table and took extra care brushing her long blonde tresses which she decided to let hang loose past her shoulders. A pair of white leather, strapped sandals with stacked heels completed the look. At last, she was ready for her very first date.

When Gene called promptly at seven-thirty and Anna told him to meet her at the Dairy Queen, he knew right away her parents didn't approve of them going out. Either she had asked them and they refused or she already knew what their answer would be and lied to them about where she was going and with whom. Either way, it meant she still thought enough of him to risk getting caught in order to keep their date.

Anna was sitting inside the burger stand at the same booth they had occupied earlier that day when Gene drove up in his blue Chevelle. Cassie had picked her up at her house and dropped her off there to wait for her date. She got up and walked outside to meet him. He pulled into a vacant parking space and got out to walk around and open the passenger's door for her.

"You look beautiful," Gene told her as he slid behind the wheel beside her. And she did. That night she was easily the most beautiful of the three Coleman sisters.

"Thank you," Anna replied, bowing her head with a shy smile. "You look nice, too." And he did. That is, without the fine, expensive wardrobe Anna had the privilege from which to choose. Hers were brand names from the most expensive clothing stores in Atlanta. His were the cheapest K-Mart had to offer. But he made sure they were clean and neatly ironed.

He had even knocked off early at the farm to run by the barbershop in town and treat himself to a fresh haircut. While in the barber chair, it dawned on him that he didn't even own a bottle of cologne. He glanced at his watch. If he hurried, he might be able to run by Wheeler's Pharmacy before they closed and buy a bottle of English Leather. He wanted British Sterling, but he knew he couldn't afford that. However, Doc Wheeler was running a closeout special that week on a boxed set of British Sterling cologne and shaving lotion. He was now convinced this had to be the luckiest night of his life. He paid for the cologne and hurried home to shower and shave. While he was washing down the dairy barn before he left that day, he gave his Chevy a quick wash and rinse before heading home. Now both he and his car were ready for the special occasion. And it *was* special, for it had been nearly a year since Gene had last been out with a girl on a date. He simply didn't have the extra time or money. But tonight, he was determined to somehow find both.

"Are you hungry?" he asked.

"Sure, if you are," Anna replied.

"Where do you feel like eating?"

"I'm not real choosey. I like most anything when it comes to food," she smiled. Anna wasn't too worried about running into her parents that night. They were having dinner at their friends' home, so any place they decided on would be safe—at least tonight.

"Do you like barbeque?" he asked.

"I love barbeque," Anna replied.

"Okay, what do you say we drive back to town and eat at Sonny's?" he suggested.

"That sounds great."

They left the Dairy Queen and drove back into town to the small, gray cinder block building beside the railroad tracks that was known for the best hickory smoked pit barbeque in north Georgia. The parking lot was small, as well, having enough spaces for no more than a dozen cars, and, on a Friday or Saturday night was normally filled to capacity. Tonight was no exception. As they pulled into the narrow parking lot, a faded red pick-up was backing out of one of the coveted spaces.

"Looks like this is my lucky night," Gene said as he quickly pulled in behind the truck. How luckier could he be? He got out and went over and opened Anna's door and helped her out. They went inside the small crowded restaurant and waited by the door until the waitress quickly wiped down the only remaining vacant table that sat in a private corner. When the table was ready, they walked over and Gene pulled out Anna's chair and seated her across from him. The restaurant was dimly lit, for which Anna was thankful just in case one of her parents' friends happened to be dining there that night.

The waitress returned and took their order. After serving them iced tea, she said it would be a few minutes before their barbeque plates were ready.

"I'm guessing your parents don't know you're with me tonight," Gene said. "Otherwise I would have picked you up at your house instead of meeting you at the Dairy Queen."

Anna flushed with embarrassment. "I told them I was going off with Cassie tonight," she confessed. "I didn't really bother asking them if I could go out with you tonight."

"You didn't think they would approve of me, did you?"

"Let's just say I didn't want to give them the opportunity to say no."

"I guess they wouldn't have much reason to approve of somebody like me anyway. I don't have money or a nice house or a decent job."

"That doesn't make you a bad person," Anna replied.

"No. Just a poor one."

"Did you ever try to get a job at my Dad's mill?"

"I did," Gene replied, taking a big swallow of iced tea. "But he wouldn't hire me."

"Why?"

Gene shrugged. "He said he wasn't hiring at the time."

"You should try again," Anna told him. "But I do have to admit, the mill has really slowed down a lot in the past few years. Daddy says polyester is destroying the cotton industry. I think he's pretty worried about the future of the mill. It's one of the few that are still operating."

"Yeah. It's hurt the farmers, too. That's why Harry started cattle farming and gave up growin' cotton."

Anna paused for a moment then confessed, "My parents are snobs," she said, changing the subject. "Always have been and always will be. They'll never change. My sisters are snobs, too. It's just the way they are."

"Obviously you aren't or you wouldn't be here. How come?"

"What do you mean?"

"What made you different from them?"

Anna shrugged. "I don't know. I've always been different from them. I've never been anything like my sisters. They've always been outgoing. I've always been shy. My oldest sister Angel, always had lots of boyfriends but I never did. In fact, you're the first guy I've ever gone out with. I wasn't even invited to the prom."

"I can't believe that," Gene replied with a look of surprise on his face.

"It's true. Amy says it's because guys think we're stuck up and don't want to get turned down. I know they think I'm a snob because I'm shy and rarely talk to anybody at school. Cassie is my only real friend besides my sisters."

"It's good to have a tight family. They're the ones who will always be there when everyone else turns their back on you."

"My parents aren't like that though," Anna explained. "My sisters care about me, but my parents always treated me different from them. I don't think they ever really loved me the way they do Angel and Amy. Angel says it's because Daddy wanted a boy instead of another girl and Amy says it's because momma didn't want any more kids after she was born and that she really didn't want me. Anyway, I've always been like an after thought to them."

"How's that?"

"Daddy always paid more attention to Angel and Amy. For instance, he would come in from the mill and pick them up and sit them on his lap and cuddle them. He'd hug and kiss them all the time and give them money to go to the store, but he never acted that way with me. He just ignored me as if I didn't even exist. Mom too, only not as much. When my sisters turned sixteen, Daddy bought both of them a brand new car and took them out and taught them how to drive by the time they were fifteen. He took them to get their learners and drivers licenses. But when I asked him to teach me how to drive, he told me to get my sisters to teach me." Anna paused once again before continuing. "We went to Olan Mills once to have a family portrait made when I was about six. The photographer was trying to get the five of us closer together so he could get all of us in the shot and he told Daddy to pick me up and hold me on his lap. He picked me up and sat me on my mother's lap instead." Anna hung her head and fought back the tears. Ten years had passed since that incident and the memory was still as painful as the day it happened.

Gene saw the pain in Anna's eyes and didn't know how to respond to her. He couldn't imagine a father rejecting his own flesh and blood. "I'm sorry," he said. "I can't imagine what would cause your father to be so cruel to his own child. My mother was Italian. Nothing like what you described would ever happen in an Italian family. To them, their kids are their life. My mother was like a lioness with her cubs where we were all concerned. My dad was the same way. And he wasn't even Italian. They treated all of us kids the same. Never showed any favoritism that I recall." He stopped. He could tell he was only making matters worse.

"You're lucky," Anna told him. "Be glad."

There was an uncomfortable lull in their conversation, and then Gene finally said, "I'll teach you to drive."

Anna smiled at him as if he were joking.

"I mean it," he assured her. "It's a stick shift, but you can learn. It's not that hard."

"Oh, I don't know," Anna, said. "A stick shift is hard for somebody just learning."

"No, it's not. That's what I learned on. Once you learn how to drive a straight shift you can drive anything."

Just then, the waitress arrived with their food. "Is there anything else I can get for you? Catsup? More barbeque sauce? How about more tea?" she asked.

"Could you bring us a pitcher of sweet tea?" Gene asked. "Save yourself some trips back to the kitchen."

"Sure," she replied. "Be right back."

"I've been working out in the hot sun all day and I'm parched," he explained.

'You work on Saturdays, too?" Anna asked.

"Saturdays, Sundays—everyday of the week, twelve months out of the year."

"You don't have any time off at all?"

"Farming is a twelve to eighteen hour a day job everyday of the year with no time off and no exceptions. Not even Christmas or Thanksgiving. Those cows have to be milked twice a day everyday and the cattle has to be fed everyday no matter what. And in between there's hay to be cut and bailed and eggs to be gathered every morning and the dairy barn has to be washed down every evening after the last milking. There's always plenty to do. My day starts at four A.M. and ends after six P.M."

"You do it all by yourself? You don't have any help?"

"Oh sure, I have help. I'm the farm foreman. I'm over four other guys. We all work our tails off. In fact, I've been there longer than anybody else. Porter has guys quittin' on him all the time. I have to hire new guys at least a couple times a year because the work is too hard, the hours too long and the pay is too low. But Harry pays me more than he does the others 'cause I'm the one that actually keeps the farm going. I've seen a lot of guys come and go in the past eight years. There's only one other guy besides me that's stayed on and stuck it out. That's Red. Me and him have worked for Harry longer than anybody else."

The waitress returned with their pitcher of tea and sat it down on the table. "Let me know if you need anything else," she said.

"You must really like working there," Anna said.

Gene looked at her and laughed. "Well I guess it beats the alternative which is unemployment. I hate it, if you want to know the truth, but it's all I got. It's steady work and I don't have anybody looking over my shoulder givin' me orders. I'm basically my own boss. I know what has to be done and I do it. And if the others don't hold up their end then I let them go and hire on somebody else who will."

"Maybe you'll have your own farm some day."

"No chance that will ever happen," he assured her. "I was born poor and I'll die poor. Nobody ever got rich workin' for somebody else and I'll be working for somebody till the day I die. I won't always be workin' for Harry though because he won't always be around. He's pretty old. But when this plays out, I'll just go to work for somebody else. It takes money to make money and I'll never have any except just enough to get by."

"Is Mr. Porter wealthy?"

"Harry? Oh, sure. He's loaded. There ain't no tellin' how much money he's worth. I don't even think he knows how much money he's got himself. His family always had money and at one time they owned the majority of land that made up this county. It was handed down from generation to generation until they all died off. Harry is the only one left and he's got everything now. But he don't let on like he's got a dime," Gene chuckled. "He's scared to death somebody's gonna try and separate him from his money. He lets on like he ain't got nothin'."

"Who's going to get it after he's gone?" Anna asked.

Gene shrugged. "Probably the State for all I know. I don't think he's even got a will. Why should he? He doesn't have any family left. Just him. There's nobody to leave it to."

They continued to talk non-stop throughout their meal without a single lull in their conversation. Despite the fact that their backgrounds and lives were so diverse, they found they shared as much in common as if they'd been the best of friends all their lives Their conversation continued long after their meal. It was almost ten P.M. and they suddenly found themselves the last of the few remaining diners.

Gene glanced at his watch. "It's too late to catch a movie," he said. "Any place else you'd like to go?"

"I can't think of any," she replied. "Besides I need to be getting back home. There's nothing left open around here this time of night anyway. They pretty much roll up the sidewalks after nine o'clock."

"What time did you tell your folks that you'd be home?"

"Ten-thirty," Anna replied.

"That's not too far away. It's almost a quarter till ten now. Is Cassie going to pick you up at the Dairy Queen and drive you back home?"

Anna nodded. "Yeah. So I guess we'd better be going. She said she'd be there waiting on me at a quarter after."

"Well, we'd better be going then."

Gene left a small tip for the waitress and paid for their meal, then drove them back to the Dairy Queen. As they left the restaurant, they drove through town past the rows of small identical mill houses where the mill workers lived. Anna noticed one had recently burned down leaving a gapping black hole in the row. It reminded her of a tooth missing in a row of teeth.

"I guess I could be living in one of those houses if I worked for your dad," Gene commented as they passed by.

"Believe me," Anna assured him. "You probably wouldn't be much better off than you are now. My dad doesn't pay his mill hands that much. You can tell that by where they live."

They finally arrived at the Dairy Queen where they sat in Gene's car and continued talking as they waited for Cassie to drive up. She appeared at exactly a quarter after ten as promised.

"Well, I guess I'd better be going," Anna sighed. "Thank you for a wonderful evening. I can't remember when I've had a better time. The barbeque was great."

"Good," Gene replied. "I had a good time myself. I hate that you had to lie to your parents about going out with me, but I'm glad you did."

Anna smiled. "Me, too."

"You think we might be able to get together again?" he asked cautiously.

"Yes," Anna replied without hesitation. "I don't know how, but I'll think of a way and let you know."

"Should I call your house or would that be a bad idea?"

"Give me your number and let me call you instead. Just tell me what time would be best to catch you at home."

"Anytime after six," he replied. "I'm home every night after say, six-thirty. Hey maybe I can take you driving next week—or even tomorrow if you can manage to slip away. I'll put you in Harry's pick-up. It's an automatic. I'll turn you loose in the cow pasture," he laughed. "You'll have a thousand acres all to yourself."

Anna gazed at his sunburned face in the dim light. He was the most handsome man she had ever seen. He was so big and strong, yet such a well-mannered gentleman with impeccable manners. He had given her a night she would always remember. And if there were anyway possible, there would be many more nights just like this one. She just had to figure out a way. Their eyes met and they stared at one another not knowing what to say next or how to say good-bye—and neither wanted to go. He wanted to lean over and kiss her, but didn't know how she would react. He certainly didn't want to mess things up now.

"Well, guess I'd better be going. Cassie is waiting for me. I don't want to be late getting home," she said.

"Call me," he said, the impatience showing in his voice. "I'll be waiting to hear from you."

"Oh, I will. Don't worry," she promised. "Good night and thanks again for a terrific evening. I had a great time."

"Me, too. And you're welcome. Call me now," he reminded her once again.

"I will. Good night."

He waited until she had climbed into Cassie's Toyota. He waved one last time as they drove away toward Coleman Hill. Anna, and the evening they had shared, dominated his thoughts as he drove home. Was it really possible to fall in love with someone after the first date? If so, then he was in love. He was deeply in love. He'd never been in love before. No girl had ever left him with the feelings he carried home with him that night. He felt light-headed. He had butterflies in the pit of his stomach. Everything she said and did kept playing over and over in his memory. He couldn't wait to see her again, to be with her, to have her near him. It would be torture waiting for her call, knowing he couldn't call her. It would be so much easier if it were left up to him to make the next move. But it wasn't left up to him. He would just have to wait. And what if she didn't call? He didn't want to even think about that. She had to call. She just *had* to.

# Chapter Three

Anna awoke that Sunday morning to the shrill chirping of a family of Blue Jays that had nested in the huge Magnolia tree outside her bedroom window. The first thoughts that popped into her head as she opened her eyes were of Gene and their date last night. Those delightful memories brought a warm rush over her from head to toe. She couldn't wait to see him again. But how? She couldn't drive and she didn't have a car of her own like Angel or Amy. And she couldn't continue to use Cassie as a cover because her parents didn't want their daughter being seen with a black girl. And he *certainly* couldn't pick her up at their house. Suddenly, her thoughts were interrupted by a knock on her bedroom door.

"Come in," she answered.

The door opened and it was Amy. "Momma told me I'd better wake you. We have about an hour before we have to leave for church," she informed her sister as she stuck her head though the crack in the door. "If you hurry, I'll do your hair before we leave."

"Okay. Sure. I'm getting up now," Anna replied, tossing the covers back.

She quickly bathed and dressed, then sat down at her vanity table and began applying on her make-up when her sister reappeared.

"You want me to put your hair in a French braid?" Amy asked, as she picked up the hairbrush and began brushing her sister's long, blonde hair.

"Yeah. That's fine," Anna replied.

"You're lucky," Amy told her sister with envy. "Your hair is so thick and heavy. You can do anything with it. Mine is like a limp dishrag. And you're a natural blonde to top it off. Girls would die to have your hair."

"Your hair is pretty, too."

"Mine is too thin and I have to perm it to keep it from being stringy. Your hair is natural. I have to sit for hours at the hair dresser's to get it to look like anything."

Anna sat still and remained quiet, absorbed in her own thoughts over last night, while Amy carefully separated and braided her hair in a beautiful, long French braid.

"You seem unusually quiet this morning," Amy commented, studying her sister's reflection in the mirror as she stood behind her and twisted the strands of hair from side to side. "How was your date last night?"

Anna's eyes immediately shot up to Amy's reflection in the mirror. "What do you mean?"

"I mean your date with that guy—his name is Longhorn, isn't it?"

Anna started to turn around and face her sister, but Amy quickly jerked her back. "Be still. You'll make me mess up. I'm almost finished."

"How did you know I went out with someone?" Anna asked, her voice filled with surprise.

"I saw you at Sonny's last night."

"You were there? I didn't see you."

"Chuck and I stopped by there for a bite to eat before going to the movies and we walked in but the place was packed and there wasn't a table available. As we were turning around to leave, I saw you with that Longhorn guy. Don't you think he's a little old for you? He graduated a year ahead of Angel. Where did you meet him?"

"At the Dairy Queen last Sunday. Remember when we went there to get ice cream after dinner? He was standing in line beside us."

"Yeah, I remember," Amy, replied. "That's the first time you ever saw him?"

"Yes. Then I ran into him again yesterday afternoon while Cassie and I were at Wheeler's Drug Store. He asked me out. I had to lie to mom and dad because I knew they wouldn't let me go out with him."

"You're right about that," Amy agreed. "They would have a fit if they knew. He's poor white trash. A redneck. What made you start liking *him*?"

"Because he's nice. And I think he's cute."

"He's also a big loser," Amy added.

"No, he's not. Just because he works on a farm and doesn't have a lot of money doesn't mean he's not a good person. He's sweet and kind and he's a gentleman."

"Where did you go after you left Sonny's?" Amy asked, obviously taking her role as big sister quite seriously.

"Nowhere. We sat there and talked until they closed and then he took me back to the Dairy Queen where Cassie met us and then she drove me home. You're not going to tell mom and dad are you? Please don't tell them, Amy," she pleaded. "I really like him and I want to see him again."

"Don't worry," Amy assured her. "I won't say anything. But I really wish you would think about this before you become anymore involved with this guy. He's not your type. I had a couple of classes with him my freshman year when he was a senior. He's dirt poor and he's not even that good looking. He was working on a farm when I knew him—milking cows. He's a loser. You are so above him. You can do so much better than that. He's half Indian or something, I think. His dad owns a junkyard and his brother weighs like four hundred pounds and is gross looking. My God, Anna, what are you thinking? Mom and dad would die if they knew you were going out with someone like him."

"I can't help what they think. They're snobs anyway. Gene is a very sweet person. I like him a lot and I'm going to keep seeing him."

"You're asking for trouble. You better never let mom and dad catch you with him. Daddy would beat you half to death if he knew."

A brief silence fell between them as Amy finished braiding Anna's hair and tied a small yellow ribbon at the bottom.

"Look," Amy advised her younger sister as she knelt down beside her. "I know how mom and dad are. Daddy is way too controlling and overbearing. We all know that. But Angel has her escape plan and I have mine. Angel is going to college so she can have a good career and make her own money. She won't ever have to depend on daddy to support her. But I'm not going to college no matter what they say. If I have to, I'll marry Chuck and leave home. At least he's from a good family with plenty of money and a good future. Besides, mom and dad like him."

"You're going to marry Chuck Willis?" Anna said, her eyes widened with surprise. "You just started seeing him."

"But I've known him practically all my life. I went to school with him and we grew up together. If getting married is the only way I can get out of this house and have a life of my own, then I'll do what I have to do."

"But I thought you wanted to move to Atlanta and go into modeling."

"I do and I will—eventually. But first I have to get away from daddy. He won't let me leave home alone. I have to make my move as soon as possible while I'm still young and pretty enough to pursue a modeling career. I can't waste three or four years in college. By then I'll be in my twenties and time will be running out. Models start out young, sometimes right out of high school because nobody will hire them when they're past thirty. They have a good eight to ten years before their careers are over. I can't wait until I get a four-year degree like Angel. And if Chuck Willis has to be my ticket away from here, then so be it."

"Do you love him?"

"Of course not," Amy replied without hesitation. "I don't even like him that much. But so what? If I really did like him it would only make it harder to do what I have to do to get what I want. Chuck is just a steppingstone as far as I'm concerned. But let me tell you something. And you remember this," Amy said, pointing her finger at her sister. "Forget that redneck loser. You can do a hundred times better than him. You're young, you're pretty and you're smart. You don't have to settle for white trash. You can marry rich and handsome just as good as you can poor and ugly. Don't forget that."

Anna stared into her sister's eyes. She saw desperation and she understood that desperation, but she didn't agree with her opinion of Gene. Amy didn't really know him. She was only looking at the surface and not the real person underneath. She was wrong in her judgment the same way her parents were wrong to judge Cassie just because she was poor and black.

"I appreciate the advice, Amy. But I really do like Gene. He's a nice guy."

"But nice isn't enough," Amy was quick to reply. "There has to be more. Being nice never got anybody anywhere. Money buys power and power gets you places. It gives you prestige. You'll never have any of those things if you settle for a guy like Gene."

"But I really like him."

Amy gave a long sigh and rolled her eyes in desperation. "Okay then, don't listen to me but if daddy ever finds out you're seeing him, there will be hell to pay. Don't you understand? It's not that he cares about you, but *what* you do. Because everything we do is a reflection on him and mom. How it makes them look is all that matters. So it's not all about us. It's about *him*."

"I know," Anna replied. "And I also know he never cared about me the way he does about you and Angel. He never really loved me the way he does you two."

Amy gazed at her sister with eyes expressing deep emotion. "Be glad," she said softly. "Be very glad. You're the lucky one."

Anna looked at Amy with curiosity. Something in her voice sounded so peculiar. Before Anna could reply, Amy stood up and turned to leave the room. "We'd better hurry," Amy told her. "We'll make them late for church."

Anna couldn't wait for church to end and Sunday dinner to be over with. All she could think about was making that phone call to Gene. After helping her mother and Amy clear the dinner dishes from the table, she waited until her parents went upstairs for their afternoon nap. Anna decided she couldn't wait until six. She was just going to have to take a chance now on catching him at home. She sat down on the sofa and nervously dialed his number. The phone on the other end rang for what seemed an eternity. She was just about to hang up when she heard a man's voice answer.

"Hello."

"Hello," she replied, her voice a little shaky. "Is Gene there?"

There was a brief pause. "Hold on," he replied finally. "Hey Gene, some little lady wants to talk to you."

Anna waited patiently. She heard footsteps on the other end.

"Hello." The familiar voice put her instantly at ease.

"Hi. It's me. Anna," she announced shyly.

"Oh, hi. How you doin'?" His voice seemed filled with surprise and excitement."

"I'm fine," she replied. "Listen, I know you told me not to call until after six but I—

"No, no, that's fine," he said quickly. "I'm glad you didn't wait that late. I took the day off and let the other workers take care of the chores today because Harry had a funeral to go to today. He asked me to drive him to Rome for the visitation and services. An old friend of his died the other day. I just walked in the door as a matter of fact."

"Oh, good. I'm glad I took the chance and caught you at home. My parents are taking a nap upstairs," she explained. "I might be able to get away and meet you a little later—that is, if you don't have anything else better to do."

"No, that's fine. What time? You want me to meet you some place?"

"My sister Amy, is going over to her boyfriend's house in a little while and I thought I would ask her to drop me off somewhere."

"When is she leaving?" he asked.

"Around three-thirty. She plans on having dinner with his family and then going to church with them. She'll be heading back home about eight or eight-thirty. Services start at seven. I told my parents I was going with her."

"Where do you want us to meet?"

"Well, she has to stop at the gas station on the way so I thought I could meet you at J&L's Quick Stop between three-fifteen and three-thirty."

"That sounds good. I'll see you then. I'll be waiting out front by the pay phone," he told her.

"Okay. See you then."

After they hung up, Anna quietly ran upstairs and changed out of her Sunday clothes into a pink gingham check sleeveless sheath dress and white flat sandals. Her hair was still braided and complimented her casual summer attire. She swapped the yellow bow her sister had tied around her French braid for a solid pink one to match her dress. She gave a quick glance in the mirror and went downstairs where Amy was looking for her car keys.

"I really appreciate you doing this for me and not saying anything to mom and dad," Anna told her.

Amy gave her sister a discerning look. "You know how I feel about that guy and I've already warned you about him. I think you're a fool for getting involved with him, but it's your life. You do what you want to, just be careful. Dad will flip out if he catches you. And I'll get in serious trouble for lying for you."

"I'll be careful. I swear."

Gene was already parked beside the public phone booth at J&L's when they arrived, just as he had promised. While Amy got out of her car to pump the gas, Anna walked over to Gene's Chevelle. He leaned across the front seat and opened the passenger's door for her to get in. The engine started with a loud roar and they drove away.

"Do you want to go by the Dairy Queen and get a sundae or something before I take you driving?" he offered.

"Yeah, that sounds good."

They sat in his car beneath a big sweet gum tree behind the hamburger stand eating a couple of fudge sundaes and talked for over an hour. A thunderstorm that had passed over earlier brought some relief from the oppressive heat, only to replace it with a thick layer of humid air. A welcomed cool breeze circulated through the car bringing with it the odor of steam rising from the hot pavement. Gene got out of the car and walked over to the trashcan behind the restaurant where he deposited their empty ice cream containers. Anna watched him as he walked across the parking lot, admiring his strong, muscular, heavyset body. He got back behind the wheel and slid down slightly in the seat, making himself comfortable. They continued their small talk awhile longer, until unexpectedly, he reached over and took Anna's hand and held it. Her heart raced. No guy had ever held her hand before. It felt fragile and dwarfed in his powerful grip.

"Are you ready to go take some driving lessons now?" he asked with a faint smile.

"Yeah, I guess," she replied nervously.

"I'll take you out to the back pasture. There's no livestock out there right now," he said. "In fact, there's nothing out there except a few oak trees and lot of rocks. As long as you can manage to dodge both, you'll be fine. That and the pond in the middle of the pasture." He teased with a grin.

"Gee," she replied. "Thanks for not adding to my anxiety."

He laughed. "You'll do fine," he assured her.

They drove out of town, turning on Highway 11 that took them straight to Harry Porter's farm. As they passed the huge, two-story wood frame plantation house with the large four, square columns that supported the front and side porches, Anna stared at the property as they went by.

"That's the most beautiful house I've ever seen," she said in awe of the once majestic southern mansion.

"It used to be. A long time ago, but it's about to cave in now. It would cost a fortune to rebuild it," Gene told her.

"It doesn't look to be in that bad of shape."

"It is though. If you want, I'll take you in it after we go driving."

"Oh, good. I'd love that," she replied.

Gene pulled off the highway onto a dirt driveway secured by a long steel gate that led into a two hundred acre pasture. He got out and unlocked the gate. He drove out about a hundred yards and stopped the supped up Chevelle. He got out and walked around to the passenger's side and opened the door.

"Okay, slide over," he instructed her.

Anna slid across the seat behind the wheel and Gene climbed in beside her. Then, for the next hour, they drove over the empty pasture as Anna became comfortable with the straight shift. She caught on surprisingly fast making smooth starts and stops after only a few tries. Finally, he told her she was ready for the highway. He directed her out of the pasture, past the steel gate and back onto Highway 11. Being a Sunday, there was little traffic. He told her to drive down the road to the long, winding dirt driveway that led up to the old, dilapidated plantation house.

"Are you sure Mr. Porter won't mind us going in his house?" Anna asked.

"Of course not. He won't mind. Besides, he's in Rome right now. He won't be back until sometime later tonight. Park here at the bottom of the steps," he said, pointing to the long steps leading up to the two-story front porch that stood about six-feet off the ground. Two enormous oak trees, at least a hundred years old, flanked each corner of the old house.

Anna pulled up and parked at the bottom of the steps as Gene instructed her to do. They got out of the car and started up the steps. The porch ceiling was so high it made Anna dizzy when she looked up.

"What's under there?" she asked, pointing to the windows beneath the high porch.

"Oh, that's just the basement," he replied. "There are another four rooms beneath the house."

The wood siding hadn't seen a coat of paint in nearly five decades yet the bare wood was still in relatively good condition with minimal decay and rotting. Kudzu vines blanketed much of the exterior and porches, threatening to swallow up the entire house. The four, enormous, square Confederate-style columns that supported the front and side porches were still astonishingly sound and sturdy. The wood steps however, gave with their weight as they climbed to the top. Gene made sure he went ahead of Anna, testing each step with his own weight before allowing her to follow. Once at the top of the steps, they found the porch floor in good condition. Gene turned the rusty old doorknob and pushed open the heavy solid wood door. The corroded hinges squeaked loudly as the door slowly opened into a twelve-foot wide foyer that ran the length of the entire house. In its era the mansion was often referred to as a *shotgun house* due to the fact one could stand at the front door and fire a shotgun straight through the foyer out the back door.

The grayish wood floor was splintered and worn down to the bare wood, all the varnish gone. The walls were cracked and peeling, exposing the bare wood slats in several places. The fourteen-foot ceilings were water stained and sagging with their antique light fixtures and dining room chandelier tarnished and coated with cobwebs. The once grand staircase was still sound except for the rickety banister with missing spindles. The ground floor consisted of four enormous rooms, two on each side of the long central hallway with a large room, jutting off to the side, forming the left wing of the house. This was added on over a half a century ago providing the main floor kitchen. The windows went from the floor all the way to the ceiling and were dotted with missing and broken panes of rippled glass. Each room displayed an enormous brick fireplace.

Anna walked into what was once the formal dining room. She gazed in wonder at the nobility and grandeur of the old southern ten-room mansion that had withstood and endured time and harsh elements for well over a century while sheltering several generations. Gene watched Anna as she explored the old mansion and found her adulation of the old ruins amusing.

"You really like this old place, don't you?" he asked, smiling at her.

"I love it. It's filled with warmth and comfort. It seems to embrace you the minute you walk in the door. I feel welcomed and safe. It makes me sad to see it rotting away. It still has so much life in it, so much love to give to another generation. Don't you think it could still be saved?"

"I don't know," Gene sighed, shaking his head. "It would take an awful lot of work. And money. It would cost a small fortune to make this place livable again. But yeah, I suppose it still has a chance."

"Where does that door lead to?" Anna asked pointing to a door behind the staircase.

"That goes down to the basement," he replied. "You don't want to go down there. It's dirty and smells musky. Besides, the steps might be rotten."

"Can we go upstairs? Is it safe?"

"It might be. Let me go up first and check it out. Last time I was up there the roof was pretty well rotted and about to cave in."

Gene climbed the stairs one step at a time, slowly testing his weight on each step as he went up. He disappeared briefly as he inspected the second floor, making sure it was still sound enough to support both their weight. Then he motioned for Anna to join him. "Be careful," he warned. "Don't put all your weight on one step at the time."

As on the ground floor, there were large fireplaces with hand-carved mantles and marble hearths inhabiting each of the five spacious upstairs rooms. She glanced up at the ceiling and saw a tree limb protruding through the roof.

"I could stay here forever," she said.

"Why? You don't exactly live in a shack," he laughed. "Your place makes this look like a cord of kindling wood. Which is about all it's good for now."

"No, that's not true. This house has more love and warmth hidden behind those walls than mine ever will have. Nothing but a cold, empty shell sits on top of Coleman Hill. This house is screaming for some nice family to lavish it with tender loving care. It still has so much comfort and shelter to offer some nice family."

Gene walked over to where she stood in the upstairs hallway and cupped her face in his hands. "I wish it were mine to give to you," he said. "But I don't have a thing to offer you. No big house, money or a fancy car. All I have are the basic necessities of life." He paused, then added, "And my heart."

He leaned closer and kissed her for the first time. Her heart pounded so fast and hard she thought it would explode. He kissed her a long time, or so it seemed. When their lips finally parted they stood there staring silently at one another, savoring that incredible moment that only a first kiss could bring.

"That's all anybody needs," she said softly. "I've been given all the luxuries life has to offer, but nothing else. No love and little affection. Which is all I ever really wanted."

"Well, that's about all I have to offer," he said. "I may not be able to give you much else, but I can give you plenty of that." He bent down and kissed her once again, this time longer and more passionately.

They stayed in the old mansion until it was time for Gene to drive her back to town. They went downstairs into what was once the front parlor and sat on the hard, wood floor and just talked and held hands. They planned their strategy of when and how they would continue to see one another without raising suspicion. It would be much easier if Anna had a car of her own. Once he had taught her to drive, she would ask her father for one. After all she said, her seventeenth birthday was next month and her two sisters already had their own transportation. It was only fair he should provide her with a car of her own. They kissed once more and proclaimed their love for one another before finally leaving.

He drove Anna back to town and waited until she was safely in the car with her sister before he drove back to his house. That night before going to bed, she slipped downstairs and phoned him and they talked briefly again, hungry to hear the other's voice once more. Before they hung up, he told her he loved her. They were words she had seldom heard—from anyone and it almost made her cry.

"I love you, too," she whispered softly before they finally parted.

Anna lay in bed for a long while that night finally drifting off to sleep. Gene dominated her every thought. Already she felt empty and alone without him. For the first time in her life, she really felt loved. Regardless of whatever Amy thought or said about him, this was the man she knew she wanted to spend the rest of her life with. It didn't matter what he had or didn't have. Anna had found her soul mate.

# *Chapter Four*

That August, Anna turned seventeen where upon her father finally agreed, after much begging and pleading on her part and a little encouragement from her mother, to buy Anna a car. Actually, it wasn't Anna who received the shiny new Mustang, but Amy instead. Anna was satisfied with Amy's two-year old hand-me-down when her father gave the new one to Amy so that she would have dependable transportation to and from Athens. However, it didn't matter to Anna, who was accustomed to her father's partial treatment. All that *did* matter was now she had more freedom.

Anna had lied to her parents and told them that Cassie and Amy had taught her to drive when actually, it had been Gene. Hours spent in the cow pasture and on back, country roads had paid off and now Anna was a whiz on both a straight shift as well as an automatic. This made it much easier to steal away and see Gene for a couple of hours several times a week without having to allow Cassie or Amy to lie for her. Thus, Anna and Gene continued to see one another regularly during the remainder of the summer until September when Anna returned to Myrick High as a senior.

By now Amy was engaged to Judge Willis' son and they were busy planning a Valentine's Day wedding. She had done some fast work and managed to get Chuck to propose by early September. However, it wasn't soon enough to prevent Ben Coleman from forcing his daughter into her freshman year at Athens. Angel meanwhile, entered her junior year there.

## COLEMAN HILL

When Anna entered her senior year at Myrick high that September, she and Gene had been dating two months. He had dreaded and put off taking Anna home to introduce her to his father and older brother. The sole reason being, he was embarrassed. He was ashamed of the five-room shack in which they lived, the junkyard out back and mainly of them. Gene loved his family but they were fat, lazy and ignorant. Both worked harder to get out of work than if they went ahead and put in an honest day of labor. He had tried to prepare Anna for the inevitable encounter, but it was nearly impossible considering the fact she came from such wealth and class and his background was filled with adverse poverty. Nonetheless, the introduction had to take place sooner or later and Gene decided it was best to go ahead and get the unpleasant task over with.

It was an unusually hot and humid Sunday afternoon. Especially hot for the end of September. Temperatures had hovered in the triple digits for almost three consecutive weeks without a drop of rain to offer any relief. The Barrow County Government Center had opened up an emergency shelter for the elderly and very poor who were without air-conditioning in order for them to escape the deadly heat. Two elderly persons and a child had already succumb to the searing heat wave. Unfortunately, from past history, the only thing that could break that kind of weather would come in the form of a terrific electrical storm. The heat continued to simmer and boil like a volcano ready to erupt until a severe storm released the pressure. Those storms were known to produce deadly lightning, damaging winds, hail and even tornadoes. The only good thing was that usually after a sudden burst of dangerous storms Georgia was blessed with cool fall temperatures in the sixties. Georgians were known for describing the drastic climatic changes saying, "If you don't like the heat wave we're havin', just stick around and you'll be wearing your long handles by tomorrow."

After church that afternoon, the Coleman family returned home to their traditional Sunday dinner, compliments from Estelle. Angel had driven up that weekend with her new roommate Tanya, as had Amy. Amy was living in a separate apartment in the same complex that her sister and roommate shared. Amy wanted her own privacy, thus she chose a one-bedroom apartment three doors down from Angel. At least that was the reason she gave her parents. The real reason being, Amy was privy to her sister's well-hidden, dark secrets which only Angel's closest college friends were aware of. In the late sixties, especially in the Deep South and American Bible Belt, homosexuality was still a deeply guarded, closeted subject. If one was either gay or lesbian, one kept their sexual preference concealed from the world, otherwise face disgrace and rejection in society. Which is precisely what Angel did. Not even her younger sister Anna was aware of her homosexuality and Amy had only recently become aware of the fact. Having been an active, practicing heterosexual since the age of fourteen, she suddenly turned to women as her sexual preference. For the past four years, she chose to use and discard men before they became aware of her intentions. Her perception of men as weak, selfish, sexual predators came from her own father whom she had grown to despise over the years. He was selfish, controlling and cunning. What disgusted her most was his ability to control everything and everyone around him except his own weaknesses. Like the other men in her life, she received great satisfaction in using him to serve her own needs. Which presently was her need for financial support and material possessions such as college tuition, living expenses, nice clothing and cars. Amy, while pretty much sharing Angel's opinion of their father, was also learning to use men for her material gains as well. And apparently, she had decided to begin with Charles Willis.

"Are you going to the Willis's for dinner this evening?" Ben Coleman asked his middle daughter.

"Yes, sir. We're going to church services afterwards," Amy replied. "They're having Revival at his church starting tonight."

"Well, you mustn't make yourself too late returning to Athens tonight," her mother cautioned. "That's an awfully long drive back. I really wish you would reconsider and leave this afternoon instead."

"Since I don't have any early morning classes it won't matter if I get back late," Amy insisted.

"Even if you leave right after church you won't get back to Athens before midnight," her father added.

"Not really, because Revival starts at six tonight instead of seven like regular services. It's only an hour long. I'll leave Myrick a little after seven."

"Well, just be careful driving back," Catherine insisted. "That's a dangerous road, especially after dark."

"Did I mention that I was going to Revival with Amy tonight also," Anna added.

"No, you didn't," Catherine replied.

"But first I'm going over to Cassie's so we can study for our Algebra exam on Monday," she added. "I should be home a little after seven."

Angel and Amy glanced across the table at one another and then at their younger sister. The girls knew Anna was walking a tightrope. One slip and it was all over. They knew how fiercely their father guarded his coveted reputation and if he ever discovered that one of his daughters was slipping around behind his back dating common white trash, his volatile temper would certainly take its toll on Anna—as well as the young man she was seeing. His reaction would surely be the same were he to discover his oldest daughter was gay.

"I don't recall you attending our last home coming," Catherine said. "What's so special about Revival at the Willis' church?"

"I like their preacher," Anna replied.

"He must preach a pretty good sermon if members from neighboring churches attend the services," Tanya observed, helping herself to a second slice of Estelle's sweet potato pie.

"Oh, he's very good," Anna, replied. "In fact, I've been considering moving my letter over to Myrick Methodist."

"Oh Anna, you're not!" Catherine exclaimed. "You were raised a Baptist. How could you consider such a thing?"

"Don't worry, Mom. She's not going anywhere," Amy assured their mother. "She just likes visiting that church. It's something different and just a passing fancy of hers. It won't last," Amy glanced over at Anna and gave her sister a playful smile.

"Well, I certainly hope not," Catherine, said. "But your sister has been spending an awful lot of time attending that church the past couple of months."

"So has Amy," Anna quickly replied in her own defense.

"Well, I can understand why Amy's been going. That's Charles' church. Besides, it's a nice place to go on a Sunday night. Much more appropriate than some drive-in movie."

"There's another place you've been spending an awful lot of time," her father said, glaring at Anna from under his dark brow. "At the Pittman's. I told you I didn't want you socializing with that black girl."

"But Daddy, Cassie is in two of my classes this year—Algebra and American History. I've been having a terrible time in Algebra and Cassie is so good at it. She's been tutoring me. She's helped me a lot," Anna explained, trying to sound as convincing as possible.

"I'm sure there're other girls in your class that are just as capable," he insisted. "White girls."

"But Cassie is my best friend."

"You can make other friends," her father said firmly, his voice filling with anger. "I've told you about hanging around that colored girl. You keep disobeying me and going over there and you'll find yourself finishing your senior year at an Atlanta boarding school," he pointed his finger at her, his voice rising louder.

Anna quickly looked up at her father from across the table, her expression filled with fear and surprise.

"That's right," he warned. "You just keep disobeying me and see what happens."

An uncomfortable silence filled the room. Anna was suddenly horrified at the thought of being sent away from her home and even worse—away from Gene.

"Well, I guess we had better go on upstairs and start packing," Angel said, breaking the silence. "Tanya and I plan on leaving around four this afternoon. We both have early classes tomorrow."

"I better get going, too," Amy agreed. "I told Chuck I'd be at his house by three." She glanced at Anna, seated beside her. Her younger sister looked sad and defeated. "Would you like to go with me to the Willis' for dinner before going to church with us tonight?" Amy asked. "I'll go over your Algebra with you while we're there if you like. You can drive your car and follow me so you won't make me late dropping you back home. How does that sound?"

"That will be fine," Anna replied solemnly. "Thanks."

After the girls excused themselves from the table, they all went upstairs to change and prepare for their individual plans the rest of the afternoon.

Anna went into her room to find something appropriate to wear to meet Gene's family for the first time. The door opened and her two sisters entered the room. They were concerned and upset over their father's outburst at the dinner table.

"Anna," Amy began. "You've got to be careful. If daddy finds out your seeing that Longhorn guy he'll go nuts. There's no telling what he might do."

"She's right," Angel agreed. "He'll flip out. It's bad enough that he thinks your paling around with a black girl, but if he finds out it's a guy, he'll kill both of you. And you can't keep using Cassie as your excuse for slipping off. Tell him you're gong over to study with somebody else in your class."

"Yeah, make friends with some white girls in your Algebra class and tell him you're going to their house instead," Amy suggested. "You don't want him to send you away. Just hang in there until you finish out your senior year and then move to Athens with us."

"You'll have plenty of freedom there, believe me," Angel assured her sister. "You can come and go as you please and see whom ever you want. But as long as you live under this roof, you'll have to obey his rules. It's only another nine or ten months and you'll be free to leave."

"That's right," Amy added. "But whatever you do, don't piss him off and make him look bad or spoil his precious image in the community because he'll do more than just take your car away. He'll send *you* away. And you don't want that."

Anna knew her sisters were right. They had all seen their father go into one of his violent rages on a few occasions whenever he didn't get what he wanted, which was seldom, or when one of them had inadvertently caused him hindrance. She knew she had to use extreme caution when dealing with their father. He could quickly turn into a raging maniac when provoked. He was rich and powerful and could back up any threat he made. Even worse, she was his least favorite. He wouldn't think twice before sending her off to a private boarding school. In fact, she was surprised he hadn't already done so.

Both sisters gave her a comforting hug and a final warning before leaving her room. Anna changed out of her Sunday clothes into a new lavender sundress that Angel had just given her for her birthday. It was the first time she had worn it. She already had in mind what she wanted to wear to compliment the scooped neckline. She went to her hand-carved cherry jewelry chest that sat on her dresser and took out the sterling silver and diamond chip, double heart necklace that Gene had given her for her birthday last month. He couldn't afford real gold, so he bought her sterling instead. It didn't matter, for they *were* real diamonds, if only diamond chips and she treasured the little inexpensive piece of jewelry as if it were a three-carat diamond. He had told her that the two entwined hearts represented their own hearts.

Anna finished dressing and met Amy downstairs. After bidding Angel and Tanya good-bye, they left in separate cars, supposedly headed for the Willis home only when they reached the end of their street, their automobiles turned in opposite directions. Anna took Highway 11 and drove the short distance to the Porter farm where she pulled up to the dairy barn and parked her 1966 dark green Mustang beneath a big oak tree out of sight. That location was her usual parking spot whenever she met Gene at the farm. From there, they would get into his car and leave, which were their plans on this particular afternoon.

As she turned off the highway and pulled up to the pasture gate, she paused to allow a pick-up truck pulling a cattle trailer filled with Black Angus to exit the pasture. One of the farm hands quickly closed the gate behind the truck to prevent some calves from escaping that were running after the truck. Suddenly the scene became apparent to Anna and filled her with sadness and remorse. The truck had arrived to take the older beef cattle to the slaughterhouse while some of the remaining herd ran after the trailer that was taking away their parents and mates. Anna looked on as the younger cattle let out pathetic wails as they ran after the trailer that carried the other cattle to slaughter. The sight made her never want to touch another piece of meat again.

As Anna pulled up behind the barn, she found Gene waiting for her as he chatted with Harry Porter. Gene had already introduced Anna to his boss not long after they began dating and the old man took an instant liking to the young girl. She reminded him of the only woman he ever loved—Olivia Cummings, who had been his childhood sweetheart and who died suddenly and tragically one week before they were to be married. He had almost finished remodeling the old plantation house when she fell ill with pneumonia and died two weeks later—only a week before their scheduled wedding date. Ollie had been the love of Harry's life. She was a slender blue-eyed blonde with a loving nature and friendly personality—much like Anna. It had been fifty years now since he buried his soul mate and future bride beneath a blossoming Magnolia tree in the backyard, not far from the old plantation house. Ollie had fallen in love with the mansion where Harry was born and raised and had spent many hours helping him remodel and restore it in preparation for them to move in following their wedding. After her death, the old house never seemed the same and Harry found it increasingly difficult as each year passed without his lovely Ollie for him to continue living alone there. Besides, the huge mansion was just too spacious for a single person. He and Ollie had intended to fill it with children—"a child or two in each of the four bedrooms," she would dream aloud with a big smile. After her death all five bedrooms remained empty, as did the five downstairs rooms except for a few pieces of antique furniture. The only portion of the house he refused to enter, after making a chilling discovery thirty years ago, was the basement. After two decades of living alone in the enormous mansion, Harry bought a trailer and moved it beside the house, where he had resided now for the past thirty years. Now, after three decades, the trailer was in worse decay than the house.

"Lookie there, ain't you about the prettiest little Southern Bell there ever was," Harry said as he watched Anna get out of her car. "You look like a cool breath of spring. I hope this old boy realizes how lucky he is to have such a sweet little lady to call his own," he said, glancing at Gene.

"Oh, I do," Gene, replied with a big grin. "She's the best thing that ever happened to me."

"Listen to you," Anna smiled as she walked over and put her arm around Gene. "You two are going to spoil me with all that flattery."

"A sweet little thing like you deserves to be spoiled," Harry smiled.

"Are you ready to go?" Gene asked, wrapping his arm around her waist and pulling her close to him in a playful gesture.

"As ready as I'll ever be, I guess," she sighed. "I'm as nervous as if I were going to an all night dentist."

"Why?" Gene asked. "They're the ones who should be nervous. You don't have a thing to be shy about," he assured her. "My family are just your average slobs."

"And mine are your average snobs," Anna laughed.

Harry chuckled. "Slobs and snobs. That about sums up your two classes of southerners. But neither of you are nothin' like your own people so you two will make a nice couple. You'll set a fine example of just good, down-to-earth, hard workin' folks."

"Come on, let's go," Gene said, leading her toward his car.

"You two go and have a good time now," Harry told them. "Son, you got somebody to be real proud of to take home."

"Bye Mr. Porter," Anna said as Gene opened the passenger's side of his Chevelle and helped her in. "It was nice seeing you again."

"You take care now and don't worry, you'll make a fine impression," Harry assured her.

Gene waved to his boss as he got into his car and they drove off. They drove the short distance to Gene's house and pulled up in the front yard. He parked beside the sagging front porch and sat quietly for a moment.

"What's the matter?" Anna asked.

"I need to ask you something before I take you in there," he replied nervously.

"What?"

"I need to know something *before* you meet my family."

"What is it?" she asked once again. Something was obviously bothering him.

He turned to face her. "I'm just afraid what your answer might be after you've gone in there."

"Gene, what in the world are you talking about," she laughed.

He hesitated another moment, then said finally, "I want to know if you'll marry me."

Anna stared back at him in stunned silence. He had taken her completely off guard. They had only been dating a couple of months.

"I was afraid to ask you after you met my father and brother and then realized what you were about to get yourself into. We can wait until next June after you graduate if you like. That will give me a little time to put some money back so I can get us a decent place to live. Maybe find a better paying job somewhere away from here. At least find one with better hours so I won't be tied down twelve to fifteen hours a day. I'm sorry I don't have a ring to give you, but I didn't have the money to get you a nice one and I was afraid if I waited until after I brought you here, you'd be tempted to say no." He paused once more. "Well, what do you say, Anna? Will you marry me?"

Anna looked at him and smiled. "Yes," she replied softly. "I would love to spend the rest of my life with you."

He pulled her closer and kissed her. "That's your final answer," he warned. "You can't change your mind and back out now—no matter what you think after you leave here today."

"Don't worry. I'm not going to change my mind," she smiled. "I'm marrying you, not your family. And so what if I am. They're part of you, so I have to love them. Right?"

"Well, I don't know about that. Wait until after you've met them."

"Oh, come on Gene, they can't be all that bad."

"I'm sorry I couldn't give you a ring. But I will. Maybe Christmas."

"Don't be silly. You already have my answer. A ring won't change that. Besides, I couldn't wear it now anyway. I'm not supposed to be seeing anyone. Remember?"

Gene reached over and took her hand and cradled it in both of his. "I want us to be married by next June right after you graduate. That will give me time to look for a better job and find us a decent place to live."

"You don't like working for Mr. Porter?"

"I won't ever make enough to support a family on what Harry pays me. Besides, Harry is so old he probably won't be around much longer. Then the State will more than likely get the farm and turn it into a housing subdivision."

"What will happen to the house?"

"Ah, it's so old and run down they'll just bulldoze it over." Gene glanced down at his watch. "Well, I guess we'd better go on in. Dad's probably got dinner on the table. Remember what I said. You can't back out now."

Anna laughed. "Oh, come on. It couldn't be that bad. Stop being silly."

It may not have been as bad as Gene warned, but it certainly was different from anything Anna had been accustomed to. Gene's father had made an attempt to clean up the place a bit before greeting their guest, but the furniture was still old and soiled with peeling wall paint and water stained ceilings from numerous roof leaks and bare light bulbs hanging from electrical cords. They drank their iced tea from old Mason jars and ate their fried chicken and potato salad from cheap paper plates. Still, Gene's father and brother gave Anna a warm, friendly welcome and treated her like family instead of a guest. They even cleaned *themselves* up as well and managed to find some clean clothes for the special occasion. In fact, Anna actually enjoyed her visit with them and really hated to leave. They gave her a friendly hug before she left and invited her to come back anytime. Gene breathed a sigh of relief when it was all over and hoped the meeting hadn't done too much damage to his relationship with Anna.

After they left his house, he drove her back to Porter's farm to get her car. They sat in Gene's Chevelle for a moment kissing, not wanting the day to end.

"I wish you didn't have to leave," he told her. "I wish we had the rest of the evening to spend together."

"So do I, but I had a really good time and I enjoyed meeting your dad and Joey. You're dad's a good cook," she smiled. "Maybe he can teach me how to cook fried chicken."

"Oh, I'm sure he'd be more than glad to. Then all he'd have to do is sit back and eat it instead of going to the trouble to cook it himself." He paused, and then added, "They liked you a lot, too. I could tell. Especially my brother. He couldn't take his eyes off you."

"Well, I've met them now and my answer is still the same. Nothing could change my mind now," she assured him. "I'll always love you, no matter what."

They kissed some more until finally Anna had to go. It was getting late. Gene saw Anna to her car and followed behind in his until they came to the highway and turned in opposite directions. That night was the happiest night of Anna's life. She was in love with a wonderful guy and engaged to be married. The next nine months would seem like an eternity.

# *Chapter Five*

The fall was the time of year in Georgia when many of its' residents displayed their most beautiful and unique handmade crafts for sale. This was especially true in the nearby Georgia Mountains where the poorest residents lived and made magnificent quilts, stained glass and furniture as well as household novelty items to earn extra income.

Aware that the young couple was running out of places to steal away and be together, Harry Porter gave Gene the day off that Saturday and suggested they drive up to the Blue Ridge Mountains to the craft festival for the day. Gene was both surprised and very pleased with the old man's offer. Harry held great affection for the two youngsters and secretly wished they could have been his own children.

Since it fell on a weekend that both Angel and Amy were staying in Athens, Anna told her parents she was driving down to Athens to visit her sisters for the day. Instead, she left around eight that Saturday morning and drove to Gene's house where she picked him up in her car and they headed for the mountains. They drove up to Chatsworth and Ellijay along the Blue Ridge Parkway, stopping at the different craft fairs they passed on their way. It turned out to be one of the best times they had ever spent together. They strolled through the craft exhibits, sampled the different southern foods that were offered from the outdoor grills and kettles and spent hours wading through the crystal clean mountain streams, enjoying the cool, fresh mountain air. When they tired, they sat down at a picnic bench over-looking the majestic Blue Ridge Mountains, ablaze in a kaleidoscope of breath-taking fall colors of orange, red and golden yellow. At one of the craft stands Anna bought two beautiful, handmade quilts, one to bring back to Harry for being so thoughtful and making their day possible and the other one she kept for herself. They used it that day to lie on beside a mountain stream as they listened to the tranquil sound of water splashing over the rocks while they made plans for their future.

They dreaded to see the day end as they got into Anna's car and headed back to Myrick later that afternoon. Before going home, Anna wanted to take Harry the quilt she had bought him. They drove to the farm and parked behind his trailer home where her car wouldn't be seen. The lonely old man was so pleased that the youngsters had ended their day by paying him a visit and presenting him with their gift that he nearly broke down in tears. Harry insisted they come in and sit with him for a while before Anna had to return home. After sharing a soft drink and some pleasant conversation, Anna said she had to leave and go home before her parents grew suspicious. Before she left, Harry asked if he could give her a hug and she gladly obliged. She returned his warm hug and thanked him again for allowing them one of the best times she and Gene had ever shared.

It was the day after Thanksgiving, one of the only two holidays the cotton mill observed and shut down. Ben Coleman sat in his glass-enclosed office at the top of a flight of stairs overlooking the ground floor of the mill. From his perch, Coleman kept a constant and watchful eye over his workers. No employees except the floor supervisors were allowed to ascend the flight of stairs and only then if the matter was significant enough to require his immediate attention.

Paul Woods, who had worked at the mill for nearly two decades and who was Coleman's dock manager, walked up the flight of stairs to his boss's office. In his hand was an inventory statement for that morning's arrival of raw cotton that was shipped by boxcar directly to the mill's receiving dock.

"Here you go, Boss," Woods said, handing over the yellow sheet of paperwork to Coleman, who sat behind a large mahogany desk. "They said we should be receiving the rest of the shipment by no later than noon tomorrow."

"Good," Coleman replied, taking the paper from Woods without looking up from his desk.

"Did you have a good Thanksgiving?" his dock manager inquired solicitously. Paul Woods was known around the mill as a *brown noser* and suck-up. He also held a reputation for *pimping* on his fellow employees to the boss.

"It was alright," Coleman replied, not bothering to look up from the paperwork before him. "Just another day out of the year. More of a bother than anything else."

Woods stood there a moment waiting for a polite inquiry from his boss concerning his own holiday. It never came. The dock manager finally turned to leave the office, but stopped abruptly as he reached for the door.

"Oh, did I mention I happened to see your daughter a few weeks back at the craft fair in Chatsworth?" Woods volunteered.

Coleman stopped what he was doing. "You saw *my* daughter?" he asked.

"Yes. I believe it was Anna, your youngest girl. Me and Faye drove up there for the weekend and happened to see her there with the Longhorn boy."

Ben Coleman looked at Woods with his cold black eyes. "The Longhorn boy?"

"I believe his name is Gene. He works for Harry Porter as his farmhand or something. You know, his old man owns that junkyard on the highway going out of town. We didn't go over and speak to them so I don't think she saw us."

"You have my daughter confused with someone else. First of all, she hasn't been anywhere but to Athens to visit her sisters and second of all, she wouldn't be seen with white trash the likes of what you describe."

Woods remained silent for a moment. "Your daughter drives a dark green Mustang with an Athens bumper sticker, don't she? It had a Barrow County license tag and the girl driving had long blonde hair. I know it had to be her."

"When was this?" Coleman shot back.

"Back the first week or so in October when the festivals opened," Woods replied.

A hot rush of rage swept over Coleman causing his face to flush an angry red. That had to be the weekend Anna said she was driving to Athens to visit her sisters at college. The last thing he needed was to have one of his mill workers catch his daughter with a piece of common white trash. Paul Woods was by far one of the biggest gossips in the mill. By the end of the day everyone in the cotton mill would know the story and by the end of the week the entire town would know—that is if they didn't already. He was worse than any woman about carrying tales and spreading rumors. It was obvious to Coleman that the only reason Woods mentioned seeing his daughter that day was to let him know he knew she was seen in public with someone beneath her.

"Well, I'll see you later, Boss," Woods said as he left the office. His mission accomplished.

Ben Coleman sat frozen with anger and rage as he pictured his youngest daughter with the boy from the junkyard. He wanted to strangle the girl with his bare hands for embarrassing him in front of his mill workers—not to mention the entire town. He glanced down at his watch. She would be getting home from school in a couple of hours. He rose from his desk and reached for his coat. He wanted to be there when Anna arrived home.

It was three-thirty that afternoon when Anna arrived home from school. She parked beside her father's black Lincoln Continental. It was unusual for him to be home in the middle of the afternoon. She went into the house and called to her mother. Her calls went unanswered. She walked into the kitchen where she found Estelle scrubbing Irish potatoes at the sink.

"Estelle, where's mother?" she asked

"Upstairs," the maid replied, not offering to turn around and face Anna.

"Is Daddy home?"

"He's upstairs with you Momma," the old black woman replied, continuing to keep her back turned.

Anna sensed something was wrong, but not until she started upstairs to her room and found five suitcases and four boxes filled with her shoes and other personal belongings, did she grow alarmed. Nearly everything she owned lie there at the bottom of the staircase. Anna sat her purse down and removed her coat before going upstairs. She walked to her bedroom where she found her father waiting for her. He was standing beside the window glaring at her when she entered her room.

"You little tramp," he growled, his black eyes glaring at her. "You've been lying about where you've been going and slipping off to be with that piece of white trash that works for old man Porter. I should kill you! You embarrass me in front of the whole town. I'll fucking kill you!"

Before Anna could escape, he lunged at her, drawing back with his fist and punching her hard in the mouth, splitting her bottom lip. She fell backwards onto the hallway floor. Before she could get back on her feet, he was on top of her, straddling her, punching her hard in the face with his fist. He hit her several times and then began banging her head on the floor and against the upstairs banister. He slammed her head so hard that it splintered one of the wooden spindles. Anna began to lose consciousness and would have passed out had her mother not come running out of her room and jumped on her husband's back, pulling him off their daughter. But Coleman was in a violent rage. He began kicking Anna with the rounded tip of his hard shoe, the blows landing on her stomach, back and legs all the while Catherine was screaming for her husband to stop. But he couldn't stop. He was in the midst of one of his violent outbursts and was finally releasing years of pent-up hatred for his youngest daughter.

"I hate you!" he yelled. "I've hated you since the day you were born. I tried to get you mother to get rid of you before you were even born and she wouldn't do it. I should have gotten rid of you myself the day you came into the world! I knew you'd turn out to be nothing but trouble!"

"Shut up, Ben!" Catherine screamed. "Stop it! Leave her alone!"

"I won't shut up," he yelled, shoving his wife away from him, slamming her into the wall. "It's time she knew the truth!"

"No, Ben! Please! Don't!" Catherine pleaded.

"I'm not your father! So don't you ever call me that again. You should have never been born. You were a lousy accident that happened because your mother wanted to get even with me and took up with another man. Well, she's had seventeen years of payback and enough is enough. You're not mine! You never were and you never will be. I despised the sight of you since the day I found out you existed. You're nothing but an embarrassment to me! A constant reminder of the mistake your mother made years ago. You get out of my house now and don't you ever let me catch you back here again or I'll kill you for sure. And I'll get away with it, too."

With that, he reached down and grabbed Anna by the arm with a violent jerk and began dragging her to the top of the stairs. Her shoulder made a loud popping sound and she screamed from the excruciating pain that shot through her upper body. It was the first sound she had uttered during the entire beating. Coleman drew back with his foot and kicked her hard in the side causing her body to start tumbling down the stairs. She rolled and slid until she landed on the bottom step. Her mother started to run downstairs after her daughter but Coleman grabbed his wife and slapped her hard in the face, spinning her around.

"This is all your fault! She wouldn't be here if it weren't for you," he shouted.

Catherine fell to the floor screaming and crying for her husband to stop, but he wouldn't—not until he had plucked the thorn out that had remained in his side for the past seventeen years. He ran down the stairs, stepping over his daughter's body and grabbed up her purse, spilling its' contents on the floor until he found her car keys.

"Now, you get out of my sight," he told her. "You gather up all this shit laying here and call your nigger friend and have her come get you because you're not leaving here with anything that belongs to me."

Estelle had run out of the kitchen when she heard Coleman raging upstairs and stood in the hallway, watching helplessly. Like everyone else, she was afraid of him. No one ever dared stand up to him, especially when he was like this and least not his colored maid. Suddenly he glanced up and saw her staring at him, his steely cold eyes shooting daggers through her.

"You get back in that kitchen and call that daughter of yours and tell her to come pick up her white trash friend and get her the hell out of my house," Coleman ordered his housekeeper. "I don't want to find her here when I get home tonight, you understand me?"

Estelle stood frozen with fear, unable to speak.

"You hear me?" he shouted again.

"Yes, sir," she replied.

Then, pointing his finger and glaring at Estelle through glazed eyes, he added, "If you ever tell anybody anything you heard here today, you won't be able to find another job anywhere in this county. You'll fucking starve to death. You hear me?"

The heavyset black woman nodded her head, too frightened to speak.

Coleman then straightened his back, adjusted his shirt collar and grabbed his jacket from the hall tree. "Remember what I said. I want her gone before I return home this evening." Then he strolled calmly out the door as if nothing out of the ordinary had occurred.

Estelle quickly ran to Anna who lay on the bottom step gasping for breath between heavy sobs. "Are you alright, child," she asked, putting her arms around her and trying to help Anna to her feet. Anna was too hurt to answer.

"Miss Catherine, we have to get this child to the hospital right away," Estelle called upstairs, but Catherine didn't reply. She lay on the upstairs landing where Ben Coleman had left her, crying and sobbing hysterically, engulfed in her own personal anguish.

"You wait here, honey," Estelle told Anna. "I'm going to go call Cassie and have her drive you to the hospital. Don't you move now. I'll be right back."

It took Cassie less than fifteen minutes to get to Coleman Hill. Anna was barely conscious when she arrived.

"You've got to get her to a hospital," Estelle urged her daughter. "Her head is bleeding real bad and I think she might have a concussion."

"But Mom, the nearest hospital is in Rome. You want me to drive her there all by myself?"

"I don't care how you get her there, just go!" Estelle told her daughter. "Take her to the Longhorns. They'll get that boy to drive her to the hospital. Here, I'll help you get her to the car."

Together, Cassie and her mother carried Anna to Cassie's car and sat her in the front seat.

"Lord Jesus, she's hurt too bad to even cry," Estelle told her daughter. "You hurry now and get her to the Longhorn's as quick as you can. You know where they live, don't you?"

"Yes, Momma. I know where they live."

"You hurry now, but don't have no wreck," Estelle warned.

Cassie left with her friend beside her and headed down Highway 11 toward Harry Porter's farm. She knew there was no point taking her to Gene's house. They would only waste time there trying to get in touch with Gene. He was more than likely out on the farm working. She drove straight to Harry's front door and began honking the horn. Porter jumped up and peered out the front window of his trailer. He didn't recognize the car or the two people inside. With his poor eyesight, he couldn't even tell how many people were in the car. When he didn't come out, Cassie jumped out of the car and ran to the front door and began banging on it with her fists.

"Mr. Porter! You've got to find Gene Longhorn. It's Anna. She's been hurt bad!"

As soon as Harry heard her cries for help, he opened the trailer door. "Who are you?" he demanded, straining through his thick eyeglasses to recognize the stranger at his doorstep.

"My name is Cassie Pittman. I'm Anna's friend. Anna has been hurt real bad. She needs a doctor!"

Harry hurried down the rickety trailer steps and walked over to the passenger's side of the Toyota.

"My God! What's happened to her?" Porter gasped when he saw Anna nearly unconscious, her face cut and bleeding.

"Old man Coleman found out she was seeing Gene and he beat her and threw her out of the house."

"Go get my truck," he said, digging into his pants pocket for his keys. He handed Cassie the keys to his pick-up truck parked beside the trailer.

"Drive up to the dairy barn and get Gene. It's after four so he should be up there milking the cows right now. Go! Hurry!" he said.

"Where's the barn?" Cassie asked.

"It's the big red barn back off the road a ways," he said, pointing toward Highway 11. "Turn in the first driveway to the right and go through the gate. It's unlocked. You can't miss it."

Cassie ran to Porter's truck and sped away toward the highway. In a few minutes, Gene's blue Chevelle came speeding into the yard with Cassie following behind in Harry's truck. Gene jumped out and ran over to Harry, who was kneeling down beside Anna in the front seat of Cassie's car. By now, Anna had already lost consciousness.

"Anna! Anna!" Gene yelled, grabbing her by the shoulders. She let out a loud moan, but her eyes remained closed. "Oh, my God! What's he done to her?" he gasped.

"Get a hold of yourself, boy," Harry said, grabbing Gene by the arm. "You got to get her to the hospital and fast. You don't have any time to waste. Put her in the truck and let's get going. I'll go with you."

"Forget the pick-up," Gene said. "We can make better time in my car."

Gene reached inside the Toyota and carefully lifted Anna out of the front seat. He then put her into the backseat of his Chevelle and Harry slid in beside her. Gene slammed the door and ran around to the driver's side and jumped in behind the wheel. The souped-up Chevy's engine roared as they sped away toward the nearest hospital some eighteen miles away. Gene was praying all the way that they would make it in time. She was unconscious and bleeding. On the way to the hospital all he could think about was what he was going to do to Coleman. He couldn't allow him to get away with what he had done to Anna. But for now, his first concern was to get her to the hospital. After that, it would be Ben Coleman who would be on his way to the hospital.

Gene and Harry sat in the hospital waiting room nervously awaiting word on Anna's condition. They had been there nearly an hour and a half. Gene sat in the uncomfortable, straight-back chair as long as he could before getting up to pace the length of the room several times in a row. He continued to alternate sitting and pacing until he thought he would scream.

"What's taking them so damn long? Do you think she's going to be alright?" he asked Harry, who remained seated.

The old man bowed his head and stared at the floor. "I hope and pray that she will be alright, son. But she was unconscious a long time." Harry's thoughts drifted back fifty years ago to a night very similar to this when he waited with anguish at his beloved Ollie's bedside. But his prayers that night went unheard and unanswered. He lost the love of his life. Was this history repeating itself? Would Anna be laid to rest alongside his Ollie beneath the huge Magnolia tree behind the house? Harry watched Gene continue to pace back and forth and saw himself fifty years ago.

"I want to kill that son-of-a-bitch," he said. "I will kill him for sure if Anna dies. I won't have anything left to live for anyway. She's all I have. I can't believe a man could do this to his own daughter."

"You better watch what you say," Harry warned him, adjusting his thick bifocals. "Because Ben Coleman can get away with murder and you can't. He's got the sheriff and every politician in the county in his back pocket. If she dies, all he has to say is she fell down some stairs and hit her head. He'll claim it was an accident and nobody will dispute his word. Not if they know what's good for them. Not even his own wife and certainly not the Negro maid."

"He'll pay for what he did," Gene swore. "One way or another. I'll make sure of that."

Harry just shook his head. There was no getting through to Gene, especially not now. He was enraged and worried senseless over his wife-to-be. "You don't want to go and do something that will get you locked up for the rest of your life. You wouldn't be around for Anna then. No. Men like Ben Coleman get what's coming' to them eventually. He'll get his, someday. Just be patient. What goes around, comes around. He's got more enemies than any man I've ever known."

"Well, right now, I'm his worst enemy."

A doctor, accompanied by a nurse walked into the room and introduced himself and asked if they were waiting for the young girl brought into the emergency room unconscious awhile ago.

"Yes," Gene replied quickly as he jumped up to greet the doctor. "How is she? Is she going to be alright?"

"Well, she has a concussion and a dislocated shoulder," the doctor told them.

"Is she still unconscious?" Gene asked.

"She's finally coming out of it. She got a pretty bad lick on the back of her head. It took seventeen stitches to close the wound and three more to close the cut over her eye. Her jaw was dislocated as well and she has a couple of fractured ribs. Her left kidney was pretty badly bruised but other than that, no serious internal injuries. The main thing that concerns me is the concussion and how long she was out. She has some brain swelling that's my major concern at the moment. But we should know more in the morning."

"Will she need any surgery?" Harry asked.

"I don't think so," the doctor replied. "At least not at this time. I'm hoping the brain swelling will go down on its own. But like I said, we'll know more by tomorrow."

"When can I take her home?" Gene asked.

"Well, we need to be absolutely sure she doesn't have any complications from the head trauma and make sure she's not passing any blood in her urine before we can discuss releasing her. If she's doing well enough by tomorrow, we'll get her up and let her move around a bit. Then when she's able to go to the bathroom on her own and she's eating well, we'll see about letting her go home in a couple of days. But we need to keep her here for observation for at least another forty-eight hours. Even then, if she goes home, she doesn't need to be left alone in case she blacks out again. If I were you, I'd have someone keep an eye on her for about a week or ten days just to make sure she's going to be alright." The doctor paused, then asked, "You said she fell down a flight of stairs?"

Gene nodded his head.

The doctor looked at him suspiciously. "I don't think she could have received the type of injuries she suffered from just a tumble down some steps. That girl was beaten within an inch of her life."

"We weren't there when it happened," Harry explained. "All we know is what we were told. A friend brought her to my house up the road from where they live in town and asked me to get her to the hospital."

The doctor then looked at Gene. "I see. And who are you?"

"I'm her fiancée," he replied.

"He works for me," Harry added quickly. "I got a farm just outside of Myrick and he's my foreman. I sent for him to come drive us to the hospital since I can't see to drive that good."

The doctor remained silent and looked at them curiously. "So neither of you were with her when she got hurt?"

"No sir," Harry replied. "We were home when her friend brought her to us."

"Who is this friend?"

"A girl she goes to school with," Gene replied. "She's their housekeeper's daughter."

"Was she there when it happened?"

"I don't know," Gene said.

"All we know is what we were told," Harry said. "The housekeeper was home with her. She called her daughter who is Anna's friend to get her to the hospital since the maid didn't have a car. The girl wasn't sure how to get to Rome the fastest way, so she brought her to my place for help."

"Look, when can I see her?" Gene asked impatiently.

"You can see her now if you like. But I can't promise she'll be awake. She's in and out of consciousness right now. That's why we moved her to ICU. We'll keep her there through the night and decide tomorrow whether or not she's well enough to be moved to a private room. She's lucky, but she's still not out of the woods completely. She could have easily died from her injuries." The doctor paused, then added, "I still have to question what *really* happened to put her in this shape. I'm still not convinced her injuries were caused merely by a fall."

Gene had no doubt who or what was the cause of Anna's injuries. The only thing he wasn't sure of was how he was going to get even with the person responsible for her being there.

The most difficult decision Anna was faced with when she was finally released from the Rome hospital four days later was where she would stay until she had fully recuperated. It wasn't so much the fact she had nowhere to go, but a matter of whom she would choose to stay with. Harry wanted Anna to stay with him at his trailer home because she would be safer there and he could keep a close eye on her. On the other hand, Gene's father wanted Gene to bring Anna home with him because there would be three people there to help care for her until she got back on her feet. Gene of course, insisted Anna return home with him.

He and Harry drove to Rome that morning and checked her out of the hospital. And it was Harry who volunteered to pay Anna's rather large hospital bill. On signing her out, Harry pulled three thousand dollars out of his pocket and handed it over to the woman behind the discharge desk.

"I'll pay you back somehow," Gene promised his boss.

"Don't worry about that," Harry told him. "Just be thankful we were able to bring her home alive."

Cassie had returned to the Coleman house after leaving Anna with Gene that afternoon, and loaded her belongings in her Toyota and taken them to the Longhorn's. Estelle assured her daughter that if they didn't remove Anna's belongings from the house that Coleman would have them destroyed when he returned. Not knowing anywhere else to take them, Cassie left them with Gene's father.

No one bothered to contact Anna's two sisters to let them know what had happened, therefore it wasn't until a week later that they were even aware that their sister was no longer at home. They were simply told that after discovering she was seeing the Longhorn boy behind his back, their father kicked her out of the house. Her parents didn't know where she had gone after Cassie left with her that day, barely conscious and badly bleeding, nor did they attempt to find out. Only Estelle and Cassie knew of her whereabouts and they were keeping quiet about the entire incident.

Gene had made room for Anna in his tiny bedroom at his house. He gave her his bed while he took the worn sofa in the living room. While he worked on the farm during the day, his father looked after Anna and saw that she was fed and cared for. Harry called to check on her every single day. Two weeks later, Gene drove her back to the hospital in Rome to have her stitches removed. On the way there and back, they discussed their plans for the immediate future.

"This frees us to go ahead and get married, you know," he told her as they drove toward Rome. "We don't have to wait until June now."

"I know," Anna replied. "But I would still like to graduate with my class."

"Well, I think the sooner we get married, the better," he insisted. "I say we go ahead and apply for the marriage license. Today. When we get back to Myrick, we can stop by the court house—that is if you're up to it after we leave the doctor."

"I would really like to return to school first and finish my senior year. It won't be that long until I graduate, just another six months before school is out."

"Well, if you insist," he replied. "Maybe by then I'll have enough money saved up for a nice wedding ring and a place to live."

"All I need is a plain gold wedding band," she smiled. "I don't need anything fancy."

"Where do you want to get married?" Gene asked. "The court house? Do you know of a church—other than the one your parents are members of?"

Anna thought for a moment, and replied, "I want to get married in Harry's old house."

Gene looked at her as if she had lost her mind. "What? You mean the old plantation house?"

"Yes."

"That old place? It's caving in. That's no place for a wedding. It would be better if we got married beneath the old Magnolia tree out back."

"No. I want to get married in the house. It's still sound. It just needs a little work, that's all. I love that place."

Gene shook his head and laughed. "I don't believe you," he said. "What is it with you and that old house?"

"I don't know," she replied. "I just feel like that's where I belong. Like it's calling me to come live there."

"I think that bump on your head is still having an affect on you," he laughed. "You mean you'd rather get married in that old rundown pile of firewood than in a church somewhere?"

"Yes, I would."

"Well, alright then," he shrugged, throwing up his hands. "If that's what you really want."

"Do you think Harry will mind?"

"Mind? No, he won't mind. But he'll probably think you're crazy, like I do. But no, he won't care if that's what you really want."

That afternoon when Gene returned from Rome with Anna, he went to Harry and told him Anna wanted to be married in the old plantation house.

"For some reason," he told Harry, "she's always been crazy about that old house of yours. Don't ask me why, but I think she'd move in and live there right now if she could. That place is all she talks about."

Harry hung his head and stared down at the ground as if looking for something lost beneath his feet. He remained silent for a long while.

"Look," Gene finally said. "I'll talk her out of it. I just told her I would run the idea by you. I know it's crazy but she really had her heart set on us getting married there."

Gene looked at the old man and thought he saw tears welling up in his eyes. "If that's what she wants, then that's what we'll give her," Harry said at last. "The bride should have her say where she wants to be married. If she wants to be married in that house, then that's where she'll have her wedding." He paused and dabbed at his eyes with a handkerchief he pulled from his back pocket. "Have you two set a date yet?"

"I want to go ahead and get married right away, but Anna wants to wait until after she graduates which will be sometime in June. The way I see it, there's nothing standing in our way now so why not go ahead and get married as soon as possible."

"No," Harry said. "Let her finish school first. She's right. She's almost through with school, another few months won't matter." A faint smile danced across the old man's wrinkled, weathered face. "A June bride," he mumbled under his breath. He thought for a moment and added, "I tell you what. You tell her that if she will wait until June to get married and finish school, I'll fix up that old place and that will by my wedding present to the two of you."

Gene looked at Harry in disbelief. "Are you kidding me?" he replied. "You'd *give* us that old place?"

"Well, not until I fix it up first and make it livable. You certainly couldn't live in it the way it is now, but I'll pay for the cost of the materials if you do the work yourself. Look," Harry said. "I ain't got no family left. No wife or kids. I ain't even got any brothers or sister, nieces or nephews. The state will get it when I die and God knows they don't need no more of my money than they're already entitled to. They get enough already in the taxes I have to pay on that thousand acres I own. I fixed that place up fifty years ago for Ollie and she never got to enjoy it. It would make me proud if somebody deserving got to enjoy it before it falls down. All it needs is some new life breathed in it. I know it would make Ollie happy if she knew some nice young couple was livin' there and raisin' a family, like we'd planned to do. And I would too, rather than watch it rot away like it is and cave in."

"Harry, do you realize how much it's gonna cost to repair that old place and make it livable?" Gene asked.

Harry nodded his head. "If you do most of the work yourself, it'll cut down the cost some. Besides, it'll be worth it just to see the look on Anna's face when you carry her across the threshold. I never got to see that look on Ollie's face."

Silence fell between them for a moment as emotion overcame them. Harry had known Gene since he was thirteen and had worked long and hard hours for the old man, never letting him down. He was responsible for the farm running smoothly. He couldn't have kept the place up without him. Gene was trustworthy, dependable and honest, as well as a hard working young man. He was everything Harry would have wanted in his own son had he been blessed with children. As for Anna, she reminded him of his beloved Ollie and looked enough like her to have been her daughter. Both were worthy and deserved only the best life had to offer. Harry would do for them what he would have done for his own children. He would see to it that his and Ollie's legacy would be left with Anna and Gene.

# Chapter Six

Anna continued to stay with Gene's family as she regained her strength and became more familiar with his father and older brother. Gene's father waited on his future daughter-in-law hand and foot—something he'd never done for anyone in his life. But Anna was special. She was sweet, gentle and kind-hearted. Meanwhile, Gene's brother Joey grew so fond of her that his affection bordered infatuation. She was the most beautiful girl he'd ever known and so far, the first one who showed him the slightest attention. During the day, while Gene was busy with the farm, Joey followed her around like a lost puppy. He now hung around the house more and spent fewer hours in the junkyard.

"You better keep an eye on that office," Joe, Sr. warned his son. "You don't want to lose any customers. Or any car parts for that matter. Somebody could just go in there and walk out with anything they wanted before you even knew they were on the property."

"The dogs will let me know if anybody drives up," Joey replied. "There ain't nothin' to do out there anyway and besides it's warmer in the house."

"Yeah, and the scenery is a little better here, too," his father added sarcastically.

Anna was in the kitchen taking her daily medications and overheard their conversation. "That reminds me," she said. "I need to go make sure the dogs have some fresh water and feed them these left over table scraps."

"You don't need to worry yourself with that," Joey told her. "I'll go check on them before it gets dark. It's too cold for you to go out."

"Oh, I don't mind. I like looking after them. My father never would let us have any pets when I was growing up. I always wanted a dog," she said, sliding her coat over her arm sling. Joey struggled to lift his weight from the sagging sofa and waddled into the kitchen to help Anna with her coat.

"You don't mind if I take them these sausage patties left over from breakfast, do you?" she asked Joe, Sr., who remained seated in the living room absorbed in one of his daily soap operas.

"No, I guess not," he replied. "You might as well go ahead and take 'em those left over biscuits, too."

Before leaving the kitchen, she sneaked a quart of milk out of the refrigerator along with the sausage and biscuits. Anna had begun spoiling the animals with special treats like milk and table scraps since she had been there, even though she knew Gene's father frowned on such practice. But she loved the dogs and enjoyed spoiling them as much as they loved receiving her special treatment.

Joey, Jr. followed Anna out the back door and down the rickety, rotting steps leading off the back porch. Each board bent dangerously low, threatening to split in half from his three hundred plus pounds. The two large, black and tan German Shepherds bounced up and down and yelped with excitement when they saw Anna coming through the six-foot Rio Grand fence that surrounded a portion of the junkyard and the dilapidated shack which served as the office. Running out of an oversized doghouse and tagging after the two adult dogs were eight six week-old pups.

"Hi fellas!" she greeted the eager animals. "Here, hold this while I pour some milk in the puppies' bowl," she told Joey, handing him the paper plate filled with sausage and stale biscuits. After tending to the pups, she divided the food up between the parents and placed it in separate bowls. "Is that good, girl? You like that sausage, don't you boy? When you finish that, I'll give you some cold milk."

Joey, watched Anna interact with the dogs as if they were small children. She seemed to get so much enjoyment from caring for them and playing with their pups. He found her childlike enthusiasm amusing and refreshing. He helped her fill their water bucket with fresh water from the outside faucet.

The dogs' attention was suddenly diverted to a car pulling up in the Longhorn's driveway and they began barking aggressively. Joey quickly closed the gate to prevent the animals from running after the intruders. Anna glanced up and recognized the familiar, convertible red Mustang. It was her sister's car.

"Who's that?" Joe wondered aloud, having never met Anna's siblings.

"That's my sister, Angel," Anna replied, her voice filled with delight. "Amy's with her."

She hadn't seen her sisters since their father had thrown her out of the house. It had been two weeks. The girls had learned of the incident from their mother, but were told she had no idea where Anna had gone. Finally they learned from Estelle, that their sister was staying with the Longhorns. As soon as they found out, they jumped in the car and hurried out to the old rundown shack outside of town.

"Come on," Anna said, giving Joe's sleeve a playful tug. "I'll introduce you." She walked past the junkyard toward the driveway where Angel had parked. She was elated her sisters had found her and greeted them with a cheerful smile and warm hug. But as she approached, the two girls were horrified and shocked at what they saw.

"Oh my God," Amy gasped as she got out of the car and walked toward her younger sister. Anna's right arm was still in a sling, both eyes were badly blackened and her lips were still cut and swollen. Above her left eye remained an angry red wound where the stitches had recently been removed.

"Oh Amy, I'm so glad you and Angel are here," Anna beamed, oblivious to the expressions on their faces after seeing her for the first time since their father's beating. "I've missed you so much," she said, wrapping her good arm around their neck and giving each a firm hug.

"Jesus, look at you!" Angel said. "My God, what did he do to you?"

"I'm alright," Anna assured them. "I still have a few bumps and bruises, but I'll be fine."

"I'd like to kill that son-of-a-bitch," Amy said through clinched teeth.

"You'll have to get in line," Joey said, standing in the background.

Anna's sisters had been so pre-occupied with her that they hadn't paid any attention to the large man standing off to the side. They glanced at him with annoyance and curiosity.

"Amy, Angel, this is Joey—Gene's older brother. Joey, these are my sisters."

"Hi there," he replied with a polite nod.

The two girls gave him a quick evaluation without a verbal response and turned their attention back to their sister, ignoring him.

"Are you sure you're alright?" Amy asked, gently pushing Anna's hair away from her face.

"You look terrible," Angel said, lightly stroking Anna's dislocated shoulder.

"I'm a lot better since I got out of the hospital," she assured them. "Gene and his family have taken such good care of me. Joey and his dad won't let me lift a finger. They've all been so good to me."

The older girls turned and once again glanced over their shoulder at Joey. "We appreciate what you've done," Amy said, finally. "It's very kind of you."

"Our pleasure," Joey replied. "We don't mind at all. It's nice having a girl around for a change."

"Listen, would you mind if we had some time alone with our sister?" Angel told him. "We'd like to speak with her if you don't mind."

Joey silently nodded his head and turned to walk back toward the house.

"I'll be in shortly, Joey," Anna told him, somewhat embarrassed by her sisters' rudeness.

"Listen Anna," Angel told her. "You can't stay here. You're coming back with us."

"You don't understand," she told her sister. "I can't go back home. He said if I ever came back there, he'd kill me."

"We don't mean back to Coleman Hill," Amy explained. "We're talking about taking you back to Athens. I've got plenty of room at my place. You can stay with me."

"That's right," Angel added. "And you'll only be a couple of doors down from Tanya and me. We'll take care of you. You don't have to stay here with these people."

"But I want to," Anna assured them. "I actually like it here. They've been so good to me. Besides, I'm with Gene now and this is where I belong. We're getting married in June, right after I graduate."

"You can't be serious," Angel insisted. "Jesus, just look at this place. It looks like the goat man's house. Do they even have plumbing in there?"

"Of course," Anna replied, rolling her eyes. "And electricity, too," she added, cajoling. "Really, this is where I belong. Gene and his family are all I have now. Besides, they treat me better and care for me more than Mom and Dad ever did. And even Mr. Porter. He treats me like his own daughter. He even paid my hospital bill. I've never had people treat me so well and be so concerned about me."

"Are you getting enough to eat?" Amy asked. "Do they have decent food on the table?"

"Of course they do," Angel told her sister. "Didn't you see the size of that guy? Looks to me like *somebody's* eating pretty damn good in there."

"You're right," Amy agreed sarcastically. "Maybe they're eating her share along with their own."

"Stop being mean. Joey is a very nice person. So is his dad. You have to stop judging people by appearances," she told them. "Gene's family may not have much money, but they're good people. And Gene is so caring."

"Are you sleeping with him?" Amy asked abruptly.

"No," Anna assured her sister. "We've never been together like that. I told Gene I wanted to wait until after we were married and he's respecting my wishes. He's sleeping on the sofa in the living room so I can have his room. That's why it hurt so bad when Dad called me those awful names." She paused and lowered her head. "He said a lot of hurtful things to me that day. But one thing he said has haunted me and I can't stop thinking about it."

"What did he say?" Angel asked.

"He said he wasn't my father."

"What?" Amy gasped, her mouth dropping.

"He screamed that he wasn't my real father and that Mom had an affair with another man to get even with him for something and got pregnant with me. Is that true?"

Angel and Amy turned and looked at one another in stunned disbelief. "Anna, I never heard either of them say anything like that before," Amy assured her. "Are you sure that's what he said? Are you sure you didn't misunderstand him?"

Anna shook her head. "No, I'm very sure. I couldn't believe what I was hearing. But then, on the other hand, it might explain why he always treated me the way he did. It was obvious he never had any feelings for me. Not the way he did for both of you. That would explain a lot."

Angel and Amy continued to stare at one another in silence. "Did he tell you who *was* your real father?" Amy asked.

Anna shook her head. "No. And at the time, I was in no position to ask any questions. I really thought he was going to kill me. And Mom just stood there and did nothing."

"Anna, we warned you about seeing this guy," Angel reminded her. "We told you how he'd react."

"How did he find out?" Amy asked.

"I have no idea," Anna replied. "He never said."

"So, Mom just stood back and let him beat you like that?" Amy asked.

Anna nodded her head. "I think she was afraid to try and stop him for fear of him turning on her. I've never seen him so mad. I think he really wanted to kill me."

Amy looked intently at her younger sister. There was something she wanted desperately to know but was afraid to ask. After all these years, perhaps now was the time. "Anna," she began. "There's something I have to ask you and I want you to tell me the truth. Don't be afraid to tell us," she paused. "Has he—"

"Look, you're coming back to Athens with us," Angel interrupted her suddenly as if she were reading Amy's mind. "We can't let you stay here. This isn't where you belong." She glanced back at Amy and flashed her a stern look that silenced any further questions.

"You don't understand," Anna tried to explain. "If Dad finds out I've moved in with either of you, he will cut off your living expenses and stop paying your college tuition. He won't give either of you another dime."

"Like I give a damn," Amy replied. "I'm getting married in a couple of months anyway and I won't be needing a damn thing he has to offer me. I'll be a Willis by then and have my own money and plenty of it at that. Chuck's grandfather is giving him a Chevrolet dealership for his twenty-third birthday. His grandfather already owns three dealerships and when the old man dies, he'll pass them on to Chuck, who's his only grandson."

"She's right," Angel added. "And I'll be graduating with a four year business degree in June. So who needs the son-of-a-bitch anyway?"

"You do. Both of you do until February and June rolls around," Anna told them. "You can't possible support yourselves *and* me and still go to school without his money. Look, I appreciate your concern and the offer, but it's best for everybody if I stay here for now. Besides, I need to remain here so I can finish out my senior year. I can't do that if I go back to Athens with you."

Angel and Amy looked at one another and knew Anna was right. They hated their father for many reasons and this was just one more excuse for them to despise him even more. He was a monster. But right now he had them all over a barrel. They needed his financial support, at least for a few more months. Soon, however, neither of them would ever need him or anything he had to offer.

With much reluctance and deep regret, Angel and Amy left their sister there where she insisted she belonged and where she assured them she wanted to remain.

"This is my home now," she said. "And these people are about to become my family. I'm really better off here than I would be anywhere else." And for now she was probably right.

Anna knew her father was a rich and powerful man, but she wasn't aware of the depth of his power or how far it reached until she borrowed Gene's car and drove to Myrick high to return to school that day. When she entered the school lobby early that morning and went to her locker, she was surprised to find the lock had been changed.

"Excuse me. That's my locker," a girl said, pushing in front of Anna, as she began turning the combination lock.

"But that's *my* locker," Anna insisted.

"Not anymore," the girl replied, opening the door and removing a book, then slamming the door shut.

Anna watched as the girl left and hurried toward her classroom. She turned and looked at the locker again, checking to make sure it was the right number. Then she walked straight to the school office and went to the front desk, where she was greeted by a fellow classmate with whom she shared a biology class. The girl worked in the office during first period.

"Tracey, do you know what's going on with my locker?" she asked. "The lock has been changed and some other girl is using it."

"Oh gosh, Anna. You look terrible. What happened to your face?" the classmate asked, ignoring Anna's question. "I heard you were in a bad accident or something."

"Yes, it was an accident, but I'm fine now," she replied, avoiding the girl's curiosity. "What happened to my locker?"

"Your father was here last week and got your school records from Mrs. Keiser. He told her that you were transferring to another school in Atlanta and wouldn't be back here."

"What?" Anna gasped, unable to believe her ears. "My father came to the school?"

The girl nodded. "Yeah. He said you weren't living here anymore. Mrs. Keiser gave him your records and he took them with him."

Anna was in such shock and disbelief that she barely remembered walking out of the office and leaving the school grounds. She got back in Gene's car and immediately went searching for him. She found him hosing down the dairy barn after the morning milking. He looked up and was surprised to see her.

"What are you doing back here," he asked. "I thought you'd be in first period by now. What are you doing, playing hooky on your first day back?"

"I don't go to school there anymore," she told him.

"What?"

"My father went there and gathered up my school records and told the assistant principal that I was transferring to a school in Atlanta. What am I going to do? I can't even finish out my senior year now." Anna covered her face with her hands and started to cry.

Gene tossed aside the water hose and walked over to her. "Hey, don't cry," he said wrapping his arms around her. "We'll figure something out. You'll finish school somehow. I'll talk to Harry and see what he says. Maybe he can think of something."

"I can't believe my father did that," she sobbed. "Why would he do a thing like that?"

"Why would he beat the hell out of you just because you were seeing a guy he didn't know? Because he's a nut. A control freak. And because he wants you out of Myrick. That's why. He thinks he can run you out of town and out of his life by kicking you out of his house and preventing you from returning to school. But I got news for him. It ain't gonna work. We're stayin' right here. I'm not runnin' from nobody and you aren't either. We'll figure something out. Don't worry. We'll get you back in school somehow," Gene assured her.

"But he took all my school records. I can't even transfer someplace else without my records. All my grades, my credits, everything—they're all gone. What am I going to do?"

"I don't know," Gene confessed. "But we'll get around it somehow. We'll talk to Harry and see if he can come up with a suggestion."

That evening after he finished his farm chores, Gene went to Harry and explained what Coleman had done.

"I'm not surprised at anything that man would do," Harry replied. "Let me think and I'll try to come up with a solution. You tell Anna not to worry. Her old man ain't the only one around here with some pull and a few contacts. I got a few myself."

As it turned out, Harry was right. He began by having Anna drive him to the courthouse where they acquired a copy of her birth certificate. Then they went to the county board of education where copies of all school records were kept and had copies made. From there, they drove over to Gordon County where Anna enrolled as a senior at Gordon County High. Harry even bought her a good, used, little Chevy Corvair to drive to and from school each day. Thanks to Harry Porter, Anna would be able to complete her education and graduate that June.

When Harry tried to give Anna a small allowance for gas and lunch money, she refused, insisting he had done enough already. Instead, she got a job at a small department store in Calhoun, a short drive away from the high school and worked after school and on Saturdays until the store closed each night at nine p.m. She earned enough money to pay for her gas and food and still managed to put back a little extra. Plus, she received a twenty percent discount on any purchases she made at the store. Anna was the happiest she had ever been in her life. She was finally with people who loved and cared about her, she was engaged to a wonderful man and she had even earned some independence and was maturing into a fine young woman.

Every other weekend, when her sisters came home from college, they slipped out to the Longhorn's to briefly visit Anna. When Amy was married on Valentine's Day to Charles Willis, she was advised by her sisters not to attend the ceremony for fear of retaliation from their father. Anna was hurt, but she knew her presence would create an ugly scene that would only ruin Amy's wedding day. In fact, she made sure she kept a low profile and out of sight around Myrick to prevent any further trouble from her father. By now, most everyone in town was of the belief she was attending a fancy boarding school in Atlanta. Very few people knew the truth, which is exactly the way Ben Coleman intended it.

# Chapter Seven

It was now April and the beginning of spring. Since December, Harry had been funding the restoration of the old plantation house while Gene had been busy doing most of the work himself and hiring out the rest. In another month, it would be ready to occupy. The roof had been completely rebuilt and all the water damage repaired. The exterior was freshly painted and all the rotting wood and broken windowpanes replaced. Gene worked long into the night, doing all the electrical rewiring and plumbing by himself. All that remained were the interior floors and walls to be refinished. There were several pieces of antique furniture and accessories that had remained in the house after Harry moved out. Things Ollie had chosen that Harry could not bring himself to dispose of. He had also stored a number of items that were still in good shape, but just needed a good cleaning, in an old barn. Harry told Gene to move them back into the house once it was completed, restoring the old mansion to nearly its original state, both inside as well as out. The house would be ready to move into by the time Anna walked with her graduating class.

That Sunday afternoon, after Anna had prepared Sunday dinner and they had all eaten, Gene returned to his farm chores. Anna then got into her car and drove down to Harry's trailer to take him a plate of food and some homemade chocolate meringue pie. She sat and kept him company while he ate.

"You sure are a fine cook," he said, digging into the large slice of pie she had brought him. "I haven't had any food this good since I went to my last church homecoming. Gene better watch out, he'll wind up bein' as big as his brother and old man. I noticed he's already putting on a few pounds since you two been together."

Anna laughed. "I'll always love him no matter how big he gets. I love what's on the inside, not on the outside."

"That's the way it should be," Harry agreed.

Anna waited until Harry had cleaned his plate before announcing she would like for him to walk next door and go through the newly restored mansion. "I haven't been in the house since Gene polished the light fixtures and hung them back up," she said. "Would you like to walk over there with me and look at how things are coming along?"

"Sure, I'll go with you," he replied enthusiastically.

They walked next door and climbed the fourteen newly repaired steps leading up to the front porch. "Gene did a good job refinishing this old door," Harry remarked as he reached for the shinny, new, brass door handle.

"He's done a great job on everything," Anna agreed. "He's worked so hard and put so much effort in everything he's done. From the road, it looks like a million bucks. It's quite impressive. Of course, even when it was run down it was impressive to me, but now I notice a lot of other people are slowing down and staring at it as they pass by on the road."

"Yeah, I noticed that myself," Harry replied. "It looks just like it did fifty years ago when Ollie and me was about to move in. It's a showplace alright, when it's fixed up."

Anna stood in the center of the wide hallway and gazed around in awe and admiration. "I can hardly wait until I walk down those stairs in my wedding gown and stand beside Gene in front of the preacher. Sometimes when I'm in class or at the department store, I catch myself daydreaming about it. I fell in love with this house the first time I laid eyes on it. I couldn't have been more than six or seven when I was with Momma and my sisters one Saturday as we were driving back from Atlanta. I remember looking over here at this big old house and thinking how much I'd love to go inside and explore it. Next to Coleman Hill, it was the biggest house I'd ever seen. And even prettier than the one I lived in. I liked the way it was built better than ours." She paused and looked around the room, admiring its majestic beauty. "Oh Harry, this is going to be such a grand place to live and raise our children. It's so big that they'll each be able to have their own bedroom."

Harry froze as he looked at Anna. Ollie had stood in that same spot fifty years ago and said those exact words. Suddenly, he saw Ollie standing before him.

Anna's eyes darted over every detail of the interior as she visualized where she would place family pictures and furniture. Her attention fell on the door behind the stairs leading down to the basement.

"You know, I've never been down to the basement before. I think I'll go and see what Gene has done down there."

"No! No, don't go down there!" The urgency in Harry's voice startled Anna and took her by surprise.

"Why?" she asked curiously.

"It's dark and damp and musky down there. You don't want to go down there. Just keep that door closed," he warned her, stepping between her and the basement door. "Besides, there's nothing down there to see. I should have had Gene nail that door shut while he was working on those light fixtures."

"Nail it shut? Oh no, Harry. Don't do that. Why can't I go down there just for a minute to look around? It's the only place in the house that I've never been."

"Listen," he said, taking her by the arm and leading her away from the basement door. "Let's finish looking at those light fixtures and then I have something I want to show you back at the trailer." He hoped to get her mind off her curiosity.

Finally, he succeeded in diverting her attention as they walked through the rest of the house admiring Gene's hard work. Then Harry used the new key Gene had given him and locked the front door behind them before walking the short distance back to Harry's single trailer. The old man escorted Anna inside his small, yet clean and neatly kept, trailer home and began by offering her a cold soda.

"No thank you, Harry. I just finished eating. I'm still stuffed from dinner."

He walked over and sat down on the sofa beside her. "Anna, there's something I've been wanting to mention to you, but I didn't quite know how to bring it up." He paused nervously and adjusted his thick bifocals.

"What is it, Harry?"

"I have something—actually, it's a couple of things that I wanted to share with you."

"Okay," she replied, looking at him curiously.

"It's back here in the spare bedroom," he said, pointing toward the narrow hallway in the rear of the trailer. He rose from the sofa and started walking down the hallway toward the tiny bedroom. He motioned for her to follow him.

With some hesitation, Anna got up and slowly walked behind him. He led her into the spare bedroom where there was only enough room for a twin bed and double dresser with an attached mirror. She watched as he bent down and slid open one of the dresser drawers. He reached inside the drawer and brought out a rather large, flat, white box and placed it on the bed. Slowly, he removed the lid and peeled back several layers of yellowed tissue paper. Then, ever so carefully, he held up a beautiful, white lace wedding gown and matching veil.

"This was to be Ollie's wedding gown. It's handmade," Harry said. "She never got to wear it."

"Oh, Harry," Anna gasped. "It's beautiful."

"Do you really like it?" Harry asked.

"Oh, yes. It's gorgeous."

"I'll offer it to you," he said. "That is if you don't already have something else in mind. If so, you won't offend me if you don't take it."

Tears welled up in Anna's eyes. "Oh, Harry. Of course, I want it. I'm so thrilled and touched that you think enough of me to offer me something so special."

"Ollie would be proud for you to wear it on your wedding day."

"I can't believe you've kept it all these years. And it looks brand new," Anna said, stroking the delicate handmade lace.

"Well, I've tried to keep it preserved. I heard if you wrap something in white tissue paper, it keeps things from turning yellow over the years."

"Oh, I hope it will fit," Anna said, holding the gown up against her and turning to admire her reflection in the dresser mirror.

"It will," Harry assured her as he stood back and admired Anna's reflection. "You and Ollie are the same size. I'm sure of it."

As Anna continued to admire the antique lace gown, Harry reached in his pants pocket and pulled out a small, hand carved, ivory ring box. "I have something else I saved," he said, taking her hand and placing the tiny box in her palm. Anna carefully laid the gown on the bed and opened the ring box. Her eyes widened when she saw what was tucked inside. It was a beautiful diamond and yellow gold, wedding ring set. The engagement ring had a solitaire diamond in the center with two smaller diamonds on each side and a matching wedding band with four diamonds.

"Oh, my gosh," she gasped. "It's beautiful."

"It's two and a half total carats," Harry told her. "I bought it in Atlanta. Ollie never got to wear the wedding band, but she wore the engagement ring for about a year. You're welcome to them, too. That is, if you and Gene haven't already picked out your wedding bands," he added.

"Oh, Harry. I don't know what to say. I didn't know how I was going to afford a wedding gown and Gene has been saving every dime he can to try and buy me just a simple gold band. I was thinking about asking my sister if I could borrow her wedding gown. There's no way we could have ever been able to afford anything as nice as what you've offered." Anna paused. "Harry, are you sure you want to give me the gown and these rings? I mean, you've already spent a fortune on fixing up the house."

"Who else am I going to leave them to? I have no family. No children to pass them down to. When I die, there's no tellin' who'll come in here and take these things. They're liable to wind up in some pawnshop. I'd rather give them to somebody deserving. It would please me to know you kept these things and passed them on down to your own children. And I'm sure Ollie would be happy with that decision."

Anna walked over to the old man and put her arms around his shoulders, giving him a warm hug. "I'll be honored to wear both the gown and the rings, Harry. I don't know how Gene and I will ever be able to repay you for all you've done for us. You've given us so much and been so kind and thoughtful. I don't know what to say. I'm speechless."

"You don't have to say anything, Anna. Just accept these things with my best wishes and you and Gene make a good life for yourselves and always be kind to one another and love one another. Do it for Ollie and me. That's the only payment I want."

Anna fought back tears as she looked at Harry and smiled. "We will. I promise. We'll make you proud of us."

"You already have," Harry said.

Anna worked long, hard hours between going to school, working at the department store until nine, making the long drive back home and studying until she fell asleep from exhaustion. Then she would get up the next morning and start her day all over again. She and Gene saw less of one another now, even though they were living under the same roof, than she did when she was sneaking around to date him. She worked at the department store on Saturdays from nine a.m. until six p.m. This left Saturday nights and Sundays as the only time she and Gene had together. But the money she made at the store was pretty good and the discounts on top of the red tag sale prices came in handy. She was able to have enough left over after gas money, to buy some nice things for their new house such as bed linens, bath towels and some nice everyday dinnerware and flatware. Whenever she made a new purchase, she would take the items to the old plantation house and put them away until the time when she and Gene would move in after their wedding day. But first, she would always take them to Harry and show him her new treasures and brag on how nice they were going to look in their new home. Harry would smile and agree, taking pleasure in her childlike enthusiasm. He was like a proud father where the two kids were concerned and his life began to take on new meaning. Watching them grow from kids courting and slipping off to be together, into mature, responsible young, adults, was now his greatest joy. They had taken his old, decaying plantation house that was falling to ruin, and breathed new life into it. Gene spent long hours, after working on the farm, restoring and building the old house. Anna spent most of her time after school and work, inside the house decorating and preparing it to become their new home. Their enthusiasm gave Harry a new lease on life and brought him happiness that he hadn't known since he and Ollie were together. In fact, the two youngsters reminded him of he and Ollie five decades earlier. He could visualize them as their very own children, and knew how proud Ollie would have been to see the way they had turned out.

Their wedding was less than a month away as Anna stood in the dining room of the plantation house, placing the formal china and stemware, that had been Ollie's mother's, inside the antique china hutch. After Harry had given them to her, she had ever so carefully washed them in the farmhouse kitchen sink and gently placed them in the one hundred year-old china hutch that had been in Harry's family since he was a small boy.

She was arranging the stemware behind the china when she heard the front door open and a girl's voice call out to her.

"Anna? Are you there?"

Anna immediately recognized the familiar voice as Cassie's. "Cassie! I'm here. In the dining room."

The young black girl entered the house through the front foyer and was awestruck at the magnificent transition the old house had undergone.

"Anna, this is beautiful! I can't believe this is the same house that was rotting down all these years. I barely recognize it. From the road, it looks like someone tore down the old one and built a new house in its place."

Anna walked over and greeted her friend with a big hug. "Oh Cassie, it's so good to see you. How are you?"

"I'm good. But how are you? Let me look at you," she said, examining Anna closely for telltale scars and bruises. "You look great. Why, you're as good as new."

"Yeah. All healed up. I'm fine now. My shoulder still gives me some trouble now and then, but other than that, I feel good."

"Oh, Anna, I'm so glad. That day I brought you out here, I didn't know if you were going to live. Your father nearly killed you. You were hurt so bad."

"I know. But all that's behind me now. I have a new life here with Gene and his family and I'm happier than I've ever been in my entire life. I can't wait for us to get married."

"Have you seen your mother since it happened?" Cassie asked.

"No. I see Amy pretty regularly since she moved back to Myrick to live with Chuck after they married. She drops by quite often. And I see Angel every other weekend when she comes home from Athens. I do miss seeing Mother though. How is she doing?"

"She's okay," Cassie replied. "But Momma says she's been drinking kind of heavy since your dad kicked you out."

"Drinking? I never knew my Mother to drink. At least nothing more than a social cocktail now and then whenever she was entertaining."

"Yeah, well, Momma says she stays up in her room a lot now and drinks Vodka all day long. Some days she doesn't even come downstairs at all."

"I wonder if Amy and Angel know about this," Anna wondered aloud. "If they do, neither of them have said a word about it to me."

Cassie shook her head. "I don't know if they do or not. Maybe they do and they just don't want to worry you. But then maybe they don't know she's drinking. Momma says she manages to hide it pretty good from everyone except your dad."

"So he knows she's drinking?" Anna asked.

"I guess so. That's what Momma says."

"That really shocks me," Anna said. "I never knew Mother to drink like that."

"Well, don't worry too much about it," Cassie told her. "Like you said, you got your life here now and it's a hundred times better than what you knew at home with your parents."

"Yeah, I guess you're right. Well, how have you been doing? Are you looking forward to graduating next month?"

"I guess," Cassie replied solemnly, her expression showing no emotion.

"What's wrong? Isn't this what we've all been looking forward to all these years? We're finally getting out of school and starting our lives."

"Yeah, well, you have a lot more to look forward to than I do right now," Cassie frowned.

Anna looked at her friend who had obvious despair written all over her face. "Cassie, what's wrong?"

Cassie turned her back to Anna, unable to face her friend and began to cry. "I messed up," she sobbed. "I *really* messed up good."

"What are you talking about? What do you mean you messed up?"

"I'm pregnant," she sobbed.

Anna was so stunned that she remained silent for several moments, not knowing what to say. "Oh, Cassie. I'm so sorry."

"It's my fault. It's all my fault."

"Well, I don't think it's *all* your fault. You didn't get pregnant by yourself," Anna said, taking Cassie in her arms and holding her close. "How far along are you?"

"About three months. I'm hoping I still won't be showing that much by graduation. I've been trying real hard not to put on any extra pounds."

"Well, you can't starve yourself, you'll harm the baby. You have the baby to think about."

"*Think about it?* That's all I've been able to think about since I found out I was pregnant. I don't know what I'm going to do, Anna. I can't have this baby."

"Does you mother know?"

Cassie shook her head. "And I don't want her to ever find out."

"But Cassie, she's bound to find out sooner or later. You can't hide something like this forever. Does the baby's father know?"

"No! And he's not going to either. He don't want no part of me or this baby. Me and him—we just had a few good times together, that's all. It wasn't nothing serious between us. Our families would have a fit if they was ever to find out we were ever seen together."

"Why? Who is he? If you don't want me to know, then that's fine. You don't have to tell me, but I swear I won't tell anyone."

Silence fell between them for a moment before Cassie finally answered. "You gotta swear to me that you'll never tell anybody, Anna. I mean not anybody. Not even Gene."

"I won't," Anna promised. "You know you can trust me."

Another silence fell before Cassie finally replied, "It's Danny Peavy."

Anna's mouth dropped. She couldn't believe her ears. Danny was a high school drop out and juvenile delinquent. He stayed in trouble more than not and worked at her father's cotton mill at the receiving dock unloading the bails of cotton that arrived on the boxcars. He was their age and from the wrong side of town. The trashy side. But more than that, he was white.

"What are you thinking about doing?" Anna asked. "Do you have any ideas?"

"I know what I *need* to do, but it won't be easy," Cassie replied.

Anna had a sinking suspicion what Cassie was referring to. It was 1970 and abortions were still illegal. Even if Cassie could find a doctor who would consent to do it, it would still be costly and dangerous. Her only other alternative would be to have the baby and put it up for adoption. But keeping a racially mixed child and raising it in a black community would be extremely difficult—especially in the south and especially in a small town like Myrick where racial prejudice was still very strong. Neither race would be willing to accept the child.

"Cassie, are you absolutely certain it's Danny's baby? I mean are you—"

Cassie nodded her head. "Yes. I'm positive. The last guy I was with was George Groves and it had been a couple of months since we broke up when I started seeing Danny. So I'm certain it's Danny's baby." She dropped her head in her hands and began to cry again. "Oh Anna, I've got to find somebody who'll take care of this. I heard there's a doctor in Alabama who'll do it for five hundred dollars if you meet him at a motel on the state line."

"Do you have five hundred dollars, Cassie?" Anna asked, knowing with all certainty that she didn't.

Cassie shook her head. "You know I don't," she cried. "But what else am I going to do, Anna? What other choices do I have? There aren't any."

"Have you considered giving it up for adoption?"

"Who's going to adopt a half white baby? My people don't want him and white folks *sure* don't. He'll wind up in an orphanage his entire childhood until he's grown. He'll never know what it's like to have a real family who cares about him. Or even worse, he'll be shuffled from one foster home to another being abused. I'd rather see this baby not ever come into this world if that's going to be his fate."

Anna understood everything Cassie was saying and she agreed. She knew better than anyone what it was like not have loving parents. But an abortion? It was just too risky for Cassie. Girls died all the time from botched abortions performed in seedy motel rooms and on kitchen tables. She couldn't bear the thought of losing her best friend to a situation like that.

"Cassie, just wait. Don't do anything right away. Please, let me talk to Gene about this."

"Don't you dare! I told you Anna, you can't tell anybody about this. I'd die if my Momma found out."

"Cassie wait. What if—" Anna hesitated. She thought for a moment before getting in way over her head. But there was no other way to help Cassie out of her situation. There was simply no other choice. "What if Gene and I took him and raised him as our child."

"What? Are you out of our mind? Don't you think you should ask Gene about that before you go volunteering to adopt some half black baby? There's no way he'd agree to something like that."

"Gene isn't prejudice. He's half Indian and half Italian himself."

"But that's different from being half black," Cassie insisted. "He's still considered white—at least by white people and he's still accepted by them. Besides, if I had this baby and turned him over to you and Gene to raise, my Momma would still have to know about it. The whole point is, to keep her from finding out." Cassie leaned forward and put her arms around Anna. "Oh Anna, you don't know how much I appreciate your offer. You're the best friend anybody could have. But I can't have this baby. I just can't."

"Where are you going to get five hundred dollars? You can't ask Danny and you certainly can't ask your Mom. And I don't have that kind of money."

"Then I'll just have to find someone who'll do it cheaper."

"And you'll wind up bleeding to death and dying in some filthy motel room," Anna warned her. "'Listen Cassie, all I'm asking is for you to wait until I've had time to talk this over with Gene. There's got to be another solution. The problem is, you don't have that many options and I'm offering you the best out of the three."

Cassie thought for a moment. "Alright," she agreed finally. "But I don't have a lot of time. I'm already three months along. If I'm going to do something, I need to do it soon."

"Good. Just promise me you won't do anything foolish until I've had time to talk to Gene. Don't worry, Cassie," she assured her friend. "We'll work something out."

"Okay," Cassie promised. "But whatever we do, we have to do it soon."

# Chapter Eight

On June 5, 1970, Anna Coleman walked with her senior class and graduated from Calhoun High in nearby Gordon County. On June 10, 1970, she stood beside her childhood sweetheart and became Mrs. Eugene Anthony Longhorn.

Since there wasn't a preacher in Barrow County who would officiate the marriage ceremony, thanks to Ben Coleman, Harry obtained an old Reverend friend of his from Rome. The Reverend had been retired nearly a decade, but was happy to travel to Myrick to officiate the wedding ceremony. At two p.m. on a beautiful Sunday afternoon, Anna and Gene were pronounced man and wife in the old Porter Plantation house that they would now call home. Surprisingly, there were twenty-three guests attending the small ceremony. There were a few that Anna and Gene had not previously been acquainted with, such as the preacher for example, but most were immediate family and close friends. The Reverend's wife came along and offered to play the wedding march on the antique piano that had been in Harry's family over a century, along with their granddaughter who sang accompaniment. Angel's roommate and love interest Tanya, brought her little niece and nephew along to serve as the flower girl and ring bearer. She also invited her older brother, who was an amateur photographer, to take the wedding photographs. Estelle had made a beautiful two-tiered wedding cake complete with bride and groom on top and Cassie served the refreshments that her mother had made especially for the occasion. Angel was maid of honor while Amy stood beside her sister as matron of honor. Anna and Gene had given Harry the distinct privilege of walking Anna down the isle and offering her hand in marriage. Their decision touched the old man and moved him to tears. It was the greatest honor anyone had ever bestowed upon him. Gene's brother Joey served as his best man. Completing the wedding party was Amy's new husband Chuck, Gene's father and the four farmhands who worked with Gene, and their wives.

That day, the decaying, rotting plantation house, which had new life once again, was hosting a very grand and glorious occasion with twenty-five people rejoicing in the celebration. The bride's sisters and best friend had done a magnificent job of decorating the downstairs with yards of white tulle, satin ribbon and huge Magnolia blossoms from the tree out back. A white lace tablecloth and silver candelabras adorned the large dining room table where Estelle had placed the wedding cake and punch bowl, along with silver serving trays filled with finger sandwiches and hors d'oeuvres. On one end of the table lay two stacks of white napkins engraved in silver foil with the bride and groom's name and wedding date. On a table in the foyer sat a small white guest book and plumb pen for the guests to sign. Beside the dining table sat a bottle of expensive champagne in a silver ice bucket for the bride and groom's wedding toast, compliments of the bride's sister and brother-in-law. The guest photographer snapped dozens of photographs throughout the ceremony and reception filling an entire wedding album. Anna made a breath-taking bride in Ollie's long, white lace wedding gown with four-foot train and matching veil. Angel had provided the bride's bouquet and men's boutonnières from a florist in Athens. And as luck would have it, Gene was able to squeeze into Chuck's wedding tux and shoes, allowing him to compliment his bride's formal attire. Thanks to Harry Porter, Anna's sisters and Estelle, the bride and groom were granted a beautiful and memorable wedding ceremony. All they, themselves, were left to supply were the groom's plain, gold wedding band, which Anna purchased with her employee's discount at the department store.

Following the reception, the photographer suggested everyone gather outside beneath the two huge oak trees flanking each side of the tall front porch for some final wedding photographs. He positioned the bride and groom on the bottom steps of the mansion and took a snap shot, then another of Anna alone at the top steps tossing the bride's bouquet into the crowd of female guests below.

The happy wedding party and twenty-five guests could be clearly seen from the highway, which ran past the old Porter plantation toward town. Passersby would honk their horns in congratulatory gestures as they sped by the celebration. One passerby was more shocked than pleased to see the gathering in front of the old, newly restored mansion. On his way home from a business trip in Atlanta, Ben Coleman was stunned to see his three daughters collected in the front yard, his youngest daughter in a wedding gown posing with her groom. He slowed his Lincoln as he passed by, unable to believe what he saw. No one had seen Anna since he had kicked her out of his home nearly seven months ago. He had not mentioned her name to his two remaining daughters, nor had they spoken of Anna to him. She had become an unapproachable subject in the Coleman household. Coleman figured she had left town with the dissembled aid of her sisters or best friend, never to be seen or heard from again. Or at least that's what he had hoped. Instead, much to his dismay, she had settled right there in Myrick with her white trash boyfriend to become a constant embarrassment to him. He clutched the steering wheel with clinched fists as he accelerated past the Porter farm into town. He would be damned if he allowed her to continue to humiliate him. He would get rid of her one way or another. And for *good* this time.

Immediately following their wedding, Harry insisted that Anna and Gene leave for a brief honeymoon in the Blue Ridge Mountains not far away. He rented a small cabin for them and provided them with enough money for a three-night, two-day stay. They returned with some beautiful memories and two roles of Kodak film before settling into marital bliss.

Gene had wanted Anna to give up her part-time job at the department store in Calhoun, but when they suddenly offered her an assistant manager's position with a substantial pay raise, along with medical benefits, Anna couldn't turn down the lucrative offer. The extra money allowed her to furnish their beautiful new home with items she couldn't have otherwise afforded, even though Harry insisted on paying for any improvements around the house that her heart desired.

When Anna came up with the idea to surround Ollie's grave and the old Magnolia tree with a three-foot, black iron post fence, it was Harry who ordered the fence installed the following week. Then when she wanted to plant rose bushes and giant Hydrangeas around the grave and surrounding yard, Harry had her drive them in his truck to the local seed and feed store to purchase the necessary gardening materials. All Anna had to do was merely mention some improvement she had in mind for the property and Harry would insist she drive them into town for everything she needed. Before long, between her salary from the department store and Harry's indulgence, the old mansion was an impressive and charming sight, both inside and out. The house began to draw attention from the townsfolk and passersby. Soon, everyone knew that Ben Coleman's youngest daughter had married Harry Porter's farm foreman and was living in Porter's old plantation house with her new husband. Some even took it for granted that Coleman had been the one responsible for restoring the house for his daughter and new son-in-law, which couldn't have been farther from the truth.

Each Sunday, Anna took her only day off from the store, to cook a big Sunday dinner for her new family. At twelve o'clock noon, everyone would gather around the large, antique dining table at the house and enjoy one of Anna's delicious home cooked meals. There was Gene's father and brother, Harry, Amy and her new husband. Occasionally, Angel and Tanya would join them on the weekends they drove up from Athens, along with Anna's friend Cassie, who was by now, no longer able to keep her condition a secret. After dinner, they would all gather on the front porch in the oversized rocking chairs for some conversation and a relaxing afternoon. The once vacant, barren house was now alive with joyous family get-togethers filled with love and laughter. It had been transformed into a comfortable and inviting home with a loving atmosphere.

Adding to their family, were three German Shepherds that Anna had acquired from the litter of pups at the junkyard and from a neighbor down the road who decided he had one too many K-9 mouths to feed. Max, was a massive, three year-old Shepherd that looked like Rin Tin Tin and was capable of showing strong aggression toward uninvited visitors. In addition, Gene's father had given Anna two female pups from his recent litter and with Max, Anna now enjoyed the K-9 companionship she was denied as a child. The three dogs soon became her constant companions and a temporary substitute for the children she had yet to conceive. The animals, which Anna had painstakingly housebroke, had full run of the yard as well as inside the house. When she had trouble coming up with a couple of German sounding names for the two pups, she turned to Harry, who named them Gretchen and Greta.

After returning home from work late one Saturday afternoon, Anna was busy tending Ollie's grave beneath the Magnolia tree, while her three four-legged companions lay close-by keeping a watchful eye. They looked up and wagged their tails in a friendly welcome as Harry came out of his trailer and walked over and joined them.

"This place has never looked so beautiful," he told her, as he watched Anna dig the weeds from around the rose bushes on each side of Ollie's marble headstone. "Ollie would be so pleased."

"I hope so," Anna replied. "I planted these pink roses just for her since you said they were her favorite. They're coming along real well, don't you think?"

Harry nodded silently, choked with emotion. Anna glanced up at him and smiled. He reached in his back pocket and pulled out his handkerchief.

"I never knew much about plantin' pretty flowers and such as that," he said, removing his thick glasses to wipe his eyes. "All I ever knew how to grow was cotton and cows. I would just go buy some pretty flowers and lay them on the headstone when I came out here to sit and talk to her. But them flowers wouldn't last more than a day."

"Well, now she'll be surrounded by pretty flowers all summer long," Anna said, straightening up and stretching her back. "It would be nice if we got a little bench to sit over there beside the grave so you'd have a place to sit when you came out here to visit with her."

Harry glanced over at the spot Anna pointed out. "You know, that would be a great idea," he said. "We'll have to go lookin' for one after you get home from the store one day next week. We'll get one of them nice marble ones like I seen at the cemetery."

"Yes, that would be nice," Anna, replied.

"You know," Harry said, bowing his head and digging at the dirt with the toe of his shoe. "I always fancied bein' laid to rest right here beside Ollie. But I figured once I was gone, there'd be nobody left to look after the graves and besides, once they tore down the house, me and Ollie would be forgotten."

Anna looked up at Harry and saw the sadness on his face. "Harry, it's going to be a long, long time before anybody tears down *this* house. Not as long as I'm alive. This is going to be mine and Gene's home for as long as we're on this earth and after that it'll belong to our children. So if this is where you want to be buried, then this is where it will be," she promised. "Right there beside Ollie." Anna paused and thought for a moment, then added, "You know, one of those marble benches with Porter engraved on it would be nice, don't you think?"

Harry's face lit up with a smile. "I think that would be real nice."

Their conversation was suddenly interrupted when the dogs leaped up and began barking aggressively and ran toward a strange car that pulled up in the front yard. It was an old beat-up Oldsmobile with a young black man behind the wheel.

"Who could that be?" Harry said, straining his eyes to recognize the unannounced visitor.

"I believe that's Cassie's brother, Simon," Anna replied. All of a sudden, her heart began to pound. Surely Cassie hadn't done something foolish without first telling her. Anna called to the dogs to be quiet and began walking toward the car.

"Anna?" the young man called out, afraid to step out of his car for fear of being dog bit.

"Simon? Is something wrong? Has something happened to Cassie?" she asked.

"No, it's my Momma. Cassie sent me to tell you she's been taken to the hospital. They don't know if it's a heart attack or stroke, but she's in bad shape."

"Where is she?" Anna asked, holding Max tightly by his collar to prevent him from lunging at the car.

"They've taken her to the hospital in Rome."

"Let me go clean up right quick and I'll be on my way. Tell Cassie I'll be there just as soon as I can get to the hospital."

Anna never made it to the hospital in time to see Estelle alive. A rapid succession of massive strokes had taken Estelle's life suddenly and without warning. She was pronounced dead soon after arriving at the hospital. Cassie was seated beside her brother in the hospital waiting room when Anna walked in. Cassie burst into tears when she saw her friend. Anna held Cassie and tried to console her the best she could.

"I can't believe Momma is gone," Cassie cried. "It happened so fast. She walked through the back door after coming home from work and just collapsed on the kitchen floor."

Anna held Cassie in her arms, unable to find the right words to comfort her. She glanced over at Simon.

"I don't think she ever knew what hit her," Cassie's brother said. "She just laid there with her eyes open, staring at the ceiling. She didn't move or speak a word. Next thing we knew, she was gone."

"I hate to say it, but maybe that's the best way any of us can go," Anna told them. "At least she didn't have to lay in bed and suffer for weeks or even months."

"No, I don't think she suffered," Simon agreed. "At least not for long."

That night, Anna brought Cassie home to stay with her until after the funeral services. Since Simon had just recently married and moved out of the rented run-down home he had shared with his sister and their mother, only Cassie remained at the house. And without Estelle's income, she wouldn't be able to meet the monthly rent payments. It was then, that Anna turned to her husband and asked Gene if it would be all right for Cassie, now six months pregnant, to come and live with them until her baby was born. He said yes. However, he was still mulling over his wife's suggestion of them adopting Cassie's baby. Raising a child was a lifelong commitment and an enormous responsibility. Raising a child that wasn't actually theirs was a very difficult decision. Raising a bi-racial child among prejudice in the Deep South would create difficulties far greater than anything they would encounter raising a child of their own. However, Gene knew that time was running out. Cassie was more than halfway through her pregnancy already and the time was nearing when he would have to give his answer one way or the other. But for now, she was welcome to stay with them until she was able to get back on her feet.

After twenty years of service to the Coleman family, Ben and Catherine Coleman offered only an inexpensive floral arrangement of yellow Chrysanthemums sent to the funeral home, along with their condolences. Harry, Gene, his wife and Anna's two sisters sat in the front of the old Negro country church among Estelle's close friends and family members, as they paid their final respects to the woman that had been such an important part of their lives for so long.

"It looks like Mother could have at least gone to the church and signed the guest book," Anna whispered to her sister Amy, seated beside her in the church pew.

"She'd have to sober up first," Amy replied.

"Is she still drinking?" Anna asked.

Amy nodded. "She started right after you left and she hasn't stopped since."

"I want to go see her," Anna said. "Maybe if I talked to her—" Anna stopped suddenly when she felt a sharp jab in her side. It was Gene's elbow. She glanced over at him with surprise.

"You can have this conversation when the services are over," he said, leaning over and whispering in his wife's ear. "This is a funeral, not a family sit-down. Have a little respect."

"Sorry," she whispered, looking down with embarrassment.

Amy glanced over at her brother-in-law with a disgusted look. Now that Amy had gotten to know him better, she found him to be overbearing and bossy. Characteristics that her own father had possessed and traits she despised in any man. Chuck knew better than to ever reprimand her in public or privately.

Anna knew in her heart that she would never be able to return home to visit her mother. Not as long as her father was alive and especially if Gene had anything to do with it. He would never allow her near Coleman

Hill. In fact, he wouldn't even allow her to travel into town alone without either him or Harry along. This was the reason she did most of her shopping and errands in Calhoun on her way home from work. Anna knew the reason for her mother's sudden drinking was due to her father's beating her senseless that day and him telling her he wasn't her biological father. His words still haunted her. She lay awake many a night wondering whom her real father was and if she would ever know the truth. Gene told her to stop torturing herself, that it didn't really matter now. But it did. And the only person who knew the truth was behind closed doors. Doors that would remain locked tight as long as her father was alive.

*Book II*

# Chapter Nine

By mid-September Anna and Gene had been married three months and were still caught up in the rapture of young love, reveling in the joys and bliss of newlywed life. Only now, they had a houseguest. Cassie, who was nearly seven months pregnant, stayed close at home and seldom left the house. She felt, as did Anna and Gene, that it was best if as few people as possible knew she was pregnant or still living in Myrick. After much careful consideration, Anna and Gene decided they would take Cassie's child to raise as their own rather than let her give it up for adoption. No one in Cassie's family wanted anything to do with the baby. They all had advised her to give it up for adoption. But they all knew the baby would more than likely never be adopted. And Cassie knew that as a single black mother, she would have much difficulty raising her baby alone. Gene's father and Joey were against the idea of them adopting the child and did everything in their power to dissuade them, as did Anna's sisters. Harry on the other hand remained supportive of their decision and saw it as commendable and unselfish.

Cassie had decided that as soon as the baby arrived she would leave for Atlanta and start life over there. She agreed to give up all rights to her child and allow Anna and Gene to legally adopt it. The three agreed to be honest with the child as soon as it was old enough to understand and tell him or her about it's background, allowing Cassie unlimited contact and visitation.

For now, Anna continued to work at the department store in Calhoun in order to buy things the baby would need after it arrived and to pay for attorney's fees. But once the baby was born, Gene insisted Anna quit work and stay home to be a full-time mom. Harry had already increased Gene's salary to help compensate for Anna's lost income once the child arrived. Both were looking forward to becoming parents and starting a family as soon as possible, even though it wasn't their own flesh and blood. They were, however, well aware of the potential problems of raising a racially mixed child in the Deep South, yet both were ready to accept the responsibility and demands.

It was a muggy and sticky September night. Cassie had dinner waiting on the table when Anna arrived home from work that evening. As usual, Harry walked next door and joined them for dinner, after which he sat in the den and chatted with Gene while Anna and Cassie cleaned up the kitchen. It was shortly after nine when Harry bid them good night and walked back to his trailer home. As he started to unlock his trailer door, he noticed a strange car parked up the road beneath some trees. Passing it off as someone with car trouble, he went on inside and gave the incident no more thought.

Since Gene had to be at the milking barn by four a.m., he and Anna were in bed with lights out no later than nine forty-five. Cassie however, usually stayed up awhile longer and watched TV downstairs before retiring to her upstairs bedroom. Less than half an hour after Cassie had turned out her bedroom light, Gretchen and Greta, who always slept indoors with the family, suddenly went into a barking frenzy, waking up everyone in the house. Max, the male Shepherd, who kept a careful watch outdoors, remained silent however.

"What in the world is going on?" Anna said, sitting straight up in bed and reaching for the lamp on the bedside table.

"Turn that light off," Gene quickly told her. "Keep the light off and wait here." He jumped out of bed and pulled on his pants. He reached for the 12-gauge shotgun he kept in their bedroom closet and loaded it. "Get on the phone and call Harry. See if he heard anything around his trailer." Ordinarily, Gene wouldn't have told Anna to bother Harry just because the dogs woke them barking, but something told him this time was different.

"Where are you going?" Anna asked.

"I'm going outside to look around. You stay here and keep the dogs upstairs with you and Cassie. Don't any of you come downstairs until I get back. It may be nothing—just a polecat or possum."

"Please be careful," Anna pleaded.

Gene closed the bedroom door behind him and met Cassie coming out of her room. "Go stay in our bedroom with Anna and keep the dogs in there with you," he told her. "I'm going downstairs to look around."

Cassie did as Gene told her and ran past him into the bedroom where she joined Anna. Gene hurried downstairs and began looking around. The downstairs was pitch dark and appeared undisturbed. He walked toward the kitchen wing and saw a bright light flickering outside the kitchen door beside the back porch. He ran and opened the door and saw flames leaping up the outside of the house. It just so happened, Anna had left the garden hose hooked up to the outdoor faucet after watering the Hydrangeas, allowing Gene to quickly grab it and extinguish the fire within minutes. Fortunately, he managed to prevent the blaze from spreading and doing more damage than just searing the brick on the basement wall around the back porch. Had it not been for the six-foot tall brick foundation supporting the wood frame house structure, the fire would have surely engulfed the one-hundred and twenty-five year-old house within a matter of minutes, burning it to the ground and taking its occupants inside with it.

Just as Gene finished extinguishing the last of the flames, he heard a gunshot and a man scream. He grabbed his shotgun and ran toward Harry's trailer where the sound had come from. There, in the front yard, he saw Harry holding his shotgun on one man while another lay screaming on the ground, holding his badly injured leg.

"Gene! Gene!" Anna called from the second story window. "Are you alright? What's going on?"

"Call the sheriff!" he yelled back.

"I found these two runnin' away from the back of the house," Harry said. "I heard Max barking at something down near the road, then a gunshot and I didn't hear him bark anymore. I got up and grabbed my shotgun and by the time I came out my door, I saw these two runnin' toward the road."

"They tried to burn the house down," Gene said. "I just put a fire out beside the kitchen door."

"Call an ambulance!" begged the injured man, lying on the ground, as he tried to control the blood flow with both hands. "I'm bleeding to death!" The shotgun blast had nearly severed the man's right leg.

Gene walked over to him and jammed the barrel of his gun into the man's groin. "You'll lose more than your leg if you don't tell me why you tried to burn down my house. Who the hell are you and what are you doing here?"

"You better listen to him," Harry urged the man on the ground. "You won't get no ambulance until you start talking."

"We was sent here!" he said, wincing in excruciating pain.

"Shut up!" his accomplice yelled. "Shut your fucking mouth."

"Who sent you?" Gene said, pressing the gun barrel harder against the man's groin.

"Nobody sent us," the other man insisted. "We did it on our own."

"Why?" Gene asked. "Why'd you try to burn us out? Are you with the Klan? Did the Klan send you?"

"Please! Somebody get me to a doctor! I'm bleeding to death!" the man cried in agony.

"Yeah," the other man confessed. "It was the Klan that ordered it."

Gene stared at the man and thought for a moment. In one way, it made sense. Perhaps word had gotten out around town that Cassie was living with them. But on the other hand, he didn't see how that was possible because Cassie rarely left the farm and when she did, she traveled to Calhoun with Anna to do the weekly shopping. For all the townspeople knew, Cassie had left Myrick soon after her mother passed away. Besides, the man was too willing to admit that he was with the Ku Klux Klan. Klansmen always wore hoods whenever they committed their acts of violence and sought anonymity.

Gene cocked the gun and once again pressed it harder against the man's genitals. "Who *really* sent you here tonight? It wasn't the Klan. I'm no fool. If you were Klansmen, you'd have burned a cross on my front lawn before you'd try to burn me out of my house."

"It was Ben Coleman," the injured man finally admitted. "Now get me help! I need an ambulance!"

"Shut up, Tillman! You wanna get us killed for sure?" his friend warned.

"Why did he send you?" Gene demanded.

"He wants you and his kid out of town," the man on the ground explained. "He said if the fire didn't kill you, then you'd have to move someplace else. Please, get me to the hospital before I bleed to death!"

"What's your name?" Gene demanded.

"Tillman Raynor.'

"Who's he?" Gene asked, gesturing toward his friend.

"You keep your fuckin' mouth shut or I'll kill you myself," the other man warned his accomplice.

"Lonnie Gill," the wounded man replied, about to lose consciousness from the pain and blood loss.

Anna appeared at the window again. "I've called the sheriff. He's on his way!"

As they waited for the sheriff to arrive, Gene's temper grew out of control as he realized the men's actions could have easily killed all of them. He began cursing the men for their actions. He left the man lying on the ground and walked over to his partner standing in front of Harry's gun. Gene drew back and slammed the butt of his gun hard into the man's face, knocking him to the ground.

"You listen to me," Gene said, pointing his gun at the man's head. "You take this message back to old man Coleman. You tell that son-of-a-bitch that if he ever comes near my family or my property again and I'll come after him myself and blow his fuckin' brains out. You hear me?"

The man nodded as he held his hand over his bleeding face.

"You tell him that! You hear?"

All the man could do was nod.

"I mean it. I'll kill that bastard if he ever tries anything like this again," Gene swore.

When the sheriff arrived, an ambulance was summoned to transport the injured man to the nearest hospital while his accomplice was arrested and taken to the county jail. By the time the deputies had taken all their statements on what happened that night and all the names of the people involved, it was almost time for Gene to get up and begin his morning milking.

"I hope they lock that bastard Coleman up until he rots in hell," Gene told Harry, as the last sheriff's car pulled out of the driveway. "He could have killed all of us tonight. We all could have been burned alive. As old and dry as that wood is, that house would have gone up like a pile of fat lighter. We wouldn't have had a chance in hell of escaping before it went up in flames."

Harry shook his head, unable to bear the thought. "You're right about that," he agreed. "But you're wrong about old man Coleman. That sheriff ain't gonna lock him up. He won't do a goddamn thing to him. He and Coleman are old asshole buddies. Ben Coleman bought him into office. Coleman tells him to jump and he asks how high. Like everybody else in this town, Coleman's got him in his back pocket. Sheriff Bowman will come up with some excuse to get Coleman off the hook. He'll claim those men were lying or either you was lyin'. He'll go scott free. Mark my words."

"Then I'll just go to the G.B.I.," Gene told him. "They'll find out the truth. I know Ben Coleman don't have *them* in his pocket."

"Not if Bowman has anything to do with the investigation. Nothin' will ever come of it. It'll all be swept under the carpet." Harry paused and removed his eyeglasses. He took the handkerchief from his back pocket and out of habit, began wiping the lenses in a circular motion. "Let me tell you something about Sheriff Bowman and then maybe you'll understand the power Ben Coleman has over this town. I've known Wilfred Bowman since he was a kid and I can assure you, he was dumb as dirt and barely got out of the tenth grade by the time he was eighteen. In fact, his teachers just went ahead and passed him just to get him out of their hair. And I'll tell you something else that hardly anybody else around here knows. He can't read a lick."

Gene looked at Harry with curiosity. "What do you mean?" he asked.

"I mean, the man never learned to read. He's illiterate. He's got that condition they call dyslexia or something like that. He can't read or write."

"How do you know?" Gene asked.

"Because that woman behind the pharmacy counter down at the drug store used to be his secretary when he first got into office years ago. She told me that's why he always rides around with a deputy who drives him everywhere he goes. He's got a driver's license, but he can't read street signs or write out reports. He lets his driver do all his paperwork."

"You got to be kidding," Gene replied in disbelief.

"No, I'm not. I swear it. He wouldn't be in office right now if it weren't for Coleman keeping him there."

"Does Coleman know about him not being able to read?"

"Sure he does. That's his leverage," Harry replied. "That's how he keeps Bowman jumping through hoops. Bowman would be out of a job if it weren't for Ben Coleman. Not to mention he'd be the laughing stock of the town."

"How'd he get through the police academy?"

"Back when he ran for office, you didn't have to go through no academy. You just ran for office and was elected by the people. That was before they changed the law and you had to go through the academy to get into law enforcement."

"Damn! So we got a sheriff who can't read or write," Gene laughed.

"And who can barely drive, as long as he don't stray out of the county where he isn't familiar with the street signs and back roads."

"I wonder what people around here would think if they knew that?" Gene asked.

"Well, half of them wouldn't believe you if you told them and the others wouldn't care," Harry replied.

Gene glared at Harry with anger and frustration. "Well, it don't matter because Ben Coleman won't get away with what he's done here tonight. I still owe him for what he did to Anna and what he put her through. I swore I'd get even with him for that. Now, he's gone way too far. I owe that bastard and I'm gonna pay him back for everything he's done—one way or the other."

"You stop and think before you go and do anything foolish, boy," Harry warned him. "You go and do something that will get you locked up for the rest of your life and you'll regret it. You got Anna to take care of. And now, a baby to consider. You can't see after a family if you're locked up in the penitentiary. The law ain't on your side here. The only side it's on is Ben Coleman's side. There's no justice around these parts. Only Coleman's way of justice. That's all that exists around here."

"So what am I supposed to do? Pack up Anna and the baby and leave the county? Where would we go? What would I do for a living? I put my blood and sweat in this house and on this farm. I've worked my ass off for this place since I was thirteen years old. It's my life. It's all I know to do. And just because I married Ben Coleman's daughter, I'm supposed to turn tail and run 'cause we're not good enough to live in his fuckin' town? Hell no! We'll see who turns tail and runs. It won't be me, I can promise you that much!"

If Harry Porter hadn't known before how deep Gene's feelings were for his land and the farm, he was more than certain of them now. Gene had grown fiercely protective of the farm and portion of property Harry had bequeathed him, as if it were his very own. And Harry knew at that moment that one day it *would* be Gene's own property. The farm and the entire thousand acres and all the prized livestock would belong to him and Anna. Harry also knew the enormous risk Gene was taking in his stand against Ben Coleman in order to protect what was rightfully his. Harry admired and respected Gene for being a man and standing up to Coleman and was behind him a hundred percent. But from that point on, they would have to use extreme caution in their everyday life and never let their guard down for a single moment. The battle had only begun and if they were to win, they would have to remain one step ahead of Coleman's evil and lawless tactics. The risks were great and the stakes high. But Harry Porter would stand behind the heir to his small dynasty and help him fight for what was rightfully his. It was all Harry had left and it belonged to the only heirs he would ever have. He would fight with his last remaining breath to preserve his final legacy.

"We better go look for Max and bury him before Anna finds him," Harry told Gene. "He's up there near the road where I heard the gunshot. Anna will go all to pieces when she finds out he's dead. You know how much she loved that dog."

And she did. Her cries could be heard from the highway as she and Cassie stood beneath the old oak tree out back and watched as Gene and Harry buried the animal that had lost his life protecting his family and their property.

"I'll get you another dog," Gene promised, as he and Harry patted down the mound of dirt around the fresh grave. "In fact, I'll get you a couple more."

"I want another Shepherd," Anna sobbed. "Don't bring home any other kind."

And he didn't. Five days later, after much searching and a quick trip to Rome, Gene returned with not two, but four registered German Shepherd dogs. Two full-grown males and two female, five month-old pups. He had located a man in Rome who owned a breeding kennel that was going out of business. The cost of four registered pedigrees was of course more than Gene could afford on his salary, so Harry paid for three of the dogs out of his own pocket. But it was well worth any price he had to pay when he saw the ecstatic look on Anna's face when they arrived home with the four dogs in the back of his pick-up truck. Before Gene had the tailgate down and the animals were on the ground, Anna began naming them.

"You're Hans and you'll be Fritz and let's see," she paused, trying to come up with a couple of strong German female names.

"How about Helga and Hannah?" Harry suggested.

"Great!" Anna agreed. "Helga and Hannah it will be."

"Whatever happened to names like Lady and Buddy?" a very pregnant Cassie asked.

"They're names for those wormy little lap dogs," Anna explained. "These dogs are noble and fierce. They're German nobility. They deserve proud names."

The following week after acquiring the pack of ferocious guard dogs, Gene and Harry went to the nearest sporting goods store, where Harry purchased four handguns and two high-powered hunting rifles with night scopes.

"You fellas must be plannin' on doing some serious hunting," the storeowner remarked as he rang up the six guns and several boxes of ammunition.

"Not really," Gene replied. "But you never know when you might need some protection around the house."

"You got enough protection here to handle an army of invaders," the man behind the counter replied. "You'll have your own Fort Knox."

By the end of the month, Harry had a four-foot high, split rail fence installed, with a padlocked gate surrounding the plantation house and property, with an electric wire running along the top rail. Gretchen and Greta stayed inside the house while the four remaining dogs had full run of the outside yard. Now, the property *did* resemble Fort Knox.

"If they get past that electric fence," Harry said confidently, "they won't be able to get past those six guard dogs. And if they manage somehow to get any closer, I *know* they won't get past this arsenal we got inside."

Their final step after securing the property was to set down some solid ground rules and guidelines for the family to follow. First of all, Gene demanded that Anna give up her job in Calhoun. Second, she could not leave the property unescorted at anytime. Either Harry, himself, his dad or Joey had to accompany her into town whenever there was shopping or errands to be done. Furthermore, everyone was armed with a handgun and permit to carry a firearm. After every conceivable precaution had been taken, Gene and Harry felt confident they had the situation under control.

Harry was right about Ben Coleman getting away with the arson attempt. Coleman's name was never mentioned in Sheriff Bowman's report. The incident was deemed an attempted burglary and arson. Period.

One benefit did rise from the incident, however. A very crucial point was conveyed. The thugs Coleman hired to try and scare his daughter and her husband out of town had failed, but not before returning to Coleman with Gene Longhorn's message. That message being, he would come after Coleman himself and *"blow his fucking brains out"* if he ever came near his family again. Ben Coleman got the message and took it seriously. It was no longer a simple matter of attempting to put the fear of God into a frightened young woman and running her out of town. He was also dealing with an angry, strapping, young man who was desperate enough to go to any length to protect his family. Not to mention he had the resources and support of old man Porter behind him. Intimidating and controlling his youngest daughter took on a whole new meaning now.

His relationship with Anna however, was only one of Ben Coleman's recent and growing concerns. For he was a man slowly losing his control and power in other areas of his life as well. His world was beginning to crumble. His three daughters were now all grown and gone. Two were married and the third, embarking on a career path of her own. His wife was slowly sinking into alcoholism and seldom, if ever, left the house and was no longer capable of playing hostess to their lavish social functions. But worst of all, his cotton empire was slowly decaying. A relatively new and popular man-made material had recently come on the scene that was seriously threatening the cotton industry and having a devastating affect on cotton farmers and manufacturers alike. Polyester was taking over the fashion industry and Ben Coleman was feeling the effects. He had already been forced to let nearly a fourth of his employees go and was now operating only one shift a day, six days a week. Production was down and so were his profits. If it continued, the cotton mill would have to eventually shut down, causing Myrick to become a ghost town. Ben Coleman was on the verge of losing everything he owned. He had already lost his family. If he lost the mill, he would be at risk of losing Coleman Hill. Everything he'd worked for all his life would be gone. He would be a broken man. The only thing remaining was his reputation in the community and his false pride. As long as he could cling to that, he would manage to salvage at least something.

# Chapter Ten

It was the first of October and Angel Coleman's twenty-second birthday. Fresh out of college with a degree in finance and business administration, she would soon be moving to Atlanta where she had found a job with a national advertising agency. That weekend, she had made plans to meet her sister Amy, in Myrick for a little family get-together before leaving for Atlanta.

Anna had invited them to her house for Sunday dinner. Amy brought her husband Chuck, and Angel arrived with Tanya. Cassie, now eight months pregnant was also present. Completing the family gathering were Gene's father and brother, Joey, and of course Harry, who probably enjoyed the get-togethers more than anyone.

The ten people sat around the antique dining table enjoying a slice of Anna's red velvet cake and a final glass of iced tea before dividing into their respective gender groups with the men retiring to the den for a long stretch and some friendly conversation, while the women collected in the kitchen for dish washing duties.

Amy had enjoyed a few drinks of her favorite alcoholic beverage before her arrival and was feeling relaxed and outspoken. Since her marriage, she had become a little fonder of the bottle than she had in the past and was now drinking quite regularly, much to her new husband's surprise and dismay.

"Don't tell me she's taking after Mother," Anna whispered, leaning over to Angel, as they stood at the kitchen sink preparing to wash the dinner dishes.

"She's been hitting the bottle kind of regular here lately," Angel admitted. "I think she looks forward to any occasion that calls for a celebration. My birthday, her birthday, the President's birthday—whatever."

"Why?" Anna asked. "What brought on her sudden fondness for the bottle? I never knew her to drink like that."

Angel shook her head and shrugged. "I don't know. I guess she's just enjoying the freedom of being able to do whatever she pleases now that she's away from Daddy." But Angel *did* know what was causing their sister's drinking. The same reason that had forced Amy to turn to the bottle had caused Angel to turn to women.

"Anna, I can't believe what you've done with this house," Amy told her sister as she placed some dirty dinner plates beside the sink. "It's beautiful."

"It is," Angel agreed. "It doesn't even look like the same old house we used to pass by when we were kids. I don't know how you managed to do it."

"I couldn't have if it hadn't been for Harry's money and Gene's hard work. They're the ones who made it possible. All I did was add a few feminine touches and a good cleaning."

"She's being modest," Cassie said, seated at the kitchen table, her swollen belly barely fitting beneath the table. "She added a lot more than a few feminine touches. Anna put in a lot of hard work and long hours making the place livable."

"Well, it's become the talk of the town, that's for sure," Amy added. "Nobody can believe the transformation this old house has gone through."

"And they came close to losing it, thanks to her dad," Cassie volunteered.

"What are you talking about?" Angel asked, unaware of what happened a month earlier. Anna had not told either of her sisters about the incident for fear of upsetting them and creating more havoc.

"Anna hasn't told you about what happened?" Cassie asked.

Amy and Angel both looked to their sister who remained silent as she continued to load the dishes into the sink.

"What happened?" Amy asked her sister. "What's she talking about?"

Anna just shook her head nonchalantly and concentrated on the dirty dishes.

Amy turned back to Cassie, looking for an explanation.

"Your dad sent two thugs here in the middle of the night to burn the house down with us in it," Cassie told them. "Harry shot one of them in the leg and Gene forced the guy to tell him who sent them. He said it was Ben Coleman who wanted to run his daughter and her husband out of town."

"Oh my God," Amy gasped. She looked at Angel, and then Anna.

"Why didn't you tell us?" Angel asked.

"There was nothing either of you could do. And besides, I didn't want to worry you."

"Did you report it to the police?" Amy asked.

"Of course we did. But they didn't do anything but arrest the men who set the fire and charged them with attempted burglary and arson. They never charged Dad with anything. I doubt they even confronted him about it."

"Probably not," Angel agreed. "He and Wilfred Bowman have always been in cahoots together. It would be real easy for Dad to get by with murder as long as Bowman is in office."

"God! That lousy bastard!" Amy screamed. "I hate that son-of-a-bitch! I wish he were dead!"

Amy's sudden outburst took everyone in the room by surprise. She had been drinking since that morning and didn't care what she said or to whom. She had been holding in a painful, dark secret for far too long and she simply couldn't keep it hidden any longer.

"Amy, you've had a little too much to drink, dear," Angel warned. "Just calm down and take it easy. Don't say something you'll regret later."

"I'm sick of protecting that filthy bastard. He's a sick, fucking bastard and it's time somebody did something! He can't go on controlling our lives and making us afraid of him."

Gene and Chuck excused themselves from the den and walked into the kitchen to see what was causing the loud disturbance.

"What's going on?" Gene asked.

"Amy's just had a little too much to drink today, is all," Angel replied, attempting to pass off her sister's outburst.

"Well, I know she didn't drink anything here," Gene said. "We don't keep any liquor in the house."

"No, she had it before she got here," Angel assured him.

"I'm not drunk! I'm sick! Sick and tired of keeping all this shit bottled up inside of me. I'm sick of all the lies and secrets." Amy began to sob. "That man is a goddamn monster and I won't keep quiet anymore about what he's done to us!"

"Come on, Amy," Angel said, taking her sister by the shoulders and leading her toward the back door in an attempt to silence her and get her away from everyone. "Let's just step outside and get some fresh air. You'll feel better."

"No! Leave me alone! When are you going to stop protecting him? He deserves for everyone to know what kind of man he really is."

"Come on Amy, it's time we went home anyway," Chuck said, as he walked into the kitchen and tried to help Angel get her under control. "Go get her purse, Angel. I'll take her home where she can sleep it off."

"What did you mean when you said you were sick of protecting him?" Anna asked her sister. "I don't understand."

"No, I don't guess you would, would you?" Amy snapped back at her sister. "He didn't come into your room at night, did he? Or did he?"

"Just get her on home," Angel told her brother-in-law, handing him Amy's purse. "Before she says something she'll regret later and makes a bigger fool out of herself."

"Why do you want to pretend it never happened?" Amy snapped at Angel. "Is that your way of coping with it? To just pretend it never happened? Well, it did! He did it to you, too. He did it to both of us! You were just strong enough and mean enough to stand up to him and make him stop."

"I don't understand what either of you are talking about," Anna insisted. "Angel, why is Amy so upset?"

"Why am I so upset? You really are clueless, aren't you? You really don't know what went on in that house."

"Amy, shut your mouth and just go home. You're drunk! Nobody wants to hear anything you have to say," Angel told her sister. "Chuck, get her out of here."

"I'm talking about all those years when Angel and I were just kids and he would come into our rooms after we'd gone to bed and make us do things. Disgusting things! I'm talking about all those years from the time we were five and six years old until we were entering our teens that he screwed us and made us give him oral sex. And with Mother in the next room! And she knew what he was doing and never once tried to stop him or go to the authorities and have him locked up because she needed his money. To this day, I can't stand the sight of a jar of Vaseline! But what always baffled me was that he never came to you," Amy said, staring at Anna. "As bad as he seemed to hate you, he always left you alone. But now we know why, don't we? He hated you because you weren't his own flesh and blood like we were. But you know what? It seems like that would have made him go after you before he turned to us. Why was that? Because he got more satisfaction out of screwing his own daughters rather than going to someone he wasn't biologically related to? That really makes him sick! But you turned out to be the lucky one. You were lucky because he never got into your bed and climbed on top of you like he did us. But it really should have been you he went after. We were his own flesh and blood. You weren't! We didn't deserve what happened to us. And he would still be doing it if Angel hadn't pulled a kitchen knife on him when she was thirteen and told him if he ever came near either of us again, she'd rip his guts out. That's when he stopped messing with us!"

A dead silence fell over the entire house suddenly. It was if someone had dropped a bomb. And in reality, they had. Harry sat in the den with Gene's father and brother in shock at what they had just heard coming from the kitchen. Everyone remained frozen in stunned silence and disbelief.

Finally, it was Angel who broke the silence. "Feel better?" she asked her sister, her voice expressing little emotion. "Now that you've finally gotten everything out of your system and out in the open, with all those years of silence broken. Now everyone knows. Are you happy now?"

Amy dropped her head and began to sob. "Come on, let's get you home," Chuck said, taking his wife by the shoulders and leading her away.

"I'll help you get her to the car," Angel offered, helping her brother-in-law remove Amy from the house.

Anna remained silent, still in shock, as she watched her two sisters walk away.

"I'll call you later," Angel said, glancing over her shoulder at Anna. "The dinner was great. I'm sorry about all of this."

"Is there anything I can do?" Anna asked, feeling helpless and ashamed.

Angel shook her head. "No. I'll call you after I help Chuck get her home."

Anna looked at Gene. His eyes were as big as saucers. She had never seen her husband with such a shocked expression. Everyone appeared stunned for that matter. Gene walked over and put his arms around his wife and held her. She looked over and saw Harry standing in the doorway. He had left the den and quietly walked into the kitchen when Amy began ranting.

Tanya walked over to Anna and gently placed her hand on her shoulder. "Thanks for having us over, Anna. The dinner was delicious. We'll be in touch later."

Anna nodded, still unable to speak.

"I'll finish cleaning up the kitchen," Cassie said, struggling to get up from the kitchen table. "You go on in the den and take it easy."

"No," Anna replied. "I'm fine. I'll finish up. You need to stay off your feet. Go on in the den and rest."

"Yeah, go on Cassie," Gene said. "I'll help Anna finish cleaning up in here. She and I need to talk anyway. We'll join you in a little while."

Cassie accepted Gene's suggestion and left them alone in the kitchen. Harry followed her, allowing Gene some privacy with his wife. Anna began busying herself with her domestic duties, still unable to process what had just happened in her kitchen.

Gene stood close behind her as she began washing the dishes in the sink. "I want you to tell me the truth," he told her. "Did he ever mess with you?"

"No. Never," she said. "I swear it. I lived in that house seventeen years and I never experienced anything like Amy said she and Angel endured. And no one ever told me that it was going on. I had no idea. I'm in shock."

"Are you sure?"

"Yes. I wouldn't lie to you," Anna assured her husband.

"If I thought he ever tried anything like that with you, I would kill him for sure. I'd kill him with my bare hands," Gene swore.

And he would have.


On November 4, 1970, Cassie went into labor. Since she had no medical coverage, Anna had summoned a midwife to deliver the baby at home. The old Negro woman had been a close friend of Estelle's and had helped bring Cassie and her brother into the world, along with a good portion of the black population in Barrow County.

Late in the afternoon, Cassie began experiencing her first labor pains. Gene was at the barn, busy with the afternoon milking. Harry was next door watching television. Anna picked up the phone and dialed the midwife, and then she called Harry. Fourteen hours later, at two-forty a.m. on November fifth, Cassie gave birth to a six pound, twelve ounce, beautiful baby girl, whom Cassie named Anna Nicole.

"We'll call her Nicky, to keep down confusion," Cassie said, as she held her daughter in her arms for the first time.

Nicky was one of the most beautiful babies Anna had ever seen. She looked more Caucasian than black. Her father had been a fair skin, blue-eyed, blonde and Cassie, herself, was a light-skinned black with light brown eyes, which explained the child's fair appearance. Both Anna and Gene were relieved to discover their newly adopted baby was so fair skin. It would make things easier on them raising a child that could easily pass for white. Cassie was simply relieved to have the entire ordeal over with so that she could now move on with her life.

Harry paid an attorney he knew to draw up the legal adoption papers, allowing Anna and Gene to become her legalized adoptive parents. Cassie signed the necessary documents relinquishing all rights to the child without a single hesitation. She had absolutely no doubt that Anna and Gene would provide her baby with a much better life than she possible could. Everyone was elated, including Harry, who couldn't keep his eyes off the tiny baby whose life had begun in the old plantation house, that was so close to ruin only a year ago.

"Already this old place has seen a wedding and a birth," he gleamed with pride. "Who would have ever thought it would be possible?"

"And it's sure to see a lot more births and weddings before all is said and done," Anna assured him with a big smile. "That's what makes a house a home." Little did she know at the time that she was already a month pregnant with their first child.

By mid-January, two and a half months after little Nicky was born and after the holiday season had passed, Cassie packed up her belongings and caught a bus bound for Atlanta to look for a job and start a new life. By then, Anna was three and a half months pregnant. She and Gene were ecstatic and Harry was walking on cloud nine. Instead of being referred to by his given name, he was now known simply as *"Papa"*. He was more like a father to Anna than her own father had ever been and no one could have been more deserving of the title.

Harry was now paying Gene more than twice what he was paying him before his marriage and since the job offered no medical coverage, Harry paid for any medical expenses they incurred, as well as anything else they would need such as a new refrigerator or washing machine. Despite the fact they still weren't even close to being considered well off, they ate better than most wealthy people. Living on a four-hundred herd dairy and cattle farm provided them with plenty of dairy products and only the finest cuts of meats to fill two refrigerators and freezers. Between that and the vegetable garden Anna planted that summer and the chickens she tended, they all ate like kings. Anna had become quite an accomplished cook and spent hours in the kitchen cooking enormous meals and baking a variety of cakes and pies for her family of four. Being an old bachelor who had survived on TV dinners and cereal for years, Harry had never eaten so well, nor looked so good. He began to add some weight to his frail, thin frame and even his coloring improved. He looked and felt better than he ever had in his life. But it wasn't *all* due to Anna's cooking. Much of it had to do with his new lease on life and his newfound happiness. For the first time in more than a half century, Harry, who had become a loner and recluse following Ollie's death, had a wonderful family to be a part of and was seldom alone. Instead of keeping to himself, shut away in his small trailer home, he spent most of his time in the house with Anna, helping care for little Nicky while she went about her daily household chores. There were times when his seventy-five year-old mind would play tricks on him and he would see Ollie at the kitchen stove removing a pan of cornbread from the oven or at the clothesline hanging out bed sheets or hoeing weeds in her vegetable garden and flower bed or rocking the baby to sleep. Suddenly he would realize it wasn't Ollie that he was watching, but Anna. Harry had spent the past fifty years of his life grieving. Now, he was too pre-occupied and too busy for grief. Like the old, rotting plantation house, he had new life breathed into him and he felt the same way he had when he was a young man—vibrant and full of life. He was a very happy man.

# Chapter Eleven

By now, Anna was well into her sixth month of pregnancy and little Nicky was five months old. The little girl had a beautiful, bounty of blonde straight hair with light brown eyes and light brown skin that looked as if she had been born on a California beach. Instead of the broad flat nose and full mouth, characteristic of her mother's race, Nicky had a small, delicate nose and Caucasian lips. To anyone who didn't know the child's true heritage, she appeared to be an exceptionally beautiful white child. As she grew in age, Anna and Gene never hid the truth of her heritage from little Nicky; therefore, she was aware of her black roots. However, since a white family raised her, she embraced the white race and although she wasn't ashamed of her black heritage, she never told anyone, not even her closest friends, that her birth mother was black. Thus, everyone assumed that Nicky was Caucasian, born to a white family.

She was certainly the apple of her father's eye as well as Harry's. Little Nicky was their Princess. The two men doted on her and spoiled her to extremes. Whenever Anna drove them to Calhoun to do their shopping, Harry would take Nicky to the nearest toy department and buy her a sack full of toys and stuffed animals.

"You're spoiling her rotten, Harry," Anna would warn him.

"Good. That's what I intend to do," he would reply, unashamed. "She's the closest thing I will ever have to my own grandchild."

"Well, you better hold some back for this second one on the way," Anna reminded him.

"Oh, there's plenty to go around," he assured her. And there undoubtedly was, for only second to Ben Coleman, Harry Porter was one of the wealthiest men in the county, between his family's old money and his dairy and cattle farm business, which were very lucrative. Besides, who or what else did he have to spend his money on? Furthermore, nothing gave him greater pleasure than to lavish his love on the children he and Ollie never had.

Since Gene still felt uneasy allowing his wife to be seen around Myrick for fear of what her father might do, he insisted they conduct all their trading in nearby Calhoun. When Harry needed his medications refilled, Gene would run to Wheeler's Pharmacy there in Myrick and get them filled himself. One afternoon while Anna and Harry had driven to Calhoun with Nicky to do the weekly shopping, Gene was busy mending a fence in the pasture near the highway when Chuck Willis happened to pass by in a brand new, red Corvette convertible.

"Shouldn't you be doing that kind of work early in the morning before the sun starts beatin' down?" Chuck said, as he pulled off the highway to chat awhile with his brother-in-law.

"The bull didn't bust out this mornin' before sun up. He broke out a couple of hours ago," Gene replied, as he reattached the barbed wire to the fence post.

"Did you find him?" Chuck asked.

"Oh, yeah. He hadn't gotten too far. Fortunately, I got him back in the pasture before somebody came along and made ground beef out of him."

"I guess it would really cost old man Porter to lose that many Black Angus steaks," Chuck surmised.

"It would cost him more if he had to repair somebody's car. Especially if they was drivin' something like that," he said, referring to Chuck's shiny new sports car.

Chuck laughed. "Yeah, I guess it would."

Gene eyed the fast, sleek automobile. "Of course, if you hit a two-thousand pound bull in that thing, you'd probably be the one windin' up ground Chuck. The bull would just get up, shake his head and walk away."

They both laughed at the idea. "I guess so," Chuck replied.

"Is that your new toy?" Gene asked, admiring the Corvette.

"Yeah. Nice ain't it? We just got it in at the dealership. It'll do a hundred and eighty. Hop in and we'll take it for a test drive," Chuck offered. "I'll even let you drive."

"I'd like to, but I guess I'd better hang around here and finish mending this fence. Besides, I'm all hot and sweaty. I might ruin that new car smell."

"How's Anna and the baby?" Chuck asked.

"They're doin' fine. Anna took Nicky and Harry with her to Calhoun to pick up a few things and run some errands."

"You still don't feel good about letting her go into town by herself?"

"Not as long as that son-of-a-bitch is still around," Gene replied. "He's the reason my house looks like a goddamn fort, with the electrified fence and pack of guard dogs in the front yard. Because of his lousy ass, my family has to live like prisoners and I'm afraid to let my wife and kid out of my sight."

"I know what you mean. Me and Amy have got our own sack of rocks to carry because of that bastard. He's the reason Amy started drinking in the first place. She carries a lot of emotional baggage because of what he did to her. I think that's why she isn't really anxious to have any kids of our own."

Gene looked at him curiously. "How's that?"

"Well—" Chuck paused. "I think because of what her old man did to her, she thinks all men are alike and she's afraid I might try the same thing with our kid. It just messed her up pretty bad."

"You know, somebody ought to catch that son-of-a-bitch alone sometime and kill him. If nothin' else, beat the hell out of him. Make him suffer a little for what he's done to his family," Gene said.

"So when you want me to help you do it?" Chuck asked, his voice expressing no signs of humor. "I'm serious. We could take him. We don't have to kill him. Just scare him so bad he'd never mess with you again. All we gotta do is threaten to tell people his dirty little secret. For Coleman, that would be worse than threatening to kill him. He'd rather die than have people know he was a fucking child molester."

Gene stopped what he was doing and leaned forward on the fence post, as he seriously considered his brother-in-law's suggestion. "I always swore I'd pay the bastard back one day for what he did to Anna." He reached up and pushed the baseball cap back off his forehead. "It would be nice not to be afraid for Anna to go into town alone. The way it is now, she's living like a prisoner in her own home."

"I bet he wouldn't ever mess with you again if he knew what we know about him," Chuck assured him. "You know, some people say money is power. But so is knowledge. All you have to do is threaten to tell somebody's dirty secrets and they're putty in your hands."

"Yeah. I know," Gene replied, remembering what Harry had told him about Wilfred Bowman.

Both men remained silent for a moment; each deep in thought over how sweet the revenge to have the upper hand on the most powerful man in the county. Gene had the most to gain. If Chuck were right, Ben Coleman would never dare come near them again. Yet both would have the satisfaction of making him suffer, if just a little, for all the pain and anguish he inflicted on their wives.

"You're right," Gene said, looking out over the pasture. "We wouldn't even have to kill him. "Just let him have a little taste of his own medicine."

It was nearing the end of May and the Memorial Day weekend was just around the corner. Barrow Country had just wrapped up its annual Civil War Days weekend where local citizens dressed up in Union and Confederate uniforms and Southern Belle dresses and staged battle reenactments over a two-day period. The affair drew people from all over the state and raised money for the Historical Society, which went toward the restoration and maintenance of the pre-Civil War homes and other landmarks around the county.

Anna was busy preparing for a big barbeque and get-together at the farm. Since there was never a shortage of meat on a cattle farm, Gene planned on grilling a whole side of beef with steaks, hamburgers and hot dogs. They had invited Anna's sisters, Gene's family and the farmhands and their families to join them. Even Cassie had promised to drive up from Atlanta for the occasion.

Anna had picked up several bags of charcoal and a can of lighter fluid for the grill. Gene had taken them out of the back of the pick-up and set them in the kitchen until the cookout. Anna was tired of them being in her way, so she began looking for another place to put them. She suddenly thought of the basement. She walked over to the back of the staircase where the basement door was, and turned the doorknob. The knob turned easily, but the door wouldn't budge. She glanced up and saw that Gene had installed a slide bolt lock at the top of the door jam. She stood on her tiptoes, but still wasn't tall enough to reach it. She went into the kitchen and grabbed a chair and pushed it against the door. By now, she was seven months pregnant and quite awkward. Being careful not to lose her balance, she climbed onto the chair and slid the bolt to the side, freeing the door. Sliding the chair out of her way, she tried the doorknob once again and the door swung open. The basement stairwell was dimly lit. The only light came from the basement windows around the bottom of the house, which were ground level. She felt along the side of the wall for a light switch and found one, but when she turned it on, there was still no light.

As long as they had lived in the house, which had only been a year, she had never been below the ground floor. Gene and Harry had remained adamant about her not venturing down there. She was given a variety of excuses and reasons from the stairs were too dangerous and she would fall, to it was too dirty and musky smelling. She was tired of their excuses. It was her house and her basement and she would go wherever she wanted. Little Nicky had just begun her afternoon nap and was sleeping soundly in her cradle in the den. Gretchen lay beside the cradle, keeping a watchful eye on the baby, while Greta insisted on seeing where Anna was venturing. Carefully, she began descending the steep, narrow steps. Abandoning caution, Greta ran on down the stairs past her. When she reached the bottom of the stairs, her hand ran across another light switch. She tried it and a light came on overhead, illuminating the enormous, full basement. The basement floor was handmade terracotta tile with cement grouting, most certainly made by the pre-Civil War slaves that built and worked the original plantation over a hundred years ago. The walls were cinder blocks that were once white washed. The basement, which was the size of the entire ground floor, was divided into four cavernous rooms.

The first room at the bottom of the stairs facing the front of the house had been the original kitchen with a huge fireplace dominating an entire wall. During that time, kitchens were often placed in the underground basement where it was cooler during the summer for the slaves while preparing meals and added warmth to the ground floor during the winter. The rooms were empty with the exception of several pieces of antique furniture. She found a wonderful, old, mahogany sideboard and an antique iron bed that could certainly be used in the house. It would take several good, strong men to move them, but well worth the effort, she thought. She stood in front of the old, brick fireplace where several, long-handled iron pot utensils still hung from the wood mantle. Inside the large fireplace a big, iron kettle sat on the hearth where many a venison stew was simmered over a century ago. Anna felt as if she had taken a step back in time. She felt like a kid exploring a mysterious and exciting new world.

She took her time investigating every nook and cranny. The basement was not dirty at all. In fact, there was only a faint musky odor. Nor was it damp. Actually, it felt quite warm and cozy. With Greta at her side, she wasn't the least bit frightened. She was drawn back to the fireplace once again where she stood, imagining the hundreds of simple, yet tasty meals prepared there over the past one hundred years. She happened to glance down at a strange looking object in the back of the hearth. She reached up and got one of the iron spoons hanging from the mantle and pulled it out of the fireplace. It was transparent and about six feet in length, resembling a strip of tissue paper. On closer inspection, she recognized it as an old, dried snakeskin. Anna tossed it back into the fireplace and hung the iron spoon back where she had found it.

"Anna!"

Suddenly, she heard Harry shouting for her.

"Anna! Where are you? Are you down there?" His voice was filled with fear and panic. "What are you doing? Get back up here, right now!"

She walked to the bottom of the stairs and saw Harry standing above in the doorway. "Why? There's nothing down here except some old furniture," she told him. "I found an old sideboard down here that I can—"

"Get up here, right this minute!" he shouted, not allowing her to finish. "You have no business down there. There's nothing there to concern yourself with. Now, you get up here! I mean it!"

Surprised and puzzled by Harry's urgent insistence, Anna did as he ordered and climbed the stairs back up to the ground floor.

"Come on, Greta. Let's go," she called to the large dog that ran past her up the stairs.

"You should never go down there," Harry scolded. "I thought I told Gene to put a lock on that door."

"He did. But I unlocked it," Anna replied.

"How? You can't reach it."

"I could when I climbed up on that kitchen chair."

"What do you mean climbing on chairs and up and down dark stairs? Are you trying to kill yourself and that baby? Don't you ever, ever go down there again!"

Harry grabbed the basement door and slammed it shut. He reached up and slid the bolt back through the lock, all the while continuing to give Anna a sound and very loud scolding. She just stood silently staring at him in bewilderment. She had never seen him so upset. She was afraid he would wake the baby. He finally stopped his verbal assault when the phone began ringing. Anna left him standing in the hallway and went to answer it. It was Cassie, calling from Atlanta, confirming her trip home for the holiday. They talked for several minutes. After she hung up, Anna walked back to the hallway where she had left Harry. He was gone.

# Chapter Twelve

If there was one thing Ben Coleman hated worse than losing a dime, it was losing face. After his unsuccessful attempt to run his daughter and her husband out of town, Coleman was forced to turn his attention toward more urgent matters such as his struggling cotton mill. Thanks to polyester, which was less expensive and faster to manufacture, and with work being sent overseas where labor was cheap, the cotton industry was entering its death throws. The thought of being forced to close down his mill was eating at him like a cancer. His usual nasty temperament was growing worse and reached its peak the day Paul Woods walked into his office with another tidbit of small-town gossip. Ordinarily, it would have gone in one ear and out the other, had it not concerned his youngest daughter.

"Oh, by the way," Woods offered as he was leaving Coleman's office one afternoon. "Did I mention my wife happened to run into your daughter over in Calhoun one day last week?"

Coleman continued to busy himself with the paperwork in front of him. "No," he replied, expressing no interest.

"I guess congratulations are in order. How come you never mentioned you were gonna be a grandfather?"

Coleman suddenly stopped what he was doing, but continued to stare at his paperwork. "How's that?"

"Your youngest daughter had her new baby with her. Faye said she was a pretty little thing. Said she looks just like your daughter, with all that blonde hair. She said she was about to have another baby in a couple more months. Faye couldn't believe it because the baby she was holding didn't look to be more than six months old. We didn't have any idea that she had gotten married. She must have run off and got hitched. Oh well, that's kids for you nowadays. Once they turn seventeen there ain't a whole lot you can do with them. Least that Longhorn boy *did* marry her. Well, I guess I'd better be getting' back down to the dock."

With that, Woods closed the door behind him and left. Ben Coleman knew that by the end of the day, if he hadn't already, Paul Woods would let the entire cotton mill and half the town know his daughter *had* to get married to a poor white trash boy and was expecting a second baby within a year's time. She continued to humiliate him. And would, until he finally put an end to it.

Harry had been battling a bad summer cold and hadn't been himself the past week. Therefore, when it came time to do the weekly grocery shopping, Gene asked his father to accompany Anna to Calhoun, since Joey was busy watching the junkyard.

"Are you sure your Dad doesn't mind going with me?" Anna asked her husband that morning over the breakfast table.

"No. What else does he have to do, but sit around the house and stuff his face? Why don't you take Harry's truck, it'll be easier for Dad to climb in and out of?"

"I would, but it's too crowded in the cab for all three of us and I have more room in the back seat of the Corvair for Nicky and groceries. I can strap her car seat in the backseat, whereas, if I took the truck, your dad would have to hold her in his lap."

"Take the Chevelle. There's more room," Gene suggested.

"I'm not that crazy about driving a straight shift. An automatic has me spoiled."

"It has you lazy," he teased.

"Gene, there's something I've been meaning to mention to you," she said, clearing the breakfast dishes form the table.

"What's that?"

"A couple of weeks ago, before we had the barbeque, I went down to the basement to just look around and see what was down there."

"What did you do that for?" Gene asked, his voice expressing concern.

"Just curiosity."

"How'd you get down there? I put a lock at the top of the door."

"I got a chair and climbed up there and unlocked it."

"You did what?"

"I know. I know. Harry's already crawled me for that," she said, trying to divert his obvious irritation with her persistence. "But my point is, when Harry walked in and found me down there, he went nuts. You would have thought I tried to parachute off the roof. What's the big deal about him not wanting me down there? You'd think that's where he keeps his money hidden." Anna paused, then laughed. "It isn't, is it?"

Gene shook his head. "No. No, it's not that."

"Then what? And why did you put a lock at the top of the door?"

"I was afraid Nicky might learn to open it one day and fall down the stairs. Look, you don't need to be going down there anyway. Especially in your condition. You could fall and hurt yourself real bad. Just stay out of there. You hear me? Don't go down there again and I mean it."

Anna gave her husband a long, curious look.

"Promise me," he insisted.

"Okay," she finally agreed. "But there's nothing down there that can hurt me. There's nothing but some old antique furniture there."

Gene got up from the table and kissed his wife good-bye. Then he went out to begin the morning milking while Anna finished cleaning up the kitchen. Around nine a.m., after dropping in to check on Harry before leaving, she strapped Nicky into the back of her Corvair and drove to Gene's father's house to pick him up. Anna had grown close to Joe Longhorn and enjoyed his company. She felt free to talk to him about any subject and considered herself fortunate to have both him and Harry as substitute fathers.

Seeing her drive up, Joey hurried out of the junkyard office and was the first to greet her as she got out of the car.

"Why don't you let me ride with you to Calhoun, instead of Dad?" he asked, looking for any excuse to spend time with his favorite sister-in-law. "Dad can watch the office while we're gone."

"Nice try," Joe Longhorn said, as he walked out of the house and waddled over to the small compact car. " I already promised Gene I'd ride with her. You need to stay here and keep an eye on things."

Anna looked at Joe, Jr. and saw the disappointment on his round face. "Maybe you can go next time," she told him. "If Harry was feeling up to it, he'd be going, but I didn't want him getting out while he's still running a fever."

Joe, Jr. turned and walked away without saying a word. He felt cheated. But then he was used to that by now. While his younger brother got the beautiful wife and the pretty babies, and the big house, he just got fatter. Anna felt bad for Joey, but she didn't know what to say to keep his feelings from being hurt.

"I hate it about Joey," she told her father-in-law, once they were in the car.

"Why?" Joe asked.

"He wanted to go with us so bad," Anna replied.

"Well, there's no use in both of us going. Besides, someone has to stay and keep an eye on the business."

They enjoyed a pleasant drive to Calhoun and had lunch at a small diner in town before returning home. Since Joe was so heavy, causing his feet and legs to hurt when he did much standing or walking, he spent much of the time sitting in the car, entertaining little Nicky, while Anna did her shopping and ran errands. She hurried and finished as quickly as possible so that she could get back home in time to start dinner.

"I appreciate you going along with us today," she told her father-in-law as they drove home that afternoon. "Harry has felt so bad the past couple of days. I just couldn't let him go."

"Oh, I don't mind at all," Joe, replied. "It gave me a chance to get out of the house and besides, I got to spend some quality time with my grandbaby. Have you heard from Angel or Amy since the barbeque?" he asked, changing the subject.

"Yes, I talked to Angel last night as a matter of fact. She said she and Tanya would try to drive up this weekend and spend Saturday night with us. If she does, I'll call Amy and Chuck and have them join us for Sunday dinner. I love it when we can all get together. My sisters and I have actually grown closer since we all left home. We spend more time together now than we did when we were younger."

"That's good, because a lot of times after kids leave home, they grow apart and go their separate ways."

"Well, I'm thankful we didn't. My sisters are all I have left now since I never see my parents. I can't say I miss my Dad, but I do miss my Mom. Sometimes I want to pick up the phone so bad and talk to her. But Gene would kill me if he ever caught me trying to get in touch with them. It's not that he doesn't want me to have anything to do with my Mother, it's that he's afraid of what my Father might do."

"Well, he's right," Joe, agreed. "I know how hard it must be not being able to have any contact with your Mother, but it's best you stay a safe distance from your old man. He sounds like a real nut."

"Amy sees Mom pretty often. She tells me she's drinking all the time now. It's so hard for me to believe because I never knew my Mother to drink as long as I lived at home. The only time she drank was when they had a party at the house."

"Well, livin' with a man like your Father is enough to drive anybody to drink."

Anna reached up to adjust her rear view mirror and noticed two men in a beat-up, Dodge pick-up had been behind them ever since they left the shopping center in Calhoun.

"You know," she confided. "My worst fear is that something will happen to Mother before I have a chance to talk with her again and ask her who my real father is. As far as I know, she's the only one who knows the truth. And if something happens to her before I find out, she'll take that secret to her grave. That haunts me."

"Auh, honey. Don't dwell on things you have no control over. What good would it do if you knew the truth anyway?"

"But it really bothers me. There's a man out there, somewhere who's my own flesh and blood and I wouldn't know him if we came face to face."

"He might not even still be alive. You don't know."

"That's just it," Anna sighed. "I don't know who he is, where he is, or even if he's still alive. And I want to know what made my Mother turn to another man in the first place." She glanced up again and saw the truck picking up speed until it was inches from her rear bumper.

"What does that guy think he's doing?" she said, keeping her eyes on the rear view mirror.

"Who?" Joe asked, turning around to look out the back window.

"That guy in the pick-up behind us. He's been riding my bumper for the last couple of miles."

Joe squinted and tried to focus on the vehicle traveling behind them. The pick-up was so close behind the small, low-slung car, that the truck's grill and hood was all that could be seen.

"Slow down and let him go around," Joe told her.

Anna eased her foot off the accelerator, allowing the truck to pass, but the driver refused to go around. They were entering a very dangerous and curvy stretch of back, country road between Myrick and Calhoun. There were fifteen to twenty-five foot drop-offs on both sides of the narrow black top road with a double yellow line down the middle for the next several miles.

"I may have to pull over, Joe. He's refusing to go around us."

"Okay then, pull over up here. Just be careful. There's a big drop-off up ahead."

Anna lifted her foot from the gas pedal and gently applied pressure to the brake. "Oh, my God!" she yelled. "I don't have any brakes!"

She looked up in her rear view mirror once more and was able to get a good look at the driver of the truck. "Oh, my God. That's—"

Before she could finish, the truck accelerated and rammed their car from behind. The force propelled the small car off the road and down a twenty-foot embankment, flipping it end over end, over and over until it finally came to rest upside down at the bottom of the embankments. It was over an hour before a passing truck happened to see the little red Corvair resting on its top at the base of the ravine. There were no signs of life in or around the car.

Gene was busy loading cattle feed into the back of the pick-up, preparing to feed the livestock when Sheriff Bowman and Chaplin Rainey pulled up in front of the pole barn. Gene's heart began to pound like a drum and he felt a sick, sinking feeling in the pit of his stomach. He knew immediately that something terrible had happened. Anna should have been home hours ago. Two of the farmhands that were helping him with the afternoon feeding, stopped what they were doing and watched as Bowman, a large man, tipping the scales at well over two-hundred eighty pounds, struggled to get out of the patrol car driven by his deputy.

"Mr. Longhorn? This is Chaplin Rainey," Bowman said, gesturing to the Chaplin who worked closely with the Sheriff's department. Whenever there was a death or fatality in the county, Rainey rode with the Sheriff to help break the news to the family. Having Rainey and Bowman arrive together at someone's home was not, by any means, a welcomed sight. "I'm afraid there's been an accident," Bowman told Gene. "Your family has been air lifted to the hospital in Rome."

Gene remained frozen, unable to speak. All he could do was stand there and listen to the horrific account of what had just happened to his entire family. Nearly everything and everyone in the world that he ever loved was in that car—his father, his wife, his daughter and his unborn child. Suddenly, his knees became weak and threatened to buckle. All the color drained from his face.

"We'll escort you to the hospital," Bowman offered. "But I don't think it would be a good idea for you to drive yourself. Maybe you should have one of these men here drive you," he said, gesturing to the two farmhands standing beside him.

Gene turned to his two helpers. "Walter, go to my Dad's house and get my brother and bring him here. Red, I'm going to get Harry. You stay here and take over until I get back."

The half hour drive to Rome was shear agony for Gene. He had no idea how badly his family had been injured or who was the reported fatality. All Bowman had told him was, there had been a serious single automobile accident with a fatality. He didn't know if it was his wife, infant daughter or his father. All he could think about was the accident that had claimed the lives of his mother and younger sister ten years ago.

He once again would have to endure the pain of burying another close family member or perhaps even the rest of his entire family. His stomach churned and his hands trembled all the way to the hospital. His brother Joey sat beside him in the front seat of the Chevelle, while Harry sat in the back. They followed behind the Barrow County Sheriff's car, speculating how the accident could have occurred on what little information they had received from Bowman. All they knew was there were no witnesses and the vehicle had left the road without leaving any skid marks. The small car had apparently flipped several times and landed on its roof at the bottom of a steep embankment.

    They were almost certain that Anna had been driving since Gene's father was too heavy to fit behind the steering wheel of the compact car. He barely fit in the front passenger's seat. They also knew that the road, on which they had been traveling, was narrow and isolated with a lot of tight, twisting curves in the foothills of the Blue Ridge Mountains. There were steep drop-offs with soft shoulders on both sides of the road. Anna being a good driver was extremely cautious when Nicky was in the car. Gene had taught her well and had kept the little Corvair in tip-top shape. He routinely checked her brakes; tire pressure, oil and water levels. He was a fair shade tree mechanic and knew that morning; her car was in good mechanical order when she left home with their baby. He wondered if there had been another car involved or if a deer had darted out in front of her. That particular area was over-run with herds of deer as well as black bear and cougars. But Bowman had said there were no skid marks and suggested Anna had taken her eyes off the road for a brief moment and lost control when her wheels dropped off the pavement. Gene, however, knew better and cringed at the thought that they may never know what really happened.

    They finally arrived at the hospital, and were taken to the waiting room by a nurse who told them to have a seat until a doctor was able to speak with them. Gene called Amy and told her what had happened. She immediately called Angel in Atlanta. Angel, in turn, called Cassie. By now, all were on their way to the hospital in Rome. Amy was the first to arrive with Chuck. They sat with Gene, Joey and Harry, and anxiously waited for a doctor to inform them of their family member's conditions. They waited for what seemed an eternity. Not long after Angel and Cassie arrived, an emergency room physician finally appeared and introduced himself.

"Mr. Longhorn, I'm sorry but we were unable to do anything for your father. He was pronounced dead on arrival. His neck was broken. He was probably killed instantly."

Gene stood there, facing the doctor in stunned disbelief and shock, unable to speak. Joey stood to his left, while Amy remained close at his other side. She reached up and placed one hand on his shoulder and the other on his arm, as if to brace him for more bad news.

"Your daughter suffered a broken arm and has some cuts and bruises, but actually, she suffered the least injuries of all the passengers in the car, probably because she was strapped in her car seat. More than likely, that's what saved her life. She is going to be fine, but we want to keep her here for a couple of days for evaluation."

Gene continued to stare at the doctor in silence. He could only stand there helplessly as he listened to this stranger announce the fate of his family.

"Your wife has gone into labor," the doctor continued. "She's stable, but in critical condition. Her back is broken and her pelvis is fractured. I think it would be best if we take the baby early."

"Is the baby okay?" Amy asked anxiously.

"We believe so," the doctor replied, sounding somewhat uncertain. "We are able to detect a strong heartbeat. But we won't know for sure until she delivers."

"Is my wife going to be alright?" Gene asked, finally breaking his silence.

"There again, I can't say for sure. We have stabilized her, but she's not out of the woods by any means. Our main concern is internal hemorrhaging. She suffered a collapsed lung and has a skull fracture and concussion. She's lost a lot of blood."

"Is she conscious?" Amy asked.

"She is conscious and surprisingly alert considering her injuries. In fact, she's been quite adamant about not allowing us to take the baby. She's refusing a C-section, but in my opinion, it would be detrimental to both she and the baby if we allowed her to have a normal delivery. She's lost too much blood and she's already weak and suffering from shock. We could lose them both if she were allowed to remain in labor. Besides, that would be impossible with a fractured pelvis."

"She was looking forward to a natural birth with Gene there in the delivery room," Amy said. "But I know we have to do what's best for both her and the baby. We can't afford to take any chances."

"All that matters is what's best for my wife and baby," Gene said. "But if it comes down to it, my wife comes first. We can have more kids, but I only have one wife. You do whatever you have to in order for her to leave this hospital alive."

"We will," the doctor assured him. "Of course, we'll do everything in our power to save them both."

"Would it be possible for me to be with my wife during the surgery?" Gene asked.

The doctor thought for some time before answering. "I'll see, but I can't make any promises. Your wife will be under anesthesia during the delivery. She won't know you're there."

"No, but I will," Gene insisted. "Can I see her now?"

"Yes. But she's being prepped for surgery at the moment. I'll have a nurse let you know when they are done."

"Can we go in with him?" Amy asked. "We're her sisters."

"Yes," the doctor replied. "But you can't visit with her for very long. The sooner she delivers the baby, the better."

"You said her back and pelvis were broken," Harry asked, after patiently waiting his turn. "Will she be able to walk?"

"Oh, yes. But not for several weeks or maybe even a month," the doctor explained. "And then she'll require months of physical therapy to get her back on her feet again. She'll be bedridden for some time. It's a miracle that she and her daughter are alive. They both are very lucky."

When they were finally allowed to see Anna, they found her in a considerable amount of pain and still very shaken. She was devastated over the loss of Gene's father. His death and the possibility of losing their unborn baby had her in a state of panic. However, there was something very important she knew she must tell her husband before they took her to surgery.

"Gene, I have to tell you something now in case something happens to me. This was no accident," she assured him. She spoke slowly and was visibly weak.

"What do you mean?" he asked.

"We were forced off the road by a pick-up truck. It was an old, faded green Dodge pick-up. They began following us just outside of Calhoun. He got right on my bumper and refused to go around. Then he rammed the back of the car and forced me off the highway."

"Did you see who was driving?" Gene asked.

"Yes," Anna replied. "And I know him."

"Who was it?" Gene asked.

"It was Danny Peavy."

"Danny Peavy?" Gene replied, his voice filled with surprise.

"Oh my, God," Amy gasped. "That's Nicky's father."

"And he's also a little punk," Angel added. "He's been in trouble all his life and in and out of jail."

"He works for your old man, doesn't he?" Gene asked.

"Yes," Anna replied.

"Do you think Daddy had something to do with the accident?" Amy asked her sister.

"She just told you, it wasn't an accident," Angel reminded her. "And of course he had something to do with it. What other motive would that little punk have for trying to kill her?"

"Maybe he found out Cassie had his baby," Amy suggested.

"No way," both Anna and Gene replied in unison.

"She never told Danny she was pregnant," Anna assured her sister. "He doesn't even know Nicky exists. Cassie only saw him a couple of times and hasn't spoken with him since."

"You're sure it was Peavy?" Gene asked her.

"Positive."

"Was he alone?"

"No. There was someone else in the truck with him, but I didn't recognize who it was. When I tried to hit the brakes there weren't any. When they rammed me from behind, I hit the pedal. It went all the way to the floorboard."

Gene knew they had to get Anna's car back. He had to find out which wrecker service towed it and where it had been taken. But his first concern was his wife and baby. He, along with Amy and Angel, remained with her until she was wheeled into surgery. He then hurried back to the waiting room and told Chuck to go with his brother and locate Anna's car and bring it back to their father's junkyard as soon as possible. There, they would go over it with a fine-tooth comb and find out what had happened to cause the brakes to fail. He was sure he already knew the answer. Someone had cut the brake lines.

Meanwhile, Gene remained at the hospital with Harry and his two sister-in-laws, waiting the outcome of his wife and unborn baby's condition. While still at the hospital in Rome, he phoned Jordan's Funeral Home in Myrick, and arranged for them to pick up his father's body. He and Joey would have to plan the funeral arrangements tomorrow.

On arriving back in Myrick, Chuck and Joey found Sheriff Bowman and asked him where Anna's car had been taken. As they expected, they received no co-operation from him. After Bowman claimed he couldn't remember which wrecker service had towed the vehicle. Joey quickly got on the phone and began calling around until he located the salvage yard that had the wrecked car. They immediately drove to the junkyard, which happened to be two counties away, and towed the automobile back to their own salvage yard where Joey locked it up behind a chain link fence with two large guard dogs.

It didn't take Joey and Chuck long to discover what had happened to cause the wreck. A quick inspection revealed the brake lines had been cut nearly in half, which allowed the brake fluid to escape. Joe Longhorn's death was no accident. It was pre-meditated murder. Yet the passenger, who was supposed to have died, had miraculously survived and was still alive to tell what *really* happened. But getting the local authorities to co-operate in order to bring the person responsible to justice would be next to impossible. They would have to take their evidence to the GBI. Even then, they risked being ignored.

"Sometimes you just have to throw caution to the wind and take matters into your own hands," Chuck told Joey as they stood in the junkyard, after confirming the wreck was actually a murder case. "Something your brother and I should have done right after we had our little discussion not long ago. But instead, we put it off. That was our mistake. Now, Coleman has made his mistake. If Gene and I have anything to do with it, he won't be making any more."

Nearly three hours after Anna was admitted to the hospital in Rome, she gave birth to a beautiful, healthy set of twins by Cesarean Section. The double birth came as a shock to everyone, including the surgeon who made the delivery, as well as Anna's obstetrician, who detected only one heartbeat throughout her entire pregnancy and delivery. Through some miracle, the paternal twins, a boy and a girl, arrived in much better condition than their mother, who now faced months of recovery and rehabilitation. The infants were allowed to go home three days after their arrival, along with their older sister, while Anna was forced to remain in the hospital a couple of weeks longer.

Since the proud parents had already chosen both a male and female name for their baby, when both sexes arrived, coming up with *two* names was not a problem. They named their son, who was first to arrive, Eugene Anthony, after his father. Their daughter was named Olivia Marie, after Harry's beloved Ollie. Before Gene was allowed to bring his children home, he was faced with the unpleasant and heartbreaking task of burying his father. Since Joseph Longhorn was unable to afford life insurance, the burden of his funeral expenses fell on his two sons. They were forced to make arrangements with the local funeral home to pay what they could until the funeral was finally paid in full. They both knew that would probably take years. Since there was no money for a cemetery plot, Harry suggested that Gene and Joey bury their father beside Ollie behind the house. With no other choice, they were grateful, and accepted his offer.

After the funeral, Gene Longhorn turned to his next task at hand— finding the man who caused his father's death and who nearly killed his wife and three infants in the process. He would then go after the man who was responsible for making his life a living nightmare. Despite the fact that Gene had a violent temper when provoked, he was not a man prone to unnecessary violence. But, this time, he had been pushed beyond his limits. He had been backed into a corner and he was coming out fighting. And he wasn't coming out alone.

# Chapter Thirteen

Chuck Willis had known Ben Coleman long before he ever met and married his middle daughter. Chuck's father, the Honorable Judge Charles Willis, III, had been a close friend of Coleman's for over two decades. They did a lot of favors for one another and socialized frequently. Chuck had attended the same schools as the Coleman girls and had known their father since he was a young boy. He never had any feelings for Coleman one way or the other, until he married Amy, and learned of what her father had done to her and her older sister.

After Chuck's marriage to Amy, he developed a kind liking for his brother-in-law Gene and the two men became good friends. Both saw what Coleman had done to his wife and daughters as vile and despicable. They were also aware that not a single, local law enforcement officer or city official would go up against Coleman, including Chuck's own father, even if they knew the truth. Coleman had something on everybody. Most people have skeletons in their closets, but in a town the size of Myrick, where gossip spread quickly and reputations were easily destroyed, those with status, closely guarded their secrets. Therefore, in order to put a stop to his rein of power, matters would have to be taken into someone else's hands besides the proper authorities. Everyone knew Ben Coleman had lots of enemies. None of them, however, had more reason to do him harm and teach him a lesson than his own immediate family—his son-in-laws included. If Chuck chose to do Coleman harm, he had an advantage over Gene. Chuck was more familiar with Coleman, and on better terms with him than Gene. They spoke on occasion, whenever he and Amy would go to Coleman Hill and visit Amy's mother. To Coleman's knowledge, Chuck hadn't any resentment toward him. But his other son-in-law was a different matter in-deed. Ben Coleman had only met Gene once when he applied for a job at the mill several years ago, and although he knew of the Longhorn family, other than meeting Gene that one time, he wasn't personally acquainted with any of them. Since he didn't leave a lasting impression on Coleman and the brief meeting occurred years ago, he most likely wouldn't recognize Gene if they came face to face. That made the matters at hand much easier. Chuck was close enough to the old man to know his routine. He knew when he arrived at the cotton mill and more important, when he left, which was usually alone after everyone else had gone home for the day. Gene would have little trouble approaching him since Coleman probably wouldn't recognize him immediately. Together, they could teach Ben Coleman a lesson he would never forget and prevent him from ever doing harm to any of their family again. Or, they could kill him.

When Amy learned that her father had tried to have her sister killed, she went into a rage fueled by alcohol. Once she was assured Anna and the three children would be alright, she left Angel and Cassie at the hospital where they were keeping a vigil at Anna's bedside, and drove back to her own home where she became quite inebriated in a short period of time. Then, she got into her car and drove straight to Coleman Hill where she confronted her father for the first time, face to face.

Amy waited late in the day when she knew her father would be home from the mill. She used her key to let herself in without knocking. After Estelle's death, the Coleman's had not replaced her with another full-time maid. Ben Coleman saw no need since their daughters were gone now and only he and Catherine were left. Times were getting hard and he felt they needed to cut back on any unnecessary expenses. Instead, he hired a housekeeper to come in twice a week to do the laundry, heavy cleaning and some cooking. Today happened to be the maid's day off.

Amy entered the den unannounced, where she found her father sorting through the mail and her mother preparing herself a mixed drink.

"You mind making one of those for me," Amy told her mother, as she walked into the room and tossed her purse on the sofa. "I might even need a couple of those before I leave here."

Her father glanced up at her with a look of disgust. "Isn't one drunk in this family enough?" he said.

"Actually, I'm really surprised that there didn't turn out to be more than just two," Amy replied. "After what you put all of us through. You're lucky you didn't wind up with more than an alcoholic, a lesbian and a runaway. You could have spawned a serial killer, which really is a shame you didn't, since they could have started with you."

"You're drunk," Coleman snapped. " Go home and sober up. Stop your babbling."

"I'll go home, but not before you hear what I have to say to you." Amy turned and faced her mother, who was seated on the sofa, seemingly oblivious to what was going on around her. "And you too, Mother. I'm going to say some things that should have been said a long time ago." She turned back and faced her father again. "I want to know why you tried to kill my sister? What did she ever do to you to make you hate her so much?"

"I don't know what you're talking about," Coleman said. "You're too drunk to make any sense. Get out of here before I throw you out. I've already got one drunk to deal with. Come back when you've had time to sober up."

"No, I'm not ever coming back here again," Amy, told him. "I just want to be sure you know why your kids hate you so bad and never want to have anything to do with you again. And Angel and I hate your guts the most because we were the ones you terrorized while we were growing up."

"What the hell are you talking about? *Terrorized* the two of you. All I ever did was give you every luxury in the world. The finest clothes, the best education, nice cars and jewelry. You're all goddamn spoiled, that's what's wrong with all of you."

"You're a liar. You just don't want to hear truth. You're afraid someone will finally confront you with the sick and disgusting things you did to your own daughters. Afraid somebody might find out you made a habit of slipping into their rooms at night and forcing them to have sex with you. Are you listening, Mother? And don't you pretend you didn't know what was going on, because you did. You knew all along! Why didn't you try to stop him? You were our mother; you were supposed to protect us. Why didn't you leave the sick bastard the first time you heard him in our room?"

Amy paused, waiting in vain for some response from her mother. "Are you listening to me, Mother? Answer me! Is the reason you let him get away with it was so that he wouldn't come to you for sex? Because if that's the reason, then it makes you just as sick and perverted as him."

Catherine Coleman sat frozen on the sofa. She put her hands up to her ears and closed her eyes, trying to escape the confrontation.

Coleman went over and grabbed his daughter by the shoulders and gave her hard shove toward the door. "Get the hell out of my house and don't you ever step foot in here again!" he shouted. "I'll kill you if you ever try to spread those vicious lies."

"The same way you tried to kill Anna? Will you run my car off a mountainous road some night? If that's the case, then you might as well go ahead and kill all three of us. Because you'll never be able to escape what you've done. You're going to pay for what you did, one way or the other, sooner or later. And I'll personally see to it."

"Who's going to believe a drunk?" he snarled.

"Because of what you did to her, Angel hates men! She can't stand for them to touch her. She likes women. She's a lesbian because of you! Are you listening, Mother? Your oldest daughter is a lesbian because your husband couldn't keep his filthy hands off her when she was a little girl. How can you stand the sight of him after knowing what he did? He's the reason you haven't seen your youngest daughter in over a year. He's the reason you haven't seen you firstborn grandchild. You have three now, did you know that? He's why Angel and I wouldn't step foot in this house if it weren't for you. Say something, Mother! Why don't you say something?"

Coleman drew back and hit Amy hard across the face with his fist. The blow spun her around and knocked her off her feet. Quickly, she regained her balance and slapped him back as hard as she could.

"Stop it! Stop it!" Catherine screamed, leaping up from the sofa. "Both of you, stop it right this minute! I don't want to hear any more."

Coleman grabbed Amy by the hair and began dragging her across the room toward the door. "You get out of my house and don't you ever show your face here again! I'll fucking kill you if you ever try to spread rumors about me. I never want to see any of you again. As far as I'm concerned, you're all dead! Dead and buried!"

Amy grabbed her purse and headed for the door. She stopped and turned to face her mother once more. "You're as guilty as he is for allowing it to go on under your own roof without even trying once to stop it. You're just as responsible as he is. And you're going to pay for what you did the same way he'll pay. While you're sitting here in this big, old house all alone, day after day, without a single visit from any of your children or grandchildren, just remember, he's the reason! Besides, I would die before I ever let him near any child of mine. You two deserve one another!"

With that, Amy turned and left the house, slamming the door behind her. She got into her car and sped away, leaving with as few answers as she had when she arrived. She never wanted to lay eyes on either of them again. Little did she know at the time, that she wouldn't.

Since Angel and Cassie had to return to Atlanta, Amy brought the twins home with her, along with seven-month old Nicky after they were released from the hospital. She cared for the three infants until Anna was released two weeks later. Once Anna was home, Amy and Harry worked together and helped care for Anna and the three babies during the day until Gene returned home at night, and then he took over. Caring for Anna and three babies in diapers was a full-time job. The doctors had insisted that Anna remain in bed for another six weeks and not be allowed to lift her children for at least three months until her back and pelvis had sufficiently healed. Joey offered to stay with Gene and help out until Anna was back on her feet. Since he needed all the help he could get, Gene gladly accepted his brother's offer. During the day, Joey managed the salvage yard and after it closed in the evenings, he went to his brother's house where he spent the night and helped Gene care for Anna and the children. Thus, between the four of them, with Amy and Harry caring for them during the day and Joey and Gene looking after them at night, it worked out well. Still, Gene had his hands full with running the farm and caring for a bedridden wife and three babies.

One evening, a couple of weeks after Anna was released from the hospital, Chuck drove out to the Porter farm. He went there that night to discuss an urgent matter with his brother-in-law. While Anna and the children slept in the downstairs bedroom, Gene, his brother Joey and Chuck gathered around the kitchen table. A few minutes later there was a knock at the back door. Gene got up to answer it and one of his farmhands joined them.

Red Moore was a powerfully built man measuring just a little less than six feet and weighing well over two hundred pounds. His muscular body was covered in freckles and tattoos and his reddish blonde hair was neatly cropped close to his head. The muscles, like the tattoos, had been acquired through years of prison life after serving sixteen years in the Atlanta Penitentiary for a double murder. On a cocaine high, Red had gone to the wrong house on a drug buy and mistakenly murdered a husband and wife. He was twenty-five years old when he was sentenced to two life sentences. Following his parole four years ago, Red returned to Myrick where his parents still resided and found steady work with Harry Porter on his dairy and cattle farm. At forty-five and still single, Red was Gene's right-hand man and a hard worker. He had no desire to return to prison life and made a sound effort to avoid trouble and walk the straight and narrow. With his youth spent as an outlaw biker and drug dealer and the majority of his adult life wasted in a prison cell, Red Moore had earned the reputation of a career criminal. His intimidating appearance and prison history only added to that reputation, despite the fact Red was working hard to change that image and turn his life around. He didn't make much money working for Porter, but it was about the only honest and steady work afforded an ex-con and it satisfied his parole officer. He and Gene got along well and were good friends. Red had been privy to Gene's problems with Ben Coleman and was aware of the recent attempt on Anna's life.

"I would have already taken care of that son-of-a-bitch the first time he put my wife in the hospital," Red assured Gene. "There wouldn't have been a second time."

Gene took Red's advice seriously now and that was the reason he was sitting at his kitchen table with Joey and Chuck that night.

"I've never in my life gone after anybody with intent to do them serious harm until now," Gene told the three men seated around him. "But then I never had any reason to until now. Ben Coleman killed my father and tried to kill my wife and kids. For that, he's got to pay. I don't consider myself a violent person, but that bastard has pushed me over the edge this time. He's made us live like prisoners in our own home. He's terrorized my family and put my wife in the hospital twice and now he's responsible for my father's death. I can't get the law around here to do anything about my situation. All they're doing is protecting him and allowing him to continue to get away with murder. I have no way of fighting back or protecting my family without taking matters into my own hands."

"In all due respect Gene, your father might still be alive if we had taken care of the bastard when we first discussed it awhile back," Chuck reminded his brother-in-law of the conversation they had by the roadside not long ago.

"I know," Gene replied with regret. "And I have to live with that the rest of my life."

"And if you don't want to have to live with your wife and kids' deaths on your conscious, we had better do something to stop him before he comes after you again," Joey told his brother.

"The thought of killing another person has never entered my mind and I never thought I'd be sitting here even considering such a thing. But he's got me backed into a corner," Gene confessed. "He's a monster and he doesn't deserve to live for what he's done to so many innocent people."

"And he'll continue doing them, if he's not stopped," Chuck added. "We're all behind you. And three of us at this table have good reason to want Coleman dead, or at least taught a fucking good lesson. Like I told you Gene, we don't have to kill him, just let him know he can't go on terrorizing people. Once we let him know we'll spread his filthy secret all over town, if he ever tries to harm you again, maybe he'll realize we mean business and back off."

"But what if he won't?" Red asked. "What makes you so sure that will make him back off and leave you alone? Coleman doesn't strike me as somebody who can be easily intimidated or scared. All you might do is just piss him off even more. It would be like pissing on a hornet's nest. He would come after you with both barrels then."

"He's right," Joey agreed. "I say we kill him and get it over with. Make it appear like an accident and be done with him."

"I know that on Saturday nights he leaves his office late after everyone has gone home and the mill has shut down until Monday," Chuck volunteered. "He leaves through the side exit where he keeps his car parked. The parking lot is dimly lit and nobody is around that time of night. That might be the best time to take him."

"But how do we make it look like an accident?" Joey asked. "Kidnap him and take him out in the woods and kill him there. Make it look like a robbery?"

"No," Red told them. "You're there waiting on him when he comes out of the mill, sneak up behind him and put a bullet in the back of his head before he knows what hit him. Then take his wallet and any jewelry he has on him and make it look like a robbery. That way, you're less likely to leave evidence behind. Keep away from his car where you're liable to leave fingerprints behind. A bullet in the back of his head right there in the parking lot. Clean and simple. Don't run a risk of leaving behind any evidence by moving the body or getting in his car."

"I think he's right," Joey agreed. "Don't leave behind any clues. They'll never know who did it."

"Alright, where do we get the gun?" Gene asked. "I've got some here at the house, but they're all registered in my name."

"No, no. You let me handle that," Red insisted. "You can't use a weapon that could be traced back to anybody. It's best if it's already been reported stolen and then after we're done with it, destroy it. Take it a part; toss it in the river in several locations. If the gun can't be found, they won't have anything to trace back to us. We'll do the same with his wallet and jewelry. We'll burn them. Don't leave any clues or prints behind that could implicate us in any way. Everybody knows Coleman has money and they'll just figure somebody tried to rob him when he was leaving work one night. But the most important thing is, what's said here tonight at this table can't leave this room," Red warned all of them. "It has to stay between the four of us. Nobody can ever know we had this discussion."

Gene nodded in agreement. "You're right."

"If we cover our asses and watch our step, we can pull this thing off without a hitch," Red assured them. "But there can't be any witnesses. We have to make sure nobody sees a thing."

The four men continued to sit around the table plotting Ben Coleman's murder until late into the night. It was Friday. Tomorrow was Saturday. The night Coleman would be leaving the mill late.

It was a hot and sticky July morning as Gene and Red finished cleaning up the barn after the morning milking. Their conversation was sparse and pertained only to the day's work ahead of them. Since their meeting the night before in Gene's kitchen, the four men had made a solid promise not to discuss anything pertaining to their plans that night in the presence of anyone.

"Nothing leaves this table tonight," Red had reminded them once more before the meeting was adjourned. "What's said here tonight at this table can't leave this room. It has to stay between the four of us."

Gene knew Red was right. If anyone knew how to handle his problem once and for all, it was Red Moore. During his days as an outlaw biker, Red had made several men disappear without a trace and without ever drawing suspicion. To his own admission, he would have never served sixteen years behind bars had he not been high the night he murdered the couple in Atlanta and been sloppy with the murder. But in some ways, Red knew going to prison for that long was the best thing that ever happened to him, for had he not done hard time, he would have probably been killed by a rival gang member or found dead from an overdose. Prison helped change his life. As to whether or not it was for the better, only time would tell. But for now, he was forced to revert back to his former criminal way of thinking in order to help a friend in desperate need of some guidance. The kind of guidance only a man with his experience could offer. There were times when violence had to be met with more violence in order to sustain self-preservation, and this was Gene's case. Red felt obligated to his friend to offer him his expertise.

As they were about to leave the barn, Chuck drove up. Gene found it odd he would be out at the farm that time of the morning. Most people were still in bed.

"What brings you out here at the butt-crack of dawn, city boy," Gene cracked, as he watched Chuck get out of his car.

"You'll never believe what's happened," Chuck told them, his voice filled with somber emotion.

"What is it?" Gene replied, almost afraid to ask.

"The Coleman's housekeeper arrived this morning to report to work and found Ben and Catherine Coleman shot to death."

"What?" Gene gasped, a shocked expression on his face.

"The Sheriff just left my house with the Chaplin looking for Amy. They thought she was home, but I told them she was here helping look after Anna."

"Looks like Coleman had worse enemies than us," Red replied.

"Yeah, his wife," Chuck said.

"Catherine?" Gene replied with disbelief.

"Bowman said it looks like she shot Coleman and then turned the gun on herself. He says it appears to be a murder suicide."

"Well, looks like his wife saved us the trouble," Red sneered, turning to Gene.

And she had. There weren't a handful of people who were sorry Ben Coleman was dead, although everyone was shocked at *how* he had died. Everyone wondered what could have possibly made Catherine Coleman to do such a thing. Most everyone in town was aware that she had recently began drinking and had given way to depression, but it was suspected that her condition was brought on by the fact her three daughters had all left home about the same time. The *empty nest syndrome*, as it was sometimes referred to. Only a select few knew the *real* reason for her actions. All that mattered to those few, was that Ben Coleman was dead and would never be able to interfere with their lives again. Justice had been served.

# Book III

# Chapter Fourteen

The double homicide stunned the small, close-knit community, especially since it involved one of its most influential families. Anna was the only daughter who was unable to attend the funeral since she was still bedridden with a broken back. But even if she had been well enough to attend, Gene would not have allowed it.

"Since you weren't allowed in their house, I'm not allowing you to attend their funeral. They wouldn't want you there in the first place. At least I know your old man wouldn't. And neither do I," he told Anna.

She understood her husband's resentment. Her father had put them all through hell, but he wouldn't anymore. They were free now. Free from fear. They didn't have to keep a low profile and travel twenty-miles out of town to go shopping for necessities. Myrick was again their town and they were free to go anywhere they pleased without fear of being seen or harmed. It was as if a weight had been lifted from their shoulders. The only thorn remaining in Gene's side was the fact that the man, who had been hired by Ben Coleman to cause the accident that killed his father, was still alive. He had sworn to find him and make him pay. But once again, fate stepped in and plucked even that thorn from Gene's side. Not long after the Colemans' funeral, Danny Peavy was shot and killed by a convenience store clerk when he and an accomplice attempted to rob the store. The man who was their adopted daughter's biological father, and the man whom she would never know, was now dead. Like Coleman, he wouldn't be missed.

Despite the decline of his cotton mill, Ben Coleman died a very wealthy man. He left behind a sizable fortune along with the failing mill and a magnificent, old southern mansion. When Amy and Angel sat in the attorney's office for the reading of their father's will, they weren't surprised to learn he had cut their younger sister completely out of everything. Her name was never mentioned. However, her sisters assured Anna they would see to it that their father's fortune would be split equally three ways. Anna insisted that it wasn't necessary and for them to split it down the middle among themselves. She assured them she neither needed nor wanted a dime of his money.

The mill, which had been losing profits and business over the past few years, was headed for closure with or without Coleman. Angel, a business major and successful advertising executive, already had plans for the crumbling business. If her strategy worked out, she and her two sisters would soon be the proprietors of a million dollar industry.

After a rough and rocky beginning, Gene and Anna were finally awarded what they so justly deserved. Once Anna had regained her health and was back on her feet, they would be on their way to a secure and happy life. Their future finally appeared bright.

On the other hand, it wasn't looking as bright for Amy, who continued to use alcohol as her way of coping with her tragic childhood. In addition to the alcohol, she began to rely heavily on prescription pain medications as well in order to ease her tremendous emotional, rather than physical, pain. As if her reliance on alcohol and drugs weren't enough to complicate her life, Amy also began a series of extra-marital affairs. Perhaps it was the combination of drugs and alcohol that encouraged her infidelity, or simply the fact that she used sex as well, in order to escape her unbearable past. Whatever the reason, Amy had embarked on a fast collision course and was headed for disaster. She was an unhappy and tormented young woman despite the fact she had money, looks, a beautiful home and a husband who adored her. Her dreams of going to Atlanta to pursue a modeling career had long vanished. She had been distracted by her younger sister's problems with their father, her mother's drinking and depression, her parents' deaths and finally, her own addictions. Instead of leaving and escaping her life there, she seemed to have sunk only deeper, as if she were being swallowed up in quick sand. Even worse, she was following in mother's footsteps.

Angel, however, was different. She was financially secure and independent with a successful career and a partner she was totally committed to. Tanya was the love of her life and the feminine half of the lesbian pair. In Atlanta, where gay and lesbian couples were for the most part, accepted and left alone, they found peace and contentment. In Myrick, they would most certainly be met with disapproval and non-acceptance. Nonetheless, Myrick was Angel's hometown. It was where her sisters still remained. It was where her roots had been firmly planted. And, it was where she planned to open a new industry. An industry that would offer much needed and better paying jobs to many of the locals and allow Myrick to grow and prosper. People would just have to learn to accept her unconventional lifestyle or go to hell. It was as simple as that.

As for Cassie, like Amy, her life was spiraling out of control. She had gone to Atlanta seeking a decent job and a fresh start. Instead, she wound up selling her soul in exchange for pursuing her dreams. An exceptionally pretty girl with an hour glass figure, Cassie found work as a nude dancer in an Atlanta strip club when she was unable to land a decent paying job elsewhere. In the club, she made more money than she ever dreamed possible, but blew most of it on drugs and the high life. Before she knew what was happening, she became addicted to cocaine and lived the fast-paced life of a party girl. While she used to return home at least one weekend out of the month to spend time at the Porter farm with her daughter and childhood friend, they now seldom saw Cassie. When she wasn't working at the strip club, she was partying with her friends, drinking and getting wasted until the wee hours of the morning. She even traveled to Florida on a few occasions to appear in low-budget porn films that were distributed around the country in adult bookstores.

The next two years, following the Coleman's deaths, brought about a multitude of changes and experiences for everyone. Some would prove to be devastating occurrences, some shocking revelations and even some glorious occasions. The future was, at the very least, uncertain, but with the help and support of this remarkably strong and united family, there would be hope and salvation for some, while sadly, desperation and destruction awaited others.

Soon after Ben and Catherine Coleman were buried, their daughter Angela left the advertising agency in Atlanta and moved back to Myrick with Tanya. They moved into her parents' home on Coleman Hill, where they quickly auctioned off all the Coleman's possessions and furnishings and re-decorated the entire house to suit their own taste.

Angela's next project was the cotton mill. Since neither Anna nor Amy knew anything about business management, they turned over their interests in the mill to their older, more business savvy sister. Angel proceeded to shut down the cotton mill, borrow against the property and use the loan to transform the one hundred year-old mill into a carpet manufacturer. The cotton industry was re-locating overseas where labor was cheap, but there was a substantial marketing need for commercial and domestic carpeting. Within a year, the mill was back in business, turning out thousands of rolls of high-quality carpeting while providing lucrative jobs, as well as benefits for the former cotton mill workers and earning Angel and her two sisters a hefty income. Since Angel was the brain behind the business, it was quickly agreed that she would be the president and CEO of the new company that she named AAA Carpet Mills of Myrick. Since Amy always excelled in math and majored in finance during her first and only year in college, Angel put her in charge of the bookkeeping and finance department. Both Angel and Amy wanted their younger sister to join them at the mill as the personnel director, but Gene refused to allow his wife to leave their small children and work outside the home. A man with old-fashioned values, he insisted a woman's place was in the home—especially *his* woman. In the following year, their family had grown even larger with the birth of another son whom they named for Gene's brother, Joey. Now, the Longhorn family consisted of four children—two girls and two boys, all less than three years of age. Therefore, Angel suggested Anna take care of the posting and billing at home in her spare time so that she could be put on the company payroll and allowed the necessary health benefits that Gene had never been able to provide for his wife and children. In turn, this removed a large financial burden from Harry, who had voluntarily been paying for their doctor's visits and medical care out of his own pocket. Anna's enormous hospital bill following the car wreck ran into the thousands, which Harry paid out of the goodness of his heart because Anna was *family*.

The new industry also provided opportunities for other family members as well. Joey was offered a manager's position in charge of shipping and receiving at the loading dock. He quickly sold the family's salvage yard and accepted his new job offer along with the invitation to move in with his brother and sister-in-law at the farm. The old shack that had been home for Joey and his father for so many years had begun to collapse and became even dangerous to inhabit. In addition, the mill offered yet another family friend the opportunity for better pay and benefits. Angel hired Red Moore as an assistant production manager, forcing Gene to lose his best farmhand. In short, everyone prospered and benefited from Myrick's newest industry, which grew rapidly and began producing the majority of carpeting in Georgia and neighboring Alabama.

Besides providing the former cotton mill workers with better paying jobs and benefits, employees worked less hours under better conditions and were allowed all major holidays along with paid vacations and sick leave. Unlike her father, Angel saw that her employee's needs were of the utmost importance. And unlike Ben Coleman, Angel was well liked and respected by all her employees. Once again, the Coleman family dynasty was back on top, only bigger and better than ever before.

# Chapter Fifteen

The day began like any other hot and muggy April day; only it would turn out to be a day that Anna would remember the rest of her life. She had just put the children down for their afternoon nap and sat down at the roll-top desk in the downstairs hallway to do some posting for Amy. She opened the exterior doors at each end of the downstairs central hallway in hopes of catching a fleeting breeze.

The four German Shepherds that kept a constant watch outside the house lay sprawled on the back porch and gave a lazy wag of their tails as Anna opened the exterior door. The other two dogs were upstairs in the children's room lying beside their beds, keeping watch as they slept.

It was tornado season in Georgia, which meant any severe thunderstorm was capable of spawning a tornado and with the boiling heat, the atmosphere was like a pressure cooker ready to explode.

Anna was now four months pregnant with their fifth child. This would give them five children, all less than three years-old, including the twins and their adopted daughter, Nicky. Amy was also three-months pregnant with her first child after three years of marriage. The family was rapidly expanding and with the carpet mill flourishing, everyone was prospering. After the passing of Chuck's grandfather, he was now the owner of three Chevrolet dealerships and a millionaire in his own right. Chuck had offered Gene a manager's position over the service department at his dealership in Myrick, but he turned the offer down in favor of remaining Harry's foreman. He had worked for old man Porter since he was a kid and Harry looked on Gene as the son he never had. One day the old man would die and being that he had no other family or living relatives, Gene felt almost certain that if he remained loyal to Harry, he would leave the thousand-acre farm to him when he died. If he did, Gene would be a very wealthy man. Rather than continue farming the land, he would sell it and turn a handsome profit from the sale. His dream was to become a self-made millionaire and never again be forced to work long, hard hours of back breaking manual labor. Although Harry paid him well, he knew he would never become rich being a farmhand. Only the farm owner made any *real* profit.

Ironically, it was now Anna who was bringing in the largest income for their family, which annoyed Gene somewhat. As co-owner of the carpet mill, she received a sizable quarterly check and for the office work she did at home, she was paid twice monthly. All together, she was earning almost three times what Harry was paying Gene, as well as providing their full medical coverage.

"Anna?" Harry called to her as he walked through the kitchen door. He normally dropped in to check on her and the children around that time each day and was returning a pot he had borrowed a few days ago to cook some grits.

"I'm in here, Harry," she replied. "I'm just catching up on some paper work for the mill."

"Here's that saucepan I borrowed the other day."

"I told you that you didn't have to give it back. I have plenty of pots and pans. You need it worse than I do."

"This one sure makes a good pot of grits," he said.

"Then keep it for yourself. I really don't need it."

"Are the children asleep?" he asked.

"Yeah. I just put them down. I thought I'd use the free time to catch up on these invoices Amy dropped by this morning. Sit down and keep me company while I work."

Harry pulled up a chair beside her.

"Can I offer you a soda or a cup of coffee?" she offered.

"No, it's too hot for coffee."

"Then how about a glass of iced tea? I just made a fresh pitcher."

"No, I'm fine. I just heard on the TV that we're under a tornado watch until eight o'clock tonight," he said.

"I'm not surprised. It's been so unbearably hot, especially for this time of year. Normally, it doesn't get as warm this early in the summer."

"You need to keep a radio or TV on to keep track of where the storms are headin'. We need to keep an ear out in case the watches turn into a warning," he suggested. Harry was terrified of bad weather like most Georgians. He had lived through two category four tornadoes and he knew the devastation they were capable of producing.

"Go get the radio in the den and bring it in here," she told him. "You never know if we might have to grab the kids and head for the basement."

"No, we don't need to be going down there," Harry was quick to reply. "We'll dive under that heavy table in the dining room if we have to."

Anna laid down the pen she was posting with and sat up straight in her chair. "Harry, I've lived in this house nearly three years now and I've only been down there once. I want you to tell me why you and Gene flip out every time I mention going into the basement. What the hell is down there that you don't want me to see? Or find?"

"There's nothin' down there for you to concern yourself with," Harry insisted. "Just a damp, musky hole. You're liable to fall down them stairs and hurt yourself bad. You don't need to be goin' down there and you sure don't need to be takin' those babies down there with you. You hear me? Don't ever take the children down there."

"Why Harry? What's down there?" she persisted.

The phone rang suddenly and interrupted their conversation. Anna got up to answer it. A sharp crack of thunder rolled in the distance as the sky grew darker outside.

"Hello," she answered. "Yes, this is Anna Longhorn."

There was a long pause on her end. Harry walked over to the screen door at the end of the central hallway and looked up at the sky.

"Oh, my God," Anna said to the other person on the phone. "Oh, no. When did it happen?"

Harry turned and walked into the den where Anna was talking on the phone. He was alarmed by the serious tone in her voice.

"What funeral home will be handling the arrangements?" she asked.

Harry knew immediately there had been a death. Suddenly, a bright flash of lightning lit up the entire house, followed by another loud clap of thunder. The house became very dark inside and the wind began to pick up. There was a storm rapidly approaching.

"I'm so sorry, Simon. I'm so very sorry. Cassie was like a sister to me. She was my best friend since elementary school. But I knew she was headed down a dangerous path when she went to work at that awful club. She was associating with some bad people. When she got into drugs, she stopped coming on weekends to visit. I knew it was just a matter of time before her lifestyle caught up with her. It's so sad."

A weather bulletin sounded over the radio announcing that a tornado had been sighted somewhere close by. Harry walked over to the radio and turned up the volume. The announcer began naming a list of counties in the path of a funnel cloud spotted on the Alabama state line and traveling east into Georgia.

"Those counties now under a tornado warning are Chattooga, Walker, Floyd, Gordon and Barrow," the broadcast warned. "People in those counties should prepare to take cover immediately."

Out of the corner of her eye, Anna saw Harry running upstairs toward the children's' bedroom.

"Alright, Simon. Thank you so much for calling. And I'm so very sorry. Call me as soon as her body arrives at the funeral home. I'll meet you there. Yeah, it looks like we're in for a pretty bad storm."

Before she had a chance to say good-bye, the phone line went dead and the lights suddenly went out. Anna hung up the phone and walked into the hallway in time to see Harry hurrying down the stairs with the baby in his arms and Nicky, the twins and the two dogs following behind him. She heard something pelting the roof and hitting against the windows and realized it was hail.

"Anna! Here, take the baby!" he said, shoving ten month-old Joey in her arms. "I'll get Nicky and the twins. Get under the dining room table. Quick! There's a funnel cloud headed this way!"

"Oh my, God! Are you sure?"

"Yes, I'm sure! I just heard it on the radio. They're telling everyone in Barrow County to take cover!"

The children began to cry and cling to their mother in panic. She hurried to the door at the end of the hallway, threw open the screen door and called for her four dogs to come inside the house.

"Get away from that door!" Harry shouted. "Get down here with the children and take cover! Don't worry about them dogs."

"Wouldn't we all be safer in the basement?"

"No! Now get over here under the table."

Suddenly it grew very dark and still.

"Mommy, Mommy, I'm scared!" cried two year-old Nicky. "I want Daddy."

Suddenly Anna remembered that Gene was probably out in the pasture somewhere and hadn't heard the weather bulletin.

"Oh my, God! I've got to go look for Gene. He doesn't even know it's headed this way. I've got to get to him!" She grabbed the keys to her car lying on the desk and burst out the door onto the front porch.

"Mommy, Mommy, wait! Come back!" the children screamed.

Harry wanted to go after her but was afraid to leave the children. Just as she ran out onto the porch, she saw Gene and two of the farmhands leaping out of Harry's pick-up and come running up the porch steps toward her.

"Get in the house, a tornado is coming!" he yelled at his wife.

Anna looked up about that time and saw the all too familiar wall cloud overhead. The sky was pitch black above light gray clouds beneath. The darker clouds were beginning to dip down and swirl in a circular motion forming a funnel cloud. The roar was deafening and sounded like a freight train on top of them.

Gene grabbed Anna by the arm and shoved her back into the house. "Where are the kids?" he yelled.

"Daddy! Daddy!" Nicky screamed, running out of the dining room with the twins toddling behind her.

Gene reached down and grabbed up the twins, one under each arm and ran toward the basement door. "Everyone get in the basement! Now!" he shouted. He reached up and quickly unlocked the bolt at the top of the basement entrance and threw open the door.

Anna grabbed the baby from Harry and hurried down the basement steps behind Gene and the twins. The six German Shepherds ran past everyone as they made their way into the basement. The two farmhands quickly motioned for Harry to go ahead of them, but he hesitated.

"Get down here now!" Gene shouted to them. "It's on top of us. What are you waiting for?"

The farmhands quickly grabbed Harry by the arms and practically carried him down the basement steps. One of them reached for the door and closed it behind them. Without any electricity there were no lights and the basement was almost pitch dark.

"Papa, I'm so scared," Nicky cried as she clung to Harry.

"It's alright, Baby. We're safe down here," he told her. "It'll be over in a few minutes."

And it was. It took less than five minutes for the funnel cloud to snake its way past the farm and on to the next county. An eerie calm suddenly blanketed the earth as the sun began to peak out from behind the clouds and shine through the windows, illuminating the dark basement.

"Is it over?" Anna asked her husband.

Gene listened for a moment, then replied, "Yeah. It's gone."

"Come on," Harry urged, as he began herding everyone toward the basement steps. "Let's get back upstairs and look over the damage."

Gene led the way and opened the basement door. "Don't anybody step outside until I've looked around first," he warned. "There are probably live power lines down everywhere. Keep the dogs inside."

"You children stay inside with me and do what Daddy says," Anna told them.

While Anna remained behind with the children, Gene, Harry and the farmhands stepped out onto the front porch to access the damage. The sun was shining bright once again, but the air was cool and crisp—almost chilly. Hail stones the size of golf balls covered the ground like a thin blanket of snow. The smell of fresh pinesap filled the air from the broken and twisted pine trees. Sirens began wailing in the distance. Dozens of trees surrounding the farm and across the road lay sprawled over the ground and blocked the highway leading into town. The two trees that remained were the enormous one hundred year-old oaks flanking each side of old plantation house. They stepped off the front porch and out into the front yard as they continued to evaluate the destruction. Miraculously, the house itself managed to escape unscathed other than some missing shingles. A large limb from one of the oaks beside the house had fallen on top of Harry's truck, caving in the roof and knocking out the windshield. Other than some minor damage here and there, the property seemed to remain pretty much intact, with the exception of one thing.

"Harry, it looks like you're gonna be staying with us for a while," Gene said, staring at the spot where his trailer had once sat. "It touched down right beside us and got your trailer."

Harry stood beside Gene, staring in disbelief. "That's the way those damn things are," he said, shaking his head. "They just dip down out of the sky and take whatever they want."

"Well, it looks like it wanted your trailer,' Gene said. "That should make Anna happy. She's been wanting you out of there and in the house with us for a long time. I guess she finally got her wish."

Of the four counties hit by the twister that day, Barrow County managed to escape with the least amount of damage and no fatalities. Only some minor damage was done to the carpet mill, but a trailer park and fire station weren't so lucky. Chattooga County was the hardest hit with three fatalities and over two million dollars worth of damage.

For Anna, it was a day she would never forget. Within a few brief moments, she learned she had lost her best friend and at the same time came close to losing her home and family. The following Sunday, she took her husband and children to church for the first time since she and Gene married. She even made Harry and Joey accompany them. Anna informed all of them that they might as well get used to it because they would be going to church each and every Sunday from now on.

Three days after the tornado had touched down in Myrick, Cassie Pittman was laid to rest beside her mother in the cemetery behind a small Negro church on a red dirt road. Cassie had died from a drug overdose after partying all night with a couple of men she met at the strip club where she danced. Anna and Gene paid their last respects and were the only white couple at the services. They brought two and a half year-old Nicky with them. Anna had, from the beginning, been honest with their daughter and explained that Cassie was her birth mother and they had adopted her. Without telling the child who her biological father was, Anna told Nicky that he had been white and that he died not long after she was born. She explained the circumstances of how and why Cassie had agreed to allow them to adopt her. She also gave Nicky the choice of whether or not to divulge her true ancestry. No one knew of Nicky's background except Anna and Gene's immediate family. People just assumed that Nicky had been born to Anna and Gene.

Perhaps the reason Anna had been so open with their daughter was due to the fact her own mother had been so deceptive with her and never divulged to Anna the identity of her real father. Catherine had died with that secret and left Anna with many unanswered questions. That quandary would eat at Anna everyday of her life as she wondered who her real father had been.

On the way home from the funeral, Nicky lay in the backseat, drifting off to sleep. She was past due her afternoon nap. Gene had taken off a couple of hours from the farm and left one of the farmhands in charge so that he would be able to attend the funeral. It had rained heavily the past few days causing the dirt road to become slippery and muddy. Their car slid and fishtailed as Gene maneuvered the steering wheel to keep the automobile between the ditches on each side of the Georgia red clay road.

"Gene, I've been thinking. Now that we have Joey and Harry with us and the baby is on the way, we could use some extra space," Anna suggested as they drove home. "Why don't we fix up the basement and put a couple of bedrooms and maybe an extra bath down there? Joey and Harry could have their own apartment. I figure since we have to make some repairs anyway from the storm damage, we could go ahead and renovate the basement."

Gene scratched his head vigorously the way he did whenever he was uneasy or approached with something that made him uncomfortable.

"It's not like we don't have the money anymore to improve the house," she continued. "I'm getting plenty of money from the carpet mill now. The house is big enough for all of us. The basement would give Joey and Harry an entire floor all to themselves. We could even put in a little kitchen down there."

"That's fine," Gene replied. "I'm sure Joey would love it, but I wouldn't count on Harry spending one night down there."

"Why?" Anna insisted. "Gene what the hell is it about that damn basement that has Harry so spooked? He's like a kid afraid of the dark. All I've heard since the day you brought me to that house is, 'Don't go in the basement. You'll fall down the stairs and hurt yourself. It's dirty and musky down there.' And it's no such thing! Now I want to know what's with you and Harry not wanting anybody down there."

Anna stared at her husband demanding an answer once and for all while Gene shifted his weight nervously behind the wheel. "Anna," he began with a heavy sigh. "I didn't want to tell you this because I was afraid it would scare you and you'd never want to go near the house again. It scared the beJesus out of Harry. That's the real reason he moved out of the house and moved that trailer beside it."

Anna's eyes grew wide with anticipation. "What are you talking about? What's in the house?"

"It's not in the house exactly," Gene explained. "It's the basement." He glanced over his shoulder at their daughter asleep on the backseat. He didn't want to upset her by what he was about to tell her mother.

'What's in the basement?" Anna asked.

"Well, they were, but they're not anymore. I solved the problem, but I couldn't convince Harry." Gene paused. He knew more than anyone how much Anna loved that old plantation house and he didn't want to spoil her passion for their home.

Anna was growing impatient with Gene. She had to know once and for all why Harry didn't want anyone going into the basement. "Gene, if you don't stop beating around the bush. For God's sake, just tell me—"

"There were some snakes dening down there at one time," he said finally, keeping his voice low, trying not to wake Nicky.

"Snakes?" Anna replied, surprisingly calm.

Gene nodded. "I didn't want to tell you because I was afraid you'd never go near the house again and I knew how much you always loved that place. But Harry went in the basement one day, years ago, and found black snakes crawling all over the place down there. He ran back up the stairs, slammed the door, packed up his clothes and went to stay in a motel down the road until he could get that trailer set up beside the house. He never went back in there again after that. Then, when I started working for him, he told me about it so I went down there and found out where they were coming in. They were getting in through a broken basement window and had started making a den down there and hatching out. There must have been a dozen or more down there."

"How did you get rid of them?"

"I went down there with a garden hoe and a big croaker sack. I just started huntin' for 'em and rounded them all up and turned them lose in the woods down the road."

"You didn't kill them?"

"No. They're not poisonous. They can't hurt you. They're just black snakes. Some people call them Indigo snakes. They can bite you if you mess with them, but they can't kill you. Actually, they're good to have around because they kill rats and mice and other poisonous snakes. As a matter of fact, I put one in the milking barn and another up at the pole barn to keep down the rat population. Joey and me used to play with them when we were kids. I had one as a pet. They're more afraid of you than you are of them."

"I doubt that," Anna said.

"Anyway, that's why Harry didn't want you or the kids going down there. I tired to convince him I got all of them and assured him I fixed the window so no more could get in, but he was always afraid there were still some down there."

Anna remained silent for a moment, staring out the car window. "Are you sure there's no more down there?"

"I'm positive. There hasn't been a snake in that basement for ten years."

"When I went down there once awhile back, I found a snake skin in the fireplace," she told him.

"Well, I'm not surprised to hear that because there were quite a few down there at the time. I'm sure they left a few snake skins behind here and there. But there aren't any more snakes down there. I made sure of it when we were renovating the house. I went down there and checked the place out good. There's nothing there that can hurt you."

Anna studied her husband for a moment. "Are you sure they can't hurt you? Are you sure they're not poisonous?"

He shook his head. "No. They're not a venomous snake. They don't have any venom. It would be like a cat bite if they did bite you. But you don't have to worry. They're none in the house now."

"Couldn't they fall down the chimney from the trees beside the house?"

"I guess they could, but I keep the flues closed in the summer and they hibernate in the winter so I doubt you have anything to worry about. Believe me, if I thought for one minute that you or the kids were in any danger, I wouldn't let you stay in that house one night."

Anna silently thought to herself and glanced over her shoulder at Nicky sleeping soundly in the backseat. "Well, I didn't let those thugs run me out of my house when they set fire to it and we've managed to survive a tornado, so I'm not going to be scared out of my home by some snakes. If you say we have nothing to be afraid of, then I trust you. That settles it," she said finally. "We're remodeling the basement and taking it back from the snakes. But don't tell Joey about it, because he might not want to move in down there if he knew."

"Don't worry about Joey," Gene chuckled. "He's the one that taught me not to fear them and which ones were dangerous. He won't be afraid to stay down there. But I still say you're not going to get Harry down there for love nor money."

"That's fine. He can have the downstairs bedroom. In a way, I'm glad that's all it was because I was afraid you were going to tell me Ollie's spirit was inhabiting the basement."

Gene laughed. "No. Nothing like that."

"That's good, because I think she's already in the house with us."

Gene turned and glanced at his wife with a curious look. "What do you mean?"

"I haven't mentioned anything to you about it, but I've had some strange experiences at times when I was alone in the house."

"Yeah? Like what?"

Anna smiled. "Well, like seeing things out of the corner of my eye when I'm at the kitchen sink washing dishes or upstairs making up the beds. I see a lot of shadows, especially upstairs. Sometimes, I smell honeysuckle real strong."

"So? There's nothing unusual about that. There's honeysuckle all around the house," Gene replied.

"Not in the dead of winter with all the doors and windows shut. Besides, Harry has told me that Ollie's favorite perfume was honeysuckle and that she wore it all the time."

"Anything else strange happen?" he asked, looking straight ahead.

"Well, I have been sitting in the den before or at the desk doing my paper work and all of a sudden Greta or Gretchen will start staring at something behind me and begin growling like they see someone standing there. I'll turn around and there will be nothing there."

"Hmm." Gene thought for a moment, then asked, "You ever been in bed and it felt like someone sat down on the foot of the bed, but when you looked up, there was nobody in the room but you?"

Anna looked at him. "Oh, that's happened to me a lot."

"Me, too," he replied.

They looked at each other for a moment, and then continued to drive in silence for another mile or so.

"Well," Gene said finally. "Whatever or whoever it is hasn't hurt us yet and we've been in the house going on four years now."

"That's right," Anna agreed. "Besides, if it is Ollie's spirit, she may be watching over us like a guardian angel. Maybe that's why the house didn't catch fire that night and maybe that's why the tornado got Harry's trailer instead of the house."

"Could be. Maybe she wanted Harry in the house with her," Gene laughed.

"Maybe it'll be *his* bed she'll be visiting next time," Anna smiled.

"Yeah, maybe it's best Joey does go live in the basement and we let Harry have the ground floor all to himself. Maybe Ollie has it planned that way for a reason."

They both laughed. "We should be ashamed of ourselves," Anna said. "Here we are leaving a funeral and we're laughing on the way home."

"Maybe Cassie will be next to pay us a visit," Gene laughed. "You never know."

Anna reached over and gave her husband a playful slap on the arm. "You're awful," she said.

By Christmas that year, Joey had moved into the basement apartment that Gene had renovated for him. The large basement now consisted of two spare bedrooms, a bathroom, a spacious living area and a full-size kitchen. The apartment was larger than the tiny shack Joey had shared with their father and it was furnished much nicer.

Harry however, refused to remain in the house with them. Instead, he stayed only until he was able to move another single trailer in the same location as his other trailer home. Despite Anna's begging and pleading for him to stay on, he insisted that the house belonged to them and he would feel like an intruder. She even confessed that Gene had told her about the snakes in the basement and that she felt neither afraid nor threatened and neither should he. Still, he insisted on moving into the trailer next door. Anna got the feeling that it wasn't the reptiles at all that kept Harry from living there, but Ollie's memory. It simply hurt too much knowing the house was meant to be his and Ollie's. She decided not to pursue the subject and as long as Harry was happy next door, that was all that mattered.

One more addition was made to the property following the tornado damage. Anna had Gene construct an elaborate six-foot, curved brick and wrought iron entrance gate at the end of the driveway with a large sign announcing, *The Porter Plantation est. 1841*. She wanted the world to know that the old plantation house was full of life and a major part of the community. Neither the thugs who tried to burn them out, nor an F-3 tornado, or snakes, or ghosts had managed to run her off the property that she so dearly loved. Nor would anything ever succeed in forcing her to leave the old plantation house she fell in love with as a child. It belonged to her now and come hell or high water, it would remain hers.

# Chapter Sixteen

It had been over two years since Angel had taken charge of her father's old cotton mill and created her own dynasty. The carpet mill was thriving and making its three owners very wealthy women. Angel was forced to hire fifty more employees just to keep up with production and she was already looking at a location in nearby Dalton to expand and open a second carpet manufacturer.

By now, with the birth of her fifth child, Anna was the proud mother of three sons and two girls. Nicky was nearly four years-old, the twins were three, Joey had just celebrated his second birthday and little Harold, whom they named after Harry and nicknamed Hal, was ten months old. Amy was also a mother now, with the birth of her twin sons, Charles, Jr. and Toby, who were born only a month after Anna delivered Hal. The family continued to grow in numbers and prosper financially. Anna and Gene had been married five years now while Amy would soon celebrate her sixth anniversary with Chuck. Amy's marriage, however, was beginning to show some serious signs of trouble, and both Angel and Anna was concerned she and Chuck may be headed for a divorce.

Angel decided it was time she and Anna put their heads together and try to think of a way to stop their sister from destroying her life and marriage with alcohol. One Saturday morning, Angel asked Anna to go with her to Walker County to see an antique dealer. She was interested in an old desk for her office. Angel and Tanya arrived early that morning at Anna's house where Tanya planned to stay and help Harry look after the children while Anna went with her sister. They would use their time together to discuss what steps should be taken to help Amy get off the booze.

"She'll never admit she needs help," Anna told Angel as they left the farm and headed toward Walker County. "She doesn't believe she has a drinking problem. She thinks she has it under control."

"Under control my ass," Angel said, lighting up a cigarette. "She drank the entire time she was pregnant with the twins and she's already been pulled over once for drunk driving. If it hadn't been for Chuck's father getting her out of that, she could of had her driver's license suspended or spent the night in jail."

"And she could wind up killing herself or someone else," Anna added. "I wish Chuck had never given her that Corvette to drive. She flies in that thing like a bat out of hell. I rode with her a couple of weeks ago and she scared the living daylights out of me. And she was cold sober. I don't want to think how she drives after she's had a few drinks."

"Something has got to be done, that's for sure. Chuck is a good man and he is crazy about Amy and those two babies, but he can't continue to put up with her crap much longer. The first time he catches her cheating on him, he's liable to kill her. Do you know what she told me?"

"What?" Anna replied.

"She said the twins weren't really Chuck's."

Anna's jaw dropped. "What? Oh, that can't be true. When did she tell you that?"

"A couple of months ago. You know neither of the boys look a thing like Chuck or anybody in his family."

"But that doesn't mean that they're not his," Anna said.

"Well, apparently Amy feels certain they aren't," Angel insisted.

"She never mentioned anything like that to me. Who does she think the father is, if it isn't Chuck?'

"Robert Ely."

"The attorney?" Anna asked with surprise.

Angel nodded. "Yep."

"He's the one that handled Mom and Dad's will."

"Well, obviously he handled more than Amy's interest in their will,"

Amy surmised. "She started seeing him right after that. Of course, she's been with a few others before and after her affair with Ely, but he was the one she saw on a more regular basis."

"Oh, my God. I can't believe Amy would do something like that. I had a suspicion she was running around on Chuck, but I never dreamed she would have another man's baby." Anna grew silent for a moment and then added, "She did the same thing Mother did. She's followed right in her footsteps. Doesn't she realize how devastated I was to learn Dad wasn't my real father? Does she know what she's going to put her sons through if they ever find out Chuck isn't their real father? What is she thinking?"

"That's just it," Angel said. "She's drinking instead of thinking about the consequences of her actions."

"Chuck doesn't know?" Anna asked. "Does he still believe the boys are his?"

"Of course," Angel replied. "She told me she would never let Chuck know the twins weren't his. But she's getting child support from Ely."

"Child support?"

"Well, actually it's hush money if you want to know the truth," Angel said. "Amy threatened to go to Ely's wife if he didn't pay her a thousand a month."

"What? Oh, that's crazy, Angel. That doesn't even sound like something Amy would do. What does she think would happen if she went to Ely's wife and told her and she turned around and went to Chuck and told him that her husband was the real father of his two sons?"

"Well, obviously she thinks she knows Ely well enough to believe he'd rather pay her child support than to take the chance of her going to his wife."

"But why would she do a thing like that? It's not like she needs the money. Chuck is a millionaire several times over and she's making a good salary at the mill. She doesn't need Ely's money."

"Well, if the truth were really known, I think she's doing it out of revenge. Ely was trying to break off the affair and Amy wasn't ready for it to end so you know the old saying, 'hell hath no fury like a woman scorned.'"

"Angel, if you weren't telling me this yourself, I would never believe it. I'd swear it was all a lie. Why would Amy do such a thing to Chuck and their children? It doesn't even sound like her."

"She told me if Ely wanted to play, he was going to have to pay. He tried to get her to have an abortion, but she refused."

"So she just let Chuck believe the boys were his?"

"That's right," Angel replied. "And let's just pray Chuck never finds out different."

"He would leave her for certain," Anna said.

"Let's just hope that's *all* he would do. He could kill her. Somehow we've got to get her into a rehab center. Or at least get her checked into a hospital to get her dried out. She's been out of control long enough. She's drinking too much, taking too many pills and driving too fast. If she keeps on, she's going to kill herself."

"What can we do?" Anna asked. "She's not going to check herself into a hospital. You know that."

"I'm going to talk to Dr. Outler. He's been our family doctor since we were kids. Maybe he can advise us on what steps to take."

"Should we talk to Chuck? If we're planning on having her admitted to a hospital, we really need to get him involved. He *is* her husband," Anna suggested.

Angel flicked her cigarette out the window and thought for a moment. "Okay. Why don't we do this? Why don't we go pay Chuck a visit at the car lot after we leave the antique shop? Amy will be home with the twins and this will be our best opportunity to get Chuck alone."

"Okay, that sounds like a good idea," Anna agreed.

As they continued driving, they passed a chain gang along the side of the road with a pot-bellied guard in sunglasses and a shotgun slung over his shoulder.

"Hey, wasn't that Jeff Morrison back there?" Angel asked as they passed by.

"Who's Jeff Morrison?"

"Oh, that's right, he was a couple of years ahead of you. He was a guy I graduated high school with. We used to hang out together between classes. Wonder what he did to get put on the chain gang," Angel wondered aloud.

"I don't know," Anna replied. "But it's bad when you pass a chain gang on the side of the road and recognize somebody you know."

They both laughed. "Yeah, but at least it wasn't a relative," Angel said.

"Well, it might be if we don't get Amy away from the bottle and she winds up killing someone in that car of hers."

Just before they reached the Walker County line, Angel hit her sister with yet another bit of shocking news. Only this time, Anna was actually as thrilled, as she was surprised.

"Anna, there's something else I've been wanting to tell you before you hear it from somebody else," Angel began.

Anna looked at her sister with dread. "Don't tell me *you're* pregnant."

Angel laughed. "No, but I think you'll be just as surprised by this if I told you I was."

"Well, what is it?" Anna asked, unable to stand the suspense.

"Things haven't been so good between Tanya and me lately. It's not working out for us. She wants me to move back to Atlanta and I'm not about to do that now. Not with the mill doing as well as it is. Besides, this is my home and where my family is and," she paused. "I've met someone else."

"Really? Who is she?"

"It's not a she. It's a man."

"A man? Really?" Anna's voice was filled with excitement. "Who is he? What's his name? Where did you meet him?"

"Well, first of all, you already know him. He's a good friend of your husband's."

"Who?" Anna asked.

"Red Moore."

"Red? Oh, my gosh! I can't believe it! Angel, I think that's wonderful. But I would have never thought the two of you would ever have anything in common. You're such opposites."

"Well, haven't you ever heard opposites attract?" Angel replied, flashing her sister a sly smile. "Ever since he came to work at the mill, we found we were attracted to one another and we began talking and then had lunch together a few times and one thing led to another and now we're seeing each other."

"Oh, I'm so glad. I really am. I can't wait to tell Gene. He'll be so surprised. But what about Tanya? Does she know you're seeing Red?"

"Yeah, she knows. She's already decided to move back to Atlanta. I told her that wasn't necessary, that she was welcomed to continue working at the mill. She's got a good job there, but she feels about Atlanta the way I do about Myrick. She says I was the only thing keeping her here anyway. Myrick is too small and quiet for her. All her family is back in Atlanta anyway."

Anna was so happy that Angel had found a man. It was difficult to accept her sister's lesbian lifestyle, but if that was what made her happy, then so be it. Anna couldn't have been happier with Angel's choice of man. She liked Red a lot. He was her husband's best friend and a real nice guy. She couldn't ask for a better choice for a brother-in-law.

They finally arrived at the antique shop in Mt. Carmel and were greeted by Tom Webber, the owner. Webber had suggested that Angel bring her younger sister with her the next time she visited his shop. He had even asked about Anna and for some reason seemed interested in meeting her. Angel found his interest a little odd, but passed it off as just plain old southern hospitality.

"Tom, this is my sister, Anna Longhorn," Angel said, introducing them. "Anna, this is Tom Webber."

Webber was an exceptionally handsome man in his late forties with salt and pepper hair and a thick dark mustache. His dark brown eyes were penetrating and intense. He was of medium height and build and impeccably dressed in an expensive, custom tailored suit. He spoke with an educated and refined southern accent. It was obvious Webber was a charming man with extraordinary class and character.

"Hello. Nice to meet you, Mr. Webber," Anna replied politely, extending her right hand.

Webber looked at Anna as if he were appraising a very rare and precious gem. He studied her carefully as he took her hand and gently shook it, continuing to hold it just long enough to cause Anna some uneasiness.

"The pleasure is all mine, I assure you," Webber replied with a faint smile. "May I say that everything I've heard about the Coleman girls being the most stunning attractions in Barrow County, are certainly true. Mt. Carmel should be so fortunate."

Anna smiled and blushed slightly. "Why, thank you. You're too kind."

"Not at all," Webber replied, not taking his eyes off her. "Can I offer you ladies a drink? Perhaps a glass of white wine or a little Mint Julep?"

"No, thank you. None for me," Angel replied.

"Thank you, but I don't drink," Anna said, declining his offer.

"Then perhaps a lemonade or a glass of iced tea?"

"No thank you, Tom," Angel replied. "We don't have long. There's some business we have to tend to when we get back to Myrick, so we're in kind of a hurry."

"Oh, I'm sorry to hear that. Very well, then, I have the desk in the back room where we do our refinishing and restorations. If you will follow me, we'll go take a look at it."

They followed Webber to the back of his elegant antique shop where several priceless pieces of furniture were in the midst of restoration.

"Oh, that's just what I've been looking for," Angel said the moment she saw the old mahogany desk. "It's beautiful."

"It certainly is," Anna agreed. "And it looks so heavy."

"Oh, that it is," Webber, agreed. "It's solid mahogany. The only veneer is on the front drawers. The rest is solid wood." As he spoke, his eyes remained fixed on Anna.

Angel continued to inquire about the desk and negotiate a price. Webber however, remained more interested in Angel's younger sister than her bid for the desk. Growing increasingly more uncomfortable with his attention, Anna began strolling about the showroom admiring the beautiful old antiques. Finally, Angel and her dealer reached an agreement and Webber returned to the showroom to write up a sales receipt and make arrangements for a delivery date. He saw Anna admiring an old vanity table with a triple mirror.

"I see you're a connoisseur of fine antique furniture as well," he remarked to Anna.

"I have to confess I know very little about them," Anna replied. "But I know what I like when I see it."

"Do you like the dressing table?" he asked.

"Oh, yes. It's beautiful. And I could certainly use it in my bedroom. I have a smaller one downstairs, but it's not nearly as large or as nice as this one. How much is it?"

"Well, that piece is solid cherry," Webber explained. "It's hand carved with no veneer."

"That means it's worth a fortune," Angel whispered, leaning over her sister's shoulder. "Just guessing, I'd say about five figures."

"Close," Webber replied. "You do seem to know your antiques, Angela."

"Just an educated guess," Angel grinned.

Webber finished writing up the bill of sale and delivery slip while Angel and Anna continued to stroll through the shop, admiring the furniture and collectables. Anna paused once again to admire the vanity table.

"I'll make you a killer deal on that vanity," Webber said, walking over to where Anna stood. "I'll even waive the delivery fee."

"If it's five figures, it would be a *killer deal* when my husband found out," Anna told him.

"Oh, I see," he replied. "I take it your husband doesn't appreciate fine heirlooms."

"No, it's not that so much as he is a very frugal man. He grew up very poor and he's always had to struggle for the bare necessities, therefore he thinks anything that isn't a necessity is a waste."

"But you're making your own money now," Angel interjected. "You don't need his approval or permission to buy anything you damn well please."

"Oh, but I couldn't afford anything as expensive as that," she assured her sister.

"Perhaps if you brought your husband by and let him look at it, he might change his mind once he saw the fine quality and workmanship," Webber suggested.

Anna smiled. "No, I'm afraid he would still insist it was way too much money. He would just tell me to go to a furniture chain and buy something that wasn't so expensive. Besides, Mother's Day has already come and gone and my birthday just passed so I can't use a special occasion as an excuse for such an extravagance."

Angel glanced at her watch. "Well, I hate to rush, but we really need to be getting back to Myrick."

"You're right," Anna agreed. "It was nice meeting you, Mr. Webber. You have a nice shop with a lot of lovely things."

"Why thank you, but please, call me Tom," he replied, reaching out to shake her hand once more. "I do hope you'll come back again soon. Bring your husband next time. I would like to met him." He continued to hold her hand and make direct eye contact, which made Anna uncomfortable.

"Well, I would," she said, removing her hand from his grasp. "But my husband runs a dairy and cattle farm and that makes it difficult for him to take much time off. He refers to his job as a 'twenty-four hour, seven day a week ball and chain.'"

"I see. Your husband is a land owner?"

"Well, not exactly. He overseas a farm for a landowner and dairyman in Barrow County. Harry Porter is his name."

"Oh, yes. I'm familiar with that name. The Porters and the Barrows owned that entire county at one time."

"Now the Colemans and the Porters do," Angel added with a smile.

"Yes, you're right," Webber grinned.

"We really have to be going," Angel insisted. "Thanks for everything, Tom. I'll be in touch."

Webber followed them to their car and opened the door for Anna. When they left, Angel couldn't help having a little fun with her younger sister.

"Well, you certainly seemed to make an impression on Mr. Webber. I thought he was going to follow us back home there for a minute. He followed you around like a puppy."

"He was really very nice, but he was beginning to make me a little uncomfortable," Anna confessed.

"Gene had better look out. He might have some serious competition there."

"I doubt that," Anna replied. "He's old enough to be my father."

By the time they arrived back in Myrick and drove to Chuck's Chevrolet dealership, he had already left for lunch. Disappointed that they had missed the opportunity to talk with him in private, Angel drove

Anna home and they decided to try and get in touch with their brother-in-law on Monday when Amy would be at the mill.

Unfortunately, Anna and Angel's plans to meet with Chuck concerning their sister's drinking problem never materialized. That same afternoon, after deciding to go home for lunch, Chuck Willis took the back way home and happened to see his wife's red Corvette convertible parked behind Myrick's only motel. He passed by the motel, brushing it off as coincidental that a car resembling his wife's just happened to be in town. However, he quickly changed his mind after arriving home to discover neither Amy nor her car was there. She had dropped the twins off with Chuck's mother and met a man at the motel. Chuck pulled into the motel parking lot and drove around back where his wife's sports car was parked. He got out and walked around to the office where he learned his wife and a gentleman had checked in about an hour earlier. In a jealous rage, Chuck kicked in the motel room door and caught Amy in bed with a man who worked at the carpet mill. What happened then made headlines in the local newspaper and sent the mill worker to the hospital and Amy to her attorney with two black eyes.

Chuck was arrested that afternoon for assault and battery and taken to the Barrow County jail. He called his father to post his bail. By the time he returned home, he found Amy and their nine-month-old twins gone. It didn't take him long, however, to find them. They were at the first place he looked. Coleman Hill. His sister-in-law, who refused him entrance, greeted him at the front door. Angel explained that she understood perfectly how he felt but under the circumstances she didn't feel comfortable allowing him to see her sister at that time and suggested he return later after a respectable cooling off period. Chuck agreed and left to drown his miseries at the only bar in town. He remained there until his brother-in-law and Red Moore came looking for him, upon Anna's request, and escorted him back to Gene's house to sleep it off. Red followed them back to the farm in Chuck's car.

For the next nine months, Amy and Chuck remained locked in a nasty divorce and custody battle over their two sons. Finally, out of regard for their children, Chuck surrendered his fight for full custody and agreed to a joint custody. He also allowed Amy to take possession of their home and two brand new automobiles. Unfortunately, their six-year marriage ended bitterly, while Amy's drinking and illicit affairs continued.

# Chapter Seventeen

Anna had just finished feeding her five children their breakfast and was washing up the morning dishes when the phone rang.

"Hello," she answered.

"Hello," replied the friendly, yet unfamiliar male voice on the other end. "Could I speak with Anna, please?"

"This is she."

"Anna, this is Tom Webber. I hope you remember me."

"Oh, why yes, I remember you Mr. Webber. How are you?"

"I'm fine. And you?"

"Very well, thank you." Anna couldn't understand the reason behind his call. It had been almost a year since she and Angel had driven to Mr. Webber's antique shop in Mt. Carmel, and she hadn't given him another thought since that day.

"I just wanted to call and wish you a very happy Mother's Day," he said.

"Well, thank you." Anna sensed that wasn't the only reason for Webber's unexpected phone call. He barely knew her. Why would he go to the trouble to make a long distance call just to wish *her* a happy Mother's Day?

"You also have a birthday coming up next month, don't you?"

"Uh, why yes. And how would you know that?"

"I remember you mentioning that your birthday had just passed when you visited my shop last year with Angel."

Anna remained silent.

"Did you ever speak to your husband about the dressing table you saw in my shop that day?"

"No. No, I never mentioned it to him to be quite honest," she replied. So, the vanity table was the reason for the unexpected phone call. He wanted to make a sale. She was now annoyed by his persistence.

"Would you still be interested in the one I have?"

"Well, it is a beautiful piece of furniture, but I know my husband and he would never consider allowing me to spend that much money on a dressing table."

"Perhaps a little negotiation might persuade him to change his mind. I would really like for you to own it. I know how much you admired it."

"Mr. Webber, if we were looking at five figures before, I'm sure if you came down to even four, it would still be more than I could afford," she told him quite frankly. "It's way out of my price range."

Anna sensed another presence in the room and turned around to see Gene standing behind her, listening to her conversation.

"Who are you talking to," he asked.

Anna shook her head and raised a finger to her lips.

"I tell you what," Webber said finally. "Why don't you and your husband drop by my shop at your earliest convenience and we'll see if we can reach a mutual agreement on the price. I feel sure I could bring that price down to one you would consider a real bargain. I would really like to see you have that vanity."

"I'm not at all sure that would be possible. But I will consider your offer and perhaps discuss it with my husband. Thank you for calling." Anna was anxious to end their conversation. Since the first day they'd met Webber had made her uncomfortable and now she found his phone call odd and unnecessary.

"I appreciate you calling, Mr. Webber. And perhaps we will speak again. Yes. Thank you for calling." Anna hung up the phone and turned around to face her husband.

"Who was that?" Gene asked.

"That was Tom Webber. He's an antique dealer from Mt. Carmel."

"How do you know him? Why is he calling you?" Gene was curious why his wife was receiving a phone call from a man she never mentioned until now and especially someone he didn't know.

"I met him last year when I went with Angel to Mt. Carmel to look at a desk she brought at his antique shop."

"What's he doing calling you?"

"While I was at his shop I happened to see a dressing table I admired and he just called to see if I was still interested in it."

"So, get it," Gene told her.

"It's way too expensive," she said.

"How much is he asking?"

"I don't really know. He never would tell me how much he wanted for it, but Angel guessed five figures."

"What! For a goddamn piece of furniture? I wouldn't pay that much for a new car or truck. That son-of-a-bitch is crazy!"

"Calm down," Anna told her husband. "I'm not even considering buying it. I didn't call him, he called me. In fact, I hadn't even given the matter anymore thought until he just called me out of the blue and wanted to know if I was still interested. Once Angel told me it was that much money, I knew better than to even bring it up to you."

Gene shrugged. "Okay. Good. Then I don't have to tell you no. Subject closed." He was a jealous man and fiercely guarded what he considered sacred—wife, his children, his home and his marriage. He didn't like strange men calling his wife for *any* reason. Amy's infidelities had only served to reinforce his keen awareness of what was going on within his own home at all times. He insisted on knowing where his wife and children was every minute of the day. That was, however, the typical mentality of most southern men in Gene's walk of life. It was *his* pick-up truck, *his* dog and *his* woman. Anna knew her husband was defensive and protective of what he considered his property. She also knew he had a nasty temper when threatened or provoked. She hoped that would be the last she would hear from Mr. Webber.

"I have to run to the feed store in town this morning, do you need anything while I'm there?" Gene asked.

"No, I can't think of anything. How long will you be gone?"

"Just long enough to pick up some sweet feed. Why?"

"Well, do you have a minute before you go because there's something I've been wanting to discuss with you?"

"Yeah, what is it?"

"Well," Anna began. "I've been thinking. Harry has been awfully good to us, letting us live in this house, practically turning it over to us. He paid all our medical bills for years until I finally started working for Angel and, well—" she paused, not knowing how Gene would think about what she was about to say.

"I just feel like we need to try and repay him for everything he's done for us over the years."

"I don't have any money to give him," Gene replied with a shrug. "He pays me just enough to take care of my family. It's not like I'm rolling in money."

"I know that. But I have some money now from the mill and after all, he did pay my hospital bills when I was in the wreck and even before we were married when my father put me in the hospital. And he bought me my first car and I just feel bad taking all that from him and now that we're on our feet, not offering to repay him for at least some of his generosity."

"So what are you saying? You want him to give you an itemized list of every dime he's ever spent on us and pay him back? That would mount up to thousands of dollars. The way I see it, whatever he spent on our medical bills, he owed it to us because he only paid me enough to barely make ends meet. I've worked my ass off for him since I was a kid. I feel like whatever he did for us, he owed it to me."

"Gene, I'm not asking you to repay him anything out of your own pocket," Anna explained. "I'm willing to pay him out of the money I'm getting from the mill. It's only right that we at least offer."

"No," Gene insisted. "It was only right that he gave us this house to live in and paid our medical expenses because he never provided any medical coverage and didn't pay me what I was worth. The money you get from the mill should be spent on the kids and *us*—not given away to somebody who doesn't need it."

"But I'm not *giving* it away. I feel like I would only be doing what was right."

"What's *right*, is that you keep whatever money you make in the family and use it for us. Harry Porter doesn't need your money. He's got plenty of his own, believe me. He's got more money than he could ever spend in his lifetime, if he lived to be a hundred years old. So my answer is no. You're not giving him any money. He doesn't need it, we do."

As Gene started to leave the kitchen, he turned and faced his wife. "Do I make myself clear?" he said finally.

"Yes. Very," she replied.

"Good. I'll be back in a little while."

As she watched her husband walk out the door, she couldn't help thinking how he had changed since she first met him. He had grown somewhat hardened and almost bitter. Or perhaps he had always been resentful toward those who seemed more fortunate than him. Over the years Anna saw her husband grow increasingly bitter toward his life and the direction it had taken. It had nothing to do with her and the children, for he worshiped the ground they walked on. They were his greatest and proudest accomplishments. Yet he wanted more from life. He wanted wealth—enough to become financially independent so that he would never again be forced to do backbreaking work for just enough money to survive. Unfortunately, like many others in his situation, he had become locked in to his way of life and just as a man drowning in quicksand; he would never be able to free himself from his own destiny. He was doomed to work long, hard hours for every penny he would ever earn, never quite getting ahead or being allowed any of the luxuries that seemed to come so easily to those more fortunate than him. Even worse, it was the final realization that he would *never* have the opportunity to enjoy those same luxuries or attain even the slightest wealth that would cause him to become increasingly bitter as the years continued to pass him by. Sadly, that was life, which had a way of stirring bitterness and regret in those who grew old without ever achieving their dreams.

Eleven months after Angel began seeing Red Moore, they married in a June ceremony at Porter Plantation. For a second time, Harry Porter walked another Coleman sister down the isle and gave her away in marriage. Among the thirty or so wedding guests was Chuck Willis, whom everyone still considered part of the family and who divided much of his time between his former sister-in-laws' homes. His two closest friends were Gene and Red. He continued to enjoy many a Sunday dinner at the Longhorn home as well as participate in holiday festivities there. The only obvious change was that Chuck was no longer legally married to Amy. Regardless, he was still very much a part of their family.

Following their wedding and brief honeymoon, Angel and Red returned to Coleman Hill where they made their home. Four months later, Angel would discover she was pregnant with their first child. Despite all the sexual, physical and emotional abuse, the three Coleman sisters were forced to endure as children, all but one emerged remarkably unscathed with a sound marriage and contented life. Apparently, it had been Amy who suffered the most damage from their abusive childhood and who carried the deepest emotional scars. Alcohol and men continued to dominate and destroy her life. She succeeded in alienating the one man who loved and cared for her more than anyone else. Truth be known, Chuck Willis *still* cared for his ex-wife despite their bitter divorce. And he would always love and care for her, not just because she was the mother of his children, but also because she had been the love of his life from the very beginning. He had taken his marriage vows far more seriously than his wife, who had only used him as a means of escape from the clutches of an abusive father. She didn't love him when she married him and that lack of emotional attachment continued throughout their brief six-year marriage. During that time, Amy had cheated on her husband with a string of men, while Chuck remained faithful and loyal. He was a good husband and provider and a wonderful father. Their divorce broke Anna's heart, for she had looked on Chuck as the brother she never had. For that reason, she refused to allow his status within the family to change. Just because he was no longer legally married to her sister, didn't mean he no longer remained emotionally attached to their family. Both Anna and Angel made it perfectly clear he was always welcome in their home and was included in all their social gatherings. This made things somewhat uncomfortable for Amy, but that was something she would have to learn to deal with.

Not long after Angel and Red returned from their Bahamas honeymoon, they joined their family at Porter Plantation for Anna and

Gene's annual July fourth celebration, complete with fireworks. Each year, around April, Gene and Red would make a quick trip across the Tennessee state line, where fireworks were legal, and purchase several boxes to ignite on the fourth of July. Everyone in the family, along with Porter's farmhands, was invited to the celebration. It would begin around noon and wouldn't end until well after dark. There was enough food and beverage for an army. Gene barbequed a whole hog, while Red grilled steaks, hamburgers and hotdogs on the charcoal grill. Several gallons of home churned ice cream topped off the feast. Everyone gathered beneath the huge oak tree beside the house in lawn chairs and lounges and around a couple of picnic tables. Gene, Red, Chuck, Joey and Harry spent much of the early afternoon around the barbeque grill and ice cream churns, while Anna and her sisters gathered in the kitchen preparing mountains of potato salad, baked beans and Brunswick stew. Meanwhile, the seven children played freely under the adults' watchful supervision. After spending hours of fun creating loud popping noises by tossing Maypops to the ground, beside the house, Gene delighted the children by riding them around the yard on the John Deer farm tractor. They all enjoyed another splendid family gathering despite the fact that just three months earlier their close-knit family had just undergone its first, painful divorce.

After the day long celebration had finally come to an end, Amy and her two-year-old sons decided to spend the night at the farm since the children wanted to sleep over with their older cousins. The next morning, when Amy came downstairs, she found Anna in the kitchen stirring a pot of grits to serve the children for breakfast.

"Jesus, what time do you people get up around here?" she asked her sister, as she walked into the kitchen where her two sons sat at the table having breakfast with their five cousins.

"I'm up every morning by three a.m.," Anna replied. "I usually have breakfast on the table no later than three-thirty because Gene has to be at the milking barn by four a.m. Those cows can't wait."

"God, I don't see how you stand it. I'd go nuts if I had to live your life," Amy told her sister. "I'd tell Gene Longhorn he'd have to get up and fix his own damn breakfast. You couldn't pay me to get up in the middle of the night to go in the kitchen and cook."

"It's not so bad. I'm used to it. Gene doesn't want me working outside the home, so this *is* my job."

"I think that husband of yours got a little pissed off at me yesterday," Amy said, walking over to the coffee pot and pouring a cup of coffee.

"You mean about him insisting that you not drink in his house?"

"What the hell is wrong with having a few drinks? It was the fourth of July for Christ's sake. He's so damn controlling and overbearing. I don't see how you live with that man. I wouldn't stay married to him for two seconds."

"Amy, you know how Gene feels about having alcohol around," Anna explained. "He's never drank and he doesn't want his kids around it. He's half Indian and Indians have intolerance to alcohol. They're very susceptible to alcoholism. His father used to drink years ago when Gene and his brother were very young and he remembers his father coming home drunk and slapping their mother around. It left a terrible impression on him. He won't allow alcohol in his house. As long as I've known Gene, I've never seen him take a drink. He threatened to kick Joey out of the house not long ago because he caught him sneaking in a six-pack of beer in his refrigerator downstairs. It's his house and he makes the rules."

"Well, he needs to lighten up a little," Amy sneered.

"Aunt Anna, can Uncle Gene take us for one more ride on the tractor before we have to go home? Please," begged Amy's son, Toby.

"Sweetheart, your Uncle Gene is using the tractor this morning to clear off some pasture land. He's got the bush hog attached to it right now," Anna explained to her nephew. "It's not safe to ride when he's pulling that thing behind it."

"What's a bush hog?" Chuck, Jr. asked.

The boy's older cousin was quick to answer the child's question. "It's a big, flat, round disk with a big old, sharp blade underneath that turns real fast and cuts down trees and shrubs," Gene, Jr. explained.

"Daddy won't let us go anywhere near it when he's got it hooked to the tractor," his brother Joey, added. "He says that blade underneath is razor sharp and can chop up a small pine tree into little pieces."

"Well, can he take it off just long enough to ride us one more time before we go home?" Toby insisted.

"Honey, once your Uncle Gene puts that thing on, it's not that easy to unhook," Anna tried to explain. "He'll give you a ride next time you come out to the farm."

The two boys, who were identical twins, loved riding on the old farm tractor more than anything else. Their uncle spent hours riding them around the farm whenever they came to visit. They each had a toy replica of a John Deer tractor that they carried in their pocket everywhere they went.

"We need to be going anyway," Amy said. "I need to run by the mill and pick up some paperwork I have to look over before Monday morning."

Anna happened to glance over and catch Amy slipping some vodka into her coffee cup from a flask she kept in her purse.

"I see you're off to an early start this morning," Anna told her sister. "Do you really think you need to be doing that when you're about to get in the car with the boys?"

"I need to make up for yesterday," Amy replied.

"Oh, poor thing. It must have been awful for you going without a drink all day."

"It was. In fact, you just may have to celebrate without me next time you have one of your little get-togethers. You might buckle under to your old man's house rules, but I'm not about to," she said, placing the small flask to her lips and downing the last remaining contents.

About that time, Gene walked in through the back door. Amy quickly hid the flask and tucked it back into her purse. Fortunately, for her, he didn't catch her.

"What are you doing back so soon? I thought you'd be busy clearing off the pasture. I didn't think I'd see you again until lunchtime," Anna said.

"Harry just realized he let his blood pressure medicine run out and he needs me to go pick up a new prescription from the pharmacy. I just remembered I left the keys to the truck in my other pants."

"Uh-oh," Anna said. "Were those the pants you wore yesterday?"

"Yes. Why?"

"I just put them in the washing machine."

"You didn't check my pants pockets before you loaded them in the machine?"

"I thought you did. You always empty your pants pockets before you hand them over for me to wash," Anna told her husband. "They could tear up the washing machine if they're still in there."

"Come on, boys," Amy told her sons. "We need to be getting on home. I have to stop by the mill on the way. Tell your Aunt Anna and Uncle Gene what a good time you had and give them a hug before we go."

The children gave their aunt and uncle a big hug and kiss before leaving with their mother. After Anna had seen them out the door, she went back into the laundry room to help Gene find his missing keys.

"Momma, please let us ride on the tractor just once more before we leave," Toby pleaded with his mother, pointing to the big John Deer parked in the front yard. "Just one ride up the driveway and back. Please. Please. Please."

"I told you we don't have time," Amy insisted, as she tried to hurry her two lively boys into the backseat of the car.

"Momma, please. It won't take a minute," Chuck, Jr. cried and begged. "Please. Please. Pretty please."

"Oh, alright damn it," Amy snapped. "Anything to shut you up. Both of you are starting to get on my nerves. But you'll have to wait for your Uncle Gene to come out."

"But he has to go to the drug store for Papa's medicine," Toby insisted. "He won't have time. Can't you take us? You know how to drive the tractor. Uncle Gene showed you how."

"Jesus! You kids are going to drive me crazy," Amy snapped at her sons, slamming the car door. "I don't know if he even left the keys in the thing."

Back inside the house, Anna and Gene were busy dragging soapy clothes out of the washing machine, searching for his truck keys.

"Well, they're obviously not in your pants," Anna told him after they had gone through the entire wash. "They must have fallen out of your pocket before you took your pants off. Where were you when you took them off?"

"Upstairs in the bedroom, beside the bed," he replied.

"Well, let's go look upstairs," Anna suggested. "Maybe they fell on the floor and you didn't hear them drop. Maybe they bounced under the bed."

"Hell, I don't have time to spend all morning looking for those damn keys. I've got work to do," Gene growled.

"Look, just go on and do your work, I'll take the kids with me and we'll go pick up Harry's medicine," Anna told him. "I'll look for the keys when I get back home."

Suddenly, they heard the tractor crank up outside.

"Who the hell is messin' with the tractor? Goddamnit, those kids better not be out there or I'll beat their asses!" Gene ran out of the laundry room and hurried for the door with Anna following behind him. Before they made it outside, blood-curdling screams from their five children, who were standing on the front porch, cut through the still morning air.

"Oh, my god!" Anna gasped, as Gene threw open the door and they ran outside.

By the time they reached the front porch, it was all over. There was nothing anyone could do. What they saw would haunt them and their children the rest of their lives. At the bottom of the porch steps, they saw Amy leaping off the tractor. Standing off to the side, about six feet away, was little Chuck, Jr. The two-year-old was covered in blood from head to toe. Blood and bone fragments were strewn in a twelve-foot perimeter around the tractor. On the bottom porch step, lay a small piece of blood soaked clothing. Amy's screams drowned out the children's cries.

"Oh, my God! No! My baby! Not my baby!" she screamed over and over.

Harry came running out of his trailer and was horrified by what he saw. All he could do was stand frozen and look on in shock and horror.

"Where's Toby?" Anna screamed to her sister. "Where is he?"

Gene ran down the steps and grabbed his nephew. Besides appearing to be in a state of shock, Chuck, Jr. was unharmed. He handed the child to Anna and jumped on the tractor. He immediately disengaged the bush hog blade. Then he yelled for Harry to get Amy back inside the house with the children and ordered Anna to call the Sheriff. Once they were back inside, he slowly moved the tractor forward, and then turned off the engine. He jumped down and ran around to the back of the bush hog.

There, on the ground, he found nothing more than a blood-drenched circle, splattered with flesh and bone fragments mingled inside what was left of his nephew's clothing. Gene collapsed to his knees and wept.

The memorial service for two-year-old Toby Michael Willis was held at Myrick Methodist Church where his parents were married six years earlier. The empty casket held only a small body bag containing the child's few remains and some mementoes of the his brief life. A favorite teddy bear, an Atlanta Braves baseball cap and the little, green John Deer tractor that he always carried in his pants pocket were placed inside. Beside the small steel blue casket sat a floor easel with a twelve by eighteen framed, color photograph of a little boy with a big grin and his light brown hair cut in a Beatles' hair cut.

The century old, three-story, red brick church in the middle of town, was filled to capacity. Many of the mourners were carpet mill employees who worked for Angel. She had shut down the mill for the day out of respect for her sister and nephew. A gesture her own father would have never considered.

Amy had been kept heavily sedated since the tragedy occurred. She and her remaining son sat in the front church pew between her two sisters. Beside Angel, sat her husband Red, while Gene sat beside Anna. Toby's father sat with his parents beside Gene. Behind them in the second pew, were the five Longhorn children seated between Papa Harry and their Uncle Joey.

After the memorial service was over, a hearse, followed by a short procession of cars containing only the immediate family, drove to Porter Plantation where the small casket was lowered into the ground beneath the old Magnolia tree where Ollie and Gene's father were buried. It was decided by little Toby's family that it would be the best place to lay his remains since the boy loved visiting the farm more than anything else. His fondest memories were there—spending hours playing beneath the huge oak trees in the front yard with his twin brother and five cousins.

The coroner had deemed the tragedy a careless accident. Fortunately, in 1975, breathalyzers weren't a common practice by law enforcement;

otherwise the boy's mother might have been charged with reckless conduct and involuntary manslaughter resulting in the death of her son. Instead, her punishment and sentence was being forced to live with the knowledge she had been the cause of the accident that claimed her child's life. Slightly inebriated and frustrated with her sons' insistence, Amy had climbed onto the farm tractor and started the engine without giving consideration to the dangerous machinery attached behind. With her foot on the clutch, she had leaned over the side of the tractor and picked up her son. In doing so, her foot slipped off the clutch pedal causing the tractor to lunge forward, knocking little Toby out of her grasp and slinging the child beneath the powerful steel blades. Within seconds there was nothing left but small pieces of bone fragments and a few shreds of clothing. Little Toby's twin brother and five cousins had witnessed the horrific accident.

Following the graveside service, the family retired to the farmhouse where they all collapsed with grief and exhaustion. Only Chuck, Sr. and his parents refused to join them, choosing to deal with their grief elsewhere in private. By his own choice, Chuck had not spoken a word to his ex-wife since the incident, nor had his parents. There was no point in laying blame. It wouldn't bring back their son or undo the tragedy. Besides, Amy was too numb with grief and the affect of sedatives to fully experience their bitter feelings toward her.

For the time being, it was decided that Chuck, Jr. and his mother would stay with Angel and Red at Coleman Hill. The day after the memorial service was held, a member of Myrick Methodist drove out to the farm to deliver some floral arrangements that had been sent to the church.

"There were so many arrangements sent that I tried to divide them up equally between you and Angel," the churchwoman explained, as she unloaded the back of her van filled with flowers. "I must have taken close to a couple dozen to your sister's house this morning. I hope you can find room for the rest in your house."

"Yes, I'm sure I can find room," Anna told her. "Thank you so much. I appreciate you being so thoughtful and going to all the trouble to bring them out here.'

"You are quite welcome," the woman replied. "I'm just so awfully sorry about the terrible accident. It was one of the worst tragedies that has ever happened to this community." As the woman turned to leave and got back into her van, she happened to glance over and see the large patch of grass, still stained with blood. She suddenly felt sick to her stomach.

It took several minutes for Anna and Harry to move the sympathy arrangements into the house and find places for them. Anna decided not to go to the trouble of sorting through the attached cards right then. She figured she would leave them on the arrangements until she felt up to removing the address cards and writing an appropriate thank you message to each person individually. Perhaps in a day or two when things settled down a bit.

That evening when Gene came in from his day's work and started upstairs to wash up before dinner, he paused to glance at some of the floral arrangements Anna had placed at the bottom of the stairs. Most were from mill employees, but one in particular caught his interest. He snatched the card from the arrangement and walked back into the kitchen where Anna was busy frying some okra for dinner. Without saying a word, he shoved the card in front of her face. It was from Tom Webber.

"What's he doing sending flowers here?" Gene demanded.

"He didn't send flowers here," Anna explained. " He sent them to the church. They were for the family. The woman from the church who brought them by this morning said that she tried to divide the arrangements between Angel and me since there were so many of them."

"Why did his wind up here?"

"Coincidence," Anna shrugged. "I'm sure she didn't go through all those arrangements and make sure she gave his flowers to me personally. Stop being so suspicious," she told him.

"Like it was a coincidence that he just happened to call here a few weeks ago to see if you were still interested in a piece of furniture he had?"

Anna turned and faced her husband. "Just what are you trying to imply, Gene? Are you insinuating I have a relationship with a man I only met once, over a year ago?"

"How do I know you only met him once?"

Anna's face turned two shades of red. "Look, I don't appreciate you accusing me of carrying on with someone I barely know. You're crazy if you think I have anything to do with that man. I barely *know* him. What do I have to do to get that through your head?"

"I just don't like the idea of a strange man calling my house and talking to my wife when I'm not around and then sending her flowers."

"I told you, Gene, he didn't sent those flowers to *me*, he sent them to the *family*," she snapped back. "He sent them out of respect to all of us—not to me personally. They just happened to wind up here, that's all."

Gene gave Anna a long, hard stare.

"You're acting paranoid," she told him.

"I just don't trust other men around my family, especially my wife."

"You don't trust men—or you don't trust *me*?" she said, turning her attention once again to the iron skillet on the stove.

"Look, I don't want to hear or see this guy's name around here ever again," he said, tearing up the card and tossing it into the trashcan as he walked out of the kitchen.

Anna shook her head in silence. His jealousy had to come from his mother's side of the family. She had heard how jealous Italian men were. Unfortunately, she was now getting some first hand experience in that old-fashioned presumption.

# Chapter Eighteen

After the death of her son, Amy fell into a deep state of depression, fueled by her continuous drinking and dependence on prescription pain medication. Her family's growing concern for her and Amy's own inability to care for her remaining son, forced them to take steps to insure her welfare as well as little Chuckie's. It was decided that Anna would bring her nephew to the farm to live with her and Gene for the time being. It seemed like a logical choice since Anna already had five children to care for and didn't work outside the home, unlike Angel, who was at the mill five days a week and had no children of her own for little Chuck to play with. Anna and Angel were forced to take the next step and admit Amy into a Rome hospital for alcohol and drug dependency. After a month and a half, she was released and began attending Alcoholics Anonymous meetings regularly. Amy agreed with her sisters that for a few months, it would be best if Chuck, Jr. remained on the farm with his Aunt Anna and five cousins.

For the first three months after Amy was released from the hospital, she seemed to have improved so that she was able to return to work and even care for her son once again. Finally, she brought her son back home with her and they settled into a normal routine. Or at least as normal as possible, despite the fact Amy was living with the knowledge she was the one responsible for her son's death. In order to help their sister deal with that enormous guilt, Angel made arrangements for Amy to visit a psychiatrist in Rome twice a week for the next couple of months. The therapist proved to be what Amy had needed all along, for it made her understand the root of her drinking and infidelities, and enabled her to resolve some deep-seeded issues. Within a year after the tragedy, Amy appeared to have her life back on track and continued to remain clean and sober. Unfortunately, the help hadn't arrived in time to save her marriage. Despite the fact Chuck still loved Amy and always would, he couldn't forgive her for their son's death. Finally, their relationship grew amicable and they remained on friendly terms.

That year proved both traumatic as well as therapeutic for their family and Anna hoped and prayed that things would finally settle down and their lives would become normal again—at least for a while.

Meanwhile, Gene was becoming increasing dissatisfied with farming. He had always hated the long hours and daily grind that his work demanded. At the age of twenty-eight and after fourteen years of back breaking labor, Gene Longhorn was ready for a new profession. A profession that would allow him regular nine to five hours, with a retirement plan and the luxury of a paid vacation now and then. Not once during their six-year marriage had he been able to break away from the farm and take his wife and children on a summer vacation. He had never been out of the state of Georgia in his life and he had always wanted to travel to Florida, but managing a farm that required constant overseeing twenty-four hours a day, seven days a week, three-hundred and sixty-five days out of the year, made family vacations impossible. His children were getting old enough now that they could enjoy trips to Six Flags and Disney World. Nicky was nearly six and would begin school in the fall. His youngest son was almost three. It was June and the perfect time for a summer vacation. For the first time, Gene decided to ask Harry if he could leave one of his farmhands in charge of things while he took Anna and the kids down to Disney World in Orlando for a week. Anna even suggested that they invite Harry to join them. He declined her kind offer, but insisted Gene take his family and have a good time.

Two days before Anna's twenty-fourth birthday, she was busy packing their belongings for their trip to Florida. They planned to leave the day after her birthday. Nicky came running into the bedroom and told her mother that a delivery truck was coming up their driveway. Anna couldn't imagine why the truck was arriving there. After all, she hadn't purchased anything large enough to require a delivery truck. Perhaps Gene had bought her a birthday gift and was having it delivered. She hurried out of the bedroom and opened the front door. She found two burly deliverymen sitting in their truck, afraid to get out. The four German Shepherds were circling the truck, barking and daring the men to get out. Anna called to her five children and had the three oldest help her quiet the animals enough to get them into the fenced backyard. Once he was certain the dogs were safely contained, the driver got out.

"Good day, ma'am," greeted a heavyset black man, as he climbed out of the cab of the truck.

"Hello," Anna replied. "Are you looking for someone?"

"Yes ma'am. Are you Anna Longhorn?" he asked.

"Yes."

"I have a delivery for you," he said, walking to the back of the truck and lifting open the door.

"Who is it from?" Anna asked.

"Blue Ridge Antiques and Collectibles," replied the deliveryman.

Anna looked puzzled. The name didn't ring a bell. "Who?" she asked.

"The deliveryman and his partner disappeared into the back of the truck and returned carrying a very large object wrapped tightly in thick mover's quilts.

"Where would you like us to set this, ma'am?"

"Um, well in the house I suppose," Anna replied, opening the front door wide enough for them to enter. "What is it?" she asked.

"It's a dressing table, ma'am. Where would you like us to place it?"

Suddenly it dawned on her. Knowing she had admired the vanity table at Webber's antique shop that day, Gene had bought her one for her birthday and was having it delivered before they left for their vacation.

"You can put it in the downstairs bedroom. I'll show you where. Just follow me," she said, leading them into the downstairs master bedroom.

After the men had positioned the large piece of furniture in the space Anna had chosen, they untied the ropes and removed the heavy quilts.

She was shocked to see the antique vanity table from Tom Webber's antique store. Certainly Gene had not purchased that one for her. It was far too expensive for him to afford. Even if he had gone in with her sisters, she doubted that together, the three of them could afford such an extravagant gift. Anna was puzzled and shocked.

"You have a good day, ma'am," the deliveryman said, as he and his partner left the house.

"Sir, could you please tell me who sent this here?" Anna asked as they were walking out the door.

"Yes ma'am. It was sent from Mr. Tom Webber's antique shop in Mt. Carmel."

Anna's jaw dropped. Why in the world would he send her a priceless antique that she could not afford? Quickly, she ran to kitchen phone and began frantically thumbing through the phone book, looking for Webber's number.

"Mommy, Mommy," Nicky screamed, running into the kitchen. "Hal is upstairs on his bed taking everything out of the suitcase you packed for him and throwing it on the floor. I told him to stop, but he won't listen."

Anna left the phone book on the kitchen table and ran upstairs to discipline her mischievous three-year-old. While she was gone, Gene walked in the back door. He had seen the delivery truck leaving their house and was curious to know what was going on.

"Anna?" he called to her. "Anna, what was that truck doing here?"

Because she was upstairs, she didn't hear him calling her. He walked down the hall into their bedroom. His eyes immediately fell on the antique vanity that had just arrived. He went over and began inspecting it. At first, he thought Anna had purchased it and hadn't told him for fear of making him angry. He opened the top drawer and found an envelope inside with his wife's name on the front. He opened the envelope and saw a note that read: *Dear Anna, please accept this dressing table as a gift for your twenty-fourth birthday. Best wishes, Tom Webber.*

Gene's blood quickly began to boil. What the hell was this man doing sending his wife such an expensive gift? Especially a man she claimed that she only met once, two years ago.

Anna returned from upstairs and walked back into their bedroom to find her husband standing there.

"You listen to me," Gene said. "What kind of a fool do you think I am? I told you I never wanted to see or hear that man's name in this house again and next thing I know he's sent you a goddamn gift that's worth more than I paid for my truck! If you're not seeing this man behind my back and talking to him, then how the hell do you explain this?" Gene shoved the envelope with the enclosed card in front of her face.

"What's that?" she asked innocently.

"You tell me! Go ahead, read it!"

Anna took the envelope from him and read it. She happened to glance up and see the children standing in the doorway. "Go outside and play now," she told them. "I'll call you when dinner is ready." They quickly obeyed and ran outside to play.

"Gene, I swear to you, I'm as puzzled and surprised by this as you are. Where did you find this card?"

"In the top drawer where you hid it," he snapped.

"Where I *hid* it? I didn't know it was there. This is the first time I've seen it. I'm not trying to hide anything from you. When the truck pulled up and delivered it, I thought it was a birthday gift form you. At first, all the man told me was it was from Blue Ridge Antiques. He already had it in the house when I asked him who sent it. Until then, I just figured it was from you. Gene, I swear, I haven't spoken to that man since he called here a year ago."

"I find that hard to believe," he told her. "I think you're lying."

"How dare you!" Anna snapped back, unable to believe her own husband would call her a liar to her face. "Gene that man is twice my age. I met him once and I've never laid eyes on him since. Don't worry; I'm not about to keep that dressing table. I'm sending it back immediately."

"You're damn right, you're sending it back because I'm taking it back myself and I'm going to have a little talk with Webber while I'm there." Gene grabbed Anna by the shoulders and shoved her up against the wall. "And if I find out that you've been lying to me, so help me God, I'll kill both of you!"

"What's going on?" Joey asked, walking into the room. He had just arrived home from the mill and heard his brother shouting in the bedroom.

Gene stared at his wife with angry determination. "Joey, you and I are going to take a little trip over to Walker County before dinner," he told his brother. "I've got some business to take care of over there."

After Joey helped his brother load the vanity into the back of Gene's pick-up, they headed for Mt. Carmel and Webber's antique shop. He didn't have any trouble finding it; the address was printed on a label attached to the back of vanity mirror. They arrived just as Webber was about to close his shop for the day. Gene got out of his truck and walked inside through the front door with Joey following close behind.

"Can I help you gentlemen?" a man's voice called from the back of the showroom. At first, seeing the two large men walk into his shop unannounced at closing time, not knowing who they were, gave Webber some cause for concern. He thought he was about to be robbed.

"I'm looking for Tom Webber," Gene announced bristly. "You know where I can find him?"

"I'm Tom Webber. What can I do for you?" he replied, walking over to greet the men entering his store.

"You can take that piece of shit back that you had delivered to my house for starters," he growled, staring Webber straight in the eye. "And you can stop contacting my wife. I don't know what you think you're trying to pull by calling my house and sending my wife expensive gifts, but I sure as hell know what it looks like."

"Mr. Longhorn, I assure you, nothing is going on between Anna and myself," Webber tried to explain. "I sent that vanity to her because she admired it the day she visited here with Angel and because her birthday is a couple of days from now."

Gene stared at Webber with a cold, angry expression. Even when he didn't attempt to appear intimidating, Gene was quite daunting due to his size and brooding features. "You expect me to believe that? A perfect stranger my wife meets once, and he remembers when her birthday is and out of the clear blue, decides to send her a piece of furniture worth thousands of dollars. What kind of fool do you take me for?"

Webber looked at Gene and then at Joey. It was obvious he was facing a pair of men that were capable of doing him great harm.

"Mr. Longhorn, I'll be more than happy to explain my intentions if you'll just sit down and allow us to have a rational conversation. Please, won't you come into my office and have a seat. Your friend is welcome to join us. If you'll just allow me, I can explain everything."

Gene stared at Webber, evaluating his sincerity. He had driven this far and gone to the trouble of returning the vanity. Perhaps Webber *did* have a logical explanation for his actions. Besides, Gene wanted desperately to believe his wife was telling him the truth. He turned and looked at his brother.

"Let's hear what the man has to say," Joey suggested.

Webber walked to the front of his shop where he locked the door, and then led Gene and his brother back to his office and asked them to have a seat. For the next hour, the two men talked while Joey sat in silence and listened to what they had to say to one another.

Anna had waited dinner on her husband and brother-in-law for as long as she could before finally feeding the children. She then told them to go upstairs and get ready for bed. She was in the kitchen washing up the dishes when Gene and Joey returned. She studied her husband's expression as he entered the room. He appeared weary and solemn as he walked over to the kitchen sink where she stood. To her surprise, he put his arms around her and kissed her on the cheek.

"Got any leftovers for a couple of hungry furniture movers?" he asked.

"Sure. I saved a couple of plates. They're in the oven. You want them now?" she asked.

"We need to wash up first," Gene replied. "Are the kids already in bed?"

"Yes. I'll start warming up your dinner while you go wash up," she told him. He was surprising calm and mellow considering his mood when he left earlier that evening. Anna was curious and confused as to what had happened.

They left to go wash up and when they returned, Anna had their plates on the kitchen table waiting for them. They sat down and ate in silence while Anna finished washing the dinner dishes. When they finished, Joey excused himself to go downstairs.

Anna pulled out a chair across the table from her husband and sat down. Gene reached over and took her hand.

"I'm sorry about this afternoon," he began. "I just get a little crazy sometimes, especially where you and the kids are concerned. I apologize for what I said to you this afternoon and for calling you a liar."

Anna stared at her husband in silence. She was dying of curiosity, but decided to allow him to finish his explanation without asking any questions.

"Apology accepted," she replied softly.

"Anna, I had a long talk with Webber tonight." He let out a long sigh and scratched his head. "I think the two of you need to sit down and talk."

"Why? I don't understand."

"Webber has known your family for a long time," he began. "He was born and raised here in Barrow County and lived in Myrick up until about twenty years ago. He owned an antique shop on lower Main Street. He knew your parents pretty well." He paused for a moment before continuing. "He helped your mother furnish her house. They became good friends."

"I don't recall ever meeting him or hearing my mother mention his name," Anna said.

"You were only about four years-old when he left here. Anna," he paused once again. "Webber and your mother had an affair."

Anna stared at her husband in stunned silence. She couldn't believe what she was hearing.

"They began seeing one another while he was helping her furnish the house, about a year after they first met. They fell in love and continued their affair for about five years. When your father found out they were seeing one another, he had a couple of thugs grab Webber one night as he was leaving his shop. They beat him so bad that they nearly killed him. He was in the hospital for a long time. Your father warned him that if he didn't leave town, he would have him killed." Gene gave his wife's hand a gentle squeeze. "Anna, Tom Webber is your father."

All the color drained from her face as she gazed back at her husband in disbelief. "He told you that?"

"Yes."

"He wanted to tell you himself, but he didn't know how or even if he should," Gene explained. "He kept hoping he would have another opportunity to meet with you, but he didn't know how to go about it. He said he thought about you constantly over the past two years, ever since he met you that day when you came to his shop with Angel."

"How does he know he's really my father?"

"He said that your mother told him when she became pregnant during their affair."

"How could she be sure I was his and not daddy's?"

"She told Webber that she and your father stopped sleeping together about a year before they began the affair. That's also how your father knew that you didn't belong to him."

All Anna could do was shake her head in silence. At last she knew the truth. The mystery was solved. She finally knew who her father really was.

"Well, are you glad you know now?" Gene asked.

Anna nodded slowly. "Yes. I am. But it's going to take time for all this to sink in. It's such a big shock."

"I know it is," he replied. Gene understood what his wife must have been feeling at that moment. She was both shocked and relieved. And she was right; it would take time for everything to sink in.

"I would like to get to know him a little better," Anna said, her voice barely above a whisper. "That is, if it's what he would want."

"Oh, I don't think you have anything to worry about there," Gene assured her. "I know he would like that very much. In fact, he told me so. I think the reason he sent you the vanity was so it would finally open that door that has been closed all these years. He figured that would be as good a way as any. He just didn't count on having to deal with a jealous husband."

Anna looked at him and smiled. "I was so afraid what would happen after you left here this afternoon. You were so mad when you left."

"Well, it's all straightened out now. Everything is out in the open. No harm done." He leaned over and kissed Anna on the lips. "I'm sorry if I hurt you this afternoon. I love you more than anything else in the world. And I admit maybe I love you *too* much. I'm a jealous man and I can't help that."

"I know. It's alright," Anna smiled back at her husband.

"Well, I guess I need to get Joey to help me move that dressing table out of the truck before he goes to bed," Gene sighed wearily.

"You brought it back with you?"

"Of course," he replied. "It's your birthday present from your father."

# Chapter Nineteen

Four days after Anna's twenty-fourth birthday, she stood at the sink washing the breakfast dishes. She had just finished feeding her children their breakfast and sent them outside to play while she cleaned up the kitchen and tidied up the house for her special guest to arrive later that afternoon. She had invited her father there for lunch so that they could become better acquainted and hopefully embark on a long and close friendship. After years of not knowing her real father's identity and fearing that her mother had taken that secret to her grave, the mystery was solved. And now, she was only hours away from sitting down with him and having their first conversation as father and daughter. She was nervous and apprehensive. She wasn't sure of what she would say to him or where she would even begin. It reminded her of her first date with Gene. After six years of marriage, that had turned out pretty well so perhaps her relationship with her father would prove to be as rewarding.

Anna stayed up late the night before baking a chocolate cake just for the occasion. Initially, she had asked Gene to drive her to Mr. Carmel to Tom's shop so that they could meet there, but Gene had insisted on her father visiting with her at the farm instead.

"It's more convenient if he comes here," Gene had told her. "I can't be away from the farm that long and besides, we don't have anyone but Harry to look after the kids while we're gone and five kids under the age of six are just too much for him to handle alone."

As usual, her husband was right. Thus, she invited Tom to drive out to the farm for lunch that afternoon. This way, he would be able to meet their children and Harry. After making sure the house and kids were spotless, she went upstairs to find something appropriate to wear. She was already on pins and needles awaiting a phone call from her sister. Angel's baby was due any day now and she wanted her sister and husband in the delivery room. After having five children of her own, Angel felt no one was better suited to be at her side during the birth than Anna; and Red wanted her there as well for his own moral support. Since the nearest hospital was miles away in Rome, Anna knew that as soon as she received word from either of them, she would have to drop everything and leave immediately. Angel had already made arrangements with her housekeeper to keep Anna's children until Anna returned home from the hospital once the baby arrived. The idea of a stranger keeping his kids didn't set too well with Gene, but under the circumstances he really didn't have a choice but to comply. She hoped and prayed that call would not come today.

After she finished dressing, she went back downstairs and outside to check on the children. She found them in the front yard with their father. A brand new baby calf had just arrived a few days ago and Gene had brought it for the children to see.

"Momma, look at the new calf," four-year-old Joey shouted to his mother. "Isn't he the cutest thing you ever saw?"

"That he is, sweetie," Anna smiled.

"Look, he's got a curl right in the middle of his forehead," five-year-old Olivia added, as she ran her fingers through the thick main on top of the calf's head. "Let's call him Curly," she said. "Don't you think that would be a good name for him, Momma?"

"I think that would be an excellent name for him," Anna agreed.

She stood on the porch steps as she watched her children lavish their affection on the newborn calf. They had grown up with all kinds of animals and got their love of them from their mother.

"Can we keep him as a pet?" Nicky asked her father.

"Well, he won't stay that cute and cuddly for long," Gene replied, leaning against his pick-up truck as he watched the children fawn over the Black Angus calf. "Before you know it, he'll weigh in about a thousand pounds and will chase you every time you try to come near him. Bein' hit by him would be like getting hit by this truck here. A full-grown bull can be aggressive, especially when there are cows around. Just enjoy him while you can."

"He's so cute," Olivia said, leaning down to kiss the calf on the head.

"You heard from Angel yet?" Gene asked his wife.

"Not yet. But I expect a call any minute now. I just hope it doesn't come this afternoon."

"Maybe not," Gene said. "Well, I better get back to work. Say goodbye to Curly and let me take him back to his Momma."

"Oh, Daddy, can't we keep him here with us a little while longer." Joey pleaded with his father. "We'll take good care of him."

"Well son, he needs to be with his Momma so he can nurse and grow big and strong."

"But you don't let the other calves nurse," little Joey said. "You make them drink milk out of a bucket with a nipple on the bottom."

"Well, that's because those are dairy calves. They have to save their Momma's milk for dairy milkin'. We fatten the dairy calves up with powdered milk and keep them from nursing so we can sell the Momma cow's milk. Curly is a beef calf, not a dairy calf."

"That don't seem fair," Olivia remarked.

"Well, maybe not, but that's the difference between the dairy and beef cattle trade," Gene told his daughter as he bent down and picked up the small calf, carrying him over his neck and shoulders as he walked back to the truck.

"Will you bring him back later so we can play with him some more?" Gene, Jr. asked his father.

"Next time I'll take ya'll up to the pasture and let you run around with him up there for awhile," Gene told them. "He'll make too big of a mess in the yard if he stays here for very long. We got enough poop to shovel with six dogs around. Besides, he's liable to get out there in the road and get hit by a car. I can't afford for that to happen."

Anna looked up and saw a car turning into their driveway off the highway.

"Looks like your company is here," Gene told her.

"Why don't you hang around for a little while and visit with him until we get better acquainted," Anna asked her husband.

"Ah, you don't need me around. You two have a lot of catching up to do. Besides, I've got too much work waiting for me. If I don't hurry, I won't get finished by suppertime."

Anna really wished Gene wouldn't leave them alone until she and her father became better acquainted and more comfortable with one another. But at least she had the children there and Harry would be dropping in later.

The first ones in the family to welcome the visitor were the six, large German Shepherds who quickly circled around the late model Cadillac, while Webber remained behind the wheel, too terrified to get out. Together, along with the children, Anna and Gene managed to herd the dogs safely into the fenced-in backyard, allowing their guest to at last safely exit his automobile. A cat lover and owner of two pedigreed Himalayans, dogs, especially large dogs, made him uneasy—as did small children.

Gene greeted Webber, then excused himself and returned to his work on the farm, leaving Anna alone with her father. She began by introducing him to their five children and explained to them that this was their real grandfather. Once that was accomplished, Anna proceeded to take Tom on a tour of the old plantation house that she so dearly loved. That turned out to be the icebreaker she was looking for. Tom began exercising his decorating expertise by offering tips on how she could add to the inviting atmosphere she had already created for their home. They chatted freely for a couple of hours, discussing antiques and decorating ideas. Before she knew it, Gene arrived for his noon break, along with Harry, who always dropped in about the same time each day and joined them for lunch. She called the children in from outside and the nine of them sat down at the large dining room table to enjoy their first meal together as a family. It proved to be quite an experience for Tom, who at forty-five had never married or been in the company of so many young children at one time. A wealthy businessman and successful antique dealer, Webber had become reclusive over the past decade and seldom sought out the company of others. Being welcomed into his daughter's family was truly an unexpected surprise to say the least. On the other hand, to suddenly become involved in such a large circle of friends and energetic grandchildren was at times somewhat overwhelming and even a bit unnerving. Yet through it all, Anna did her best to put her father at ease and make him feel welcome in her home. If nothing else, the experience offered Tom the opportunity to get to know his daughter on a more personal level and see firsthand, the kind of person she had become; and he was very proud of what he saw. Besides being a very warm and caring young woman, she was a devoted wife and loving mother who was totally dedicated to caring for her family.

After they had finished eating, Gene left to return to his farm work and Harry took the children outside to play, leaving Anna and her father alone once more. Tom helped her clear the food and dinner plates from the table and return them to the kitchen. While she washed the dishes, he sat at the kitchen table and they began the conversation that both had longed for yet never expected to take place.

"You're nothing like Catherine," he began.

Anna gave him a somewhat puzzled look. "Do you mean that in a positive or a negative way?" she asked.

"I mean it in the most positive way," he replied. "You're mother was somewhat self-absorbed and spoiled, for lack of a better description. But you, on the other hand, are one of the most unselfish and unspoiled people I've ever met. You have a warmth about you that you're mother never possessed. I would have to say Angel is more like your mother."

"I'm afraid my middle sister Amy is the one most like Mother. She followed right in her footsteps. Angel is the strong one."

"Perhaps I don't know any of you as well as I thought," he confessed. "But then how could I? I never had the opportunity or pleasure of knowing any of you on a personal level. What little I knew was what Catherine told me."

"Did she talk about us very much?" Anna asked.

"Not really. But then she rarely spoke about your father either."

"Then what did the two of you talk about when you were together? That is, if you don't mind me asking," Anna added.

"Well, mainly we talked about how unhappy she was with her life and what a mistake it was for her to marry your father."

"If she was that unhappy with him, then why did she continue to stay with him all those years?"

"She fell into the same trap a lot of insecure women fall into," her father explained. "Your mother had always been wealthy and spoiled and she was used to having anything she wanted. That's the reason she married your father, because he continued to offer her the lifestyle to which she had become accustomed. She had never known any hardship and she was afraid if she left him, she would lose everything."

"Did you love her?"

There was a long silence. Finally Webber answered. "There's a difference between an affair and a *love* affair. Your mother and I cared a lot about one another, but we were never in love."

"So was it just based merely on sex?"

"In the beginning perhaps. But after awhile, it went beyond just sex. Your mother and I were a lot a like. Neither one of us were looking for a commitment when we met. We were *in like*, not in love. I was someone she could talk to and trust. In turn, I enjoyed her company. To her I was a temporary means of escape from an unhappy marriage. I think you're mother began her affair with me because she wanted to get even with your father for something. At least that's the impression I got."

His words jolted Anna. She suddenly remembered what her father had told her during the beating he gave her. *"You were a lousy accident that happened because your mother wanted to get even with me and took up with another man."*

"What did my father do to make my mother want to get even with him?"

Tom shook his head. "I have no idea. But I know that there was never any great love or romance between your mother and myself. We answered certain needs each of us had at the time. That's all. I suppose to be quite honest you could say your mother and I were two of a kind. We were somewhat cold and detached."

"What did you think when she told you that she was pregnant with your child?"

"Well, I was certainly shocked, that's for sure," Webber confessed. "You see, I was told by my doctor many years ago that I could never have children. I believed all along that I was sterile. Therefore, your mother and I never worried about our relationship resulting in any consequences. When she became pregnant, we were both stunned. And since she hadn't slept with your father in quite sometime, that made it impossible for her to convince him that the baby she was carrying was his."

"So he knew from the very beginning I wasn't his child."

"I'm afraid so."

"That explains why he hated me so badly."

"The entire situation was very unfortunate," Webber confessed. "It should have never happened. I'm truly sorry for the pain you've had to endure all these years and having to go through life not knowing who your real father was. But at least now you know the truth. If that's any consolation."

"It is," Anna replied. She considered telling him about the abuse her sisters had suffered at their father's hands—abuse different from her own, but she decided not to reveal their past. Perhaps for the same reasons she chose not to delve into her story of abuse and rejection. What point was there in telling him something that didn't matter now one way or the other. It was in the past. There was nothing anyone could do or say to change things. Life would go on, one way or the other. After their conversation however, Anna suspected that the reason her mother began her affair with Tom was to get even with her father for molesting their oldest daughters. What other reason could there have been?

As she spoke more with the man whom she discovered was her real father and came to know him better, she realized that she was no more like him than she was her mother. In fact, she wasn't like anyone in her family. She was completely different, with her own personality. What had made her so distinct, causing her to become painfully shy and introverted, in the end, was to her benefit. She was a better person because of it. She was able to feel great love and compassion and enjoyed caring for others. No one else in her family, not even her real father, seemed to share those qualities. Becoming acquainted with her father had been an eye-opening experience and she was grateful for the opportunity, because now, she was actually proud of who she was and the person she had become. Still, she couldn't help feeling a slight sense of disappointment, for while he was a man much different from Ben Coleman, he wasn't quite the man she had expected or hoped to find.

With both her sister and husband at her side during the entire labor and delivery, Angel gave birth to a healthy eight-pound baby girl whom she named Savannah Georgia Moore. Anna pleaded with her sister to come up with a more suitable name and even hinted that her niece would grow to resent her mother's sense of humor. Angel, however, insisted on sticking with the name Savannah so that the child could be called Anna after her aunt, and Georgia, because that was Red's mother's name.

Anna returned home from Rome and her sister's bedside early that evening after spending the day assisting with her new niece's arrival. Angel had gone into labor in the wee hours of the morning. Anna got up as she normally did at three a.m., fed her husband breakfast, and then left the children in Joey's care until they got up. Joey made sure they were fed and dressed, then dropped them off at Coleman Hill where Angel's housekeeper saw after them until Gene was free to pick them up and bring them home later that evening.

It was still daylight when Anna drove up and found her five children in the front yard with their father. Gene was sitting on the front steps watching the kids romp and play with the new calf they had named Curly. He knew when he allowed the children to become affectionate with the calf that he was making a serious mistake. He had already learned that lesson with Anna after allowing her to accept a newborn calf as a pet. Nine months later when he butchered it for their freezer she became so irate that she wouldn't speak to him for two days. She cried and yelled at him for being mean and callous and refused to eat a single bite of the meat placed on their table for months. It was then he learned that he shouldn't allow his family to name something that would eventually wind up on their plate. Still, they were farm kids and would have to learn the hard facts of life on the farm sooner or later.

"Momma, look at Curly," Joey said, as he hugged the calf tightly around the neck. "Look at how much he's grown in only a few days. He's gettin' real big and strong."

"Oh, he has grown," Anna agreed. "Pretty soon you won't be able to put your arms all the way around his neck. He'll be too big. They grow really fast."

"Well, what do we have?" Gene asked. "A niece or a nephew?"

"We have a beautiful eight-pound niece," Anna replied. "Savannah Georgia Moore."

"I hope the kid grows up with a sense of humor," he said. " With a name like that, she'll have to."

"They're going to call her Anna," she replied.

"Oh, that won't be confusing, will it?"

"Well, we already have two Gene's and two Joey's, so I guess she figured why not two Anna's."

"Why can't we call her Little Ann?" their oldest daughter Nicky, suggested.

"Yeah, or Annie," six-year-old Olivia added.

"That's a good idea," their mother agreed. "Maybe we'll do that."

Anna walked over and sat down beside her husband on the front steps and watched their children run around the yard with the calf. She rubbed her eyes and yawned.

"Tired?" he asked, putting his arm around his wife's shoulders and pulling her close to him.

"A little. The drive back was worse than sitting around waiting all day for the baby to arrive. I just wish we had a hospital closer by."

"Well, the way this town keeps growing, maybe we will one day,' Gene replied.

"Have the children already eaten?" Anna asked.

"Yeah. We just ate a little while ago. Are you hungry?"

"I could eat."

"Good. I saved you a plate. I have it in the oven warming." He leaned over and kissed his wife on the cheek. "I missed you. I don't like it when I don't know where you are."

"Well, you knew where I was," she replied. "I just wasn't at home."

"That's what I mean. I don't like it when you're not home where you belong."

"Well, I'm home now and hopefully there won't be anymore trips to the hospital for awhile. Maybe by the time Angel has her next one, we'll have a hospital closer by."

Gene gazed at his wife lovingly. "You ever think about us having another one before we get any older?"

Anna turned and looked at him. "Don't you think five mouths to feed is enough?"

"Well, I figure we need to make it at least an even half dozen," he grinned.

"I think five is plenty, at least for the time being. We just got our last one out of diapers."

"Well, come on Momma," he said, giving his wife a playful squeeze. "Let's go get you something to eat and put the kids down for the night." He stood up and stretched. "Come on kids, it's time to take Curly back to his momma."

"Oh, Daddy, can we ride with you back to the pasture, please," begged Olivia.

"Okay, hop in the truck and let's get goin'. It'll soon be bedtime." Gene reached down and scooped the calf up and swung him into the back of his pick-up.

"Can I ride in the back with him, Daddy? Please! Please!" Joey asked his father.

"Okay, but don't stand up while I'm driving down the road. You and Gene ride with Curly in the back and let Hal and the girls get in the front with me."

Anna watched as her husband and children drove away and felt so very blessed. She had a wonderful family that was loving, caring and very happy. But most important, they were *normal*. They weren't dysfunctional and emotionally damaged the way her family had been. Her own children would never have to suffer the way she had as a child. For that, she was so very thankful.

Twice a year, every spring and fall, Gene and Red would slaughter enough beef cattle to fill their freezers for the coming year. One weekend in April, Red came out to the farm early Saturday morning to help Gene with the job at hand. Since Red was a convicted felon, he was not allowed to have any type of firearms in his possession. That didn't, however, prevent him from using Gene's firearms on the farm for target practicing, deer hunting and the slaughtering. His weapon of choice for killing the beef cattle was a thirty-eight-caliber magnum. Gene, however, preferred his twenty-two rifle.

"You're gonna need something bigger than that peashooter to take out those bigger heads," Red told his brother-in-law. "Something like this thirty-eight."

"I've never had any problem with my twenty-two," Gene insisted. "It gets the job done."

"Do the kids know you plan on putting their little buddy in the freezer this time?" Red asked, gesturing to the three hundred pound, nine-month old Black Angus steer standing beside the oak tree in the back of the pasture.

"No, I just figured I'd let them find out later after they'd missed him for a few days. If they had their way, he'd be walking around here until he died of natural causes."

"They're gonna be mighty upset when they find out," Red told him.

"Well, he's just good eatin' size now. If I let him get any older, I'd have to turn him out to stud and I've got too many of 'em runnin' around here now. They just cost me in feed. He's just the right age for some tender steaks and, besides, if he gets any bigger he could hurt the kids while they're playin' with him."

They stood beside Gene's pick-up as they loaded the gun and prepared their hunting knives for the slaughter. After shooting the steer in the head, they immediately slit the animal's throat and allowed him to bleed before hoisting him into the back of the truck and taking him to the butcher to divide into hamburger, steaks and roasts. Curly was their second steer that morning and their last.

The half-grown steer stood still beside the tree, grazing nonchalantly, unaware that he was about to become prime choice beef.

Gene aimed his rifle straight at the animal's head and made the whistling noise he had always used to call the calf to his side whenever he took him to the house to play with the children. The calf quickly looked up, expecting as usual to be loaded into the back of the pick-up for some recreation with the children. Instead, when he raised his head, Gene fired off a single shot directly between his eyes. The calf let out a distressed wail and staggered for a few seconds before collapsing to the ground.

"See, I told you this twenty-two would get the job done," Gene said, as he and Red turned around and went for their hunting knife to finish the job. Just then, a deafening roar sounded overhead as three fighter jets passed over the pasture.

"Damn, what the hell are those jets doing flying over here?" Red said.

"I don't know but I've heard them fly over a lot here lately. They're probably comin' from that air base down in Warner Robins," Gene said, as they peered up at the sky.

"Don't they know the war's been over now for six years?"

"I think Harry said he read in the paper that they were flyin' some training maneuvers around here. Every time they fly over, they nearly scare the cattle half to death."

"Yeah, and you don't want 'em runnin' any meat off," Red added. "That's why we used to shoot any stray dog that got in the pasture and started runnin' after them."

"Well, I guess we better get this job over so we can get old Curly to the butcher shop before they close this afternoon," Gene said, taking his attention from the sky overhead.

"Hey! Where the hell did he go?" Gene gasped, as he looked back at the spot where the calf had fallen.

"Damn, I never seen one get up and run after you've popped him between the eyes," Red replied in astonishment. "He must have run into the woods over there."

"Ah hell, now we've got to go run him down and drag three-hundred pounds of beef all the way back up here to the truck."

"I told you that you should have used my thirty-eight," Red reminded his brother-in-law. "I know he won't get up after I pop him between the eyes with that."

They hurried into the woods that linked the pasture with the house and began searching for the wounded calf. They looked everywhere, but the calf was nowhere to be found.

"How the hell did he get away so fast?" Gene growled angrily. "I know he couldn't have gotten very far. Damn!"

"Well, he's got to be close by around here somewhere," Red told him.

"Hell, I don't even see a blood trail," Gene said. "I know I hit him."

Suddenly, they heard the children scream up at the house. "Oh shit!" Gene gasped. "He's done gone up to the house. Goddamnit!"

Quickly, they jumped into the truck and headed for Gene's house. They drove up and found Gene's five children and Chuck, Jr. standing in the front yard screaming and crying hysterically as they gathered around their beloved pet calf. Anna came running out the front door when she heard the children scream.

"Oh, my God!" she gasped. "What's going on?"

"Curly! Curly! You're hurt!" screamed Olivia as she ran to the calf and flung her arms around him.

"Oh, no! He's been shot!" cried Joey, who perhaps loved the animal the most of all the other children. He had spent many an afternoon after school running and playing with the calf.

"Gene, what have you done?" Anna screamed to her husband.

"He got away from us when we were—" Gene stopped, unable to finish in front of the already hysterical children. He glanced over his shoulder at Red, who looked on helplessly. Neither of them knew what to do next. The calf bellowed and staggered about as blood dripped from the wound between his eyes.

"Daddy, Curly's hurt bad. Do something!" screamed Nicky. "Who could have done such a thing to him?"

"You've got to get him to a vet quick!" yelled Gene, Jr.

"Yeah, that's what we're gonna do right now," Red finally said, tapping Gene on the shoulder. "Let's load him up in the truck and take him on down to Doc Griffin's."

Gene glanced up at his wife who was trying desperately to drag the children away from the wounded animal and get them back into the house. She looked over at Gene with an angry glare. "I can't believe you could let something like this happen," she snapped at him. "What were you thinking?"

"Hell, I didn't do it on purpose! I ain't never had one get away from me before," he told her as he and Red struggled with the calf to get it in the back of the truck.

"Daddy, you weren't going to take Curly to the butcher shop, were you?" seven-year-old Nicky sobbed to her father. She and her twin brother were the oldest and the quickest to catch on to why their mother seemed so upset with their father.

"Daddy! You weren't, were you?" Olivia gasped, turning to their father.

Gene looked at the children with tears streaming down their faces, obviously traumatized by the sight of their calf being sent to the butcher. The sight broke his heart, yet still, he had to put food on their table somehow.

"Well hell, how else do you think your mother puts steak and gravy on your plate?" he snapped. "Do you think it just falls from the sky? You kids know where beef roasts and hamburger come from. You've lived on a cattle farm all your life for Christ's sake. It's time you learned we have to kill some steers in order to eat. You're farm kids, you need to start acting like them and toughin' up a little. You can't make a pet out of every cow and steer walking out there in the pasture. We'd starve to death if I let you do that!"

"But why did you have to pick Curly?" Joey screamed at his father. "He was special!"

"He'll be even more special when he's sittin' on a platter in the middle of the Sunday dinner table," he told his son.

"I hate you!" the boy screamed at his father as he ran back into the house. "You're mean! You didn't have to kill Curly!"

"He's right," Olivia yelled as she and the other children followed behind their brother.

"I can't believe you let this happen," Anna told her husband.

"Ah hell, they'll get over it," Gene said as he and Red climbed back into the truck and drove away. "They're farm kids. They need to stop actin' like a bunch of city kids."

Anna watched as the truck pulled out of the yard with the wounded calf bellowing loudly in the truck bed. She dreaded going back into the house and facing the children's hurt and anger toward their father. She glanced over and saw Harry standing at the bottom of the porch. He had come running out of his trailer when he heard the children screaming.

"Well, I guess them younguns' are gonna be livin' off beans and tatters for a while," he said, shaking his head. "I don't want to be sittin' at *your* table when you serve up the next pot roast."

"I think Gene just went to a lot of trouble for nothing because I don't believe any of us will be eating meat anytime soon. He can eat it all by himself as far as the kids and I are concerned."

And she was right. Neither Anna nor the children ate a single bite of red meat for the rest of the entire summer, and it was nearly a week before the children spoke to their father again.

# *Chapter Twenty*

Since the tragedy of little Toby's death, Gene and Anna didn't have the heart to hold their annual July fourth cookout. It had been five years since the accident and they wondered if enough time had passed for them to finally put the tragedy behind them and move on. After much forethought, they decided to go ahead and invite everyone to the farm for the fourth.

It was an unusually hot and steamy July. Everyone tried to stay cool with gallons of sweet tea and ice cream. This time, the get-together was more like a family reunion with Anna's father joining in the festivities that year. Besides his daughter, her husband and their five children, there was Angel, Red and their four-year-old daughter Little Ann, Amy, Chuck, their son Chuck, Jr., Gene's brother Joey, Harry and of course the farmhands and their families.

The men, as usual, gravitated together around the outdoor grill and ice cream churns beneath the large oak tree outside, while Anna and her sisters gathered in the kitchen preparing their individual side dishes. The women enjoyed Tom's quick wit and Southern charm as they went about their cooking tasks while at the same time, tending to their children's needs. Somehow, Tom felt more at ease in the kitchen around them than mingling with their macho husbands around the barbeque grill. It didn't take Tom long to discover that he had little in common with his newfound son-in-law and the other men. Tom was a man who enjoyed professional manicures and salon-styled weekly haircuts. His hands had never been calloused or dirty and while Gene and his brother-in-laws were comfortable in faded blue jeans, T-shirts and work boots, Tom dressed in designer sports clothes and polished loafers. He was definitely more of a ladies man than a working class man as were his counterparts.

After making an earnest attempt at being cordial with the other men and soon discovering he had little to add to their conversation, he excused himself and went inside where he felt more at home with his daughter and her sisters.

"Papa, come push us on the swing," nine-year-old Olivia and her younger cousin Little Ann begged, running up to Harry, as he relaxed in a lawn chair with the other men.

"Let Harry rest," Red told his daughter. "It's too hot for him to try and keep up with you youngun's. I'll come push you in a little while. Y'all just go on and play among yourselves until lunch is ready."

""Y'all need to find a cool spot somewhere and just settle down for awhile," Gene added. "It's too hot to be runnin' around and playin' so hard. You'll get overheated in this kind of weather."

"I wish you had a pool like we do at home," Little Ann told her uncle Gene. "We could all go swimming. That's how we cool off at our house." Even at four, the child was quite a little firecracker, taking after both her parents. With raven hair and dark brown eyes like her mother, she was feisty and very mature for her age. Already she was running rough shod over her older cousins.

Harry struggled to get up out of his webbed lawn chair as he took the two girls by their hands and began walking toward the rope swing Gene had hung from one of the old oak trees in the front yard. "I don't mind swingin' these little girls around for awhile. The time will come soon enough when I won't be able to play with 'em. I better enjoy it while I can," he said as he disappeared to the opposite corner of the house with the children.

"I have to admit a pool sounds pretty inviting right now," Chuck grinned.

"Yeah Gene, why don't you put a swimmin' pool in out back," Red suggested to his brother-in-law in a jesting manner. "There's plenty of room back there for one."

"Harry don't pay me enough to afford no pool," he replied. "He barely pays me enough to put food on the table."

"Then get Anna to come up with the money," Red suggested. "I know she's got it."

Gene remained silent, choosing not to respond to his brother-in-laws reference that the women in the family were the ones with all the resources. While the fact ate away at Gene's self-esteem, it wasn't a problem with Red, who enjoyed his wife's success. It allowed him a brand new Harley Davidson and enough pocket money to do most anything he wanted whenever the notion struck him. He had been poor and deprived all his life and now that he was finally able to enjoy some well-deserved luxuries, it didn't matter to him that it was his wife providing the money.

Chuck watched Harry disappear behind the house with the children and noticed that he was still able to walk with relative ease considering his age. "He still gets around pretty good for an old man," he commented as Harry left.

"How old is he now? About seventy-nine?" Red guessed, glancing up at Gene.

"How about eight-five," Gene told them.

"You gotta be kidin'," Red replied in astonishment.

"Nope. He'll turn eighty-five in August," he said, flipping over a large rack of spare-ribs on the grill.

"I can't get around myself as good as he does now," Joey added, as he tossed back his third Coca-Cola since they had been sitting there.

"How you been getting' along with your newfound daddy-in-law?" Chuck asked Gene with a sly grin.

"We get along okay, I guess. We don't have much in common though. He seems to enjoy spending his time in the kitchen with the other womenfolk rather than hanging out with the guys," Gene replied, a hint of sarcasm in his voice.

They all snickered and laughed at the reference to Tom's masculinity—or more honestly, his *lack* of masculinity.

"He does seem to be a little too much in tune with his feminine side," Red sneered.

"Yeah, I noticed he does have a little light step in his stride," Chuck added.

"Well, I guess he really doesn't have much in common with any of us if you come right down to it," Gene admitted. "I mean he don't know nothin' about farming or mill work and he don't know nothin' about working on cars and I bet he's never been on a tractor in his life. So I guess he figures he wouldn't offer much to the conversation out here."

"I guess the only thing he knows is fancy furniture," Chuck agreed. "That and how to hang curtains. So I suppose he would get along with women a little better than he would with us."

"Yeah, Anna's already had him to help her re-decorate the house with a bunch of fancy antiques and foolishness," Gene said. "The house looked fine before. We didn't need to change nothin' in my opinion."

"Well, at least they shouldn't have cost you that much," Chuck replied. "He could let her have them at cost."

"They didn't cost me nothin'," Gene assured him. "Anna used her own money if she had to pay anything at all. I can't afford nothin' like that. Not farming for somebody else for a livin'."

"Yeah, it kind of pisses you off to see somebody like Webber, who ain't never had to work for a livin'," Red surmised. "I'm married to money and I still have a job at the mill five days a week."

"Nope," Gene agreed with his brother-in-law. "You and me won't ever make nothin' cause we don't own a carpet mill or some fancy antique shop or even a car lot," he added, glancing over at Chuck, who sat silently listening to his two former brother-in-laws complain about having to work for a living.

"Now Gene, you know good and well, I told you that you could come work for me and be my service department manager at the dealership," Chuck quickly reminded him. "I'd pay you a hell of a lot more than Harry's paying, plus throw in some medical benefits to boot and you wouldn't have to work nearly as hard and about half as long."

"Ah, you know what Gene's holding out for," Red grinned. "He's waitin' for Harry to kick the bucket so he can get a hold of this spread and divide it off into tracts of land and sell it for a fortune to some big land developer. He'd be able to buy his own fuckin' dealership then. To hell with working for you."

Chuck laughed. "Yeah, I guess you're right. Then I'd have me some serious competition. Next thing I know, I'd have a Ford dealership sittin' across the street."

"Ford my ass," Gene sneered. "It'd be a Cadillac dealership. I always wanted me a Coup DeVille."

"With Anna's money, she ought to be able to supply you with at least a couple of Coupe Devilles," Chuck kidded.

"She's too busy buyin' furniture we don't need," Gene replied. "I know one damn thing, if I never see another fuckin' cow or steer again as long as I live, it'll be too soon for me. I'm sick of bein' tied down to this farm. You ain't got no life as long as you're a farmer. It ain't nothin' but livestock and pastures twenty-four hours a day, seven days a week. No time off for nothin'. Anything would be better than what I do for a livin'. There's no way in hell that I'd ever let my sons become farmers. It's one hell of a way to have to put food on the table."

"I know I haven't missed a single day of it since I've been at the mill," Red agreed. "Compared to mill work, I got a cushy job now. Pays a hell of a lot better, too. I put in my eight hours and I go home. None of that three a.m. to seven p.m. shit."

"Well, just keep hangin' in there, pal," Chuck advised his ex-brother-in-law. "The old man can't live forever. Hell, you already got the house. And it's a fine place, too. You and Anna have made it into a showplace, that's for sure. I imagine if you wanted to, you could sell it for at least a couple hundred grand. Maybe more."

"Not if Anna has anything to say about it," Joey said, finally adding to the conversation. "She wouldn't take a million bucks for this old place."

"He's right," Gene agreed. "She'd die before she'd give up this place."

"Gene, are the ribs about ready?" Anna called to her husband from the front porch.

"Yeah, I'm takin' them up now," he replied.

"Good, because I've got everything ready to put on the table. Where's Harry?"

"Swingin' the kids."

"Well, tell them to come on. It's time to eat."

Gene removed the last of the meat from the grill and placed it on a couple of large platters. He called to Harry to bring the kids and get ready to eat, and then he and Joey took the food into the house.

"You know," Chuck told Red, speaking in a low voice as they began walking up the porch steps. "Gene's gonna be in for a big shock if Harry kicks the bucket and winds up leavin' him nothin' after he's stuck it out on this farm all these years."

"He's gonna be more disappointed if the old man don't wind up even leavin' him this house," Red added, glancing over his shoulder to make sure Harry wasn't within earshot. "You know Porter never signed anything over to them saying it was theirs to begin with. They ain't got no deed or nothing saying the property even belongs to them. For all I know, he's just lettin' them live here while Gene works for him. He ain't got no more than squatter's rights if it comes right down to it."

"I guess you're right," Chuck said. "Damn, he'll be one disappointed son-of-a-bitch if that happens."

Red shook his head and laughed. "Jesus. That would really be somethin', wouldn't it?"

By 1980, seven years after Angel had taken over the cotton mill and turned it into a carpet manufacturer, she and her two sisters were millionaires. The company that had begun on a relatively modest scale was now having difficulty keeping up with the increasing demands for more carpet products. Rather than open a second mill in nearby Dalton, as she had originally planned, Angel decided it would be better for Barrow County and it's residents if she simply expanded her present building. She bought a sizable track of land adjacent to the old building and built on to the mill, more than doubling it in size. Besides manufacturing carpet, she began producing floor and ceiling tile as well. Before long, Myrick became known as one of the largest carpet and tile manufacturers in the entire southeast and a billion dollar a year industry. In fact, the mill had become so large and employed so many workers, that people were moving to Barrow County in droves from all over Georgia and Alabama, seeking the well-paying jobs that the company offered. Soon, the county became so populated and prosperous that it was rumored that Barrow County might soon receive its much needed and long-awaited hospital. Myrick was beginning to grow and expand with more residents and businesses arriving everyday. Within three short years, the small town had nearly doubled in size. Thanks to Angel's business savvy sense and ingenuity, carpet was to north Georgia, what oil was to Texas. The Coleman girls had managed to build a dynasty that even surpassed their own father's empire and were now far wealthier than he had ever been.

Now that Amy finally had her life back on track and was no longer drinking or abusing prescription medications, she was able to accept more responsibility in helping her sister manage their growing business and became the accounting and bookkeeping manager as well as co-owner of the mill. They pleaded with Anna to join them and become active in the company's management, but Gene still refused to allow his wife to join her sisters in the family business and work outside their home. Thus, she continued caring for their five children along with Amy's four-year-old son and Angel's infant daughter. Since Anna was ordered to remain home and neither of her sisters wanted to leave their children in day Care, they sent them to the farm for Anna to look after while they worked at the mill. With five children of her own what were two more to care for?

While caring for six active children and a newborn baby, Anna was also looking after Harry, who at eighty-five, his health was finally beginning to decline. Despite her continuous pleadings, Harry refused to move into the house with them. Instead, he chose to remain in his little trailer home beside the house.

Despite the fact the carpet industry had grown so vast that Anna was no longer needed to help Amy with the bookkeeping at home, she still continued to draw a regular salary from her third share holding in the family business. And with the company's expansion, Anna was earning a fortune by just staying at home and looking after their children. Still, like her sisters, she enjoyed some of the luxuries that having money allowed her. That Christmas, she was able to buy her husband the Cadillac Coupe Deville he had always wanted. Unfortunately, he never had the time to drive it. Whenever he ran errands for the farm, it required the use of his truck. On weekends, he only drove it to church. While her sisters went on to become powerful business tycoons, Anna settled into a domestic rank as the chief family caregiver. Her husband was a relatively young man with old-fashioned ideals. He was also a very jealous man who wanted his beautiful wife kept safely at home where he could keep a watchful eye on her at all times. The fact that she was also one of the most independently wealthy women in the state continued to gnaw at his pride and self-worth. As he watched his wife grow richer as time passed, his bitterness toward his own lot in life grew stronger. All he could hope for was that one-day all his hard work and loyalties would pay off and he would own all the rich farmland on which he toiled day after day after day. Had it not been for marrying Anna or the fact that Harry had given them the old plantation house in which to live, he would have never stuck with the farm as long as he had.

Going into town to do the weekly errands and grocery shopping had become a major chore and nearly impossible task for Anna, with seven young children all under the age of ten. Leaving the house and enjoying a leisurely shopping trip alone was a luxury she seldom experienced. She had plenty of money, yet no time to spend it. Therefore, when school began in the fall, she was elated. With her five children, along with her niece and nephew in grammar school and kindergarten, Anna was free to be away from the house from eight-thirty a.m. until almost three in the afternoon.

Fridays were reserved for marketing and errands. On this particular Friday, Harry had asked Anna to take him into town and drop him off at his lawyer's office. At eighty-five years-old and with his failing health, Harry felt it was time to begin revising his will, although he didn't tell Anna or anyone else of his intentions. He merely asked if he could accompany her into town and be dropped off at his attorney's office while she ran her errands.

After doing so and before heading to the supermarket, Anna decided to drop by her father's new antique shop on Main Street. He and Anna had grown close over the past four years and Tom decided to open another shop there in Myrick not far from where his original shop had been years ago. With the success of his second shop, he decided to move back to his hometown in Myrick in order to be closer to his daughter and grandchildren. The children were a little older and more mature now and didn't seem to get on his nerves as much as they had when they were younger. They had grown into very well mannered and well-behaved children and he didn't mind being in their company as much now.

"Well hello there," Tom greeted Anna with a friendly smile and a kiss on the cheek, as she walked into his shop that morning. "You're out and about mighty early today."

"Harry had an appointment at his attorney's office this morning so after dropping the kids off at school we came on into town. He's still over there. I'm just waiting for him to finish so I can pick him up and go on to the supermarket."

"Those kids sure are growing up mighty fast, aren't they?" Tom said.

"Too fast," Anna replied. "I can't believe Nicky will be ten soon. I keep telling Angel that she and Red need to have another one. Before long Little Ann will be all grown up and gone before they know it."

"Well, I suppose her husband doesn't believe it necessary to keep her barefoot and pregnant the way yours did," Tom smiled, sarcastically. "But then I suppose that's Gene's way of keeping you on that short leash he has you tied to."

"You had better not let him hear you say that," Anna warned.

"You know, if you could ever manage to break off that leash, I could set you up in your own business. With your love of fine furnishings and flare for décor and my expertise and experience, you would be a big success in this business."

"That does sound exciting," Anna had to admit. "I would love to own my own business one day."

"And why shouldn't you? Angel has made quite a name for herself in the business world and Amy hasn't done so bad either. You deserve some success of your own. And besides, why not exercise some of that passion for the finer things in life you obviously inherited from your father? I'll have to leave my little dynasty to someone when I pass on. Why not my only daughter?"

"That's a long way down the road from now," Anna said. "I'll be a grandmother and you'll be a great grandfather by then."

"Well, all the more reason while there's still time for me to pass on my knowledge and teach you the ropes."

"Perhaps one day," Anna replied. "Maybe I could have my own shop and become an interior designer after the kids are grown. I'd really like that."

"And you would be wonderful at it," her father told her.

"First I have to get these children raised. Right now they're young and they need me."

"You need to start devoting more time to yourself," Tom said. "You're still a very young woman. In my opinion, too young to be tied down to a husband, five children of your own plus your sisters' two kids, not to mention an eighty-five year-old man. You give too much of yourself. You need to save a little time for yourself and do what *you* want to do instead of always having to do what's demanded of you. If I had been around while you were coming up, you would have never married so young and you would have certainly furthered your education. I would have insisted that you go on to college and make a career for yourself before settling into a life of domesticity."

"Believe it or not, Ben Coleman had the same plans for me and I didn't listen to him either. The day I met Gene Longhorn at the Dairy Queen ten years ago changed my life forever. I was going to marry him come hell or high water."

"And it didn't change your life necessarily for the best, as I see it," Tom replied.

"Well, I don't know about that. I could have done a lot worse. Gene has given me a good life. I've been very happy with him. And we're still very much in love, five kids and a decade later. I wouldn't trade my life with him for anything."

Her father smiled and shook his head in bewilderment. "Well then, I guess that's all that matters. As long as you're happy."

The phone in Tom's office interrupted their conversation suddenly. "Excuse me while I get that. I sent my assistant to the post office this morning and I'm having to handle the shop by myself until he returns."

"Oh, that's alright," Anna told her father. "I have to be going anyway. I need to go on to the supermarket before I go home and I have to see if Harry is finished at the lawyer's office."

"Stay right there," Tom insisted. "I'll be right back."

Anna began strolling through the shop as she waited for her father to return.

"Anna, that was Gene on the phone," he said, hurrying out of his office. "There's been a bad accident. Amy's been in a wreck."

"Oh, no! Where is she?"

"They're taking her to Rome," Tom told her. "You go ahead and hurry on back home. I'll take care of Harry. What lawyer is he with?"

"He's at Roy King's office, next door to the courthouse."

"Go home and meet Gene. I'll bring Harry back home when he finishes there."

Anna did as her father suggested and hurried home where Gene was waiting for her. When she arrived, he was on the phone with Angel. Their first concern was whom they would get to look after the children while they were at the hospital.

"Maybe I can get Tom to help look after them," Anna suggested.

"No," Gene said firmly. "I'm not having somebody who's never changed a diaper in their life taking care of my kids. Joey can stay here and handle things. If he needs any help he can call Red. Besides, the kids are old enough now to look after themselves."

About an hour later, Gene, Anna, Angel and Chuck were sitting in the hospital waiting room waiting for word on Amy's condition. All they knew so far was that Amy had left work not long after she arrived at the mill that morning to run to the bank and make a deposit. Speeding as she normally did, she floored the Corvette she was driving and sped through an intersection ignoring a red light broad siding a large delivery truck. The impact was so great, that her small sports car slid beneath the truck nearly decapitating her. She was in such serious condition, that she was airlifted to the Rome trauma center. For the next two hours her family sat in the patient waiting room waiting for a doctor to give them word on her condition. Finally he appeared and introduced himself. His news was devastating.

"She's lucky to even be alive," he began. "Her neck was broken and her spinal cord severed. She has a concussion, but she is conscious. Her back and pelvis were fractured."

"Is she going to be alright?" Anna asked.

"I don't know. We have her on life support. She's unable to breath on her own right now. The next seventy-two hours will be crucial. We'll know more after that time."

"Can we see her now," Angel asked.

"I'm afraid not. We're prepping her for surgery. There's some internal bleeding we have to stop immediately. We may have to remove her spleen."

"How long will the surgery take?"

"I have no idea. Possible two or three hours, maybe longer. After that, she'll move to recovery in ICU. A couple of you may be allowed in to see her then, but no more than two of you at the time and only for about five minutes."

"Once she's out of the woods and recovering, will she be able to get up and begin therapy to walk again?" Anna asked, remembering her own painful road to recovery following her own accident.

The doctor looked at Anna and shook his head. "I'm afraid she won't be able to walk," he told her. "Her spinal cord was severed. She's paralyzed from the shoulders down."

"You mean she'll *never* be able to walk again?" Angel asked.

"I'm afraid not," the doctor replied.

"Are you sure?" Chuck asked.

The doctor nodded in silence. "She has no sensation or feeling from the shoulders down."

"Could it be possible that the paralysis might be only temporary?" he asked.

The doctor shook his head. "She's paralyzed. The paralysis is permanent. She'll never be able to walk. The spinal cord doesn't grow back. Once it's severed, the patient suffers permanent paralysis."

With tears in her eyes, Anna turned to her older sister as if looking for an answer or some sort of comfort. She had neither. All Angel could do was put her arms around her sister and hold her.

"She's going to be okay," Angel told her. "She'll pull through this. Then we'll deal with whatever else we have to face. This family has been through worse. We'll pull through this crisis the same way we have all the others. One day at a time."

One day at a time turned into one month after another until finally five years had passed since the accident. Following the accident, Amy spent the first year at Shepherd's Spinal Clinic in Atlanta where she went through ten months of painful physical therapy and rehabilitation. Paralyzed from the shoulders down, Amy had no use of her arms or legs and was confined to a motorized wheelchair as a quadriplegic. Being confined to a wheelchair twenty-four hours a day was bad enough, but it was the breathing tub and catheter that made Amy's condition even more unbearable. Her paralysis had also robbed Amy of her ability to breathe on her own without the aid of breathing tube inserted in her throat and neck. It also meant she had lost the ability to control her bodily functions. Her condition demanded she have a full-time nurse eight to ten hours a day.

After being released from Shepherd's, the family was faced with the difficult decision of whether or not Amy would be sent to a nursing home, where she would live out the remainder of her life and receive the constant care she required or go home to live with Anna or Angel. Neither wanted to see their sister be confined to a private nursing home surrounded by strangers. Thus, after a long and painful discussion, it was decided that Amy would live with Anna and Gene on the farm since Angel worked at the mill each day and couldn't provide Amy with the full-time care and attention she required. It would also allow Chuck, Jr. who was now twelve-years-old, to be reunited with his mother since he had been living at the farm with his aunt and uncle after her accident.

The first year after Amy was allowed to come home was the hardest. Anna had to be taught by a registered nurse how to care for her sister's physical and medical needs, which were tedious and unrelenting. Since Amy was unable to feed or bath herself, Anna was forced to care for her sister as she would an infant. Yet no matter how burdensome it was for Anna, it was better than allowing her sister to waste away in a nursing facility away from her family. By the fifth year, Anna grew comfortable with Amy's needs and with the help of a nurse and physical therapist that visited twice weekly, the once insurmountable tasks became routine.

On the positive side, Amy's enormous medical bills were one burden the family was not forced to deal with. What her health insurance didn't cover, her disability did and when that fell short, it helped having a couple of millionaires in the family. Between Chuck and Angel, Amy didn't lack for anything. Her ex-husband and sisters saw to it that Amy was more than well cared for—physically, financially and emotionally.

Fortunately, for Anna, all the children were old enough by now to care for themselves. Little Ann, the youngest, was now nine-years-old. Chuck, Jr. was twelve and Nicky, the oldest, was fifteen. Nicky and her fourteen-year-old sister, Olivia, were of a tremendous help to their mother in their aunt's care. They helped Anna feed, bath and dress Amy. They were at the age where they could also help with other household chores such as the cooking, washing and helping look after the younger children. In addition to helping care for their aunt, they also had to help look after Harry, whose health was rapidly declining. At ninety, his body seemed sounder than his mind at times. He was becoming increasingly forgetful and had to be reminded to eat and take his daily medications. Needless to say, Anna was grateful for her two daughters.

While Anna devoted her life to the care of her children, husband, quadriplegic sister and a senile old man, Gene continued to sweat and toil on the farm day after day, all the while despising his lot in life more and more with each passing year. As long as Harry Porter lived, Gene was trapped. He was locked into a way of life he never wanted but was forced to accept out of poverty and lack of alternatives. He kept telling himself if he could just hold out until Harry died, he would have a good chance at becoming financially secure for the rest of his life and free of the farm once and for all. The exact number of years left in his sentence remained to be seen. Yet one thing was for certain, the longer it took, the bitterer he became.

Their three sons, ages twelve to fourteen were deeply involved in sports as well as Amy's son, who was the same age as Gene's youngest boy. Gene refused to allow the farm to prevent him from attending his kids' ballgames. Whenever there was a game, Gene was right there on the front row along with his ex-brother-in-law, Chuck. One evening they sat in the bleachers proudly cheering on their sons' athletic accomplishments while discussing their lives and families.

"You know, I don't think I've ever told you how much I appreciate you opening your home to Amy instead of allowing her to go to a nursing home," Chuck told Gene. "I know it's a tremendous burden on Anna and it can't be easy on you either. I know you and Amy weren't on the best terms. She never was one of your favorite people and vice versa."

"Well, if there's one thing I've learned in this life, you do what you have to do and not always what you want to do. We all have obligations. That's just part of life. You do it and make the best of it for as long as you have to. Anna is my wife and Amy is her sister, so there was never any doubt in my mind what the right thing was to do. Sometimes you just have to take what life hands you."

Chuck nodded. "Yeah. And life doesn't always turn out the way you plan it. When Amy and I married, I figured we'd always be together till death do us part, but it didn't work out that way. You don't know how lucky you are to still have Anna and a solid marriage."

"Oh, I do, too. I'm very lucky to have her. She's the best thing that ever happened to me," Gene assured him. "I couldn't live without her. There are times when I want to walk away from that damn farm so bad I don't know what to do, but she and the kids are the reason I stay."

"Anna's always loved it there," Chuck replied.

"Yeah, but that's only because she ain't never had to work it the way I have. I went to work there because I was too young to get a job anywhere else and because my old man needed the money. And I been stuck there ever since. Sometimes I think I should have left this place instead of going to work for Harry and gone down to Macon or Atlanta and found work down there. But if I had, I would probably never met Anna, so I guess everything happens for a reason."

"If that's the case, then how come things happened in my life the way they did?" Chuck asked him. "How come I wound up divorced with my ex-wife in a wheel chair the rest of her life?"

"Well Chuck, you have to look at things realistically. What happened to Amy and between you two wasn't your fault. You never cheated on Amy or drank yourself into a hospital and you weren't the one driving the car that day when she plowed under a truck. None of that was your doing."

"No, I guess you're right," Chuck replied, staring out across the ball field. He continued to remain silent for a while as they watched their sons' team score another touchdown. Finally Chuck said, "You know, I'll always love her. As far as I'm concerned, Amy's still my wife. Since we've been divorced I've never cared for anybody the way I cared for her. It'll be ten years this April since we split up and I love her as much today as the day I married her. I guess that's how I was finally able to forgive her for Toby's death. There was a time when I thought I would never be able to say that, but I do. I forgive her for everything."

"Why didn't you try to get back together with her?"

"Because I could never trust her. See, I knew all along that the only reason Amy married me was to get away from her old man. Amy never really loved me. She just used me to escape. And I accepted that. I thought after a while, she'd grow to love me the way I loved her. But I don't think Amy is capable of loving anyone. She sees all men the way she saw her father. I don't' think she ever really liked men. She just used them."

Gene thought for a moment, and then replied, "Well if that's the case, I guess maybe I could say that Anna used me to escape her old man the same way."

"Yeah, but fifteen years later you guys are still together. You've had five kids. I was only able to have two and that's because I kept on insisting that we start a family. Amy never wanted kids to begin with. It was me who wanted a family. Now, Chuckie is all I got left. I don't even have a wife now."

"You're still young," Gene told him. "You can find yourself another woman and start over. It's not too late."

Chuck shook his head. "In the ten years we've been divorced I've only dated three other women and never once came even close to tellin' one of them that I loved her. Now Amy on the other hand had lots of men after her when we split. But I just couldn't stop loving her long enough to find somebody else I wanted to be with." He paused once again, as if reflecting over his life. "No, I think in all, your life turned out a hundred times better than mine. You don't have a damn thing to bitch and moan about. You still have Anna and five terrific kids and they're all in good health. Me? I got nothin'."

Gene remained silent as he thought over what Chuck said. Finally, he had to agree. His life was pretty damn good after all.

# Book IV

# Chapter Twenty-One

In July 1986 the twins, Gene, Jr. and Olivia, turned fifteen. The following November Nicky would turn sixteen. Chuck, Jr. would soon be thirteen. The children were growing up fast and time continued to march on with little change. Anna continued to care for her sister and nephew. Gene continued to work the farm and Angel was not only the manager of one, but two successful carpet mills. Since she was no longer able to expand the one in Myrick, she was forced to follow through with her original plans and open a second mill in Dalton, Georgia. AAA Carpet Mills of Myrick and Dalton were now supplying carpet and tile for most of the entire North American continent and even some countries overseas. In Forbes 500, she was listed number nine as one of the wealthiest women in the United States. Her sisters' wealth grew along with hers. As shareholders and part owners, Amy and Anna were now multimillionaires themselves.

Now that Tom Webber was living in Myrick, he spent a good portion of his free time at the farm with Anna and his five grandchildren. Webber grew closer to his daughter and five grandchildren as he became older and realized he was alone and had no other family or friends. He found, to his own surprise, many of his afternoons spent on a ball field with his son-in-law and Chuck Willis, watching his three grandsons and their cousin honing their athletic skills. He also insisted on paying for his two granddaughters' piano and ballet lessons and looked forward to those weekends when he took them to Atlanta to the art museums and ballet.

On those weekends, he would also take them shopping at the most expensive stores the city had to offer and buy them designer clothes and accessories. Finally, Gene put his foot down and refused to allow his daughters to continue to be spoiled. Although he wanted his children to have more than he was forced to have growing up, he didn't want them to grow up being spoiled and pampered. He was also resentful and jealous of the affection and attention another man was lavishing on his two daughters, as well as his wife. Gene was the kind of man who was annoyed by the presence of *any* man in his family's life other than himself. Still, Tom spent most Sundays at the farm gathered around the table with the rest of Anna's family, enjoying one of her delicious home cooked Sunday dinners. Despite the years he lost with his own daughter, he was present at each of his grandchildren's birthday celebrations and every holiday gathering. He felt bad for the time he missed watching Anna grow up, but considered himself blessed to have her and her children in his life now.

Anna was his greatest accomplishment and he was so proud of the beautiful and caring woman she had become. And he was just as proud of his five grandchildren. Taking after their mother and two aunts, Nicky and Olivia had grown into magnificent young women and were so beautiful in fact, that they frequently competed in local beauty pageants, walking away with the title and crown. The three boys were handsome, strapping young men like their father. They were all honor roll students who worked hard alongside their dad on the farm and were popular star athletes at Myrick High. They were all well-mannered, respectful and fiercely devoted to their family. Despite a few early traumas in their childhood and some family hardships, they all had turned out to be well-adjusted and responsible young adults.

Anna continued to be her sister's primary caregiver except for the weekly visits from the registered nurse who kept tabs on Amy's general health issues. On one such visit, the nurse asked Anna if she could speak to her privately before she left. Anna led her into the kitchen while Amy remained in her bedroom.

"I think we need to take Amy in for a routine mammogram," the nurse told her. "I found a lump in her left breast while I was examining her."

"Oh no," Anna groaned.

"Now let's not jump to conclusions. It's probably nothing, but we need to play it safe and get it checked out."

"Alright," Anna agreed. "When do you want me to bring her in?"

"Let me make an appointment at Barrow County hospital and I'll call you as soon as I find out when they can see her."

Angel took off work the next day and together, she and Anna took their sister to the new hospital there in Barrow County where Amy was given a mammogram. They were told they would know something in a couple of days after the radiologist had read the results. That Friday, Anna received a phone call from Amy's doctor. He wanted Amy back in his office as soon as possible for a biopsy. Another week passed before more test results arrived. This time the news was not good. Amy was already in the advanced stages of breast cancer.

The following year and a half was exhausting and painful for Amy as well as her family. After having a radical mastectomy, she was given chemotherapy followed by radiation treatments. After eighteen months, the doctors felt confident the disease was in remission. But by Thanksgiving, Amy's cancer had returned and spread rapidly throughout her entire body. The doctors sent her home with less than six months to live. Hospice was called in and her family braced themselves for the worst.

Anna remained at her sister's bedside every waking hour of each day. By now, her medical knowledge was well rounded and exceptional. She insisted on doing as much as possible for Amy. She even administered injections and oxygen and changed Amy's disposable undergarments when necessary. She turned her frail, thin body from side to side every few hours to prevent bedsores from developing. After she had done all she could to answer her sister's physical needs, Anna would sit on the side of the bed and rub lotion on Amy's body while talking to her until she finally drifted off into a morphine induced sleep.

Frequently, Chuck would come to the house and spend a couple of hours at his former wife's bedside, holding her hand and stroking her forehead as they discussed their son and Amy's last wishes for him.

Chuck, Jr. was the one who was taking his mother's illness the hardest. Watching his mother die a slow, agonizing death after spending the last eight years confined to a wheelchair, was more than the young man could bear. Remembering his mother's struggle with alcoholism and being separated from her while she was in rehab when he was still a young boy was difficult enough. Then after the car accident that paralyzed her and put her in a wheelchair for nearly a decade, he felt a tremendous sense of loss. Now, to stand by helplessly and watch his mother succumb to cancer was devastating. Amy had always been so vibrant and alive. She was a spirited woman blessed with more than her share of physical beauty. Yet now, she was only a shell of the woman she had once been. Her beautiful, curly brown hair was all gone, along with her eyebrows, taken from her by the chemotherapy. Her once curvaceous body was fragile and skeletal-like. The vicious disease had taken her beauty as well as her spirit and it was difficult for anyone to accept, especially her fifteen year-old son. Were it not for the comfort and support from his father and mother's family, he would not have been able to make it through the crisis.

Christmas 1988 was not the joyous occasion at the Longhorn house that it normally was. Amy continued to linger painfully near death with each day growing worse than the day before. Anna continued to care for her dying sister with the help of the Hospice professionals. Nicky was eighteen now and enrolled in nursing school in Rome. She commuted the distance to and from college each day so that she could remain at home at least part of the time to help her mother care for her aunt.

Inspired by her grandfather's influence, seventeen year-old Olivia chose to follow in his footsteps and become an antique dealer and interior designer. An honor role student who was allowed to skip the tenth grade, Olivia graduated that June from high school, a year ahead of her class. Tom insisted on paying for his granddaughter's education and enrolled her at the Atlanta Institute of Design in Atlanta. On weekends, when she returned home, she worked with him at his antique shop where she would be employed after earning her degree.

Her twin brother Gene, also an honor student who was allowed to graduate a year early along with his sister, was now attending Georgia Tech in Atlanta on a football scholarship and was majoring in engineering. Joey was an exceptionally bright sixteen year-old whose love of animals led him to decide to become a veterinarian. At fifteen, and much to his father's chagrin, Hal announced he wanted to become a farmer and raise dairy cattle. Needless to say, Gene was doing everything in his power to discourage his youngest son from traveling down the same path he had been forced to travel.

At ninety-three, Harry was requiring more of Anna's attention. His frail body had at last caught up with his declining state of mind and now, besides being senile, he stumbled and fell quite often. Anna feared that he would either forget and leave the stove on and catch the trailer on fire or fall while getting out of the shower and lay there for hours before one of them found him. Like most people his age, Harry had his good and his bad days. On those good days, he seemed alert and lucid and could remember incidents in minute detail that occurred nearly eight decades ago. On the bad days, he had trouble remembering names and daily occurrences and stumbled about easily losing his balance. With a dying sister and a feeble old man to care for, Anna more than had her hands full.

The week after Thanksgiving, Anna busied herself putting up the Christmas tree and decorating the house for the holidays. With her sister lay dying she wasn't exactly in the Christmas spirit, yet she proceeded to go through the motions for the children's sake.

On a Wednesday night following Thanksgiving, Anna sat at her sister's bedside as she did every night, talking to her and attempting to make her as comfortable as possible before she drifted off to sleep. That same afternoon the Hospice nurse had taken Anna aside and warned that her sister's time could be any day now.

"Keep check on her legs and feet," the nurse advised her. "If they seem cold and begin turning purple, call me."

"I don't understand," Anna replied.

"Death begins at the feet and travels up. That's one of the first signs. Oh, and remember," she added. "No water. Her body is shutting down. Her kidneys are no longer able to process fluid intake."

"You mean I can't even offer my sister water if she's thirsty?"

"I'm afraid not, dear. It would only make her more uncomfortable. The best thing we can do for Amy now is to allow nature to take it's course and not prolong her suffering."

After helping her mother settle Amy in for the night, Nicky asked Anna if she needed her to sit up with Amy just in case she happened to need help.

"No sweetie, I think I can handle her alone," Anna told her daughter. "You go on to bed and get some sleep. You have classes tomorrow and I don't want you making that long drive to Rome and back on little or no sleep."

"Okay, but don't hesitate to wake me if you need anything," Nicky told her mother before going upstairs to bed.

Anna sat down on the side of the bed and placed a cold cloth on Amy's forehead. She had been in and out of consciousness all day. At brief times she was able to talk with some sense, but most of the time she lay in a morphine induced stupor. Tonight however, she seemed more alert and talkative than she had been in weeks.

"How's the pain?" Anna asked. "Do you need something to help you sleep?"

Amy's eyes remained closed and she was barely able to shake her head in silence. Anna could tell that her sister was growing weaker by the day.

"Can I get you anything?"

"Another body," Amy whispered, managing a faint smile.

"I wish I could," Anna replied, returning her sister's smile. "I wish I had the power to make you well and have you get out of this bed and back to your old self again."

"My old self is what helped put me here in the first place," Amy said, barely above a whisper. "But even if I had never been speeding that day and had the accident, I would have still gotten sick."

"That's right," Anna agreed, stroking her sister's forehead. "You had absolutely no control over that."

"But at least I would have still been able to go to some of Chuck's ballgames and been more involved in his life over the years. Now, when he needs me the most, I won't be there for him."

"Chuck is going to be alright," Anna assured her sister. "He still has his father and he has us. Between Chuck and Gene and me, we'll see to it that he turns out fine."

"I've had a lot of time to think about my mistakes and I've made so many. The worst part is, the people around me also had to pay for them."

"There's no use in blaming yourself for everything that's happened," Anna told her. "We have only so much control over our own lives, the rest is left up to fate and dumb luck, or whatever you want to call it. People say life is what you make it, but I don't believe that. I think life is thirty percent left up to you, twenty percent dumb luck and fifty percent fate. I always thought our lives were pretty much already mapped out for us from the time we were born."

Amy seemed to drift off to sleep for a moment, then her eyes opened and she looked straight into her sister's eyes. "I never could figure you out," she whispered softly.

"What do you mean?" Anna replied with a curious smile.

"You always seemed so happy with so little. That day Angel and I drove out to Gene's father's house and we saw you living in that rundown shack we couldn't believe how happy you seemed. And then when Harry gave you this old house that was caving in, you were the happiest person in the world. You would have thought he had given you a mansion to live in."

"Well he did. It just took some time and a little elbow grease to polish it up a bit," Anna laughed softly.

"Of the three of us, you always seemed to have the least, but you never once complained or seemed to have any regrets."

"That's because I don't have any regrets and nothing to complain about," Anna replied. "I have a wonderful husband, five beautiful children, a beautiful home, no financial worries and I have my health. What could I possibly have to complain about?"

"You've always worked constantly and never had any time for yourself. You've spent your life doing for other people. You live in the kitchen cooking three meals a day for nearly a dozen people, seven days a week. And when you're not doing that, you're taking care of kids, washing clothes, scrubbing floors or tending a vegetable garden. Angel and I used to wonder how you managed to keep up the pace and not go nuts. We always blamed Gene for keeping you pregnant and not ever letting you out of the house. He never allowed you to have a life of your own. Only the life he let you to have. We never could figure out what you saw in him from the beginning. He was a loser when you met him and he still is. He has no education, no money, except yours, and if it weren't for Harry, you'd still be living in a shack. You could have done so much better."

"And I could have done a lot worse. I've done just fine. I'm happy with my life. Gene's been good to me. I never went hungry and he never abused the children or me. Just a little controlling at times, is all," Anna smiled. "He's a wonderful husband and devoted father. He would do anything in the world for us."

"Well, I guess I could say the same about my other brother-in-law," Amy said. "Talk about a loser. At least yours wasn't an ex-con. I guess some people are satisfied with what they can get. I always believed you could marry rich and handsome as well as you could poor and ugly."

"And where did that philosophy get you?" Anna asked with a knowing smile. "You had it all. A rich and handsome husband, a beautiful home and a wonderful son."

"I guess I threw it all away, didn't I?"

"You let it slip through your fingers. Sometimes, we're our own worst enemy. It never mattered to me if Gene had two dimes in his pocket or was the handsomest man in town. All that mattered was he was good to me and loved me no matter what. Money doesn't make happiness. We make our own happiness."

"I guess you're right," Amy replied softly. She began drifting off again, her eyes closing, her head resting slowly on the pillow. In the next moment, she opened her eyes once more and seemed to pick up where she left off.

"You know," she said. "I look at your two girls and I see you and Angel. Nicky is the most like you. She's the caregiver. She's very sweet and loving. Always ready to do for others. But Olivia is more like Angel. She's strong and independent. Ambitious. It's a good thing you didn't have a third daughter. She could have turned out like me."

"You didn't turn out so bad," Anna told her sister. "You did alright."

"I could have done a lot better. I should have gone into therapy and gotten help a lot sooner than I did. It might have kept me from making some of the mistakes that helped destroy my life. And Chuck's."

"Like what?"

"It could have saved my marriage for one thing. Therapy made me understand why I did the things I did. I drank and took pills to numb the pain I carried around from childhood. I married Chuck to get away from Daddy. I cheated on Chuck and used men the way I used drugs and alcohol, to numb the emotional pain I felt. And in a sick way, I felt I was getting even with men by using them the way I was used by Daddy. If I hurt them first, they didn't have a chance to hurt me."

"Knowing that now, what would you have done differently?"

"I wouldn't have married Chuck."

"But Chuck has always loved you. He still does. And he was always so good to you. Besides, you wouldn't have had two wonderful children."

"It didn't matter," Amy said. "I was incapable of loving any man. I married Chuck because he offered me freedom. And I should have never had children. It wasn't fair to bring a child into my messed up life. Chuckie would have been much better off being born to someone else like you and Gene. To parents who loved one another and who could give him a stable home life. That's why all your kids turned out so good."

"Chuck isn't turning out bad. He's a fine boy," Anna assured her sister. "He's smart and a good boy. And he loves both of his parents very much."

"I should have done what Angel did," Amy sighed heavily. "I shouldn't have married and gone on to college and moved away from Myrick and become independent the way she did. She escaped without having to use a man the way you and I did. She did it all on her own. She was always the smartest and toughest of the three of us."

"None of that matters now," Anna told her sister. "We were all three different people with very different personalities. It's only natural that we took different roads in life. And besides, happiness has to come from within. We can't expect someone else to make us happy or rescue us from the past. Expecting someone else to offer us happiness is like using drugs or alcohol to find an escape. You have to look deep inside yourself and make *you* happy with the person you are. No one else can give it to us. You just never learned how to do that."

"Maybe I never knew what to look for. I still don't. Maybe some people are just destined to be miserable all their lives no matter what they do. I just never could find happiness, no matter how hard I tried. Maybe

I just looked in all the wrong places." Amy tried to shift her body and winced in pain.

"Are you alright? Can I get you something?" Anna asked.

"The pain is worse in my back. I can't go to sleep. I just want to go to sleep and make the pain go away," she began to sob.

"I'll give you something to help you sleep," Anna told her sister as she got up from the bed and began preparing a tiny cup filled with a dose of morphine. She held it to Amy's lips and watched her sister's body begin to relax as the painkiller took its affect.

"No one could have taken better care of me all these years," Amy whispered. "If I lived to be a hundred, I would never be able to repay you for all you've done for Chuckie and me."

"You're not supposed to repay me. I'm your sister. We're all supposed to look after one another. That's what families are for. Besides," Anna teased, placing another cold cloth on her sister's forehead, "I just may consider taking up nursing after the kids are gone."

"Sure. Like Gene Longhorn is going to let you out of his sight long enough. He's the reason you have two daughters who've never had a steady boyfriend between them. He always managed to scare off every guy they tried to go out with. I'm surprised they didn't try to get away from him the way I did Dad."

Anna remained silent. Under other circumstances, she would have quickly come to her husband's defense, but she felt there was no need now. This was the first time Amy had been able to carry on a conversation with her in weeks. She decided to let her talk as long as she was able.

Finally, she saw Amy begin to relax and drift off into a painless sleep. "I feel good knowing Chuckie's with you," Amy mumbled, barely above a whisper. "That's one less thing I have to worry about."

"Chuckie's like one of our own," Anna assured her. "He's lived here on the farm most of his life. He's more like a brother to my kids than a cousin. This is his home and it always will be."

Anna was thankful for the morphine. It was the only thing that gave her sister relief from the excruciating pain that had taken over her entire body. Yet as she watched Amy drift off into a deep sleep, she hated for their conversation to end. It was the first time in weeks that Amy had the presence of mind to express her thoughts to anyone. It was almost like having Amy back again. She continued to remain at her sister's side as she watched her find peace and freedom from suffering in her sleep. Anna felt alone and sad. She selfishly wanted her sister to wake up again so they could talk some more. Finally, Anna slowly rose from the edge of the bed.

"Is Chuckie here?" Amy whispered, startling Anna.

"No sweetie. He's upstairs asleep," she replied, tucking the covers securely around her sister's body.

"Tell him I love him," she said, her speech slurred and her eyes still closed.

"I will."

That night Anna didn't have the heart to leave her sister's side. She took the afghan that was hung over the back of the Boston rocker in Amy's room and placed it across her lap as she sat down in the chair at the foot of her sister's bed. She leaned back and stared out the window over the moonlit lawn. It was freezing outside but warm and cozy inside the old plantation house. Anna sat thinking how may weddings, births and deaths the old house had witnessed before she came to live there and began counting the ones that occurred since she and Gene moved in eighteen years ago. Each of their five children had been born in that very room with Gene at her side. Even Cassie had brought Nicky into the world right there in that same room. She wondered how many more it would witness and what would happen to the house she so dearly loved after *she* was gone. She hoped she would be as fortunate as Amy to draw her last breath there in a warm, comfortable bed among familiar surroundings with her family in the adjoining rooms. She began to drift off to sleep with those comforting thoughts, despite the fact that her sister lay dying only a few feet away. There was something about that old house that made even the most horrific times seem bearable.

Anna awoke suddenly to the sound of muffled whispers in the room. She glanced at the clock on the bedside table. It was a little after midnight. She had been asleep a little over two hours. She listened and heard her sister talking to someone. She and Amy were the only ones in the room, yet her sister appeared to be speaking to someone beside her bed. Anna got up from her chair and went over to the side of the bed.

"You're wearing my favorite shade of green," Anna heard Amy say to someone. "It's such a pretty dress."

"Amy," Anna said, placing her hand on her sister's arm. "Who are you talking to sweetheart?"

There was a long silence. Anna waited for Amy to drift off back to sleep after waking from her dream.

"Olivia," Amy answered suddenly, her voice barely above a whisper. "She wants me to go with her."

"Honey, you're dreaming. Olivia is at school in Atlanta. She won't be home until tomorrow. Go back to sleep."

Anna stood over her sister's bed, waiting for her to drift off to sleep once again. After making sure Amy was sound asleep, she went back to the rocking chair and pulled the afghan up around her neck. She closed her eyes and fell fast asleep. When she awoke, she looked at the clock. It was almost three a.m. Time she went into the kitchen and began preparing her husband's breakfast. Gene would be getting up soon to do the morning milking. She got up from the rocking chair and walked over to the bed and felt of Amy's feet. They were ice cold. She reached up and felt of her hand. It was also cold as ice and hard. Her sister was gone.

# Chapter Twenty-Two

Amy was buried beside her son beneath the old Magnolia tree where Ollie and Gene's father were buried. Amy had told her sisters that was where she wanted to be laid to rest. Services were held at Myrick Methodist Church with family, friends and co-workers attending. The graveside service was small and intimate with only the immediate family present. The children came home from college to be at their mother's side for the funeral. It was a bitter cold, yet sunny day that Anna and Angel laid their sister to rest. At thirty-eight, Amy was far too young to have died so soon. Actually, her body had gone long before her actual death. The past eight years had been spent confined to a wheelchair, paralyzed from the shoulders down, unable to feed or bath herself. However, the last year and a half had been by far the worst, spent in unrelenting pain and deterioration. The cancer that claimed her life was only insult to injury.

That Christmas was the worst time Anna could ever remember since little Toby had died. There was no reason to celebrate. No one was in a festive mood. It was a sad time for everyone, especially Chuck, Jr. Yet somehow, they made it through the holidays and began the New Year with a bitter mixture of sadness and hope.

It was 1989 and the children were all nearly grown now with the two girls and oldest boy in college. Only Joey, Hal, Chuck, Jr. and Little Ann remained in high school. All but Olivia and Gene, Jr. still lived at home and they returned from college every weekend.

By now, Gene and Anna had been married almost nineteen years and still Gene continued to work the farm, hating every minute spent in the brutal sun and bone chilling cold, milking, feeding and caring for livestock.

Angel continued to run the two carpet mills and devoted most of her attention to her work, leaving little time for her husband and daughter. Thirteen year-old Ann spent more time at her aunt and uncle's farm than she did at Coleman Hill. She and her father were extremely close and Little Ann was quite a daddy's girl. She spent hours riding on the back of his Harley while they took short trips together to places like Stone Mountain and Helen, Georgia.

One morning Gene walked into the kitchen for a glass of iced tea after returning from the morning milking. Anna was busy washing some freshly picked turnip greens in the kitchen sink to have for dinner that night.

"There's nothing like fresh greens, but God I hate cleaning them. They're such a pain," Anna said, as she sprinkled some salt and baking soda over the mound of greens piled high in the kitchen sink.

"You ought to try milking three-hundred head of cows at four a.m. if you want to know what a real pain in the ass is," he told his wife.

"Well, maybe one day you won't ever have to do farm work again," she replied. "Gene, you do understand don't you, that you don't have to continue working this farm. You can quit anytime you get ready. We don't need the money. I'm making enough from the mill to more than take care of us the rest of our lives. We're millionaires in case you don't know it."

"No, *you're* a millionaire," he told her. "I don't want to have to live off my wife's money. I want my own money. What kind of a man would I be if I let my wife support me? No. I want to make my own fortune. I'm not livin' off yours."

"Alright then, do you have any idea what you would like to do if you ever did quite farming? What kind of business you'd like to own?"

"Yeah. Nothing. I'd like to do nothing the rest of my life."

Anna glanced over her shoulder at her husband. "Nothing? You'd have to do something in order to keep from going crazy. After working as hard as you have all your life, you couldn't stand being idle and just sitting around all day."

"You wanna bet? After doing farm work for nearly thirty years, I deserve to sit on my ass and do nothing for a change. I haven't slept past three a.m. since I was thirteen years-old. I'd like to know what it's like just once to sleep till seven in the morning and not have to get up and milk a heard of fuckin' cows."

"Gene, watch your language. You didn't used to talk like that. You've been hanging around Red too long. You're liable to slip up and talk like that in front of the children."

Gene walked into the den with his glass of tea and noticed a new print hanging over the sofa. "Where'd that come from?" he asked.

"What?" Anna replied.

"This picture over the sofa in here."

"Oh, that. Dad brought it by this morning on his way to the shop. He thought it would look nice with my color scheme in the den."

Gene stared at the expensive reproduction for a moment. "What was wrong with the one you had hanging up there?"

"Nothing. He just thought that one would look better."

"Is he queer?"

"What?" Anna asked, surprised at her husband's bluntness. "Of course not. What makes you ask something like that?"

"How come he's never married?"

"I don't know. I guess he just never found the right woman. Just because he never married doesn't mean he prefers men. Your brother never married and he isn't gay."

"Joey would be married right now if he wasn't so fat. He loves women but he repulses them. It's a shame too, because Joey would have made a good husband." Gene walked back into the kitchen and sat his empty glass on the counter. "I've got to run into town for a few things at the seed store. You need me to pick you up anything while I'm there?"

"No, I don't think so," Anna replied. "Hal is driving Harry into town in a little while for his doctor's appointment and I told him to stop by the grocery store for me. I had so much to do today around the house that the kids being out of school today for the teacher's meeting turned out to be a blessing in disguise. I'm glad Chuckie decided to hang out with his dad today. They need to spend some quality time together. He's come to look on you more as a father figure than he does his own dad."

"Well, to tell you the truth, he wanted to hang around here today and help me out around the farm, but I told him he needed to go spend some time with Chuck," Gene confessed.

"Really? I'm glad you told him he couldn't. He needs to be around Chuck more, especially now that Amy's gone."

"Hey Mom, I need the keys to the car. It's time I took Papa to his doctor's appointment," Hal announced, walking into the kitchen.

"Is it that late already?" his mother asked. "They're laying beside my purse in the hall on the desk. Get a twenty out of my wallet to take with you to the grocery store. Don't forget, I need a bag of cornmeal and some grits. And be sure you hang on to Harry's arm while he's going into the doctor's office. Don't let him fall."

"I won't."

"You be careful now," Gene warned his youngest son. "You watch out at that dangerous intersection goin' into town. Be sure you stop at that stop sign. Those tractor trailers flyin' through there will T-bone you."

"I will Dad. Don't worry, I'll be careful," the boy promised.

"Take forty dollars out of my wallet instead," Anna told her son. "You probably need to gas up the car while you're out."

"Yes, ma'am. I will."

After their son had left, Gene kissed his wife on the cheek and went back to his farm work while Anna continued doing her household chores. Sixteen year-old Hal went next door to the trailer, got Harry and helped him into his mother's Monte Carlo.

"You be sure to watch out at that intersection up the road," Harry warned the boy. "That's always been a dangerous intersection."

"I will Papa," Hal replied. "Momma wants me to stop by the store on the way home and pick up a couple of things for her and then I gotta gas up."

"That'll be okay," Harry told him. "We got plenty of time. I'm in no hurry. When you get to be my age, there's no need to hurry in the first place and in the second, you ain't able to."

"I need to get home in time to help Daddy with the afternoon milkin'," he said.

"You like workin' with them cows, don't you, son?" Harry asked, turning to the boy.

"Yes, sir. I like working the dairy better than I do the beef cattle though."

"Why's that?"

"'Cause I love animals and I don't like to think I'm carin' for them just so they can be loaded up on the truck and taken to the slaughter house. Me and Joey want to take over the farm someday when Dad retires. That's why Joey wants to go to vet school, so he can take care of the cows and we can run the farm."

"That's good. That's real good," Harry told the boy. "That makes me feel proud to know that I got somebody I can hand my land down to and keep it going after I'm gone. I don't want to see the farm sold off after I'm dead. I'd like to know it'll always be there even when I'm long gone."

"It will be as long as Joey and me are still around. Daddy keeps sayin' if he has anything to do with it, he'd sell it off to a land developer and let them make a big subdivision out of it. But me and Joey don't want that to happen."

Harry turned and looked at the boy. "Oh, no. No. That farmland has been around a couple hundred years. That's some of the richest pastureland in the state. We don't need to see that happen," Harry insisted. "When did you hear your Dad say that?"

"Ever since I was a kid," Hal replied.

"I tell you somethin', son. That land will make you a decent livin' and put food on your table when companies and factories are layin' people off left and right. People always need milk and beef. You'll never be out of a job and will always be able to put plenty of food on your own table and clothes on your kids' backs as long as that farm is still goin'. It's a lot of hard work with long hours, but that farm will be there when all them factories shut down. Why just look at how it's already outlived the cotton mills. No, you don't want to give up the farm. That'll be your livelihood and bread and butter as long as you're willing to work it."

"Yes, sir. I know," Hal agreed. "But Dad's sick of working it. He says he don't want no more part of it."

"Well, he's lucky to have had it all these years, is the way I see it. He needs to be thankful it was there to pay his salary when nobody else would hire him. If it weren't for me and that farm, he and your Momma would have gone hungry and wouldn't have had a roof over their heads."

"Well, Momma loves the farm. She always has. She's happy there. It's Daddy. He's the one who don't want to farm no more."

The farm was all Harry had and it had been his life since he could remember. The thought of having it sold off and made into a housing subdivision sickened him. As long as Gene was alive, Harry felt the farm would live on. But now, he was finding out different. If his sons wanted to take it over and continue farming, then they were the ones entitled to it. The farm had been handed down from generation to generation for over two centuries. Why should it have to cease with his passing? If Gene had grown too lazy to continue working it and wanted to make a fast and easy killing by selling it off to a land developer, then he didn't deserve it. The farm belonged in the hands of someone who cared enough to keep it alive—the same way Anna had cared enough about the old plantation house to keep it alive. Harry needed to know that *both* would still be around after he was gone and if all Gene saw in it was a way to make a fast buck, he didn't deserve it.

Anna pulled into the parking lot of Sonny's Pit Bar-B-Que beside her sister's Lincoln Continental and parked. Angel had asked Anna to meet her there for lunch that day. Since Anna didn't have to pick Angel's daughter up from school until three that afternoon, they had plenty of time to have a nice, leisurely lunch and catch up on some girl talk.

Angel was seated at a corner table smoking a cigarette as she waited on Anna to arrive.

"I'm sorry I'm running late," Anna apologized. "Have you been waiting long?"

"No. I just got here myself a few minutes ago. I had to stop by the bank on my way and the line at the drive-thru was a block long."

"Well, I just left the antique shop myself. I thought I'd never get away from Dad," Anna said. "He had to show me some new things he got in the other day and then we began talking about Olivia. She has another year left at school before she gets her degree and Tom is so excited about having her come work with him. He's already talking about taking an ad out in the Myrick Sun announcing her joining him in the business as his interior designer. He said he would put an announcement in the Rome paper as well. He's so proud of her. You would think she was his own daughter."

"I'm sure that makes Gene happy," Angel smiled with a hint of sarcasm.

"Are you kidding? Gene is so jealous of Dad's relationship with Olivia that I can't even mention his name around Gene anymore without setting him off. And I'm sure Dad senses his resentment because he seems uncomfortable around Gene when he comes over for dinner."

"Well, to be honest, I think Chuck, Red and Joey kind of side with Gene and gang up on Tom sometimes," Angel admitted. "You've got four rednecks in the same room with one educated, refined southern gentleman. If you want to know the truth, I think they're probably even a little jealous of him."

The waitress walked over to their table and took their order, then disappeared into the kitchen to get their iced tea. Angel extinguished her cigarette and reached in her purse for another one.

"Angel, it's none of my business, but you seem to be smoking a lot more than you used to. It's not good for you, you know."

"You're right," Angel replied, lighting up. "It's none of your business."

"Dad stopped smoking cigarettes right after we first met and smokes cigars now. I guess one is just as bad as the other, but he smokes less now since he switched to cigars," Anna said.

Angel sat silent for a moment as she gazed at her sister across the table. "I've been wanting to ask you something," she said. "What made you decide to start calling Tom, Dad? I mean, you never knew him as your father and you were strangers up until the day you walked into his shop."

"Well, we've known each other almost fifteen years now. And he *is* my biological father. We discussed it and he just said he thought it would be nice if I started calling him Dad instead of Tom. Tom *did* seem a little impersonal. Why? Does it bother you that I call him that?"

Angel shrugged. "It's nothing to me really. I just wondered. You know, I still can't believe that Olivia will be through with college in another year and Nicky will graduate nursing school this June," she said, changing the subject. "Or that Ann will be thirteen in June. Where does the time go?"

"I don't know," Anna sighed, shaking her head. "I can't believe Gene brought me here on our first date twenty-one years ago. This June we'll be married twenty years."

"Yeah well, it'll soon be fifteen years for Red and me. Of course, we may not make it to sixteen the way things are looking now."

"Amy, what's going on? You never mentioned any trouble between the two of you before," Anna replied, obviously surprised by her sister's revelation. "Is something wrong?"

"There's nothing really wrong" Angel shrugged. "Nothing except I'm tired of him is all. The marriage has finally run its course."

"What in the world are you talking about? Run its course? Are you saying you don't love him anymore?" Anna asked.

"I never loved him to begin with," Angel replied nonchalantly. "Our common ground was lust and we all know that can only last so long before it finally fizzles out and you're left with nothing."

"You never loved Red? At all?" Anna replied.

"No."

"Then why did you marry him?"

"Why not?" Angel shrugged. "I think everybody should try marriage at least once, maybe even have a kid. Just for the experience if nothing else. Now I can say I've been there, done that and it's time to move on."

Anna stared across the table at her sister in disbelief.

"Oh, don't look so surprised," Angel told her. Then leaning in closer she added in her low sultry voice, "Look, you and I both know that people in small, hick towns like Myrick don't accept gays and lesbians. I knew that if I came back to Myrick and took over the mill and tried to become successful, people around here wouldn't accept my lifestyle or me. However, if I were married and a practicing heterosexual like everybody else around here, they'd leave me alone. And obviously I was right because it worked out just fine."

"So you married just for that reason? You didn't marry Red because you loved him?"

Angel shook her head and shrugged. "No. You said yourself you couldn't figure out what if anything we had in common to begin with. And the answer is nothing. Red and I are total opposites. Okay, we had a thing going and it was good enough for us to decide to get married, but I've always gone back and forth."

"What do you mean?" Anna asked, appearing confused.

"I mean I like sleeping with men as well as women. Only women a little more."

"But I thought—"

"Look," Angel said, trying to explain her feelings to her naïve sister. "A leopard doesn't change its spots. I like to be with women more than I do men. But I also like a little variety now and then. It would be nice if I could have my cake and eat it too, but it doesn't work that way so at times, I'm forced to make a choice."

Anna stared at her sister in silence. "I see," she replied finally.

"Listen, Ann is almost thirteen. She's basically living with you and Gene and has been since she was a baby. She looks on you as parents as much as she does Red and me. I'm too busy with my career for the wife and mother role. I—"

"Is there someone else?" Anna asked, interrupting her sister.

"No. Not at the moment as far as I'm concerned," Angel replied. "But Red has been having his own little flings here and there for awhile now. But what do I care? I really couldn't care less who he sees. As long as he doesn't bother me."

"Are you telling me he's been seeing other women and you've known about it?"

"Sure, I know," Angel shrugged.

"And you don't care?"

"Of course not. Why should I care if he's seeing other women? I don't care about him. I don't care about the marriage. We don't have a marriage anymore. We never did really. I needed him in the beginning and now I don't need him anymore. It's as simple as that."

Anna stared at her sister from across the table. She couldn't believe what she was hearing. "You make it sound like the past fifteen years have been no more than an experiment for you. You used Red to serve your purpose and now you're kicking him to the side. I can't believe you,

Angel. That doesn't even sound like something you'd do. Amy maybe, but not you."

"Of course it does. Look, you're nothing like me. You were nothing like Amy. You've always been the total opposite of us so I don't expect you to understand or relate to anything I do. I do what's best for me. What makes me happy and Red doesn't make me happy anymore. I'm ready to move on."

"If you don't care anything about your husband, then what about your daughter? Doesn't Ann matter?"

"Of course she does. I love her dearly. But I can't stay married just because I have a kid. If that were the case, nobody would ever get divorced. The truth is, I'm a much better businesswoman than I am a mother. Now you, on the other hand, were born to be a mother. You're *mother earth*. The perfect little wife and homemaker. That kind of thing never appealed to me. But you were made for it. That's why Amy and I dumped our kids on you. You were much better mother material than either of us. I'm not saying Amy and I never loved our kids. She did and so do I very much. But both of us had other issues to deal with besides motherhood and pie baking."

"It kind of sounds like you're making fun of me," Anna replied, taking offense.

"No. I'm not making fun of you. Actually, I'm paying you a compliment in an off-handed way. Homemaking is a lost art. You are a dying breed. It's commendable that you do your job so well and Amy's kid and mine are better off because we were fortunate enough to have you as our sister. But we weren't cut out for marriage and motherhood." Angel reached across the table and took her sister's hand. "Anna, I don't think you realize just how special you are. You are one in a million. You're the caregiver in the family. You're sweet and loving and caring. You're everything Amy and I never were or could be. You're the backbone in this family whether you know it or not. You're the one everyone turns to in time of need. Everybody thinks I'm the strongest of the three sisters, but I'm not. You are. I could never do what you do."

"But you were the independent one. You never needed anyone. Besides, running a corporation is a much bigger responsibility than running a household. I certainly couldn't do your job."

"And I couldn't do yours," Angel smiled. "You deserve a crown just for staying married to Gene as long as you have."

"Why do you say that? I love Gene more than anything else in the world. He's my life. We've had some pretty bad things happen to us, but we've always pulled through it because we've had each other. I've never been able to figure out why you and Amy felt the way you do about him. He's a wonderful man and the kids couldn't ask for a better father. What's he ever done to make you and Amy feel the way you do toward him?"

"Anna, Amy and I always knew that you could have done so much better. You had so much potential. You're beautiful, intelligent and not a lazy bone in your body. You could have joined us in the business and been such an asset. Or you could have left Myrick and done so much more with your life. We just could never figure out what you saw in him, is all."

"I love him. I fell in love with him the first time we went out. I knew he was the man I wanted to spend the rest of my life with from that very moment. But I guess you and Amy couldn't understand that because neither of you were capable of loving anyone other than yourselves."

Angel remained silent. There was nothing more she could say. Her sister was right. They were incapable of love but there was a reason for that.

"Okay. You're right," Angel finally had to agree. "Amy and I are very different from you, but then you never had to go through what we did. Dad never damaged you the way he did us. Maybe if he had, you would have turned out more like us." Angel paused and snuffed out her cigarette when she saw the waitress arriving with their food. "Maybe that's why you turned out to be so *special*," she added.

Anna stared at Angel in silence while the waitress placed their meal on the table. "Is there anything else I can get for you?" she asked before leaving.

"No thank you," Angel replied.

"Alright, just holler if you need anything."

After the waitress had left them alone, Anna continued to stare at her sister across the table. Finally she replied, "I want to know why you and Amy always seemed to hold it against me that he never sexually abused me. Was it jealousy? Would you rather he had? Because if he had then I would have turned out just as screwed up as the two of you?"

Angel started to say something, but Anna cut her off. "I think you're forgetting something," she added. "I didn't exactly escape unscathed. He abused me too, only in a different way. We were all abused. I wasn't exactly his golden fair-haired child, you know. He hated me worse than he did either of you. He was an evil man who destroyed everything and everybody he came in contact with. So no, I'm not *special* by any means."

"Look, I know he abused you, too. I'm not saying I wish he had turned to you the way he did us," Angel tried to explain. "He just didn't damage you in the same way."

"So is that my fault?"

"No, of course not. Look, maybe I am a little jealous because you wound up more 'normal' than the rest of us and were able to meet the man of your dreams and have a long and happy marriage. I didn't mean to piss you off."

"Well, you did," Anna snapped. She was hurt by what her sister had said and Angel knew it. Anna had always been the more sensitive of the three and her skin wasn't nearly as thick as theirs.

"Listen, I didn't invite you to lunch today to argue or start a fight," Angel explained. "I invited you here so that we could talk and I could break the news to you about Red and me before you heard it from someone else. This is a small town and people talk." Angel paused and looked at her sister, who was quietly eating her food and seemed to have decided to tune her out for the rest of the visit.

"So, you are definitely planning on divorcing Red?" Anna said finally, after a long silence.

"I suppose so," Angel sighed. "And the sooner the better. No use in prolonging the inevitable. Of course, it's going to cost me to get rid of him. He's not going to be so willing to give up the cash flow he's become accustomed to. I figure I'll offer him one lump sum and he can go his merry way."

"How do you think the split will affect Ann?"

Angel shrugged. "I don't think it will matter much to her one way or the other. She's never with us anyway. She'll be fine. As long as she's with you she'll be okay."

They continued to eat their lunch, neither having anything else to add to the conversation. Finally, feeling bad about the way their visit had turned out Angel tried to apologize to her sister.

"Anna, I didn't mean to insult you or hurt your feelings—"

"You didn't," Anna cut her off quickly. "I know you well enough by now. I know how you feel about me. And my husband. You've had plenty of opportunity to make yourself more than clear on lots of occasions. But I've never been judgmental of you *or* Amy. I never ridiculed either of you for what you did or who you were. And God knows I had more right to than you ever did with me." With that, Anna removed her napkin from her lap and placed it back on the table. "I have to be going or I'll be late picking up your daughter from school," she added with a hint of sarcasm. She began digging in her purse for her wallet.

"Lunch is on me," Angel told her. "Don't bother."

"Fine," Anna said, tossing a ten-dollar bill on the table. "At least let me take care of the tip." She got up and slid her chair back under the table.

"I'll call you later," Angel said. "Look Anna, I'm really sorry about today. I didn't mean—"

"I'll talk to you later," Anna said cutting her off as she turned and left the restaurant.

All the way home Anna couldn't get their conversation out of her mind. She felt hurt and angry. She didn't want to believe her sister had said those things to intently hurt her, but she did, rather she meant to or not. She knew Angel was only being honest. And maybe sometimes the truth did hurt, but Anna had heard the same song over and over from both her sisters until she was sick of hearing it. And she was sick of them running her husband down.

Gene walked into the kitchen from the afternoon milking and found Anna in the middle of preparing dinner. He also found her unusually solemn and preoccupied.

"How was your lunch with your sister today?" he asked, digging in the refrigerator for a cold soda.

There was a long pause before Anna answered him. She knew if she were honest and told him everything that was said, he would be angry and that was something she always tried to avoid. She knew her husband's temper was quick and fierce.

"Fine," she finally replied.

Gene leaned against the kitchen counter and took a long drink from the soda can while studying his wife silently. He watched her body language and knew something was bothering her.

"Did you two have words?"

"No," Anna replied simply as she continued peeling potatoes over the sink.

"Did Angel say something to piss you off?" he persisted.

Suddenly Little Ann walked into the kitchen, interrupting them. "Can I have a glass of chocolate milk?" she asked.

"Not now, Ann," her aunt told her. "You'll spoil your dinner. We'll be eating soon."

"I'm going next door to check on Harry," the vivacious thirteen year-old said, as she quickly turned to go out the door. "I'll be back and help you finish fixin' dinner in a little while."

As soon as she had closed the kitchen door behind her, Gene turned to Anna and said, "I bet if you smelled her breath when she gets back, you'd smell chocolate."

"Oh, I know," Anna replied. "She's doesn't fool me. She's not going to check on Harry. She's going over there to make a glass of chocolate milk. Harry keeps milk and Hershey's Syrup in the frig not because he likes it, but because the kids like it and it entices them to come over."

"So, what went on between you and Angel this afternoon?" Gene asked, returning to their conversation before they were interrupted.

"Did you know that she and Red were about to split up?" Anna replied, preferring not to go into what was really bothering her about their luncheon that day.

Gene finished his soda and crushed the can in his hand before tossing it into the trash. "No, but I'm not surprised," he replied. "Is that what she told you today?"

Anna nodded. "She said she was seriously considering a divorce because she didn't love him anymore and that he had begun to see other women."

Gene nodded silently.

"Has Red said anything to you about things not being right between them?"

"Well, I knew for a long time that Red felt neglected because she spent more time at the mill than with him and Ann. She already succeeded in pushing her daughter away. That's why she's living with us instead of at home with her parents. But I guess since Angel can't send her husband over here to live, the next best thing is to divorce him. That sister of yours is a real piece of work."

"Did you know Red had been seeing other women?" Anna asked.

"I had a feeling he's been playing around with some waitress at Sonny's. And then there was some girl at the mill he'd taken for a ride on his motorcycle a few times. But then I figured it didn't really bother Angel or she'd do something about it."

"Well, obviously she is because she's going to ask him for a divorce. She said—"

Suddenly they were interrupted again when Ann came running through the kitchen door. "Aunt Anna, come quick! Harry's fallen and he's unconscious. He's hit his head and he's bleeding."

"Oh, my God!" Anna gasped, dropping the potatoes in the sink as she and Gene ran out of the kitchen to Harry's trailer.

# Chapter Twenty-Three

Harry's stroke robbed him of his ability to care for himself but left him alive. He was unable to feed, bathe or dress himself. He was unable to go to the bathroom without assistance and was confined to a wheelchair. Still, at ninety-five, he remained alert, at least most of the time, and maintained the will to live. After a two-week stay in the Barrow County Hospital, the doctors informed Gene and Anna that they had done all they could for Harry and suggested he would be much better off in a nursing home where he could receive round the clock care. Anna however, insisted on bringing him home where she could care for him. Gene quickly sided with the doctors and urged his wife to take their advice and admit Harry into a nursing home there in Myrick. For the first time since they were married, Anna stood her ground and refused to obey her husband's demands.

"I wouldn't let my sister be sent to a nursing home. I brought her home where I could care for her, and she lived eight years longer than she probably would have otherwise. I will do the same for Harry," she insisted.

"It's different," Gene said. "Harry's already ninety-five, there's no way he'll live another eight years. Besides, you can't care for a man all by yourself. He needs to be in a nursing home where they can bathe and dress him. You can't do any of that."

"I can get a nurse to come in for five or six hours a day to help me the way I did with Amy. At least let me try to care for him," Anna pleaded. "If it doesn't work out, then we'll discuss other options. But at least let me try."

Reluctantly, Gene gave in, but only after something Red had told him. "Maybe if you bring the old man home with you to live out his last days, he'll leave everything he's got to you—the farm, his money, everything. After all, he doesn't have anybody else to leave it to."

Gene decided his friend had a point. At least with Harry under their close supervision, he could make certain no one talked the old man into turning over any of his property to them. Gene figured if anyone deserved any of his assets, it was certainly him. He had worked hard all his life for Porter; the least the old man could do to repay him was to remember him in his will.

Anna brought Harry home and settled him in the downstairs bedroom that Amy had occupied. Nicky, who was still living at home, was now a registered nurse at the new Barrow County Hospital. She helped her mother find a home healthcare nurse to come to the house each day to bathe and help care for Harry. Once again, Anna gladly and unselfishly accepted the responsibility of another invalid. The role as the family caregiver seemed to come naturally to her. Whether it was caring for a demanding husband, her five children, her sisters' children, a dying sister or an old man, Anna did her best and never once complained.

In June of 1992, Gene and Anna celebrated their twenty-second wedding anniversary. That same month Angel and Red's divorce became final and their seventeen-year marriage came to an end. Their sixteen-year-old daughter Ann lived with her Aunt and Uncle and saw her parents on weekends when the entire family gathered at the farm for Sunday dinner. Still considered part of the family, Chuck continued to join them as well as Red. Nineteen-year-old Chuck, Jr. attended college at the University of Georgia in Athens where he studied business administration and finance. After earning his degree, he would join his father in the car business. His two cousins, Joey and Hal also attended college there. Joey was studying veterinarian medicine and Hal was working on a four-year degree in agriculture. Both had hopes of taking over the farm one day. All three boys shared an apartment together off campus in Athens.

While all the children were smart and ambitious, it was Gene, Jr. and Olivia who perhaps became the most successful, while at the same time, achieving recognition as local celebrities. Gene, Jr. was a star quarterback for Georgia Tech and had just earned his four-year degree in textile engineering. Yet his future as an engineer with his aunt's company was about to be put on hold indefinitely after learning he was one of the twenty top players in the United States who had made the first round pick to join the Atlanta Falcons. If he chose to sign on with the NFL team, he would receive a hefty two million for his first year. His father advised his son to grab the money and run—literally. His aunt's carpet mill would just have to wait awhile longer for its new engineer.

Gene's twenty-one year-old twin sister had also gained celebrity status. That year, after earning a three-year degree in art and design, Olivia Longhorn was crowned the reigning Miss Georgia. Tom Webber was satisfied to wait for his granddaughter to complete her reign before settling in to work as an interior designer in his new furniture store. Tom had bought a franchise to a national furniture chain and opened up an Ethan Allen store in Myrick.

With much of the credit going to Angel and her carpet mill, Myrick had nearly tripled in size over the past two decades. Businesses by the dozens were opening their doors and new residents were settling there by the hundreds. New housing subdivisions were springing up everywhere and Gene couldn't wait to get his hands on the thousand-acre spread and open another subdivision himself. No longer known as a small cotton mill town, Myrick, Georgia was compared in size and productivity to Rome and Athens as one of the largest textile manufacturers in the United States. AAA Carpet Mills now shipped its fine quality carpeting and tile abroad, as well as all over the United States.

The Colemans and Longhorns were now household names in North Georgia and were among the wealthiest families in the state. Gene was counting on one day owning a large chunk of the county, which would allow him to attain some of the wealth his wife and sister-in-law shared. As it remained, he was still a lowly farm worker earning a modest living while married into one of the wealthiest families in the South. Gene longed for his own wealth and status and knew the only way he would ever achieve his dream was to wait patiently for Harry Porter to die.

Porter Plantation now equaled or surpassed Coleman Hill as one of the major landmarks in the county. The once decaying one-hundred and fifty year-old plantation house had been restored and beautified into one of the most stately and majestic historic sites in the South. As one of the few remaining working plantations in the South, the old mansion had graced the cover and pages of several national magazines and hardcover books. With her father's help, Anna had turned the house into a showplace. Georgia Public Television aired a thirty-minute segment on the history of the old pre-Civil War plantation and interviewed its present owner, Anna Longhorn. The house became a popular tourist attraction as travelers on their way to the Blue Ridge Mountains slowed and stopped to snap photographs of the historic mansion which was also home to the reining Miss Georgia and Falcons star quarterback. No one was prouder of the old mansion than its owner who was also responsible for turning the crumbling plantation home into a grand showplace. To Anna, the house was like one of her children that she had nurtured and cared for and now rewarded her with pride and fulfillment.

Besides caring for an invalid old man, Anna was also caring for her fifty-one year-old brother-in-law who had recently retired from the carpet mill on disability. After developing diabetes, the disease was taking a toll on his nearly four hundred pound body and threatened to rob him of his left foot and leg. Joey now walked with a cane and seldom left the house. Unable to climb the stairs to his basement apartment, Anna had turned her living room into a second downstairs bedroom for him. Embarrassed by his size and inability to walk without a struggle, Joey seldom left the house except to see his doctor. He sat in an over-sized chair in the den all day and ate.

Even though Harry's body had failed him and he was no longer able to care for himself physically, remarkably at the age of ninety-seven, his mind remained relatively strong, despite the fact he still had his good days and his bad. He had fought to remain independent for as long as he could and giving up his little trailer beside the house was a devastating blow. Now he was solely dependent on Anna for his care and he greatly appreciated the fact that she had refused to allow him to be sent to a nursing home. She had always been like a daughter to him and now as he neared his final days, she cared for him as if he *were* her real father. Harry loved Anna just as much as if she had been his own flesh and blood. Were it not for her, he knew he would be completely alone as he wasted away in a nursing home surrounded by strangers.

Nevertheless, Anna had a full plate between running a household and caring for two invalids as well as her sixteen-year-old niece. Ann was a good child, although she had inherited her mother's high-spirited, outspoken nature. She was a tomboy, heavily involved in 4-H in school and loved competing in the local rodeos where she had won more than a dozen blue ribbons and trophies for barrel racing and calf roping. In 4-H, she had won first prize for raising the best heifer at the Barrow County Fair. With her mother's dark hair and sultry good-looks, the teen-ager could have easily followed in her cousin Olivia's footsteps and become a local beauty queen, but she had no desire to do so. Instead, she chose to spend her spare time working on the farm beside her Uncle Gene and riding horses. Ann remained close to her own father as well and enjoyed long afternoon rides on the back of his Harley with a stop at the local Dairy Queen. No longer a resident at Coleman Hill, Red now lived on five acres of land in a modest brick house not far from Porter's farm. He continued to work at the carpet mill and after purchasing the house, had managed to bank the remainder of the generous settlement his ex-wife had given him in the divorce.

"Aunt Anna, guess where Daddy took me driving this afternoon?" the teen-ager announced as she bounced through the back door into the den where she found her aunt and Joey shelling a large pan of fresh butter beans.

"There's no telling," Anna replied, glancing at her brother-in-law and giving him a wink.

"He let me drive all the way through town to the Quick Stop and then to the county line and back. All by myself!"

"Well, not *all* by yourself," Anna replied. "He was in the truck with you the whole time."

"Of course. But I drove all by myself the entire way. Daddy said I'm ready for my driver's license now and that he'll take me down to the DMV Saturday morning."

"That's great," Anna replied. "Just remember that driving a car is a big responsibility. Not only do you have your life at stake, but other people's as well."

"Oh, she's a good driver alright," Harry said, as he sat in his wheelchair beside Anna. "I've seen her drivin' my old truck through them pastures since she was old enough to see over the steering wheel."

"That's right," Anna agreed. "Gene taught her to drive the same way he taught me twenty-three years ago. And the same way he taught his nephew and five kids."

"He must have done a good job 'cause none of 'em has had a wreck or gotten a ticket yet," Joey added.

"And they all learned on that ole' truck of mine," Harry bragged.

"That and that old Chevelle of his," Joey said.

"I love that old car," Ann said. "I love driving a straight shift. It's so cool. I wish Uncle Gene would let me have it when I get my driver's license."

"Oh, I'm sure your mother will make sure she puts you in a shiny, brand new BMW or Corvette," Anna assured her niece.

"No, I'd much rather have Uncle Gene's old Chevelle. That car is the boss."

"Well, first you're going to have to convince the *big* boss to let you have it and I don't think you're going to get Gene Longhorn to part with his vintage Chevy," Anna told her. "He loves that old car as much as he does me. Maybe even more."

"But you bought him that Cadillac a couple of years ago. What does he need with two cars?"

"Well, one he loves to show off and the other he can't part with," Anna said told her niece.

"Who can't part with what?" Gene asked as he walked into the room unexpectedly.

"Your niece wants you to give her your old Chevelle when she gets her driver's license this weekend," Anna informed her husband. "I told her you couldn't part with that car."

"No, I'm not ready to give it up just yet," Gene agreed. "You'll just have to talk to your rich mother about buying you a car of your own."

"That's what I told her," Anna replied.

The phone rang, interrupting their conversation. "I'll get it," Ann announced quickly, running for the phone in the kitchen.

"I need to call Red and get him up here so we can get some meat in the freezer," Gene said, sitting down on the sofa beside his wife.

"Yeah, it's about that time again," Harry said. "And try not to let the thing get away from you this time and have it come wandering up to the house."

Joey began to laugh. "That was the first time I ever heard of one doin' that," he chuckled.

Anna glanced over at her husband who seemed to be preoccupied with his niece's phone conversation in the next room. "Who's she talking to?" Gene asked.

"I don't know," Anna replied. "Obviously it's not for me or she would have called me to the phone. Maybe it's Red."

"It better not be a boy," Gene told her. "Ann! Who are you talking to?" he yelled at his niece from the den.

"It's Carl, a boy I go to school with," she replied.

"You know you ain't supposed to be talking to no boys! You get off that phone before I come in there and kick your tail. I mean it, right now!" he shouted.

Gene waited until he finally heard his niece hang up the phone.

Ann walked back into the den and plopped down in a corner chair. "Why can't I talk to boys?" she demanded. "I'm sixteen years old. I'm getting my driver's license this Saturday. It's stupid! All my friends my age are already dating."

"Why? Because as long as you live under my roof you'll abide by my rules," he told her. "Just like everybody else. You'll live by my rules the same way my own daughters had to and they couldn't talk to boys or go out on dates until they were sixteen and a half. You've got a few more months to go and then we'll discuss it. But until then, the subject is closed."

"But my Mom doesn't care if I talk to boys or go out on dates," she insisted.

"Well, you're not living with your mom, are you?" Gene reminded her.

"And I really don't think your father wants you going off with boys just yet either," Anna added. "In fact I heard him say myself that you should wait a while longer."

"But I'm *sixteen*," she pleaded. "It's stupid! All my friends have been dating since they were fifteen."

"I'm not responsible for your friends," Gene told her. "I'm responsible for you and I say no phone calls or dates for a few more months. It's not like you have to wait until you're legal age—just a few more months. Neither of my daughters was allowed to have anything to do with boys until they were sixteen and a half and that's still the house rules around here and you will abide by them as long as you're under my roof. Subject closed."

"You're not my father so I don't need your permission," Ann declared.

Gene leaned forward and gave her a stern look. "What did you say to me?"

"Savannah, let's discuss this later," Anna insisted. "Don't talk back to your uncle. You know better."

"You listen to me, young lady. You'll do as I say or you'll get out of my house."

"Fine! Then I'll leave!" she snapped, as she jumped up and stormed out of the room.

"Ann, don't do this, please," Anna pleaded with her niece. "Let's all just calm down and discuss this later."

"No, let her go," Gene said. "But you be sure you pack up everything because you won't be coming back here. You go back home to your mother. Let her take care of you for a while. But I can tell you one thing, she doesn't want you!"

"Gene, please—"

"No, she needs to hear the truth," he insisted, getting up from the sofa and following his niece. "Why do you think she sent you here to live with us? I'll tell you why, because she's too busy playing a big shot business tycoon to be a mother to her own daughter. Who do you think sat up with you at night when you were sick and who takes you to all those rodeo competitions? I'll tell you who, your aunt and me. Not your mother. So go ahead and move back to Coleman Hill and see how you like it there. She'll give you plenty of freedom to go out with boys and stay out all night because she doesn't care what you do as long as you stay out of her hair. And when you turn up pregnant, don't think you're comin' back here. You're her problem then! Not mine. So go on, get out of here. I'll drive you home after dinner myself."

The sixteen year-old stood in the hallway and glared back in silence at her uncle. She knew better than to say anything more to make him angrier. It was better to get yelled at by him than to get slapped across the face and she knew that would come next if she continued to provoke him. Finally she turned and ran upstairs to her room. Anna stood up and started to follow her niece but Gene grabbed her by the arm and stopped her.

"Leave her alone," he snapped. "Let her go. This is between her and me. This is my house and whoever lives here follows my rules. That goes for my wife, my kids *and* my niece. It's my way or no way. Simple as that."

Gene turned and went into the kitchen for a glass of tea. Anna glanced over at Joey and then Harry who sat silently observing the confrontation.

"She's just young," Harry said. "She'll straighten out in time. She's just goin' through that stage they all go through. She knows where she's best off. Just give her some time to cool off and think about it."

Joey nodded in agreement. "He's right. She's still a kid. And she's just got a lot of her mother in her. She's feisty and wants to see how much she can get away with."

"Well, she won't get away with much as long her uncle has any say in the matter. He won't put up with her shenanigans. I don't know which is worse, dealing with a stubborn husband or a temperamental teen-ager. I'm just thankful this is the last one. All the others are grown. I wouldn't want to go through this again, that's for sure. Our own kids were never like her," Anna said. "They did what they were told and never talked back."

"That's because your kids were scared to death of their father," Joey told her. "They all knew he would knock them down if they back talked or challenged him. Even the boys knew better. She'll learn one day. She's just tryin' you."

"I'm just glad this is the last one we've got to raise," Anna confessed.

"Well, get ready," Harry warned her. "'Cause they'll be grandkids coming along pretty soon."

"Yeah, but their parents will be the ones to have to deal with them," Anna told him. "It won't be our concern then."

"Not if they're still livin' under this roof," Joey laughed. "Not as long as my brother is head of the household."

Anna shook her head. "My sister doesn't know how lucky she is not to have to deal with a moody teen-ager. After raising seven, I'm surprised I'm not down in Milledgeville at the state mental hospital."

"If that girl don't watch her mouth, somebody will be goin' to the hospital," Joey grinned.

"Well, it's not over yet," Anna sighed. "We've got six down and one to go. After Ann is raised, it's up to the kids to raise the next generation. Mine and Gene's job is done."

"I got news for you," Harry said. "As long as you've got kids, your job ain't never done. You'll be a parent and a grandparent till the day you die."

"I guess you're right," Anna replied. "I can't wait to have some grandbabies I can spoil."

"And you'll feel toward them grandchildren the same way you felt toward your own," Harry said. "In fact, you'll spoil them even more. I just hope I'm still around when some of those grandbabies arrive."

Anna looked at Harry and smiled. "I'm pretty sure you will be," she said. At least she hoped he would.

# Chapter Twenty-Four

It was the middle of January in North Georgia and bitter cold with a foot of snow on the ground and another two inches predicted before nightfall. Anna had managed to make it through Christmas and New Years with a bad case of the flu that had left her with bronchitis. She had coughed so much over the past month that her sides felt as if she had been kicked by a mule. Normally, she was able to shake off minor illness, but this time was different. She attributed it to stress and exhaustion. Besides caring for Harry, which was a full-time around the clock job, and waiting on her brother-in-law hand and foot, she was also tending to her daily household chores of cooking three meals a day, washing clothes and cleaning the house. Aside from everything else, she was in the midst of planning her oldest daughter's June wedding. Nicky was engaged to be married that summer after meeting an emergency room physician at the Barrow County Medical Center where she worked. Nicky had asked her mother and sister to drive down to Atlanta to look for a wedding gown at David's Bridal Salon that weekend. Yet with Harry requiring constant care and with Joey refusing to wait on himself least not Harry, Anna had been trying to find someone to fill in for her at the house for several hours on Saturday. She knew Gene couldn't because of his farm chores, which began at four a.m. and ended at six p.m. She couldn't ask her niece because Ann had already made plans to join them in Atlanta for the day. Finally, out of desperation, she called her sister at the mill and asked Angel if she would mind coming to the house and keeping an eye on Harry and

Joey while she was gone. Her sister, however, let her know very quickly and quite frankly that babysitting an old man and a fat slob was not on her agenda.

"Maybe you could find a nice, dependable black lady to look after them for you," Angel suggested. "Saturday and Sunday are my only days off and I don't care to spend one of those days babysitting an old man and a pig."

"You don't have to get nasty about it," Anna replied. "I just thought you might be able to help me out for a few hours. It's not like I've ever made a habit of asking you for favors."

"Look Anna, I've always thought you took on too much," Angel explained, realizing she had come across as sounding arrogant. "No one could even attempt to keep up the pace you maintain. You're going to wind up killing yourself. That husband of yours needs to open his eyes and realize how much you do and hire a goddamn maid or part-time helper to do some of the household chores and take some of the work off you. I don't know what he's thinking, expecting you to do everything you do around that house plus look after an old, invalid man and that lazy fat ass brother of his. I have a full-time housekeeper and I don't turn my hand when I come home."

"But you work all day at the mill, I don't," Anna replied. "Besides I know what Gene would say if I complained. He would insist that I put Harry in a nursing home and I'm not about to do that."

"Well, maybe he needs to ship his brother off to a nursing home also," Angel said. "If he's so fucking helpless that he sits on his fat ass all day asking you to bring him a glass of tea or a bag of chips, he needs to be in a nursing home. Maybe they would put him on a diet and make him lose some of that lard. I swear Anna, you put up with more crap that any person I know. I would have left Gene Longhorn twenty years ago. In fact, I would have never married him in the first place. You don't have to stay with him and be a slave to any man. You get enough money from your share of the mill to support yourself quite comfortably. You don't need a man to support you."

"I don't know why you say things like that Angel. I love Gene and I enjoy taking care of him. It's just that right now with this wedding coming up and the holidays I have a little more on me than usual. Never mind though, I'll find someone else to help me out on Saturday."

Later, when Anna made the mistake of telling her husband that her sister had refused to help her that weekend, he flew into a rage.

"What an ungrateful bitch! After all you do for her, she won't give you a few hours of her precious time," he yelled. "Why didn't you remind her you were raising her damn kid because she's too busy to look after her herself? And she won't give you a few hours of her time after all we do for her?"

"Oh, it doesn't matter," Angel shrugged. "I'll make do somehow."

Finally, it was Red who offered to spend the day looking after Joey and Harry after Gene had told him of the incident between his wife and sister-in-law.

"Hell, I don't mind," Red offered. "I don't have anything else to do. It's too cold to ride the Harley in the snow. Just tell me what time to be there."

Olivia was through with college and living back at home now. Her time was divided between working with her grandfather at Ethan Allen and fulfilling her duties as the reigning Miss Georgia. Nicky was also living at home and working at the hospital in the emergency room. Gene, Jr. was busy quarterbacking for the Atlanta falcons, while his two younger brothers and cousin were off at college in Athens.

Nicky drove her mother's Chevy Suburban to Atlanta that Saturday with her mom, sister and cousin, Ann. They had asked Angel to go, but she had other plans that day.

Anna hadn't slept well the night before. She had been up all night coughing. Her greatest fear was that she would infect Harry and cause him to become ill. At nighty-seven, his frail health would not tolerate an upper respiratory infection. She really didn't feel like making the trip that day, but since Nicky had already made an appointment at the bridal salon and Red had been so kind to offer to sit with Joey and Harry, Anna felt obligated to go.

After leaving the bridal salon, they did some shopping and had lunch at a nice Atlanta restaurant. Anna had been noticeably quiet throughout the day and barely touched her lunch.

"Are you alright, Mother?" Olivia asked, as they sat at the table finishing up dessert. "You barely ate a thing."

"I haven't regained my appetite since I had the flu," Anna replied. "I'm just not very hungry."

Nicky reached over and felt her mother's face and forehead. "You're burning up," she said. "Here, take some Tylenol. I know I have some in my purse."

"You look pale," Olivia said. "Maybe we'd better go on home and come back another weekend. We have plenty of time before the wedding."

"Oh, I wanted to go to Cumberland Mall before we go back home," Ann pleaded. "I wanted to look for a new outfit there."

"Sure," Anna told her niece. "We'll go. I'll be alright."

After leaving the restaurant, they drove to the Mall where they continued shopping for several more hours. Anna felt exhausted from all the walking and was starting to feel a little queasy, but she didn't want to spoil the day by complaining. Finally, around five p.m., they decided to go home. As they were about to leave the Mall and enter the parking garage, Anna's legs felt like rubber and everything went black. She collapsed just inside the Mall and fell unconscious. Nicky told a store security guard to call an ambulance and within a half hour, Anna was rushed to St. Joseph's Hospital.

Nicky rode in the ambulance with her mother while Olivia and Ann followed in Anna's car. Nicky remained at her mother's side as she was whisked to the emergency room while Olivia and Ann waited in the patient waiting room. Olivia decided she had better call her father and let him know what was going on for fear he would become concerned when they hadn't arrived home on time. Gene insisted on driving down to Atlanta immediately to be at his wife's side despite his daughter's pleas to wait until they knew more about her condition. He made the hours drive in less than fifty minutes. Gene had just arrived and was talking to Olivia when the emergency room doctor and Nicky entered the waiting room.

"I've admitted Anna for closer observation," the doctor told them. "She's too sick to be moved right now. We have her on oxygen and an IV. She's dehydrated and suffering from double pneumonia and bronchitis.

Her left lung is nearly collapsed and she's suffering from exhaustion. She's a very sick woman. Her condition was critical when she was brought in. It would be best if she stayed here through the weekend until Monday. I wouldn't advise moving her before then. If that lung collapses, she's in trouble."

Gene refused to leave the hospital until he could take Anna back home. He told Olivia she was just going to have to take time off from her Miss Georgia duties to stay home and take over until her mother was released from the hospital. Then he phoned Red and asked him to take over the farm until he returned. Meanwhile, Nicky and her sister drove back to Myrick with Ann. Nicky did not want to leave her mother, but decided it was best to go home, gather up a few things for herself and her father and return to the hospital later that evening. She planned on staying with her father at the hospital through the night and return to Myrick again in the morning. Angel had promised to drive down to Atlanta Sunday morning and stay until late that afternoon.

Not long after Angel arrived at the hospital the next morning, Nicky left Atlanta and returned to Myrick to help her sister take over their mother's duties back at home. As it turned out, leaving her Aunt Angel alone with her father was a big mistake.

While Anna slipped into a peaceful sleep later that afternoon, Gene and his sister-in-law got into a confrontation outside the hospital as Angel stepped outside to smoke a cigarette and Gene walked across the street to pay the parking attendant.

"I've decided to put Harry in a home," Gene told Angel as he paused on the hospital steps before going back inside to his wife's room. "It's too much on Anna to care for him. He should have been put in one when he first came out of the hospital with his stroke."

"Why don't you consider putting Joey in there with him?" Angel suggested, taking a long drag from her cigarette.

Gene gave Angel a hard glare. "What makes you say something like that? Joey doesn't need to be in a nursing home."

"Well, he seems pretty helpless to me the way he has Anna waiting on him hand and foot. He needs to get up off his fat ass and burn some calories instead of sitting around all day stuffing his face."

"Joey's a diabetic. He's on disability. He could lose his leg if he's not careful."

"If he'd stop stuffing his face and lose some of that weight he might be able to get up and do for himself instead of making Anna wait on him. You know, my sister wouldn't be here if you didn't allow her to work herself to death. She works from sunup to sundown and never slows down. She's raised seven kids and waited on you, Harry and your brother hand and foot for the past twenty years. She never takes any time out for herself. She's always thinking of everybody except herself. She doesn't even take time to go get her hair or nails done. She's been a slave to you and that farm almost her entire life. You knew she was taking on too much. You should have hired some help for her a long time ago. That's the least you could have done."

"And the least *you* could have done was stay at the house for a few hours while she came here to help Nicky look for a wedding dress. Why don't you mind our own goddamned business?" Gene snapped back. "You got a hell of a lot of nerve telling me how to run my life when you can't even run your own life. You're too damn sorry to raise your own daughter. Instead you ship her off to live with us and let your sister raise her. But you failed to add her name to the list while you were naming off your sister's responsibilities. Are you forgettin' who raised your kid for you? And what about the husband you ran off?"

"You can kiss my ass," Angel sneered back.

"And you can kiss mine. You better learn how to take care of your own business before you tell somebody how to run their life. You think just because you own that fuckin' carpet business you're some goddamn big shot."

"At least I've got a business. All you've ever done is milk somebody else's cows for a living. You wouldn't have a pot to piss in or a window to throw it out of if it weren't for Anna. You think Harry Porter would have given you that old place of his if it weren't for her? And if it weren't for me making sure she got what was due her, you wouldn't have been able to feed or clothe those five kids of yours. That's why you're such a control freak, because that's all you ever managed to have was control and dominance. You couldn't make any money or have anything on your own so you controlled everybody around you. I never could figure out what the hell my sister ever saw in you in the first place."

"I tell you what," Gene said, bitterness and anger filling his voice. "You get your ass back in that fancy car of yours and go back home. I don't want you around my wife. We don't need you or your fuckin' attitude. You just go on back home and mind your own fuckin' business."

"Fuck you! Who are you to tell me what to do? That's my sister in there."

"And that's my wife. And I can take care of her myself. I don't need you for a damn thing! So get your ass back home and take care of your own goddamn business." Gene turned to go back into the hospital.

"You're not telling me what to do! I'm not your goddamn wife for you to boss around and make your personal slave! I'll leave when I get damn good and ready!"

"Okay, when you do decide to leave, swing by my house first and pick up that smart mouthed brat of yours because I'm tired of putting up with her. She's got a smart-ass attitude here lately, anyway. But I guess that's because she takes after her mother."

"You damn right, I'll get her," Angel snapped back. "I don't want her around a redneck loser like you anyway. That's why I got rid of her father. You both are just alike. Nothing but a couple of white trash rednecks."

Gene stopped and whirled around to face his sister-in-law. People outside as well as inside the hospital were beginning to stare. "At least I can keep my marriage together and raise my own kids without someone else raising them for me. That's a hell of a lot more than you're ever been able to do. I wouldn't call somebody a loser if I were you. You're nothing but a fuckin' high and mighty snob just like your parents and your sister, Amy. And that's another thing, who the hell do you think took care of your sister for eight years so she wouldn't have to go to a nursing home? Who changed her diapers and bathed and fed her like a baby? Not you! You were too busy playing big shot tycoon. I tell you what. Don't you ever step foot in my goddamn house again because I don't ever want to lay eyes on you! You stay away from us. All of us! You fucking dyke!"

"I got news for you, that's not even your house! You wouldn't even have a goddamn roof over your head if it weren't for Harry Porter. You don't have shit! All you've got to your name is squatter's rights and after the old man is dead, you'll be out on the streets with nowhere to live!"

Gene's temper was about to explode. If he didn't walk away soon, he would hit her right there in front of everyone. And if he ever hit her the first time, he was afraid he wouldn't be able to stop. Had she been a man, he would have already knocked her out cold.

"You heard me," he seethed, putting his face inches from hers, his eyes wild with rage. "You go back home and you get that kid of yours and don't you ever darken my door again. I'll sic my dogs on you if you ever step foot on my property again."

"They're not even your dogs. They're Anna's! You don't have shit! The only thing you own is that twenty-five year-old junk car and you wouldn't have that if you hadn't found it in your old man's junkyard!"

Before he knew what he had done, Gene drew back with his closed fist and hit Angel so hard that she fell backward flat on her back and tumbled down the hospital steps. The next thing he knew, two burly security guards and a hospital orderly were holding him until the police arrived. Meanwhile, Angel was helped back into the hospital where she was treated in the emergency room for a fractured jaw and head lacerations.

Nicky and her Uncle Chuck were forced to drive back to Atlanta late that Saturday night and attempt to bail Gene out of the Fulton County jail. Chuck made sure he brought enough cash with him to post bail for his ex-brother-in-law, however, it was Sunday morning before they could get him out of jail. Angel was treated at the hospital emergency room for a hairline fracture of her right jaw and a large gash in the back of her head, which required eleven stitches. She was released late that Saturday night and after refusing Nicky's offer to drive her back to Myrick, she drove herself home.

When Anna awoke later that evening and found her husband and sister gone, she asked the nurse where they were. She was told that both had left the hospital and would return later that night. It was nearly midnight and Anna was sound asleep by the time Nicky arrived back at the hospital with her father. They decided not to wake her and put off breaking the news of the incident between Gene and Angel for as long as possible. Neither wanted to upset Anna and run the risk of causing her more stress. Chuck returned home after posting Gene's bail, leaving Nicky and her father at the hospital with Anna.

Meanwhile, after returning back to Myrick, Angel picked her daughter up from the farm and brought her back to Coleman Hill. Gene phoned Red and asked him to look after the farm until he returned home on Monday. He agreed. For the time being, Olivia would remain at home and look after Harry and Joey until her mother got back on her feet.

After spending Sunday in the hospital with her husband and oldest daughter at her side, the doctor told Anna she could be released from St. Joseph's, but only on the condition that she be transferred immediately to Barrow County Medical Center. Nicky immediately got on the phone and made arrangements for a room to be ready for her mother when they arrived. Nicky and her father drove Anna back to Barrow County and admitted her to the hospital there. Still, she knew nothing of the fight between her sister and husband that sent Angel to the emergency room and Gene to jail. Gene forbade any of them to allow Anna to have any phone calls or contact with Angel and explained her absence to Anna as her being busy at the mill.

Anna spent the rest of the week in the hospital. Her husband and children were constant visitors, yet she found it odd that she had not seen nor heard from her sister in nearly a week since the day she was admitted to the hospital in Atlanta.

During the week that his wife was in the hospital, Gene was busy, but not just with the farm. With his two daughters' help, he did some quick searching and with Nicky's influence, found a nursing home just outside of Myrick that would accept Harry immediately. Normally, the waiting period to have an elderly person admitted to such a facility could be months to a year. But Nicky knew who to contact and at her father's urging and insistence, she was able to accomplish the impossible and convince the old, rundown nursing home to take Harry that same week. Both Nicky and Olivia begged and pleaded with their father to be patient and wait a little while longer until they could find a better facility—one that was cleaner and better staffed. But he refused. With Ann back in her mother's care, Gene was determined to finish cleaning house. When his wife returned home from the hospital, she would now only have two people to care for—himself and his brother, Joey.

That Friday morning when Anna was due to be released from the hospital, she was finishing her breakfast as she waited for the doctor to arrive and confirm her plans to go home. Tom had offered to come to the hospital and take his daughter home so that Gene wouldn't have to leave the farm, but Gene refused his offer. He was beginning to view Webber as a threat and wanted him away from his family. Gene Longhorn was extremely territorial where his family was concerned and resented his wife and daughters growing close to any man other than himself. Besides, he looked on Webber as effeminate and sissy. Any man who didn't get his hands dirty in order to make a living wasn't really a man in his opinion.

As Anna ate her breakfast, she watched the early morning edition of the local news. It was the first time in a week she had seen any local or national news. Suddenly her oldest son's picture was shown across the television screen and Anna grabbed the remote and turned up the volume. To her shock and amazement, the news item was not about Gene, Jr., but his father instead.

"The father of Atlanta Falcons quarterback Gene Longhorn, was arrested last Sunday in Fulton County and charged with domestic violence against his sister-in-law Angela Coleman, owner of AAA Carpet Mills of Myrick and Dalton. The incident occurred outside St. Joseph's Hospital where the two became involved in a heated argument resulting in Gene Longhorn, Sr. striking Ms. Coleman and fracturing her jaw. Longhorn was arrested and released on bond early Sunday morning. Ms. Coleman was treated at St. Joseph's and released on Sunday. Coleman presently has a restraining order against her brother-in-law who is scheduled to appear in court on Tuesday where he is expected to plead guilty to assault and battery. Longhorn could face up to a year in jail and a five thousand dollar fine if convicted on the charges. No word on what caused the dispute."

Anna sat up in the hospital bed in shock. She couldn't believe what she had just heard. Could this be why she hadn't heard from Angel since last Sunday when she was admitted to the hospital in Atlanta? Could it be why every time she called home, either Joey or Olivia answered and never Ann, who always ran for the phone every time it rang? And what had happened between her sister and husband to cause such a violent episode to erupt.

"Well, good morning. How was your breakfast?" Nicky smiled as she entered her mother's room, dressed in her nurse's uniform. She had just gone on duty, but wanted to check in on her mother before heading for the emergency room where she worked. "Are you ready to go home?"

"Nicky, I just saw on the news that your father was arrested for hitting Angel. They said she had a broken jaw and that she had a restraining order against him. What in God's name is going on? What's happened since I've been in here? Why hasn't someone told me about this?"

"Mom, we didn't want to upset you," Nicky explained. "You were very sick and you didn't need any added stress. We were going to tell you after we got you home."

"Did your father really hit Angel and break her jaw?"

Nicky nodded slowly. "He did," she told her mother. "They got into an awful argument outside the hospital and Dad's temper got the best of him. He hit Aunt Angel once, but hard enough to knock her out and fracture her jaw. They arrested Daddy and took him to jail. Uncle Chuck bailed him out of jail. When Angel got back to Myrick, she went to the house and got Ann and took her back home with her."

"My God! I can't believe this. What happened to cause your father to behave like that? What were they arguing about?"

Nicky gave a heavy sigh and sat down on the edge of the bed beside her mother. "Aunt Angel blamed Daddy for being responsible for you winding up in the hospital. She accused Daddy of putting too much on you and allowing you to care for uncle Joey and Papa. Then Daddy threw it up to her that he was raising her daughter and one thing led to another and it escalated until Daddy's temper got the best of him and he hauled off and punched Angel and knocked her down the steps."

Anna covered her face with both hands and fought back tears. Nicky put her arms around her mother and tried to comfort her. "We couldn't tell you because we didn't want you upset at the time. You were too sick.

Angel is okay. It was a small, hairline fracture in her jaw. They didn't have to wire it shut or anything like that. She had to have a few stitches in the back of her head when she fell backwards down the steps. The doctor let her go that same night. As long as Aunt Angel has the restraining order against him, Ann can't come to the house because Angel and Daddy can't have any contact. Olivia and I have been talking to her and trying to convince her to drop the charges against him before he has to appear in court tomorrow."

Anna shook her head and wiped away the tears. "Your father's temper will be the death of me yet," she sighed. "I can't believe he did this. There was no sense in it."

"It's partly my fault," Nicky confessed. "I should have never left Daddy and Aunt Angel alone and gone back home. I should have stayed there at the hospital, but I felt I had to get back home to help Olivia look after Uncle Joey and Papa."

"How is Harry?" Anna asked. "Every time I've called home he's either asleep or the home nurse is caring for him. I haven't spoken to him in a week since I went into the hospital. Does he know about any of this?"

Nicky dreaded breaking more bad news to her mother. Her father being arrested and charged with assault and battery was bad enough. Learning that her father had put Harry in a nursing home might be more than she could handle. It was sure to break her mother's heart and again, it was all her father's doing.

"Mom, there's something else that happened while you were gone," Nicky began.

"What? Has something happened to Harry?"

"No, he's fine. It's—"

"What? What is it Nicky?"

"While you were away, Daddy put Papa in a nursing home."

"What! Oh no, he didn't!"

"Mom, calm down. Papa is okay. Nothing happened to him; it's just that Daddy felt taking care of him was too much for you to handle, especially after coming home from the hospital. Maybe when you're back on your feet and stronger, we can talk Daddy into bringing Papa back home."

"I can't believe your father would go behind my back and do such a thing knowing how I felt about Harry going to a nursing home in the first place."

"I know. That's why we didn't want to tell you. We all knew how upset you would be," Nicky replied.

"Where is he? What nursing home did he go to?"

"Myrick Manor."

"Myrick Manor! That place is deplorable! It's filthy and understaffed, not to mention old and rundown. He'll die in there. Why in the world did your father put him there of all places?"

"Because it's the only nursing home that could take him on such short notice. There was a waiting list of a year or more at all the others."

"Myrick Manor should have been condemned and shut down ten years ago," Anna said. "That place is horrible. I've heard that they actually abuse patients there. I read in the paper that they have lawsuits against them for beating patients and neglecting them—not feeding them and allowing them to fall and get hurt. What is your father thinking?"

"I guess he was thinking of you when he did it, Mom. One of the things Daddy and Angel fought about that day was Angel accusing him of allowing you to take on too much and take care of too many people."

"Oh, that's ridiculous! It's my fault that all this has happened. If I had taken better care of myself while I was sick and not overdone things, I would have never wound up in the hospital and none of this would have happened. I've managed to take care of that house and seven kids along with Harry all my life. I just let myself get rundown and then I got pneumonia—that's all. I'm only forty years-old. I'm not a feeble old woman. I'm perfectly capable of taking care of Harry. I've been doing it for nearly twenty-four years."

"I know Mom, but you know Daddy. He can be very hardheaded and stubborn at times. It's either his way or no way at all. Olivia and I begged him not to put Papa in that nursing home, but he just wouldn't listen." Nicky knew the thought of having Harry sent away would break her mother's heart, but once her father made up his mind to do something, there was no stopping him and it would only mean a big argument if anyone tried. Right now, her mother didn't need to be upset.

"Listen Mom, why don't we do this," Nicky suggested. "The doctor wants you to go home and rest for the next couple of weeks. He doesn't want you overdoing things. Olivia and I will do most of the housework and cooking. We've already had a talk with uncle Joey and told him that he needs to look after himself more and not expect you to wait on him so much. He's not helpless, he can do more for himself than he lets on. Now, in a couple of weeks when you're back on your feet again, we'll all sit down and have a talk with daddy about bringing Papa back home. Maybe then we can convince him to get him out of that nursing home. But for now, let's not rock the boat. He's already upset enough over this thing with Aunt Angel. If Olivia and I can get her to drop the charges against him, then maybe he'll be in a better mood and a little easier to convince. But if you insist he bring Papa home right now, it will be like going up against a brick wall and you don't need anymore stress right now. Olivia and I will take you to visit Papa in the meantime. It'll only be for a couple of weeks at the most until things settle down. Trust me Mom, it's the best way to handle the situation for the time being."

Anna thought over carefully what Nicky was saying and decided that she was right. It wasn't just the best way to handle Gene's decision, but perhaps the *only* way. He was a very difficult man to reason with at times, but when he was angry, he was impossible. "You're right," Anna agreed at last. "But I need to at least talk to Harry and make him understand this move is only temporary."

"I'll take care of that, Mom," Nicky assured her mother. "I'll drop by the nursing home on my way home from work and check on Papa and have a long talk with him. I'll handle everything. Don't you worry."

Anna couldn't help but worry. Harry was nearing his ninety-eighth birthday and his health and mind were very fragile. He needed the kind of personal care only *she* could give him. She honestly believed that had it not been for all the tender loving care she had lavished on Harry over the past few years, he wouldn't have lasted this long. Where he was now, he would only receive abuse and neglect. She had to get him out of that awful place and as soon as possible.

"Mom, I hate to run, but I have to report to the emergency room for work. I'm already running late. Daddy will be here any minute to pick you up," Nicky said, giving her mother a kiss.

"Nicky, one more thing," Anna said. "What did Red say when he heard about your father hitting Angel?"

Nicky smiled. "He said Daddy was the only one with the balls to do what he had wanted to do for years."

# Chapter Twenty-Five

After a great deal of convincing, Nicky and Olivia were able to get Angel to drop the assault charges against their father along with the restraining order. Gene didn't have to appear in court that Tuesday as scheduled. He did, however, have a criminal record with a felony charge of assault with intent to do bodily harm. His daughters weren't able to do much as far as getting their father and aunt to forgive or forget. There remained as much hostility as ever between the two. As for Ann, Angel refused to allow her daughter to return to the farm. She went so far as to have Red pick up their daughter's two horses and take them to his five-acre spread and keep them there. Angel had not been in contact with her sister since the incident and felt for now it was best they didn't talk to one another. Angel wasn't angry with Anna, but she knew there was no point in discussing the matter with her sister. She had been with Gene for nearly twenty-three years and nothing would ever change. Her sister was under Gene's thumb and would remain there. Anna wasn't strong enough to stand up to her husband and Gene knew it. It was best for all, for now at least, some distance was put between Angel and her sister.

Anna did as Nicky suggested and didn't nag Gene about taking Harry out of the nursing home and moving him back to the farm. She did however call Harry at Myrick Manor and talk to him every single day on the phone. Anna could tell that he was very sad and didn't like being there, but understood why Gene had done what he did. She promised Harry that as soon as she was fully recovered and back on her feet, she would come get him and bring him home. She assured him that she would have never allowed him to be sent there had she not been away in the hospital. He said he knew that, but Anna could tell by his voice that he was homesick and heartbroken.

Anna asked Nicky and Olivia to drive her to Myrick Manor to visit Harry the following Saturday. After breakfast, the two girls drove their mother to the old nursing home just outside the city limits in the worst part of town. The sprawling red brick facility was decaying and crumbling, much like its patients inside. As soon as they walked in the front door that opened up into the lobby and patient visiting area, the pungent smell of urine and feces was overpowering and nauseating. As they walked across the tile floor toward the nurses' desk, their shoes stuck to the floor from Lysol mixed with urine. Old people in wheel chairs and walkers lined the hallway and sitting area, many with their hands and arms curled with arthritis, straining through thick bifocals to see who might be possibly coming to visit them. A few stared silently as the three women passed by, trying desperately to recognize them in hopes it was a relative who had arrived to rescue them from their dreadful environment.

"You go get you some of that fried chicken I left in the kitchen now," said a toothless old woman in a wheelchair as she reached out and grabbed Olivia by the wrist as she passed her. Not knowing what to do or say, Olivia smiled politely at the old woman and kept walking.

The patients all looked dirty and in need of a bath. Those who still had some white hair remaining looked as if it hadn't been combed or washed in weeks. Even the nurses' uniforms appeared soiled and wrinkled.

"God, this place gives me the creeps," Olivia whispered to her mother and sister as they approached the nurses' station. "I don't see how anyone could work here let alone be a patient. I think I would rather die first."

"If you're not nuts when you come in here, you sure are by the time you leave," Nicky added.

"People don't last long once they're put in a nursing home," Anna told her daughters. "That's why I never wanted Harry coming here. Or Amy for that matter. It's the beginning of a quick end."

Suddenly they heard an earsplitting shrill scream from one of the patients down the hall as she sat in her wheelchair, rocking back and forth feverously. She seemed to be in her own world, oblivious to her surroundings.

"Can I help you?" a black nurse asked from behind the tall counter.

"We're here to see Harry Porter," Anna replied. "Could you point us to his room?"

The nurse behind the desk stopped suddenly and looked up at Anna and the girls. "Are you a close relative?"

"My name is Anna Longhorn. Harry lived with us up until a couple of weeks ago. My husband and daughter had him admitted here week before last."

"Mrs. Longhorn, I just tried to call you at home a few minutes ago. Mr. Porter fell ill during the night," the nurse told her.

"Oh, my God. What happened?" Anna gasped.

"We believe he must have suffered a stroke. He doesn't seem to recognize anyone and his speech is slurred. The right side of his body seems to have been affected."

Anna covered her mouth with her hand as tears began to fill her eyes. "Oh no. I was afraid something like this would happen."

"Has a doctor evaluated his condition yet?" Nicky asked.

"No, our doctor hasn't come in today to make his rounds."

"You mean to tell me you didn't call a doctor as soon as you found him in that condition?" Nicky demanded.

"Well, he didn't appear to be in any urgent distress. Patients have mini strokes all the time. It's just part of their declining condition. As long as he seems to be breathing—"

"Your first priority should have been to get a doctor to evaluate him immediately," Nicky snapped back, interrupting the woman. "If it *is* a stroke, then he requires hospitalization right away. The sooner he receives medical attention the better the chances are of preventing further damage."

"My daughter is a nurse," Anna explained. "Could you at least let her take a look at him and see what she thinks?"

"He isn't in any immediate medical danger," the woman replied. "All of his vital signs are normal."

"It doesn't matter!" Nicky said, her voice rising in frustration and anger. "If you suspect he's had a stroke, you should have called in a doctor immediately. Now where is he?"

The nurse stared back at Nicky with a cold, hard look. Slowly she slid her chair back and stepped out from behind her desk. "Follow me," she said, her voice expressing obvious irritation. She led them down a long dimly lit corridor to the last room on the left. She opened the door and stepped aside, allowing them to enter the tiny room containing two twin beds separated by a dingy, tattered white curtain. The man in the first bed was lying on his back and began babbling something that was inaudible as they entered the room. He reached beneath the covers and held up something that appeared to be a partial set of dentures. In the bed beside him, lay Harry, staring straight up at the ceiling, his hands curled beneath his chin. His right eye and the corner of his mouth were noticeably drooping and a stream of drool was flowing down his chin and neck. The tortoise shell frame bifocal glasses that he always wore were gone.

"Oh Harry," Anna began to sob. "What have they done to you?" She reached down and took his gnarled hand and leaned over and kissed him on the forehead. He felt cold and clammy and was shaking uncontrollably. "He's cold. Don't you have another blanket we can put over him?" she asked, turning to the nurse.

"I'll see," the woman replied, quickly disappearing from the room, never to be seen again.

"Harry, it's me, Anna. I have the girls with me. We're going to get you out of here," she told him as she brushed a strand of thinning gray hair from his forehead. "Oh sweetie, how do you feel? Are you in any pain?"

He didn't answer. His eyes remained in a fixed stare. Every few seconds, his body would quiver as if he were having hard chills. Anna removed her own coat and placed it over his thin, frail body.

"Move Mom," Nicky told her mother, gently pushing her out of the way. "Let me look at him. Olivia, go out to the car and get my medical bag."

"Oh Harry, please say something," Anna pleaded, the tears running down her cheeks. "Please answer us. Let me know you're all right. I can't bear to see him like this."

As she stood there looking down at Harry, she thought back to the first time she met him. He was old even then, but still vibrant and active. She remembered all the good and kind things he had done for her and her family over the past two decades, paying for all their medical bills when they had no money, offering them a home to live in, buying her a car and insisting she finish school before marrying Gene, playing for hours with her children, always having their best interest at heart. And this was how she repaid him for all his love, kindness and generosity.

"Mom, go back to the nurses' station and demand that they give you a clean blanket," Nicky told her mother, bringing her out of her deep thoughts.

Anna did as her daughter said and in a few moments returned with a blanket and found Olivia standing at the foot of the bed while Nicky began checking Harry's vital signs.

"He needs to be in a hospital," Nicky told her mother. "His pulse is very weak and his blood pressure is extremely low. I'm going to go call for an ambulance to transfer him to Barrow County. You and Olivia stay with him and keep talking to him while I go to the nurses' station and use their phone."

Nicky hurried out of the room and went down the long corridor to the desk where she found the black nurse sitting down looking over some medical charts. "I need to use your phone," she told the woman.

"Is it a local call?" the nurse asked.

"Of course, it's a local call," Nicky snapped. "I'm calling Barrow County Medical Center and I'm sending for an ambulance—something you should have done hours ago."

"I'm afraid I'm the only one with the authority to do that here," the woman said.

Nicky ignored the woman and reached over the counter and picked up the phone herself. "Now you listen to me," she said. "My mother is Anna Longhorn and my sister is Angel Coleman. They have enough money between them to hire however many lawyers it takes to have this rat den shut down and your job along with it. You're not dealing with some poor white trash family who doesn't have enough money to put their grandfather in a decent facility. Besides, I work for Barrow County Hospital and I can report you to Human Resources and have this place condemned." Nicky began dialing the hospital's number. After making arrangements for an ambulance to be sent to the nursing home, she hung up and turned to walk back to Harry's room. She stopped suddenly and turned around to face the woman behind the counter once more. "If that man in there dies, I'll do everything in my power to have this place shut down so that you won't kill any more patients. This place is a disgrace and so are you."

Nicky turned and hurried back down the corridor to Harry's room. She cursed herself for allowing her father to talk her into helping him put Harry there. Now, she just hoped and prayed they could get him out of there and get him some decent medical help before it was too late.

They succeeded in moving Harry out of the nursing home before he died, but not before some serious and permanent damage was done. The stroke had all but killed him. He was completely paralyzed on his right side and left him barely able to communicate with the inability to speak clearly. After a week in the hospital, he did however, begin to appear more responsive and was able to recognize Anna and her two daughters, but few others. He was now a complete invalid, unable to do even the simplest task for himself.

Still, Anna was determined to bring Harry back home to live out his final days. Her husband however, was just as determined not to have him back home. They argued for days over the matter. The girls were annoyed with their father for his callous indifference for Harry's welfare.

"Hell, the old man's almost ninety-eight years-old," Gene snapped at his daughters. "He can't last forever. You can't help him live any longer by bringing him back here."

"Maybe not," Olivia said. "But at least he will be more comfortable and happier surrounded by people who love him instead of being cared for by strangers."

"But your mother can't give him the kind of care he needs. He needs a nurse to see after him. He can't even go to the bathroom by himself or bathe himself. Your mother couldn't possibly continue to care for him in the shape he's in now. He needs round the clock nurses to feed him, turn him and change his diapers. Your mother can't do all of that. It's impossible."

"But I would find someone who could do all of that," Nicky insisted. "Mother has the money to hire a full-time nurse to come stay with him. She did it with Amy. Besides, Harry's the only grandfather we had growing up and he's been like a father to Momma."

"Well, he's not her father and he's not your real grandfather," Gene said flatly. "He's not even a blood relative."

"How can you be so cold after all he's done for us?" Olivia asked.

"All he ever did for me was provide me with a job I hated to go to everyday of my life."

"That's not true," Nicky said. "He gave us this house to live in."

"Yeah, a hundred year-old house that was about to cave in. And besides, I did all the work to make the thing livable. All he did was provide the materials. Besides, your mother repaid him ten fold. She took care of him, cooked for him and babied him all these years. He got his pay back."

The two girls couldn't believe their father could be that hard-hearted and turn his back on the man who had helped them all of his life. Finally, they decided there was no use in trying to reason with him. It was like talking to a brick wall. The older he got, the more unreasonable and bitter he became. Truth be known, Gene would have been relieved to have Harry out of the way. He felt confident Harry would leave the farm to him and once he did, Gene would be free for the first time in his life. He had even gone to the trouble of contacting Harry's attorney and learned that Harry had been to his office twice in the past ten years to update his will. Although the attorney would not divulge any more information than that, Gene knew the old man had no other living relatives or friends other than himself and Anna. There was no one else to will his assets to and he knew Harry would never allow the state to have his property. At forty-five, Gene would finally be financially free to do whatever he wanted for the rest of his life. And if he decided to do nothing more than go fishing all day and play with his grandchildren, then so be it. He had more than paid his dues all his life and had earned his loafing rights.

Finally, after arguing with Gene for days, Anna accepted defeat and with Nicky's help, began searching for a reputable nursing home facility to admit Harry. With Nicky's influence and Anna's financial resources, they found a very capable and well-staffed nursing home in Rome that took Harry immediately. After spending two weeks in the hospital at Barrow County, Anna had him moved to Rome by ambulance where he would receive the best quality care money could buy.

She and Nicky followed behind the ambulance the day he was moved to the nursing home and made sure he was settled in and made as comfortable as possible. Anna had paid twice the normal monthly fee in order to have Harry put in a single occupancy room just outside the nurses' station. She even purchased a special lift chair recliner for his room along with an air mattress to discourage bedsores. She and the two girls hung Priscilla sheers at the double window and placed family pictures around the room to create a warm and homey atmosphere. By the time they were finished, the room looked like anything but a hospital room.

The day they moved him there, Harry was having one of his bad days where he was barely coherent and didn't appear to know what was going on around him. Anna wished that *she* could have been so lucky, for it broke her heart to finally have to leave him all alone there. She cried and didn't want to leave as her daughters practically had to drag their mother away. She continued crying all the way home and half the night. Her greatest fear was not that Harry would be neglected or mistreated where he was, but that he would die there, alone and confused. If she had to lose him, she wanted him to slip away peacefully surrounded by his family and the people who loved him, inside the house he and Ollie had intended to be their home. As it appeared now, that would not be possible.

# Book V

# Chapter Twenty-Six

That June on her parents' twenty-third wedding anniversary, Anna Nicole Longhorn married Dr. Bradford Bailey. The couple was married at Myrick Baptist Church in an elaborate wedding ceremony with over three hundred guests attending. The bride's mother and grandfather spent a small fortune on Nicky's wedding, which turned out to be the social event of the year in Myrick. Tom Webber saw to it that every minute detail from the church flowers to the wedding cake was carried out to perfection and he was personally responsible for the reception decorations and catering. All the bride's father was responsible for was proudly walking his oldest daughter down the isle. Olivia stood beside her sister as her maid of honor while the bride's three brothers and cousin Chuck served as ushers. After much begging and pleading, Anne was finally able to convince her mother to allow her to participate in her cousin's wedding as a bridesmaid. At first, Angel chose not to attend her niece's wedding, but after Anna's persistent urging, she agreed to bury the hatchet long enough to be present at the ceremony. She and her estranged brother-in-law still had not spoken since their violent confrontation five months ago and despite the fact Angel had finally agreed to attend the wedding, she absolutely refused to participate in the reception afterwards at Porter Plantation.

"It's best that I don't come," Angel declined. "It's not that I have anything against you or Nicky. I love you both dearly. But I don't want to be in the same room with that husband of yours."

"But Angel," Anna pleaded. "Nicky is your niece. I'm not asking you to bury the hatchet with Gene, all I want is for you to be present at the reception so that you'll be included in the wedding pictures. You're the only sister I have left now. I want you in my daughter's wedding album. The reception won't last more than an hour, and you can leave as soon as the photographer finishes taking the bride's family photos."

"But I would still have to pose with the bride's father and besides, I was warned never to step foot in that house again."

"But Angel—"

"Look sweetie, I'm afraid I'm going to have to decline this invitation," Angel insisted. "I'll be at the church for the wedding, but I won't stay for the reception." She paused, her voice taking on a more solemn tone. "Anna, I don't want you to think that I'm not coming to the wedding just to be mean or vindictive toward you or Nicky. I love you both with all my heart. You're all I have left now. But I don't ever want to lay eyes on that husband of yours. He has some serious mental problems."

"No, Gene just has a bad temper, that's all. He always has, ever since I've known him. It's just gotten a little worse over the years," Anna tried to explain in her husband's defense.

"No. It's a lot more than that," her sister insisted. "He reminds me in some ways of Daddy. The day may come when he turns on you."

"Angel! How could you possibly say that?"

"Open your eyes, Anna. Can't you see how over-bearing and controlling he is with you and the kids? He's got a violent temper just like Daddy. Don't you remember how Daddy used to go into rages and yell and curse whenever things didn't go his way? Do you remember how he wouldn't let any of us out of his sight until we were in college and nearly grown? Mother lived in constant fear of his rages and went out of her way to keep from provoking him, the same way you do with Gene. The kids were scared to death of making him mad or upset. No wonder you had such perfect, well-behaved children. They were terrified of their father."

"That's not true, Angel. Gene was and still is a strict parent who demanded respect from his kids, but he was never violent with them. He would spank them when they were small if they needed it, but he never beat them."

"No, but he taught them to fear him all the same," Angel replied.

"I don't appreciate you comparing Gene to Daddy," Anna said finally. "He has never abused any of the children—sexually or physically. They all love him to death. Gene is a good man and a wonderful father. I won't stand for you running him down."

It was no use. Her sister was blind to her husband's faults. Blinded by her love for him. To her, he had no faults. Yet he had succeeded in driving a wedge between her and anyone who threatened to come between them. He had managed to isolate his wife from the world and keep her all to himself. That was exactly what he wanted and precisely what he had accomplished.

The one thorn that remained in his side, besides his father-in-law, was Harry. Anna absolutely insisted that he attend the wedding.

"How the hell do you expect a ninety-eight year-old invalid man in a wheelchair to even know where he is let alone be able to participate in a big wedding?" Gene insisted. "He wears diapers for God's sake. He can't even communicate. He doesn't even know what day of the week it is."

"But he knows more than you think," Anna replied. "He knows Nicky is getting married. I've told him about the wedding and she's even taken Brad to meet him. I want him there, Gene. He belongs there."

"You beat all," Gene said. "He belongs in a nursing home. Not a fucking wedding."

After days and weeks of pleading and begging, Anna was finally able to convince her husband to consent to checking Harry out of the nursing home just for the day in order to attend their daughter's wedding. Gene however, refused to go with Anna to the nursing home and get him. She had Gene, Jr. and Joey drive to Rome and bring him home for the wedding and reception. It was the first time in five months since Harry had been home and immediately following the reception Anna's three sons drove him back to Rome. His presence turned out to be well worth the effort for Harry seemed to be exceptionally alert that day and aware of where he was and what was going on. He sat in the isle beside the church pews where the bride's family was seated with tears streaming down his face as he watched Nicky walk down the isle and say her vows. He seemed to recognize a small portion of the wedding guests even though he was unable to carry on a conversation with anyone except Anna and her children, who had managed to develop their own means of communication through their weekly visits with him. Gene had little to do with Harry, much to Anna's dismay, but did speak to him briefly before the ceremony and after the reception. Anna felt it was because Gene felt ashamed for putting Harry in the nursing home, although everyone else knew differently. Gene simply didn't want Harry around anymore. He had served his purpose and Gene was just waiting for the end, which couldn't arrive soon enough as far as he was concerned.

Following the wedding ceremony, the bride and groom drove to Atlanta where they boarded a small plane and flew to Tybee Island near Savannah for a five-day honeymoon. The wedding came off without a hitch and everyone involved couldn't have been happier. Anna and Gene felt fortunate to see their oldest daughter marry a wealthy and successful doctor and now looked forward to becoming grandparents.

Six months after their oldest daughter tied the knot, their youngest daughter married. That December, three weeks before Christmas, twenty-one year-old Olivia married David Livingston, a successful Atlanta dentist she had met during her reign as Miss Georgia. Through Anna's insistence, Harry was once again present at their second daughter's wedding. Now, both their daughters were happily married and settled down. While Nicky chose to remain in Myrick where she lived with her physician husband, Olivia moved to Buckhead, Georgia near her husband's dental practice. As a wedding gift, Tom Webber set his granddaughter up in her own interior design business in Atlanta.

Gene, Jr. was still quarterbacking for the Atlanta Falcons while his two younger brothers and cousin remained at college in Athens.

Meanwhile, Harry continued to slowly waste away in the nursing home. Anna made the hour-long trip at least once a week to visit him. She would have gone more often if Gene had allowed her. Her pleadings with her husband to accompany her on some of those visits went ignored. Since he wouldn't allow her to travel to Rome alone, she usually took Nicky or Ann along.

"Gene, Harry will be ninety-nine this coming August," Anna told him. "He won't be around much longer. You need to go see him."

"What's the use," Gene told her. "He doesn't even know he's in the world let alone when anyone comes to visit him. You're just wasting your time."

Anna however, knew differently. Harry usually recognized her and looked forward to her visits. She would bring him some fresh home baked pie or pastry treat and take him into the dining hall where she fed him and they would have a long chat. Anna of course, did most of the talking while Harry sat silently and listened to every word she said, sometimes smiling and nodding and at other times he would attempt to verbally respond. Many times she would bring pictures of the children, of Ann riding her horse in the local rodeo competitions, of Gene making a touchdown and of Nicky and Olivia with their husbands. Then on Sundays when Olivia and David drove up from Atlanta, they would drop in and spend a few minutes with Harry on their way to the farm for their Sunday family get-together.

During one of her visits to see Harry, something happened that prompted Anna to stand up to Gene and make a demand for the first time since she insisted he be present at the daughters' weddings. While she was feeding Harry his lunch one afternoon in the dining room, he suddenly looked at her and spoke quite clearly for the first time in almost a year.

"Take me back home," he said.

At first, Anna was so taken by surprise that she couldn't believe what he had just said. "What did you say?" she asked.

"I wanna go home," he said once again, a sad pleading expression in his eyes.

Anna glanced over at Nicky, who was seated across the table beside Harry. "You want to go home, Papa?" she asked him, placing her hand on his shoulder and gently rubbing his back.

"I don't like it here. I want to go home and be with Ollie."

Nicky looked at her mother. "What does he mean?" she whispered under her breath.

"Sweetie, Ollie is in heaven," Anna told him in a soft, gentle voice. "She's not at home. Do you mean you want to go visit her grave?"

"I want to go home with you and see Ollie," he repeated, his mouth quivering as he struggled to form his words.

"Alright then," Anna told him. "I'll take you home. But I can't today. They won't let me. I have to give them a twenty-four hour notice before I can check you out of here. But I'll bring you home for Christmas," she promised. "And we'll put some fresh flowers on Ollie's grave while you're there."

Harry nodded his head as tears filled his eyes. It broke Anna's heart to have to leave him there after each visit. She wanted desperately to bring him back home with her. For the first time in her life, she was resentful toward Gene for not allowing her to bring him home where he belonged.

As they were driving back to Myrick that afternoon after their visit, Nicky turned to her mother. "He must think Ollie is at home," she said. "I guess in his confused state of mind, he thinks she's still alive."

"Well, in a way she is," Anna replied. "He feels closer to her at the farm than where he is now. He knows his time is almost up and he wants to be where he last remembers being with her. I don't want him there anymore. I never did. He belongs at home with us."

"But Mom, you can't provide the care he needs. He's really better off where he's at. I'm afraid I'm going to have to side with Daddy this time."

"He would have never gotten in this bad of shape if your father hadn't gone behind my back and put him in that horrible place. He was fine as long as he was at home with me."

"You don't know that for sure. He might have had that second stroke anyway, regardless."

"I don't believe it," Anna insisted. "He wants to come home and be with us. We're the only family he's ever known. It broke my heart when he asked me to take him home and I couldn't. I won't be satisfied until I get him back."

"Mom, Daddy will never let you do that. And besides, how are you going to care for him. You're not a registered nurse."

"You can help me find a live-in nurse. I'll pay for one out of my own pocket. I have the money. I took care of Amy for eight years."

"But this is different. Papa is a man. He has a catheter."

"So did Amy," Anna replied.

"But it's different with a man. Believe me, I know. I'm a nurse. I have to catheterize men all the time and it's more difficult than with a woman. You can seriously injure a man if you don't know what you're doing."

"So I'll have a nurse there to care for his medical needs."

"Mom, I want you to listen to me," Nicky said with a heavy sigh of frustration. "Daddy has things at home just the way he wants them right now. He has you all to himself. The only people he wants you caring for are himself and Uncle Joey. My father is a very jealous and possessive man. He likes things just the way they are now. You're all he wants and needs. He doesn't want anybody else around robbing him of your attention."

"But Harry won't live much longer. He'll be ninety-nine this August. I want him home during his last days. It's where he belongs. Not in some nursing home with strangers caring for him."

Nicky shook her head in frustration. At times her mother could be as hardheaded and determined as her father. Regardless of what anyone said, she was going to try and bring Harry back home once more before he died. But first, she would have to convince her husband to allow it and Nicky knew that wasn't going to happen.

That night after dinner, Anna took a deep breath and decided to approach her husband about bringing Harry home. She waited until Joey had settled in front of the television to watch his favorite Wednesday night late shows. When Gene went upstairs to take a shower, Anna followed him a few minutes later.

"Gene, I need to talk to you," she said, as he stood shaving in front of the bathroom mirror.

"I'm listening," he replied, as he lathered his face with shaving cream.

"While Nicky and I were with Harry today he said something that really surprised us."

"Yeah, what was that?"

"He said he wanted to come home. He said he wanted to be with Ollie."

Gene stopped what he was doing and looked at his wife under his brow. "Come on now," he said. "You know he's out of it. Ollie's been dead almost seventy-five years."

"But actually, I knew what he meant. He wanted to come back here and visit Ollie's grave once more before he died. And—" she paused, almost afraid to say what was really on her mind. "I think he knows his time is very near and he wants to come back here to die."

"Anna, how many times have we been through this," he said. "You keep insisting on bringing him back here when you know good and well that's impossible. You can't take care of him in the shape he's in. He's in the best place he could possible be for his age and the condition he's in."

"But I can bring in a full-time nurse. It won't be any bother. You wouldn't even know he's around. Gene, he looked straight at me and said he wanted to come home."

Gene threw down his razor and turned to Anna. "Now you look straight at me and I'll tell you something myself," he snapped back. "You're not bringing the old man back here. He's right where he belongs. You cannot physically care for a man with his needs. And you're not wasting good money on a private nurse. Now I'm sick and tired of hearing about it. The answer is no and that's final. Period."

He turned back toward the mirror and continued shaving. Anna stood there in the bathroom staring at her husband in silence. At the risk of making him even angrier, she had to make one more attempt to persuade him to let Harry return home just once more, if only for a couple of days.

"Gene, I'm going to ask you just once more and only because it means so much to me. If you won't let Harry come back here to live out his last days, then will you at least let him come back for the Christmas holidays? Just for a couple of days. Please. If you don't do it for any other reason, just do it for me. Do it if you love me at all."

Gene jerked a towel down from the wall rack and dried his face and hands. He turned to his wife with an angry, disgusted look. How much longer could the old man possible hang on and cling to life? He was nearly a hundred years-old for Christ's sake.

"Okay," he replied, giving her an angry glare. "I tell you what. I'll make a deal with you. If you can promise me that you'll never mention taking him out of that nursing home again and drop the subject once and for all,

I'll agree to let him come back here for one day and one night only and that's all! But after that, he's gone and I don't ever want you to ask me again. Do you understand me?"

Anna smiled and went over to her husband and put her arms around him. "Yes. I promise," she agreed. "Thank you. You've just given me the best Christmas present I could have. You don't have to give me anything else."

It wasn't exactly what she had hoped for, but it would have to do. It was better than nothing. And frankly, it was more than she had expected.

# Chapter Twenty-Seven

Christmas Eve Day, Anna along with Nicky and Gene, Jr., drove to Rome and checked Harry out of the nursing home for two days and drove back to Myrick. Anna was as excited as a child. She couldn't wait to get Harry back home. Her enthusiasm was bittersweet, however, for she knew it would most likely be for the last time. Nicky had offered to spend the night at the farm so that she could help her mother with Harry and then she and her brother Gene would go with their mother to drive him back to Rome later Christmas Day. Olivia and her husband had also made plans to spend the night at the farm since her three brothers and cousins would be there over the holidays. The children had all remained close and despite going their separate ways once they left home, they continued to keep in contact and looked forward to times like this when they all could be reunited at the farm with their parents.

Anna had pleaded with her sister to come with Ann and join them, but she flatly refused. Then she pleaded with her husband to apologize to Angel and finally bury the hatchet and he too, refused. Since Ann had turned seventeen that June, she was free to make her own decisions, so she chose to spend Christmas at the farm where her father was sure to be over the holidays. Anna felt heartsick that she and her sister had been alienated. Angel was all she had left and because of Gene, her sister refused to attend any family functions or gatherings. Angel on the other hand, didn't mind not being included during the holidays for she had reunited with her former partner Tanya, and the two were now back living together at Coleman Hill. Therefore, they had their own plans for the holidays.

Everyone was excited to have Harry home for Christmas. It was the first time he'd been back to the farm in almost a year. He wasn't in the same condition as before he left, but he still knew where he was and recognized his family. Gene was perhaps the only one who wasn't as thrilled to have the old man back, if only for one day and night. Harry had become a thorn in his side and as long as the old man was alive, he remained locked into a life he hated. As he saw it, the only way he would ever be free was for Harry to be out of his way.

So far, this Christmas, in comparison to last year's was much happier. Anna wasn't sick with pneumonia, there were no elaborate wedding plans, and now with the addition of two brand new son-in-laws, their family was growing. The old plantation house was filled with festivity, mountains of food and a lot love and laughter. All seven children were there along with Chuck Willis and Red Moore. The fact that Chuck and Red had been once removed by divorce made no difference. Their son and daughter still spent more time at the farm than they did at their own parents' homes. The two men were still considered family and always would be. The same applied to Tom Webber, who also joined them for the holidays, despite Gene's obvious distain for his father-in-law, which stemmed from his jealousy over Tom's fondness for Anna.

Christmas Eve was spent with everyone dipping their plates from the large buffet table Anna had prepared in the dining room, then gathering in the den where they swapped amusing stories they all had growing up on the farm. The one story that was always shared whenever the kids got together, despite it's horror at the time, was the day their father and Uncle Red decided to put some fresh meat in the freezer.

"To this day I see Curly standing there with a bullet hole between his eyes every time I try to eat a piece of meat," Olivia confessed, to everyone's laughter.

"And I can't even look at a carton of milk with Elsie the Cow on it without thinking of him," Nicky added. "She has the same little curl in the middle of her forehead that Curly had."

"Come to think of it, your Momma has one of his brothers sittin' in there on a platter at the table," Gene added. "In fact, David's chowin' down on him right now."

They all laughed aloud as they turned to Olivia's new husband, who was holding a plate containing a healthy portion of roast beef and gravy.

David Livingston, the refined, well-bred Atlanta dentist from one of the wealthiest families in the South, turned to his bride with a confused look on his face. "What are all of you talking about?"

"Daddy made the mistake once of allowing us to have one of his beef calves as a pet. We named him Curly because he had a lock of curly mane on top of his head, and Daddy used to bring him up to the house for us to play with when we were little. Then one day he and Uncle Red were slaughtering some beef cattle and Daddy decided it was Curly's time. Daddy shot him in the head before cutting his throat and while their backs were turned, Curly jumped up and ran back to the house while we were all in the yard playing. He came staggering up to us with a bullet hole between his eyes whaling in agony and it upset us so bad we couldn't eat meat for months and wouldn't speak to Daddy for a week."

"And when Daddy and Uncle Red came looking for him and found Curly in the yard with all of us gathered around him crying and screaming, Uncle Red told us that somebody else had shot him and he and Daddy were going to take him to the vet," Nicky laughed so hard that she couldn't finish the story.

"So he and Uncle Red loaded him into the back of Daddy's pick-up and took him back to the pasture where they finished slaughtering him," Olivia added, completing the story.

Everyone roared with laughter. Anna glanced over at Harry sitting in his wheelchair, and even he had a big grin on his face. Obviously he understood everything they were saying.

David looked at his wife in horror and disgust. "And you find that story amusing?"

"Well, it wasn't funny at the time, of course," Olivia admitted. "But now that it's over, it's pretty funny."

"If you're going to be in this family David, you're going to have to get used to our sense of humor," Nicky told her new brother-in-law. "We're not like most people, we've learned to find humor in almost everything, even tragedies. It's our way of dealing with things that life throws at us."

"It's called red-neck humor," Red added. "Or a Southerner's way of coping with life."

Olivia's husband looked at the people seated around him and knew he had entered a family nothing like his own. He looked down at the food on his plate and suddenly lost his appetite. He even felt sickened and repulsed. His family would have never found anything amusing about something so macabre.

"Old Curly tastes pretty good, don't he?" Gene asked, teasing his new son-in-law as the young man got up to return his plate to the kitchen. Again, everyone laughed.

"I'm sorry," David said. "I don't find anything amusing about that story."

"Well son, where do you think all those steaks and roasts you been eatin' all your life came from?" His father-in-law replied. "They came from cattle farms and slaughterhouses, just like that beef roast you're eatin' right now. We may have been poor as dirt, but we ate the finest grade A and prime cuts of meat for free when you was paying through the nose for it."

"David grew up in the city," Olivia explained with a smile. "He's never even seen a real cow or bull up close."

"Is that right?" Gene said. "Well, next time I get ready to butcher up another one, I'll give you a call and have you come on down here and help Red and me get 'em ready for the table. You can have your choice of either shootin' him in the head or slittin' his throat. You just have to tune out their wails and screams while you're doin' it."

"Yeah," Red added. "They don't scream for long. Maybe you could just hug him to death," he chuckled.

The room again filled with laughter.

David looked at Gene and Red with disgust and disbelief, then turned and left the room. He was gone for several minutes before Olivia finally got up to go check on her husband.

They continued to laugh and talk, swapping past memories and simply enjoying being reunited once again until finally Gene announced it was time for him to go to bed in order to get up early the next morning.

"I'll have a big breakfast ready around seven after Gene finishes the morning milking," Anna announced. "Then we'll open our gifts afterwards."

Nicky and Gene, Jr. helped their mother prepare Harry for bed there in the den after everyone had excused themselves and gone up to their rooms for the night. Ann volunteered to sleep in the den so that she could keep an eye on Harry in case he needed anything. As it turned out, Harry turned out to be less trouble than expected and seemed even more alert and responsive than Anna found him at the nursing home.

"I would give anything if Gene would let me bring him back home for good," Anna told her two children as they helped their mother settle Harry in for the night. "I can tell a difference in him already in the short time since he's been here."

"He does seem happier and more alert," Nicky agreed. "I think he's really happy to be back home. I'm glad Daddy agreed to let him come home for Christmas."

"I'm sure it would make a big difference if he were here all the time rather than being kept in an institutional environment being cared for by strangers," Anna said.

She watched her oldest son change Harry into his pajamas while telling the old man, that he had always known as "Papa", how glad he was to see him again and how well he looked. Finally, when they finished settling Harry in for the night, Anna approached her son about talking to his father.

"Gene, maybe if you talked to your father about letting Harry come back home, he might listen to you," she suggested.

"Mother, no," Nicky told her mother firmly. "You know as well as anyone how Daddy feels about keeping Harry here. Don't get him started. Just be glad he agreed to let you bring him here for Christmas. Don't push your luck."

Anna lowered her eyes and remained silent.

"I'll talk to dad for you, Mom," Gene told her, giving his mother a comforting hug and a kiss on the forehead. He couldn't bear to see his mother sad or hurt. He loved her more than anyone else in the world. "I can't promise it will do any good, but I'll try."

"Mom, I wish you wouldn't do this," Nicky said. "You know how Daddy is. It's Christmas. Don't make him mad and ruin it for everyone."

"Mom's not doing anything," Gene told his sister. "I'm the one doing the talking. I'll handle Dad."

"Maybe if you just got him to agree to allow Harry to stay just one more night and then Nicky and I will take him back first thing the day after Christmas," she pleaded with her son.

Gene nodded. "Okay, Mom. I will. You just stay out of it and let me talk to Dad."

Anna put her arms around her son and hugged him. "Thank you, Gene. Maybe he'll agree if you ask him."

Much to everyone's amazement, Gene succeeded in convincing his father to allow Harry to remain there one more night. Anna was very grateful to her son. This was certainly turning out to be one of the best Christmases they had in a long time. If only she could have had Angel join them the holidays would have been complete. Next year perhaps.

On Christmas day after all the presents had been exchanged and everyone was miserable from over-eating, they all settled in the den for a few more cherished moments of family togetherness before turning in for the night. Everyone hated to see their wonderful holiday gathering come to an end. Chuck and Red had left with Chuck, Jr. and Ann a little earlier, as had Tom, and now all that remained were the immediate family. Harry sat in his wheelchair beside Anna and appeared to be enjoying the conversation even though he was unable to add anything. Every time the children would reminisce over a childhood experience and laugh aloud, a smile would flicker across his lips. Finally, the evening grew late and as usual, Gene was the first to excuse himself for bed. After everyone had gone upstairs, Nicky, Olivia and Gene, Jr. began helping their mother prepare Harry for bed once more before returning him to the nursing home the next morning. After settling him on the sofa bed in the den, the children kissed him and their mother goodnight and left Anna and Harry alone. Anna sat down on the side of the bed and carefully removed his new tortoise frame glasses from his face and placed them on the table beside the bed. It was his last night there and she wanted to savor every moment.

"I wish I could keep you here with me forever," she told him, as she took his frail, bony hand in hers and gently caressed it. "I can't tell you how much I've missed you not being here. If it were left up to me, you would have never left. I blame myself for what's happened because if I hadn't gotten sick and gone into the hospital, you'd still be with us."

"Don't blame y-y-yourself," Harry stammered, struggling to form his words. "I know it's been h-h-hard on you b-b-but it's for the b-b-best. If I h-h-had my choice, I'd r-r-rather be here too, but I k-k-know you can't take c-c-care of me a-a-anymore."

Tears began to fill her eyes. "Oh Harry, you don't know how much I miss you. I would give anything in this world if things could be different. You're more like a father to me than my own father. And my children still look on you as their grandfather and always will. You've been so good and kind to us. All of us. I could never begin to repay you for everything you've done over the years. It seems so unfair that Gene won't let me continue to take care of you now."

Harry just looked at her with sadness in his eyes and gave her hand a gentle squeeze. There were so many things he wanted to tell Anna, but the second stroke had made it too difficult for him to speak. He wanted desperately to tell her that she had always taken better care of him than he could have ever asked for. He wanted to tell her that he would always love her like a daughter. He wished now that he had said all those things while he still had the ability to speak.

Anna began to cry. "Oh Harry, I love you so much and I don't want to see you go back to that awful place."

"It's n-n-not so bad t-t-there. They take g-g-good care of me and t-t-they're kind enough. But y-y-you always gave me s-s-something they c-c-could never give me. Love."

Tears fell from Anna's cheeks onto the blanket. "Oh Harry, I know it's selfish of me, but I don't want to lose you. I can't bear the thought of life without you. I don't want to let you go."

Harry reached up slowly with a trembling hand and wiped away a tear from her cheek. There was so much he wanted to tell her that might ease her sadness. He wanted to say that he had lived long enough—perhaps too long. He was ready to die. Death was no longer something he dreaded the way a person her age might dread it. It was simply that there was nothing left to keep him there. He had done everything, tasted everything good there was to taste, seen most everything there was to see, been most everywhere he wanted to go—nothing was new or exciting anymore. Now, the worst thing about dying was leaving behind the ones he loved and cared about the most. But he still had one more thing to look forward to. He had someone special waiting for him. She had been waiting far too long and he was ready to be reunited with her at last. And one day, a lifetime from now, he would be waiting for Anna and the children. Both he and Ollie would be there, waiting for them.

Anna gently laid her head down on his chest and closed her eyes tightly, trying to stop the tears. Harry placed his hand on her back and patted her softly.

"Oh Harry, I love you so much," Anna sobbed.

"I love y-y-you t-t-too, Anna," he replied. "Y-Y-You'll always be m-m-my little girl."

There was no use trying to stop the tears anymore. There were just too many. Anna continued to lay there with her head on his chest for a long while until finally she heard Harry's breathing become rhythmic and then she knew he had fallen asleep. She straightened up and as she watched him sleep, she wished that she could somehow make time stand still so that tomorrow morning would never come and she wouldn't have to let him go. She continued to sit there for a long, long time until her head nodded and she drifted off to sleep in an upright position, still holding his hand.

"Olivia."

Anna jerked awake with a start. She wondered how long she had been asleep.

"Olivia." It was Harry. He had spoken clearly without the slightest stammer.

"No, sweetie, it's me. Anna. Olivia is upstairs sleeping," she whispered softly.

"My—my f-f-favorite green dress—She's wearing the g-g-green dress—I bought for her—b-b-birthday. The one with the yellow—f-f-flowers." His voice was weak, his breathing raspy and shallow.

He was dreaming of Ollie, Anna thought. She wondered if he dreamed of her at the nursing home or if it was because he was back at home and felt closer to her there. Suddenly, Harry opened his eyes and looked straight ahead, past her, as if someone had walked into the room and was standing behind her.

"Ollie," he stammered, his voice shaking with anticipation. "C-c-come here, let me l-l-look at you."

Anna remained very still and continued to hold his hand. "You're dreaming, Harry. It's me, Anna."

"She wants—wants me to—to c-c-come with her. She's—c-c-calling me to. She wants me—to go—"

Finally, his eyes closed once again and he appeared to be drifting back off to sleep. He was old and tired and wanted to join his beloved Ollie. Most likely he would very soon—sooner than Anna wanted. After all these years, he still longed to be with the only woman he had ever loved. He had waited over seven decades to join her and he was ready to be reunited with his soul mate and the love of his life. And soon, his wait would be over. Anna continued to sit there with him as she watched him sleep peacefully. She didn't want to leave, but she knew that Gene would be angry if she didn't come upstairs to bed. She leaned forward and kissed him gently on the forehead. "Goodnight, Harry. I love you," she whispered, pulling the blanket up around his neck. "I'll see you in the morning."

But she wouldn't.


Anna never got the opportunity to take Harry back to the nursing home the next morning. He passed away quietly and peacefully in his sleep during the night. Even though everyone was expecting his death at any time, his passing devastated Anna. She sobbed inconsolably at the funeral home and during the church services. At the gravesite, Gene and Nicky had to help her back to the house when the preacher completed the services. Not since her sister's death, had Anna grieved so hard and for as long. Surprisingly, Harry's death proved to be a turning point in the bitter feud between Angel and her brother-in-law. Angel decided to overcome her hostility toward Gene and attend Harry's funeral. It didn't mean she was willing to let bygones be bygones, it simply meant that she had set aside her existing animosity long enough to attend the funeral services out of respect for her sister.

Just as Harry requested, Anna buried him beside Ollie, beneath the old Magnolia tree out back. Each day, Anna would go visit Harry's grave where she placed fresh flowers and sat on the garden bench, talking to him as if he were still alive. As the weeks passed, her grief eased and she didn't seem as sad and despondent. With the holidays behind her and the boys back at college, Gene, Jr. playing football again and her daughters married with their own lives, Anna settled into her old routine of caring for her husband and brother-in-law.

Meanwhile, Gene was chomping at the bit impatiently waiting for Harry's will to be read. His life would remain at a standstill until the will was probated. Unfortunately, Harry's attorney had taken an extended Christmas vacation in the Bahamas and the will could not be read nor processed until his return, which was expected around the middle of February. Gene comforted himself with the thought that he had waited thirty-three years for this day to come, therefore waiting a few more weeks wouldn't make that much difference.

Since there would be no more weekly visits to Rome to visit Harry at the nursing home, Anna busied herself going through the boxes of Harry's personal belongings that she found in his trailer. One day she found a battered shoebox filled with old photographs dating back seventy years or more. Most of them were photographs of people she assumed were Harry's family and relatives. Finally, she came across one photograph where she immediately recognized the people in the old, faded picture. It was a photograph of Harry standing beneath the old Magnolia tree behind the house with his arm around an attractive young woman in a floral dress. They were both smiling and appeared very happy. Anna studied the black and white photo carefully. She knew the woman standing beside Harry had to be Ollie. She turned the picture over and saw where someone had written on the back. The jumbled scribble was difficult to read. It was in pencil and had faded along with the photograph. She strained to read the handwriting. At the top was a date. It read *March*

*14, 1917.* Harry would have been twenty-two years-old then. Beneath the date, she studied the scribbling until she finally was able to make out the words. It read: *Ollie and me after church—wearing my favorite green dress.*

Harry had mentioned a green dress the night he died. Anna remembered another occasion a green dress was mentioned. The night Amy died. Anna sat on the side of her sister's bed as Amy called out to Olivia and mumbled something about a pretty green dress. She turned the photograph over and studied the image carefully. She remembered Harry's last words. *She's got a pretty green dress on. The one with the yellow flowers. It was my favorite.*

Anna suddenly remembered the conversation in the car between Gene and herself driving home from Cassie's funeral that day and how they laughed about having strange experiences in the old plantation house and wondered if it might be Ollie's spirit roaming about. Only it wasn't so funny now that she thought about it. Ollie had been there in the room both nights when Amy and Harry had died. As silly as it might sound, Anna felt comfort knowing Ollie had been there to accompany Harry and Amy out of this world and into the next. She only hoped that Ollie would be there for her when her time came.

# Chapter Twenty-Eight

The first thing Gene planned to do once Harry's will went through probate was to move his trailer away from the house. He planned to give it to one of the farmhands whose home had recently burned. Those plans, however, didn't stop there. Through Nicky's husband, Gene got the name of an Atlanta land developer and real estate broker and began discussing dividing up the thousand-acre farm into two-hundred, five-acre residential lots. Gene's slice of the pie would equal in excess of five million dollars. For the first time in his life he would have money—lots of money. His *own* money. Anna was a multi-millionaire in her own right, thanks to her sister looking out for her interests in the mill. Gene, on the other hand, had nothing to show for his toil except calloused hands and sunburned flesh. He lived in a magnificent mansion and drove a brand new truck and a Cadillac, which Anna had bought for him, but he had no savings and little in his pocket. His wife was the one with all the money.

A couple of weeks after Harry was buried, Nicky learned she was pregnant with their first child. The baby was due in August. Anna and Gene were ecstatic, especially Gene, who knew he would soon have plenty of time on his hands—as well as money, to devote to his new grandchild.

Finally, the second week in February arrived and Harry's attorney returned from his winter vacation. Anna called that same week and made an appointment to begin processing the will. Since the attorney was busy catching up with his appointments and court dates, the earliest he could meet with them would be the first week in March. Yet as luck would have it, before their appointment with the attorney took place, something happened to put their future on hold indefinitely. Four days before they were scheduled to meet with the attorney, a fire broke out in the courthouse basement destroying much of the records on file along with two attorney's offices. Among those records were all existing copies of Harry Porter's will. Since Porter's attorney occupied one of the offices destroyed, there were no copies left. Except one. The one Harry was given to keep in his personal possession. Until that copy surfaced, the estate could not be settled. For the next year, Anna and Gene turned their house, as well as Harry's trailer, upside down looking for that will.

On August 12, 1994, Nicky gave birth to a beautiful and healthy, eight-pound baby boy. She named her son after his father and christened him Bradford Edward Bailey, Jr. Once again, Angel set aside her resentment and was present at her great nephew's christening. Still, she refused to speak to her brother-in-law or even acknowledge him, but she now refused to allow him to stand between her and her family. For that, Anna was extremely grateful and thankful.

However, while their family slowly began to heal old grievances, another crisis arose. This time, it involved Nicky and her husband of one year. Shortly after the birth of their son, Nicky's husband was puzzled by the physical characteristics of his son. About three months following his birth, Brad, Sr. noticed his son's hair was a little too dark and curly for a child of blonde, fair-skinned parents. His eyes were brown while his parents' eyes were blue and his skin tone was just a little too dark for that of a Caucasian baby. Bailey's first concern was the obvious—his son had been accidentally switched in the hospital nursery. After a quick and thorough investigation, his initial fears were laid to rest. His next thought however, was even more disturbing. His wife had been involved in an affair—with a man of another race. To clear that up, he had to confront Nicky.

After much thought concerning the matter, Nicky chose not to tell her husband of her true heritage when they first met. Why should she? She had never told anyone else that her birth mother had been black. Not even her closest friends. For all they knew, Anna *was* her birth mother. In fact, no one knew the truth except the midwife who had delivered her and she was now deceased. It wasn't that Nicky was ashamed that her mother had been black or that she was adopted, it just made things less complicated to pass as white in a white society. Besides, the subject never came up because Nicky appeared as Caucasian as the other members of her family. Yet no one ever suspected that the black genes Nicky carried would show up in her children even though she was married to a fair-skinned, blonde husband. The truth about Nicky's heritage however, had finally surfaced.

Nicky had spent the day preparing her husband's favorite meal when he came home from the hospital that day. She had already fed the baby and put him to bed a little early so that she and Brad could spend some quality time together. She greeted him with a big smile and warm hug when he walked through the door that evening. When she found him somewhat unreceptive, Nicky just thought he had experienced a difficult day at the hospital. By the time dinner was over, and Nicky was clearing the table, she was well aware that her husband's mood wasn't all due to a hectic day at the hospital. She knew something was deeply troubling him when he announced that they needed to have a talk.

"What's wrong?" Nicky asked, as she loaded the dishwasher.

"I'm going to ask you something Nicky, and regardless of the consequences, I want you to be completely honest with me."

Nicky stopped what she was doing and looked at her husband. "Okay," she replied simply.

"I want to know what's been going on behind my back."

"What are you talking about?"

"I'm talking about what were you doing while I was at the hospital twelve to fourteen hours a day, six days a week."

Nicky shook her head in puzzlement. "I don't know what you are talking about," she replied. "For the past three months I've been right here taking care of the baby."

"And before that?"

"Before that, I took two months maternity leave. What are you getting at?"

"What about *before* the baby was born. Were you having an affair behind my back?"

"What?" Nicky had to laugh at her husband's absurd charges. "What in the world would make you ask me such a thing?"

"I'm not stupid—or blind," Brad replied. "I can look at that baby and see he's not mine."

Nicky was in such shock all she could do was laugh in her husband's face. She was aware that their son was dark complexioned and might be mistaken for Latino, but not *black*. And never in a million years would she have thought that her own husband would think their child could be racially mixed. A lot of babies had different complexions than their birth parents. It didn't mean that they were mixed. Perhaps she was in denial. She had been able to pass for white, so why not her son?

"Are you joking?" she said. "What in God's name are you talking about? No, I never cheated on you. You're the only man I've ever been with. You know that. Are you out of your mind?"

"That baby isn't mine," he insisted flatly.

"What do you mean?"

"I mean that's not my son. His father has to be black."

"That's ridiculous," Nicky replied. "You're his father."

"Well, there's one way to find out for certain. I can have some tests run at the hospital. And I will."

"Go right ahead. Be my guest," Nicky told him. "You have my full co-operation. But I can save you the trouble. It's not the baby's race that's in question. It's mine."

Brad looked at his wife with surprise. "What?"

"My mother—my birth mother was black. My father was white. I was adopted when I was born."

Brad's mouth dropped. A look of bewilderment came over him.

"I never told you because I didn't think it mattered. I never told anyone for that matter. No one ever asked. Everyone just assumed I was Gene and Anna Longhorn's natural child. So if my son's ethnicity is in question, it's due to my heritage, not my infidelity. Now, I have a question for you. Does it still matter if our son doesn't grow up to be blonde and blue-eyed like his father? Or would you still disown him because he's not a hundred percent white?"

Brad remained silent and stared at his wife as if searching for an answer. "Why didn't you tell me your real mother was black?"

"Would it have mattered?"

Once again, an uneasy silence fell between them.

"Well," Nicky said. "I guess it would have. Does that mean you would have never married me had you known?"

Silence continued to fill the room. Finally, her husband replied. "This is the deep South, Nicky. Times haven't changed that much for us here. It's hard growing up with your race in question. I'm a doctor with a high profile to maintain in the community. If I was able to question my son's heritage, don't you think others will as well? It's not like we adopted him. Everybody knows he's our own child. That complicates matters."

"Oh, I see," Nicky replied. "We can't pass him off as adopted so therefore people will assume you couldn't possible be his real father. People will either think as you did that I had an affair with a black man or they'll know the truth—that I'm half black. Either way, it would be detrimental to your reputation and high standing in the community, because it matters more what people might think than how you feel about your wife and son."

"Why didn't you tell me, Nicky? Why did you keep it a secret?"

"A secret? I didn't keep anything a secret. It's not like I was ashamed of anything. I was raised in a white society by white parents and have always considered myself to be white. It never crossed my mind that if I married a white man that my children might show black characteristics. Perhaps that was naïve of me. Or maybe even stupid, but it doesn't matter. He's my child and I love him regardless. It shouldn't matter what color his skin is or what texture his hair. He's a human being. He's our son."

"No. He's your son," Brad replied coldly. "I've worked long and hard to get where I am. I have a spotless professional reputation. Something like this could ruin me if it got out."

"Oh, for God's sake. Get over it," Nicky scoffed. "You're so full of yourself. This is 1994. We're not living in the 60's anymore. Or maybe some of us are." She paused and gave her husband a hard stare. "So what you're saying is, if you would have known that I was only half white, you would have never married me. Is that right, Brad?"

"No," he replied. "I would have never dated you."

Nicky suddenly felt sick to her stomach. She was heartbroken, but she would be damned if she let him know what she was really feeling inside.

"Okay, so do you want a divorce?" she asked flatly.

"That's something I may have to consider," he replied.

"Oh, don't bother," she told him. "I'll make it easy for you. I'll file for a divorce. You needn't bother. I don't like the idea of being married to a racist. But more important, I don't want my son being raised by one."

"I'm sorry, Nicky. It's not that—"

"Don't. You've said enough," she told him. "I don't need to hear anymore. You've made your feelings perfectly clear. I'll make it easy for you. I'll see an attorney first thing tomorrow and my son and I will be gone by the end of the week. You won't have to be bothered with us anymore. You'll be surprised how quickly we can get out of your life."

With that, Nicky walked out of the room and went upstairs to begin packing. Then she phoned her mother and told her she and the baby were coming home.

By the time another holiday season had come and gone, so had Nicky's brief marriage. One year and nine months was as long as it took to produce a son and end her marriage. A few weeks after Nicky moved back home and filed for divorce, she was stunned to discover she was pregnant with another child. That didn't stop her from going through with the divorce. In fact, she didn't even bother to tell her soon-to-be ex. After all, what difference would it have made?

By February of 1995 Nicky, now three months pregnant, was living back at home with her six month-old son. Despite the fact that Nicky was due to deliver in August, she returned to work, but not at the hospital. She found employment at a private physician's office in Myrick. A month later, her former husband left Myrick to live in Atlanta where he opened a private practice. Nicky, nor her two children, ever heard from him again and it was many years before Bailey learned he was the father of *two* children.

That May, Hal and his cousin Chuck, graduated from the University of Athens after earning their degrees in agriculture and business administration. Chuck went on to work with his father at his Chevrolet dealerships while Hal returned home to settle into farming with his father. Joey remained at the University to finish earning his degree in veterinarian medicine. Gene, Jr. was entering his third year with the Atlanta Falcons and had just signed another three-year contract worth nine million. Olivia continued to live with her dentist husband in Buckhead, which was the wealthiest area in Atlanta. Angel's daughter Ann, was now enrolled at the University of Georgia in Atlanta, where she studied business administration and finance.

Anna had two of her five children back home as well as a new grandson. Once again, she had plenty of people to care for. It had been nearly a year and a half since Harry's death and still, his will was nowhere to be found. Anna had all but given up on ever finding it, when suddenly one day as she was unpacking some boxes Hal had brought back home with him from college, she found it. Harry had given Hal some momentums before he left for college and there, in an old wooden box along with some old Indian arrowheads and an antique gold watch, was the copy of his Last Will and Testament. When Anna opened the envelope and saw what it was, she screamed out loud. Nicky went running upstairs to see what had happened.

"Mom, what is it? What happened?" she gasped.

"Go get your father. I've found Harry's will!"


Anna and Gene sat in the attorney's office anxiously awaiting the reading of Harry's will. Neither had a clue as to what it contained. Since Harry had changed his will at least twice in the past ten years, even his own attorney couldn't remember much about the specifics. Finally, a year and a half following his death, his assets were about to be divulged and distributed.

"Okay," the attorney sighed. "Let's see what we have here."

As Anna and Gene sat in front of the big mahogany desk, listening intently as the lawyer began to read the old man's Last Will and Testament, Gene's heart began to pound wildly. Finally, he would have something to call his own. The house they had lived in all those years had never legally been his. His wife or either Porter had bought the cars he drove. He owned no land or property. He had no money in a savings. The only thing he had his name on was a thirty year-old car. At last he would have something of his own.

"To Anna Longhorn, I leave my plantation home and surrounding five acres on which it rests.

"To Olivia Longhorn and Anna Nicole Longhorn, I leave one-hundred and twenty-fifty thousand dollars each."

Gene took a deep breath in nervous anticipation. To his knowledge, the only asset Porter had remaining was his thousand-acre farmland. Naturally, he expected Harry to leave the house to Anna and any money he had to be divided up among their five kids. But the farm certainly would be left to him. After all, who else was left to will it to?

"To Eugene Longhorn, Jr., Joseph Longhorn and Harold Longhorn, I leave one-thousand acres of farmland and my dairy and beef cattle business to be divided up equally three ways."

Suddenly all the color drained from Gene's face. His body froze in stunned disbelief as the attorney continued reading the will.

"I leave this property and the business to the three individuals mentioned above on the stipulation that said land and business continue to remain in tack and in full operation for ten years following my death. After ten years, said land and business may be sold and or divided if desired by the three above mentioned individuals and only the three above mentioned individuals."

Anna turned and glanced at her husband, looking for his reaction. His expression faded from shock to disappointment to anger.

"And last, to Gene Longhorn, Sr. I leave my truck and my trailer home."

Gene didn't hear another word the attorney said from that point on. He had heard all he needed to hear. Repeatedly, he shifted his weight in the chair. He was anxious to leave. There was no point in remaining there another moment longer. As soon as the attorney stood and offered his hand in a final parting, Gene was halfway out the door. Anna remained long enough to accept the attorney's handshake and offer an apology for her husband's rudeness before hurrying to catch up with him. By the time they had reached their car in the parking lot, his face was red as a beet and he was livid.

"That son-of-a-bitch! I give him thirty-four years of my blood and sweat and what does he give me in return? A goddamn twenty year-old truck and a fuckin' leaky trailer!"

"He gave us the house, Gene. He gave us a place to live when we had nothing. He provided you with a job that supported your family for the past twenty-five years. He paid all our medical bills for years. He even paid for our wedding. Harry's done plenty for us over the years. Maybe he felt that he'd already given us enough and now it was time to leave something for the kids. Maybe you're expecting too much."

Gene swung the Cadillac out of the parking lot and squealed the tires as he left town and headed for home. "Too much! That old bastard couldn't have survived the last thirty years if it hadn't been for me. He would have lost that fuckin' farm three decades ago if I hadn't run it for him. I killed myself keeping that goddamn place going and all I get in return is a lousy broken down truck and a leaky trailer!"

"But Gene, it's not like he left us nothing. We have the house and five acres. And we still have the farm. Harry just didn't leave it all in your name. Gene, Jr. doesn't care anything about the farm or working it and God knows it's not like he needs the money, so I'm sure you're more than welcome to his share of it. And as for Joe and Hal well, all they ever wanted was to farm so I don't see why things can't remain the same only you can sit back now and let them do most of the hard work while you just oversee things. You'll still have a decent income and be able to settle into semi-retirement."

"A decent income! After thirty-four years I expected a hell of a lot more than that! Do you realize what I could do with that land if it would have all been left to me? I could sell it and be a multi-millionaire. Fuck semi-retirement! I'd never have to work another goddamn day of my life. But no! That bastard had to screw me over after I gave him my life."

"Gene. Don't be so bitter. Be thankful for what we have. We have a lot more than most people ever dream of having."

"No! *You* have more than most people ever dream of having. You're the one with all the fuckin' money. You and your goddamn sister. Me? I don't have a fuckin' thing to my name except calluses and blisters."

His high speed and careless driving was beginning to frighten Anna. He had already run two red lights and a stop sign before hitting Highway 11. She wanted to warn him to slow down but it wouldn't have done any good. His rage was out of control, which was the only time Anna was ever truly fearful of her husband.

"You know that's not true, Gene. You have everything I have. What's mine is yours. Everything I own is yours. It always has been. You're just as wealthy as I am. That's why I've never been able to understand why you always said you never had anything. You *do*. You're worth millions. If I died tomorrow everything I have would be in your name and your name alone. You'd be a multi-millionaire. Don't you understand?"

Anna's eyes were on her husband so she never saw the tractor-trailer that slammed into their car at the dangerous intersection a little more than a mile from the farm. Gene never saw it either. In fact, he was so preoccupied he never recalled approaching the stop sign that they routinely warned their children about. The truck hit their Cadillac Deville on the front passenger door and the sound of the impact could be heard a mile away. The crash flipped the heavy automobile over several times and through a split rail fence, landing upside down in a nearby cow pasture. Gene was ejected from behind the wheel and thrown some fifty feet from the car and knocked unconscious. Anna, who was wearing her seatbelt, took the full force of impact and was pinned inside the front seat among the twisted wreckage. The driver of the Kenworth rig slid to a stop a hundred yards down the road. Customers at the gas station and corner convenience store on both sides of the intersection immediately stopped what they were doing and ran toward the mangled car and truck to offer assistance while the store keepers quickly dialed 911.

The shaken truck driver slowly climbed down from his mangled rig, clutching his cell phone and after realizing the authorities had been notified, he dialed his boss.

"Yeah, I'm okay," he told his boss. "But I'm not sure about the people in the Caddy. I can't believe this is the first accident I've had since I hit that Black Angus twenty-five years ago at night a couple of miles down the road. Damn! I hope those people are going to be okay, but it looks pretty bad."

Within minutes, sheriff and state patrol cars along with two ambulances arrived on the scene. It took a rescue unit nearly fifteen minutes to free Anna's body from the front seat. By then, her husband was already in an ambulance and on his way to the Barrow County Medical Center.

After arriving in the emergency room, Gene opened his eyes and saw a team of nurses and doctors working frantically, scurrying around him as he lay bleeding on the gurney. He heard their voices and commands but made no sense of what was being said. His back and legs felt as if they were on fire and he was having difficulty breathing. He couldn't remember getting out of bed that morning and had no idea what he was doing there. He tried to speak but couldn't. Over and over he tried to call out to someone. Finally, he managed to make a sound as he called out to the one person he wanted most.

"ANNA!"

# Chapter Twenty-Nine

The sprawling white church on Main Street where Anna attended since she was a child and where she was baptized, was filled with mourners. Everyone in Myrick had known the Coleman family for decades and remembered young Anna fondly as the shyer yet friendlier of the three Coleman girls. Over the years they watched her mature and grow into a pillar of the community and embrace local celebrity hood as one of the wealthiest and most respected citizens in the county. Despite her affluence and wealth, she always greeted everyone she passed on the street with the same warm smile and friendly hello. Although there had been whispers at one time concerning her choice of husband and having married beneath her, she remained respected and well liked as she matured into womanhood and became a devoted wife and loving mother. She left Coleman Hill, a local landmark and embarked on creating her own Southern legacy—Porter Plantation, which like Coleman Hill, would continue to be handed down from generation to generation. It was a Southern tradition.

Sadly, at the age of forty-three, Anna Longhorn left her legacy much sooner than she should have, leaving behind five grown children, one grandchild and another grandbaby on the way. She also left behind a grief-stricken and guilt-ridden husband. His beloved wife of twenty-five years was dead because of his careless and irresponsible behavior. Had he not let his temper get out of control, she would still be alive. Little did he realize as he was ranting over being left with so little in the will, he still had his most cherished possession sitting beside him? His wife. Now because of his temper, he no longer had her. He had destroyed the most precious thing in his life, the person he loved most in the world—his soul mate. He would have to live the rest of his life knowing he was responsible for her death.

In the accident report, it was stated that he simply became distracted and didn't recognize the stop sign. He was merely charged with reckless driving and failure to yield a stop sign. Had anyone known for certain the actual circumstances causing the accident, he could just as easily been charged with vehicular homicide., Not until later when he was released from the hospital on the day of his wife's funeral, did he breakdown and confess to his children that their mother had died because of his own reckless behavior. Their reactions ranged from shock to anger and resentment. Their father's temper had finally resulted in dire consequences. Yet the one most infuriated by his actions was his sister-in-law. He had succeeded in robbing Angel of her best friend and only remaining sister. She felt nothing but contempt and loathing for him. *The day may come when he turns on you*, she had told her sister years ago. Her words seemed profound now.

His children were sympathetic, yet still resentful more toward their father's actions than him. They knew how passionately he loved their mother and how much she meant to him. She was the one great love of his life. Still, as their oldest daughter stood over her mother's casket, Nicky recalled what her mother had said the day she was released from the hospital with pneumonia. *"Your father's temper will be the death of me yet."* And so it had been. In two days she would have celebrated her forty-third birthday.

When Gene approached his wife's coffin in the church sanctuary, seeing her lifeless body for the first and last time, he broke down in tears and sobbed uncontrollably. His life was no longer worth living. He screamed that it should have been him lying there. He fell over the coffin and cried so hard that his three sons had to physically restrain him.

Anna was laid to rest beneath the old Magnolia tree beside her sister, her nephew, her father-in-law, Ollie and Harry. Only the immediate family was present at the graveside service. There were Anna's five children, her infant grandson, her sister, brother-in-law, two former brother-in-laws, her niece, nephew and her father. Gene's sobs were heard above the reverend's eulogy. His two daughters stood at his side and tried to console him, yet he was inconsolable. He watched as his wife's coffin was lowered into the ground. He insisted on remaining there even after everyone returned to the house where they gathered around the dining table. His daughters tried desperately to persuade their father to join them inside, but he refused.

"You go ahead," he insisted. "I want to be alone with your mother a little while longer."

After everyone left and her grave had been covered with dirt, he knelt down beside the grave and began speaking to his wife in whispers. He remained there for nearly an hour, begging for forgiveness and proclaiming his love for her, begging God to take him as well so that he wouldn't have to remain on this earth, forced to live with what he had done.

"He's breaking my heart," Nicky cried, as she stared out the window at her father kneeling beside their mother's grave. "I don't know what to do or say to him that will help ease his pain."

"There's nothing you can say to him," Olivia told her sister. "It's just going to take time. But he'll never get over his guilt. He'll have to live with this the rest of his life."

"I hope it eats at him like a cancer everyday," Angel said, as she walked up behind her nieces at the window. "My sister would be alive right now if it weren't for that bastard. He killed my only remaining sister. As much as I despised him before, I hate him even more now. And I didn't think that was possible."

The two girls ignored their aunt's angry words and continued to stare silently out the window at their father. They understood how their aunt felt, but still, he was their father and they knew he never deliberately meant to hurt their mother. She was his life.

"I wish it would have been him that died," Angel added, as she continued to spew her venom. "My sister never hurt a single person in her entire life. She was everything that was good and kind. She was my best friend. I'll never forgive him for what he did."

The girls continued to remain silent, their backs turned to their aunt. What was there to say? Regardless of what he had done, he was still their father.

"I hope he's happy now. Now that Anna is gone he has all her money, the house, everything. He's finally that big shot he always wanted to be. But he paid for it. He paid for it dearly. The son-of-a-bitch finally got what he wanted. He—"

"Knock it off, Angel," Red told his ex-wife as he walked over and stood beside her. "Go sit down somewhere and shut the fuck up. Nobody wants to hear your opinion. He's going to have to live with what he's done and that's punishment enough. He doesn't need you to twist the knife in his back."

"He's right," Nicky agreed.

"Mom wouldn't want us laying blame on Daddy anyway," Olivia added. "It wasn't her nature to blame anyone for anything. She would want us all to stick together and help him through this."

"Well, you'll just have to leave me out of your little support group because I feel nothing but loathing for him," Angel told her nieces. "He's nothing but a money hungry animal to me. He's still white trash and that's all he'll ever be."

Red suddenly grabbed Angel by the shoulders and shoved her away from the window. "You've had your say, now shut up! He's still these kids' father and if nothing else you should show them enough respect to keep your fucking opinions to yourself at least for one day. Now go sit down somewhere or I'll break your other jaw."

Everyone in the room looked on in stunned disbelief as the two firmly stood their ground. They all knew Angel was a spitfire and that Red was capable of backing up his threats. One of them had to back down or there would be a violent confrontation. Finally, it was Angel who turned and walked out of the room.

Silence remained for sometime until Red spoke again. "Your Dad's going to need a lot of help to get through this," he said, placing his hands on each of the girls' shoulder. "I'm always around if you need me for anything. All you gotta do is pick up the phone and I'll be right over."

Olivia turned and looked up at him with tears in her eyes. "Thank you. You don't know how much that means."

"I think I'll be going now, but first I need to go say a few words to your Dad," he said, before kissing each girl goodbye.

After he had walked away, Olivia turned to her sister. "I've decided to move back home for the time being," she said.

Nicky looked at her with curiosity. "What about David's dental practice and your decorating business?"

"I'll take a brief leave of absence. I have people working for me who can take over while I'm away."

"What about David?"

"He's a big boy. He can take care of himself for a while. We have a housekeeper who can look after him until I return. Daddy needs me here worse than I'm needed at home."

"How long will you stay?" Nicky asked.

"As long as I feel like I'm needed. If there's one thing Mother taught us, it was that our family comes first."

Nicky nodded in agreement. "You're right. I guess I need to go ahead and take an early maternity leave even though I'm not due until August, and this is only June."

"That might be a good idea," Olivia agreed.

"Daddy needs us both right now. And Gene will be able to be here too, since football season won't get underway for a couple of months. Joey won't have to return to college until September, so we'll all be here at home for a while. Maybe by then, Daddy will have time to collect himself and adjust a little. Right now, he's still in shock. At least the boys can be here to help him with the farm work for the time being. And you and I can take over Mom's place, doing the cooking and housekeeping."

"And somebody needs to look after Uncle Joey," Olivia added.

"I've got news for you," Nicky told her sister. "Uncle Joey is just going to have to learn to look after himself from now on. He relied on Mom way too much. He can do a lot more for himself than he lets on. He's crazy if he thinks I'm going to wait on him hand and foot the way she did. Most of his problem is laziness anyway."

Olivia nodded her head in agreement. "He's really going to miss her," she said.

Nicky turned and gazed out the window at her father. "We all are. But Daddy's going to miss her most of all."

# Chapter Thirty

On August 6, 1995, Nicky gave birth to a baby girl she christened Anna Nicole, after herself and her child's maternal grandmother. A couple of weeks later, her sister filed for divorce from her dentist husband sighting irreconcilable differences. The marriage had been on shaky ground for several months and although Olivia had not admitted it at the time, her decision to return home after her mother's death, had been actually a trial separation. Olivia decided, after a couple of months back home, to sell her Atlanta business and go to work for her grandfather at his Ethan Allen store in Myrick. After selling her interior design business and dissolving her marriage, Olivia returned home to help her older sister care for her two children and look after their grieving father.

With her ex-husband back in Atlanta, Nicky sought employment at the Barrow County Hospital as head nurse over the third floor. She arranged to work three-day weekends, Friday thru Sunday with sixteen-hour shifts. That allowed her to remain home with her children Monday thru Thursday. Then from Friday thru Sunday, Olivia took care of her niece and nephew while her sister pulled double shifts at the hospital.

Despite the addition of two babies and three of the Longhorn children back at home, the big old house had an air of emptiness throughout. It just wasn't the same without its mistress there in charge. Gene was a broken man. No matter how hard they tried, the children were unable to console him. Not even his two young grandchildren were able to pull him out of his deep state of depression. Without his beloved Anna, he had lost all his will to live. To make matters worse, his grief was compounded by guilt. There were days he had to force himself to get out of bed in the mornings. He barely ate enough to maintain his strength and he began to lose weight. Where he was once outspoken and quick to voice his opinion, he now seldom spoke to anyone. He was literally grieving himself to death. To ease his emotional pain, Gene Longhorn began to do the unthinkable—at least for him. He began to drink. A non-drinker all his life, he had refused to consume alcohol because he had seen the effect it had on his father while he and his brother were growing up. His father was a mean drunk who became abusive and often violent while under the influence. Therefore, Gene had vowed never to touch a drop himself.

About four months after Anna's death, however, Gene began drinking after work late in the afternoon and continued until he went to bed at night. His daughters did everything to discourage his drinking, but with no success. One Halloween night, Gene began drinking particularly heavy that evening. Refusing to join his family at the dinner table that night, he went out on the front porch with a bottle of one-hundred proof Jim Beam and drank until the quart bottle was empty. He leaned against the huge square pillar that supported the front porch and cried. He prayed for God to take him. All he wanted was to join his wife. He got up and staggered behind the house to the old Magnolia tree where Anna was laid to rest. He knelt down beside her grave and pleaded for forgiveness. He sat there sobbing until dark fell.

Inside the kitchen, his three children, two grandbabies and brother were gathered around the dinner table.

"Do you think we'll have many trick or treaters this year?" Olivia asked her sister.

"I don't know. Last year Mom said she had quite a few. But the house is so far from the main highway they'll probably hit the houses easier to get to. Besides, I think all the 'Beware of Dog' signs pretty much scare them away."

"Before you know it," Joey said, pointing to his niece and nephew. "These two will be out knocking on doors."

"It won't be long," Olivia agreed, wiping her young nephew's mouth with a damp washcloth.

Olivia was wonderful with the children. She was the perfect built-in babysitter. She loved caring for her niece and nephew and looked forward to having them all to herself on the weekends while her sister was at the hospital.

"You know, I'm so glad you decided to come back home," Nicky told her sister. "I'm just sorry about your marriage to David not working out."

"Oh, well," Olivia shrugged. "Better to realize early into the marriage that it's not going to work rather than stay together and live a lie in misery the rest of your life. I knew after just a couple of months that we weren't meant for one another. We were such opposites. I guess it was because our backgrounds were so different. He grew up rich and spoiled and I grew up poor and disciplined."

"I wonder what Mom would say about us divorcing so soon and coming back home to live. Would she think we were failures?" Nicky suggested.

"No, she would never think that," Joey replied. "She loved her kids more than anything else in the world and she just wanted all of you happy. I'm sure she'd feel bad that your marriages didn't work out, but she would be very happy to have you back home."

Hal glanced up at the kitchen clock. "Dad's been out there a long time," he said. "Maybe I better go check on him."

"Yeah, he'll be pretty liquored up by bedtime," Joey told him.

"You need to try and get that bottle away from him if he hasn't finished it by now," Nicky told her brother.

"I wish he'd eat something," Olivia said. "All he wants is his liquor. He's going to get sick if he doesn't stop drinking so much and start eating more."

Hal got up from the table and went outside to look for his father. Within a few minutes, he came hurrying back in. "Olivia, we've got to go find Daddy," he said. "He's taken the truck and left."

"Oh, my God," Nicky replied. "He can't drive in his condition. What is he thinking?"

While Nicky remained behind and cared for her two young children, her brother and sister jumped in Olivia's car and began driving around looking for their father's silver-gray Silverado pick-up. As they approached the fatal intersection where their mother had been killed only four months earlier, they saw a car loaded with small children dressed in a variety of Halloween costumes pull into a gas station.

"Watch out for the little kids running around," Olivia told her brother as he slowed down for any children that might dart out in front of them. "It scares me knowing of all nights, this is the one night Dad decides to take the truck out and go driving around after consuming a bottle of liquor."

"Well, maybe we'll find him before long," Hal told her. "He couldn't have gone too far."

"This intersection creeps me out," Olivia shuddered. "I try to avoid it every time I have to drive into town. I'll go two miles out of my way to keep from driving through it."

"Well, I don't feel real comfortable driving by here myself, but it's not helping anything to keep avoiding it," Hal told his sister.

"I guess you're right," Olivia agreed.

They continued to drive toward Myrick where they passed through town searching for their father's truck. Satisfied that he wasn't in town, they headed back toward the dreaded intersection once more as they decided to hit some of the back, country roads.

As they neared a sharp curve about two miles out of town, down a dark, rural, gravel and tar road, they saw a kaleidoscope of flashing blue lights parked on opposite sides.

"I wonder what's happened here?" Hal mumbled as he approached the patrol cars.

"I don't know, but slow down," his sister warned.

"Maybe it's just a license check," Hal suggested.

As they approached closer to the sheriff's patrol cars, they saw a vehicle partially hidden in the woods. They strained their eyes to see through the darkness and were stunned and horrified to recognize their father's pick-up.

"Oh, my God, Hal! That's Daddy's truck. Pull over," Olivia told her brother.

Sheriff Wilfred Bowman had been the Barrow County sheriff for over twenty-five years. He had known the Longhorn family since Gene and his brother Joey were kids and watched Gene's own kids grow up and knew each of them by name. When he happened to look up and recognize the car, he jumped across the ditch and walked over to their car. Hal slowed to a stop and Olivia rolled down her window.

"Hal. Olivia," Bowman greeted them as he leaned his head down even with the passenger's window. "I'm afraid your father's been in an accident. They've taken him to Barrow County Medical Center. I'll send one of my deputies to escort you there."

"Is my father hurt bad?" Olivia asked, her voice filled with fear.

Bowman paused or a moment before replying. "I think he got banged up pretty bad. You better get on over to the hospital. I'll have Lieutenant Harris escort you over there." Bowman motioned for one of his deputies to come there.

"Lieutenant, escort Gene's family to the hospital and see that they get there safely," Bowman told his deputy.

Harris nodded and hurried toward his patrol car. Within minutes, Gene's children were at the hospital emergency room. They were led into a patient waiting room and waited to speak with a doctor. It was almost a half hour before the emergency room physician appeared. The moment Olivia saw the look on his face she knew her father was already dead.

# *Chapter Thirty-One*

On November 3, 1995, Gene Longhorn was buried alongside his wife of twenty-five years. No one ever knew for sure if Gene's fatal crash was an accident or intentional. His late model Silverado left the rural highway at a high speed and hit a large oak tree head-on. There were no visible skid marks before impact. The weather was good, the moon was bright and no other vehicle was involved. There were no apparent reasons why the truck would leave the road and crash into a tree. The only known fact was that Longhorn's blood alcohol level was nearly three times the legal limit. Therefore, it was assumed that he must have passed out at the wheel.

His forty-seven years had been spent eking out a meager living in the broiling sun and freezing cold, doing backbreaking labor on land that would never belong to him, living in a house that was never in his name. He went through life without ever owning anything more valuable than a car or truck. Yet his most cherished asset wasn't any material possession at all. It was his beloved wife. How ironic that he would finally attain all the wealth he ever imagined at the cost of losing the one thing that meant the most to him. Anna had been the only thing that ever really mattered to him and when he lost her, he lost the will to live. He spent his life reaching for something far beyond his grasp, only to discover, when he finally attained it; he still had nothing without the one thing that mattered most. He already had everything he could possibly ask for or would ever need and sadly, he had to lose her to realize it.

Their original owners were all gone now, but Coleman Hill and Porter Plantation would continue to live on without them. Handed down from generation to generation, the old, stately, Southern mansions would continue to stand proud as they witnessed more births, wedding, deaths and holidays—good times as well as bad, housing a multitude of bittersweet memories and perhaps even the spirits of some past owners.

Angel Coleman remained in her parents' home on Coleman Hill and would pass the town landmark down to her only daughter. The Longhorn's five children would continue to live on the thousand-acre Porter Plantation where Nicky and Olivia would raise Nicky's two children in the nearly two-hundred year-old plantation house. Their three brothers would return to build their own homes on the same property where they would continue running their dairy and beef cattle business while raising their own families on the land they were born and raised on and cherished. The Old South would live on through the traditions handed down from generation to generation, creating the legacies that would outlive them all.